TELMENU SAIMNIEKS

TELMENU SAIMNIEKS

The Lord of Telmeni

Guntis Goncarovs

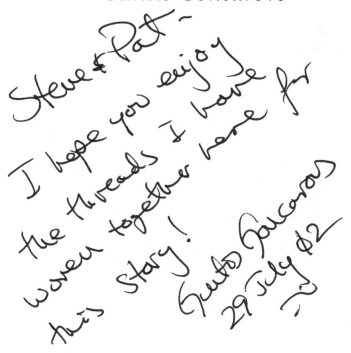

Steve & Pat —
I hope you enjoy
the threads I have
woven together for
this story!
Guntis Goncarovs
29 July 02

Writer's Showcase
San Jose New York Lincoln Shanghai

Telmenu Saimnieks
The Lord of Telmeni

Writer's Showcase
an imprint of iUniverse, Inc.

For information address:
iUniverse, Inc.
5220 S. 16th St., Suite 200
Lincoln, NE 68512
www.iuniverse.com

ISBN: 0-595-22448-2

Printed in the United States of America

To Joan:
If not for you, this would still only be a dream.

Though at the house of the widow Pshenitzyn, in Vyborg, days and nights passed peacefuly without any sudden violent changes in its monotonous existence, and though the four seasons followed each other as regularly as ever, life did not stand still, but was constantly undergoing a change; but the change was slow and gradual as are the geological changes of our planet: in one place a mountain slowly crumbled away, in another the sea was washing up silt or receding from the shores and forming new land.

—Ivan Goncharov, "Oblomov"

Contents

Historical Preface

Latvia physically sits on the Baltic Sea, a northern extension of the North Atlantic Ocean which is surrounded by the Scandinavian Peninsula. Latvia has an eastern border with Russia, a country which has several times in the past laid claim to the territory of Latvia for its own. It is sandwiched between two other small Baltic countries, Estonia to the North and Lithuania to the South. The capital city of Latvia is Riga, which sits near the Baltic Sea on the Daugava River.

The land of Latvia was settled by descendents of Ghengis Khan late in the first millennium, and soon became known as the Livs or the Livi. Many folk stories of the Livi have been handed down through the ages, and many of the holiday celebrations, such as Jani (celebration of the summer solstice) have evolved from the ancient paganistic rituals of the Livi. Latvia's agrarian roots evolved from these early settlers.

In the Thirteenth century, Teutonic Knights from Germany over-ran the Livi and established the castles and cities of Latvia, most prominently Riga and Cesis. Since that time, the Russians have coveted the land because of its ice-free ports. In the Sixteenth century, the first Russian rule was established. By the Seventeenth Century, Poland was in control until The Swedes invaded and took over. Russia retook the Latvian lands in the Eighteenth century, and grew firmly entrenched until the local people began struggling for independence in the early Twentieth Century.

This story begins in the early 1900's, when Latvia was under the rule of Czarist Russia and their ruler Nicholas Romanov. During this time, all Latvians were subject to Russian rule, which included service in the Czarist military. Nicholas faltered early in World War I, which signaled to many Latvians that it was the time for their eventual break from Russia. In 1917, with the war going poorly for the Russians, Nicholas was deposed by a Communist System. Many Latvians returned home to begin their fight for independence. A militia was formed, and much like the American Revolution, against the odds of now Soviet Russia and Germany, the Latvians won their independence in 1920.

The further history of Latvia is not addressed in this story, however, it remained tumultuous until 1990 when the former Soviet Republic of Latvia, regained its independence as a free and self-governing country.

Riga, Russian Controlled Latvia

2 May 1912

Captain Voldemars Vechi sat on a cold concrete bench across from Riga University in his full dress uniform. Consumed by his thoughts, he ignored the queer, curious glances of workers headed to their early drudgery behind machines in the manufacturing end of the city. Leering young boys scooting on their way to school didn't faze him either. Even the dampness left from overnight showers seeping through the seat of his pants went unnoticed. His only preoccupation was what he needed to say to his fiancee, as he gazed at dawn's first light piercing the dark blue sky.

Oh, for the simplicity of youth, he lamented, perplexed at how complex his life had become. He grew increasingly anxious the more he wondered how Otilija was going to react to his plan. Years ago, I wouldn't have even cared, much less felt so damned nervous. I would have just left a note and been off, he thought.

He removed his cap and placed it next to him on the bench. He ran his hand across his bristly short blonde hair, then pensively stroked at the ends of his thin handle-bar mustache. Sunlight glinting off the polished metal insignia of his cap caught his eye. He'd been proud of his stature as a Captain at only twenty-eight years old.

No other Latvian in the Czarist cavalry had moved so quickly through the ranks.

He sucked in a deep breath and gazed into the beautiful spring Riga offered, hoping the pleasant diversion would assuage his tension. This city had always made him feel good. And especially so after a cleansing spring rain, when it sparkled with a freshly washed appearance. Tulip gardens teeming with moisture laden blossoms rolled in response to the gentle breezes as if they were oceans. Her emerald hedgerows sparkled, the dark leaves rinsed clean while tiny white fragrant blossoms peeked through. Even the cobble-stoned streets and concrete sidewalks had been washed clean of their sullied pall of black and gray industrial dirt.

His wandering eyes finally settled on the closed, third-floor windows of the University's worn, red brick walls. He counted three square framed glass windows back from the right and stopped. In the office where Otilija worked, sheer, yellowed curtains remained closed.

Still not there, he thought. Good, maybe I can catch her before she goes in. He leaned forward, slipped his buttocks back on the bench, then rested his chin on top of his fisted hands. Looking at the sidewalk, he started mulling over how he'd break his news.

But before he could rehearse even one line, an approaching figure caught his attention. When he looked up, the grace of her movement alone convinced him the woman was Otilija. Her flowing, full-length sapphire blue dress elegantly brushed the sidewalk. Snow-white lace extended up from her bodice to cover her neck. A blue silk ribbon tied in her hair framed her head as if her face were a delicate spring flower. As she drew closer, her almond-shaped, brown eyes sparkled in the morning sunlight.

"Good morning, Otilija." Voldemars stood up from the bench. He smartly tucked his stiff-brimmed cap under his arm, then strutted directly toward her.

"Voldemars. What a pleasant surprise." Her thin lips twitched at the corners.

"I hope you don't mind my announcing in public that the more I see you, the more I feel I'm in love with you."

"Oh, Voldemars." Otilija blushed and dipped her head. "I honestly did not expect to see you at all today. I thought you—"

"Had maneuvers?" he finished for her. An impish grin sprouted onto his face. His nose twitched, reacting to the delicacy of her lilac scented perfume. "Well, what would you say if I told you I had decided not to play soldier. For today?"

He offered a bent arm to Otilija in a gentlemanly manner. She responded in kind, tipping her head and slipping her arm into the crook of his elbow.

"And that I was going to spend this wonderful spring day with the most beautiful woman I know," he said as they started across the street.

"I simply would not believe you, Voldemars," she replied stiffly, yet playfully. She glanced up into his pale green eyes. "Tell me, how I could ever believe that? Of all the soldiers in the Czar's army, you are the one he can always count on. Captain Voldemars Vechi would never shirk his duties. You are much too disciplined and conscientious—"

"I know we were supposed to get married next month," Voldemars blurted, but when his eyes met Otilija's, her suddenly piercing stare whisked the words from his lips.

Was my approach careless, he wondered. He tried to read into her deeply-set, widened eyes. Hoping to recapture his broken train of thought, he glanced away and quickly searched his mind. Instead of words, though, a sense of betrayal rushed in.

"I'm sorry, let me rephrase that," he mumbled, still cringing. "I'd like to get married. I mean I think it would be better if we get married now. Instead of waiting."

"Now? Why now? I thought we already decided that—"

"Uh, something has come up. There's been a change in plans," he babbled. "Our group has been transferred—"

He stopped suddenly as a waft of onion tainted perspiration rose from underneath his collar. He had no idea what his orders were going to be. Assignment was two weeks away, and Command had maintained surprisingly tight control over the information. But he had to think of something.

"Well, it really doesn't matter where we're going."

"You're confusing me, Voldemars. Please, tell me exactly what you're trying to tell me."

"What matters is that if we're married, you can come with me. That's an officer's privilege, you know, to take his wife. The military has housing for—"

"Voldemars, stop. Just stop for a moment. I still do not completely understand." She held out one hand as she pressed at her temples with the other, as if to keep her thoughts from spilling out. Her eyes grew cold and calculating. "You will be back in a month, won't you?"

Voldemars' eyes did not waver.

"So we can still have the wedding then, can't we?"

"I…I honestly don't know when I'll be back. And I don't know if I can even get leave then," he admitted. An embarrassed blush pushed a stronger odor from his open pores.

"But you will get leave sometime, though, yes?"

"I presume so."

"Could we wait until then?" Her voice trembled slightly, yet remained firm.

Voldemars' jaw dropped open. Stumped, he combed his mind to find a logical but more urgent reason to counter with, but failed. She was right.

You are all I think about now, Otilija, he thought as his eyes glassed over.

"Oh, Voldemars," her voice gently interceded. "You know how much I want to marry you. But you know I'd like to have a traditional wedding. With everyone there?"

Ever since I met you last year, my life finally has meaning. A purpose, Voldemars thought.

"If we get married now, no one will be here for the ceremony."

He felt fear and loneliness at the thought of their separation. I can't imagine a day passing without being able to talk to you or touch you, he thought.

"Your parents said that they can not make it here until next month. And Otomars, oh how Otomars would be devastated if he did not get to perform his traditional 'big brother' duties!" Otilija tittered as she pantomimed her brother's characteristic preening, thrusting out her lower jaw as she puffed out her chest and swaggered two steps.

Voldemars remained silent and sullen, thinking, I feel so much more alive now that we're—

"For heaven sakes, you know how much he likes to act like my overseer."

"But, Otilija. I want you to be my wife. Now," he pleaded. "An officer's wife. Someone to be respected and revered. As you should be—"

"And what about what I want, Voldemars." Her expression immediately iced over as her voice grew louder. Voldemars simply hung his head and absorbed her censure. "Have you considered that I might feel something else may be important right now! The wedding ceremony is just as important to me. Just as important as it is to any woman. A woman's wedding day belongs to her. Then is the most important thing for her to feel respected and revered. Not after."

"I just thought you'd like to be known as Captain Vechi's wife?" he tentatively offered.

"Ha! Captain Vechi's wife? And then what? Do I just become some baggage that you carry from campaign to campaign?" She scolded him with her finger pointing directly at his chest. "Or will I be just another of those damn ribbons you wear only on your dress uniform? A decoration to be taken out when there's no battle to get mixed up in?"

Otilija spun and stomped away in a huff. She stopped at the curb, crossing her arms in front of her emphatically. She looked at the school for a moment, then turned and glared back.

"No, Voldemars. Do you hear me? No! I am not ready for that. And to be perfectly honest with you, I don't know if I will ever be." She snapped her head around. Her lips quivered as she glared at the windows on the third floor. Her face had grown flushed in rage. "And another thing you should think about, Captain Vechi. I don't know if I am ready to give up who I am. I am happy being just a bookkeeper in Riga. I am happy just being Otilija Braze for now. I am happy just being the daughter of a common factory worker. Can you understand that, Captain Vechi?"

"But, Otilija, you are important to me. Can't you see that? You are all I have now." He tried not to whine, but felt his pleading tone seep through.

"I am all you have now?" She pantomimed surprise, propping her hands on her hips, then continuing sarcastically. "Well, Captain Vechi, if that is truly the case, then it is your own fault. If you weren't so damned obsessed with becoming the Czar's most important soldier, you might still be on speaking terms with your father."

He felt skewered.

"Sometimes I wonder if you even realize what you did to him, leaving the way you did." She relentlessly challenged him. "Did you ever think that being a Latvian hero in a Russian army may not be what your father wanted from you? Maybe all he really wanted was for you to be his son."

Her words stung, but his own guilt reminded him that she was right. He was selfish, and he never took the time to listen to anyone other than himself. He was always in too much of a rush to prove his manhood.

"You know, Voldemars, if you would only step back and watch yourself sometimes, I think you would be truly amazed." Her tone had relented a bit, and even began sounding a bit more empathetic. "You are so consumed by playing soldier that I think you have lost perspective of who you really are." Her angry, flushed face glowed. She sucked in a deep breath, then exhaled forcefully, all the while glaring at Voldemars.

"I know you could just put your time in the army and then leave, but why do I sense you will not?"

Otilija stopped, allowing Voldemars an opportunity to respond. Instead, he chewed on his lower lip and remained silent.

"You are just another body to them, Voldemars. As expendable as a pair of shoes. Can't you see that? You will never be that famous general you dream about!"

Again, he was silent.

"I have to go now. I am expected at work. As menial as bookkeeping may seem to you, it still needs to be done," Otilija announced as she turned. After taking only two steps, she spun and lashed out again. "Maybe a month or so apart will do us both some good. And if it is more, then that is all the better. Perhaps then you will decide what it is you really want...whether you want to be mortal and marry me, or keep on imagining you are the modern day reincarnation of Lacplesis."

Otilija stopped for a moment as if to let her words sink in. Again, Voldemars did not respond.

"And maybe that will give me enough time to sort out whether or not you are the right one for me." Otilija turned and stomped across the street, toward the tall oak doors of the University. When they closed behind her, Voldemars again stood on the concrete sidewalk, alone.

❋   ❋   ❋

Still bewildered and confused by Voldemars' actions at the University that morning, Otilija sauntered out into her mother's garden for a therapeutic stroll. It was a warm day even though the sun hid behind ribbons of mottled pink clouds which were fringed at both their crests and bases by a pastel blue. Trying to clear her head, she released her brown hair from its restrictive bun, then wandered through the freshly sprouting cabbage, bending over to touch the tiny purple heads as she passed.

When the gently pungent aroma of onion greens titillated her nose, she stopped and looked up. In the scallion patch ahead, her mother, Doroteja had set a three-legged stool next to the bed, then carefully set her tools down. She pulled her fine, auburn hair under a red kerchief, then tied the scarf's ends behind her head before gently easing down into a comfortable sitting position on the stool. She leaned forward and started her ritual spring harvest preparations.

First, she inspected her knife, gently scraping the edge with her finger to assure it was still sharp. Satisfied, she nestled her oval reed basket in her lap, then moved the handles out of the way before bowing her head and reciting her own brief prayer for a fine harvest season. She leaned forward, bunched up a handful of the thin, emerald spikes in her curled hand, then eased her knife across their base.

Otilija craned her neck and closely watched the blade sever the spikes and free an ooze of clear fluid onto her mother's fingers. Doroteja laid the greens into her reed basket then grabbed another bunch, and again, carefully stroked her knife through the thin tubes, but then oddly stopped and cocked her head.

"Now this is unusual. My little city girl walking in a vegetable garden," she said with a gentle soothing voice. Without looking back, she carefully set her knife and the freshly cut greens into her basket. Pivoting on her seat, she turned and faced her.

"Come sit with me, mazulis. Tell me what's troubling you."

Otilija knew her mother meant nothing other than affection with her diminutive, but it still bothered her to be referred to as little girl.

"Oh, nothing. Just coming out to visit," Otilija lied. Embarrassed, she glanced down to her feet and blushed. She scratched her toe back and forth at the ground, contemplating whether she was even ready to talk.

"Nothing?" Doroteja's doubting expression was topped by her lifted eyebrows. "This from the girl who spends all of her time at University with her nose in a book? This from the girl who's already figured out what she's going to do with her life? This from my little one who has already grown up faster than I would have liked?"

Otilija watched her mother's face grow as consoling as she'd ever been. A warm, tiny grin blossomed on her face as she tipped her head to her shoulder.

"You will excuse me for not believing you, dear child, but the only time you have ever come out here was when you needed some advice."

I should be handling my own affairs now that I am twenty-five, Otilija thought, still hesitant to admit her problem.

"I don't mean to make light of whatever's bothering you, Otilija, but I'm your mother. And since I am your mother, I can usually tell when something is wrong, even if you are grown up."

"Oh, Momma, it's Voldemars," Otilija sighed noisily as she plopped down between the rows of onions. She crossed her legs and brought them up underneath her dress, then perched her head on her hands.

"Ah, your soldier. He's got you thinking, has he? And by the look on your face, my dear, I'd guess that one of you is getting cold feet?"Otilija sighed heavily, then absently weaved her hands through the foot tall scallions. She snapped one off and slipped it into her mouth before any of the extract could ooze out. Doroteja reached into the patch and mimicked her daughter.

"Mmm, still needs another week or so," she said as she slipped it into her mouth.

"I don't know if I'll ever understand him, Momma."

"Is he putting you off again?"

"Actually, no. He wants to get married now instead of waiting until after Jani."

"You know I wouldn't be too worried about that," Doroteja rambled while she carelessly listened to her daughter. "Sometimes men just need—" She gasped, then coughed, almost choking on the onion. "Good Lord, child. You don't have to, do you?"

"Oh, no, Momma. I've been good," Otilija defended.

"My goodness, child. You do know how to make your mother gray." Doroteja released a relieved sigh. She reached over to Otilija and stroked her wavy brown hair.

"Then, he does have some reason for getting married now, doesn't he?"

"Yes. I mean, he says he does. Oh, honestly, Momma, I'm not really sure at all. He said it is because he is being shipped out on assignment." Otilija stumbled through her words.

"That can't be everything that's bothering you," Doroteja prodded.

"I think what bothered me the most was that he couldn't look me in the eyes when he said that. He wouldn't say where he was going, or for how long, but he still wants me to go with him!"

"Oh?" Doroteja frowned, apparently trying to hide a snicker. "If I were you, I'd be quite relieved that he wants you to go with him, and not leave you behind. You know how soldiers can be."

"But, Momma." Otilija slapped her hands onto the ground in protest. "If we get married now, there'll be no ceremony. And there's just no time to get anything ready by Saturday. And Otomars can't make it. He's still stationed in Petersburg at least until Jani arrives. And Voldemars' parents can't make it here on such short notice. And there's just not enough time for me to get ready. I haven't even talked to the dress-maker about a dress." Otilija stopped rambling long enough to draw a deep breath. She simmered and collected her thoughts for a moment. "And I just can't convince him of that. He's so…he's just so damned bull-headed."

Doroteja giggled, then tried to hide her smirk behind her hands. Baffled by her mother's response, Otilija stopped munching the onion stalk.

"I guess you are starting to realize what I've been going through for years," Doroteja placed her open hand on her daughter's shoulder, then compassionately peered into her eyes. "Men are an enigma, my child. They seem to always have complete control of every last detail, and pride themselves at that."

"But Momma, it's not just that—"

"Patience, my child, let me finish. When emotions are involved, though, especially heart-felt ones, they've absolutely no control. I don't think there's a woman alive who could say that she understands why they do what they do."

"But, Momma, it's just not like him. Not Voldemars. He has always understood. He has been so considerate with my feelings. He's always been a patient gentleman."

Doroteja gazed into Otilija's brown, almond-shaped eyes while she gently stroked her daughter's hair.

"I simply can't understand why he's acting this way now. Especially since he knows how much I want my ceremony?"

"From what you've told me about Voldemars, he's a man of great feeling. In that way, he's quite unlike other men," Doroteja said in a subdued tone.

"So, then why is he being so stubborn."

"Dear child, all men are stubborn. Look at Poppa. Stone faced and serious about everything. It's all I can do to get him to even crack a smile. And your brothers, well, they are just like Poppa. But your Voldemars, though, has a bit of a different character to him. Very different."

"But—"

"Think about what he's saying, Otilija. Look hard into what he's really saying. It doesn't sound like he's doing anything out of selfishness or stubbornness. I think he's doing this just because he loves you very much."

Otilija's eyes widened like saucers. She gazed deeply into her mother's eyes and read her sincerity. "Do you really think so, Momma?"

Doroteja nodded with a slight smile. "And I'd say that you're very fortunate to have a man like Voldemars interested in you," she added.

Otilija gazed at her mother, squirming as she thought. "So, then you think we should get married now?"

"Dear child, you're a grown woman now. You can think for yourself. What I think isn't important." Doroteja stood up, bent over, and picked up her reed basket and stool. She offered her hand to Otilija, then helped her up to her feet.

"Take your time and think it over," Doroteja offered as they headed toward the house. "But do remember, Otilija. This isn't the first time a man has disappointed you, and speaking from experience, believe me, it will not be the last. But when it all comes down to the end, I really don't think that Voldemars will disappoint you very much."

South of Riga, Russian controlled Latvia

16 May 1912

*L*ike a band of locusts, a flock of infantry soldiers frantically attacked a group of three steam-driven locomotives, stripping every piece of metal which identified the machines as the property of the Russian Imperial Army. Pressed and carved emblems rained to the tracks, leaving flat black mechanized horses bland and without identity. At the same time, another hoard of men slipped through the eerie fog-shrouded evening and swarmed between a parade of stock and passenger cars. They broke formation, formed smaller teams, then muscled the train cars into a long chain behind the stripped engines and slammed the hitches together. While soot-faced engineers sparingly fed the furnaces shovels of coal to maintain the boilers at the ready, the hoard disappeared into the woods as quickly as they had appeared.

From the depths of the surrounding forest, a single file of cavalry appeared at eighteen hundred hours. They were dressed in traditional olive green field uniforms. The horses sauntered at a durge-like pace, carefully stepping over surface roots that webbed the grounds. Obedient to their mounts, the horses bunched, eight in a pack, soberly waiting for their next command.

The riders dismounted, loosened their wide leather girths, and led their horses toward the open doors of the stock cars. One-by-one they entered, their steel shod hooves clomping onto the wooden ramps as they were led plodding into the holds. As one soldier sauntered out of the car, his saddle under one arm, the next in line led his mount up the ramp and into the car. When the group was finished, the rickety door was wheeled shut and secured. The soldiers then dutifully marched toward the front of the train, through steam clouds billowing from beneath the idling engine, and boarded their designated passenger car.

At precisely nineteen-hundred hours, soot-faced engineers hurled overloaded shovels of gleaming black coal into the gaping mouths of the furnaces. Instantly, the fires raged to life as the train master fixed his gaze on the smudged, oversized pressure gauge above the boiler. As he watched the black needle jerk to life, he absently groped for the steam admission valve. His fingers twitched in anticipation until the needle edged past the one o'clock position, then he yanked the knife switch down. Spinning in place, he faced his sweat soaked laborers and barked for more and more chunks to be hurled into the glowing oven.

Choking, thick black smoke exhaled from the bulged mouths of the stacks as inside, steam hissed past the opened valves. Metal pipes quivered as the steam hammered within them. A stale, damp aroma escaped from loosely fitted pipe joints and tainted the air. The black iron beast sighed deeply then groaned to life. Unoiled wheels screeched as they started to roll over rusted rails. Steam oozed in clouds from the belly of the train.

Slipping at first, the massive drive wheels of the lead engine squealed as they took hold of the large gauge track. The engine spasmed forward, and then in series, each connecting clasp of successive cars clicked together until the entire train moaned slowly forward.

The train chugged southward, noisily clicking over the steel rail's narrow expansion joints. Voldemars sat in reticence next to Gunars, a soldier ten years his elder who'd taken him under his tutelage. Resting his forehead against the damp glass, he peered through the window at the pall of thick fog. He watched blurred images of fragmented, dead tree stumps mystically take form, then magically disappear back into the soupy cloak resting over the bog. The stench of decayed matter trapped within the heavy sludge filtered through the cracked open windows and lingered in the car.

Voldemars closed his eyes and accepted the odor as part of his new life. As his mind wandered, he pictured the bogs along the Gauja River. He conjured the legends of the mythical Lacplesis, the medieval folk hero whose story his father reverently recited to him when he was a little boy. He let his eyes slip closed, and while the gentle rocking of the train lulled him to sleep, he heard his father's voice telling the legend of 'The Bear-Slayer.'

"In the thick, magical woods of Valka, nestled in the white birches of the Gauja River valley, our long forgotten ancestors, the Livi, once thrived in peaceful harmony with the land." His father's deep, musical voice resonated in his head as clearly as if he was standing right beside him. "But the Huns and the Tartars, brutal invaders that felt no shame in slaughtering the peaceable natives, hoarded in like plagues, threatening the Livi's existence. Knowing they were no match for the battle-hardened soldiers, the remaining Livi huddled around a ring of sacred fires and summoned the Great Spirit for guidance.

"Suddenly, the birches around them quivered, then swayed as a great wind rushed through the boughs. The sachem stood, spread his arms wide, and let the wind ripple through the tattered skins which covered his golden skin. With his shoulder-length, honey colored hair flowing behind him, he lowered his head and faced his people.

"'Join me. Spread your arms and take to the sky. As spirits, we can wait together for the heir of the land to arrive. When Lacplesis arrives, we will return as we are now, but forever free of incursion.'

One by one, the Livi stood and spread their arms to the wind, then vanished into the evening, leaving only their fires flickering in the still forest.

Five hundred years had passed when the sachem's spirit discovered an abandoned baby boy at the same place their fires had once burned. He spotted a she-bear near-by, who had also noticed the child. Starving and emaciated from days of unsuccessful foraging, the bear reveled in the thought of feasting on the infant's tender flesh. As the bear circled the boy, saliva dripping from her sharp incisors, the sachem realized this was exactly how the Great Spirit had said they would discover Lacplesis. He summoned all of the Livi spirits from the birches and rallied to the child's welfare. Relentlessly, the bear continued to weave around the spirits and get to the squirming infant.

After two hours of sparring with the bear, the sachem confronted the bear and promised to keep her fed forever if she chose not to devour the infant, but to nurse and nurture him as if he were her own cub. Tired and hungry, she relented and complied with the sachem's proposal.

Years passed. The once frail boy developed into a massive, superiorly sculptured warrior, filled with a fierce, indomitable spirit. The proud Livi spirits watched Lacplesis ride like the wind through Lielvarde's green forests and amber meadows, his long, golden hair tossing about his wide, sturdy shoulders. Through his open bear-skin vest, his bronze, muscular chest protruded proudly as he sat tall and proud on the back of a pure white Arabian.

He learned many things from his adopted mother. Assisted by the Livi spirits, she also taught the boy how to defend himself against any challenge; man, beast, or the ever-present evil.

One day, as Lacplesis returned from a foraging expedition, he discovered his mother was being attacked by a huge male bear. Fear froze him briefly as he realized this beast was twice his size. The startle lasted but a moment until a sudden, wild rage exploded within him. He sprung at the huge bear and wresting him from atop his surrogate mother. A protective instinct spurred, he pinned the male with lightning speed, grasped the animal's blood covered jaws and pried them open with his bare hands until they shattered.

His battle won, Lacplesis returned to the she-bear's side and dropped to his knees. Her lifeless body, however, lay quiet in a deep pool of blood. Grieving, he buried his head into her chest and wept.

The Livi spirits circled the warrior, themselves distraught by the scene which had played out before them. In their hearts they knew that Lacplesis had earned the right to sit on the throne of the Castle of Light at Lielvarde, and so honored him."

"I'm going to be like him when I grow up," little Voldemars had vowed.

"Many good years passed while Lacplesis benevolently ruled over Latvia. Warm, golden sun always bathed our emerald hills, sapphire lakes, and cool, birch filled valleys. But in the shadows, the Black Knight, the epitome of evil, grew jealous of Lacplesis and his lands. He vowed to wrest the Castle of Light from Lacplesis and all of Latvia's lands with it."

Voldemars heard his Poppa's voice growl as he hunched over, craning his neck and hooding his eyes as if he was the scheming villain. "So, while Lacplesis slept, the Black Knight snuck into the castle and wrested the key right from Lacplesis' hand."

"Not if it were me!" Voldemars' boyish voice had bellowed with mature resolve as he leapt to his feet and flailed an imaginary sword at his imaginary adversary. "I wouldn't let the Black Knight take anything from my people!"

"Cackling fiendishly and so loud that his taunts echoed all through the Gauja Valley, the Black Knight rode away into the dark, dreary night, while behind him, the Castle of Light sunk into the bogs of northern province of Vidzeme," Poppa's voice had grown quiet and sorrowful. "Dark, ominous clouds rolled in from the east, shrouding Latvia in a pall of despair.

"But the Letts, stalwart and hopeful, maintained in their hearts that someday, somehow, Lacplesis would find a way to return and again rule over Latvia. And when he did return and declare his victory," Poppa's voice regained its melodious baritone again, "The Castle of Light would rise from the swamps, silhouetted by a glorious sunrise, and Lacplesis would appear mounted on his mighty white stallion. His arrival would then forever clear the sky of the ominous clouds which had shrouded Latvia for centuries."

Squealing train wheels startled Voldemars awake. He cracked his eyes, then slid them open further when he realized it was still dark. Shaking his head vigorously, he groped for the window, then rubbed a circle in the condensed vapor. In the faint twilight, he saw a small village. Dull, wind-cracked and rain-stained clapboard covered each small house. Thatch roofs had grown olive green with moss, edges hanging over the three small windows on each side.

"Welcome back to the real world, Voldemars," Gunars voice chuckled as the engines lumbered to a halt. Steam clouds plumed a screen thicker than the already ubiquitous fog. "You must have had a hell of a dream. You were thrashing so much I thought you might tip the train over."

"What's going on? Where are we?" Voldemars turned to Gunars.

"Polish border, I'd say."

"Hmm," Voldemars grunted as he continued his gaze out the window. Through the mist he watched two sentries move toward the train, then stop at the engine. The train-master hopped down from the grated platform, opened a satchel, then presented the guards with an envelope. After slipping the flap open, the sentry withdrew the message and held the paper close to the lantern the engineer held.

The sentry immediately stiffened, then folded the message back together and returned it to the satchel. He pointed to the south, then held his hands parallel in front of him at one distance, then widened them. The engineer nodded and climbed back aboard the train as the sentries returned to their post.

"We're going further in, Gunars," he grumbled, shifting in his seat to get comfortable.

"Border reconnaissance. Has to be," Gunars whispered with a twinge of anxiety in his voice. His squared face and wide opened eyes showed his concern.

"Six months at the front. I guess there's nothing we can do about that now, can we?" Voldemars shrugged his shoulders, as he looked at Gunars.

The seasoned veteran, though, had already slumped back asleep. Voldemars squirmed a little more, the closed his eyes again.

The train again lurched forward, silently chugging into the Polish countryside. Lulled by the gentle rocking of the train on its way south, he tried to clear his mind, but the thought of what he promised Otilija about his plans kept stabbing his mind like a guilt pang. He couldn't believe how naive he'd been in believing the Russian command wouldn't send him to the front so soon after being married. He thought he had it all planned out, but this secret mission had disrupted everything.

Six months, he grumbled to himself. He sank deeper into his seat. I can survive six months, he thought, closing his eyes.

Voldemars felt himself suddenly thrust forward, catching himself before he tumbled onto the floor. He shook his head, then propped his eyes open.

"What…where are we?" he asked Gunars. As he asked he realized everyone on the car was preparing to leave.

"I think we're about to find out," Gunars groaned as he fumbled to button his tunic. He nodded toward the front of the car where Colonel Vasily Plotnikov, their regiment commander stood in dim light. He was short in stature, but what he lacked in height, he compensated greatly for in grim demeanor. His dour expression emanated gloom as he rhythmically and impatiently slapped his riding crop in his open hand. A wave of silence followed by reluctant attention rolled from the front of the car to the rear.

"This is as far as we can go by train." Plotnikov started. His face screwed up like he had caught wind of a rotting carcass. "We will set up camp just beyond the woods, where our scouts have identified a secure clearing. But I caution all of you. We are in hostile territory. Anyone here, anyone, is potentially an enemy.

"You are also expected to exhibit proper discipline. It is critical to our mission that it be maintained clandestine. Improper actions here could plunge us not only into battle, but even start a continental war. Any disobedience will be promptly disciplined."

No one stirred. Plotnikov's words hovered like the dense fog outside. Pompously, the colonel strutted down the aisle of the car, glowering at each soldier.

"I see I have your attention. Very good. Unload your mounts and gear, assemble formation by rank, and wait for your orders outside the train. We will discuss our mission and strategy at day break."

Plotnikov continued through and exited the rear of the car. As the door closed behind him, a collective sigh rose, followed by the resumption their now silent preparations to leave.

In the quickly fading twilight outside the train, doors to the horses' cars slid open, planks dropped into place and the animals clomped off in single file. Mounted and assembled behind Plotnikov, the special regiment waited and watched as the train backed away toward Russia. As it disappeared in the mist, the regiment then turned and headed cautiously into the dark forest of birch and oak trees.

Voldemars' thoughts wandered as he followed Plotnikov toward the decaying odor of the marshy bog. He hated him already. He had never hated his commanding officer before, but he never served under an officer as curt and demeaning as Plotnikov. Duty and honor was always his mission, but each officer he had served before this poor Napoleonic impostor had easily earned his respect.

He remembered his first encounter with Plotnikov, back at the processing station south of Riga. He had seen his arrogant swagger as he stiff-armed his way through the rear door. His sour, ferret-like face had glowered over the room in disapproval as the door slammed behind him. At the sudden silence, a tiny but still perceptible grin stretched across his gaunt cheeks. He snapped his heels together, then strutted through the center of the room, ordering soldiers to immediately take their seats with only his glance.

Pivoting smartly, he clapped his polished boot heels together, then after a momentary frown, he mechanically reached inside his jacket and pulled out a torn-edged envelope. He puffed into the opened end, then slipped his thin fingers in and extracted a letter. With a flick of his wrist, he snapped the letter open, held it at arms length, and forcefully cleared his throat.

"I am Colonel Vasily Plotnikov, your regiment commanding officer. It is my duty to inform you that due to the clandestine nature of this mission, as of this minute, you are hereby restricted to this compound." His scratchy, low pitched voice annoyed Voldemars. He glanced up, seeming to expect the announcement would elicit sudden disapproval. Not disappointed with the negativism of the room, he pruned his lips and grimaced, then waited for the clamor to quell enough for him to be heard again.

"By order of First Army General Rennenkampf, you have been selected and assembled as an 'expeditionary force' for His Majesty's

Service. This mission will include penetration behind German lines, and therefore, may incur engagements with the German Army.

"We will board trains and depart for the front tonight. For security reasons, further details of your assignment will be discussed only after we arrive. Additionally, since we will be continually on the move, all you will be allowed to take with you will be supplies immediately necessary for survival. If our mission is successful, we should return home in six months."

Six months. Voldemars remembered being stunned. How am I going to be able to explain this one to Otilija? It's bad enough that I'm going alone after promising her otherwise. Now it is six months instead of one. Is she even going to believe me?

"You will be given sufficient time to write letters home this afternoon," Plotnikov had informed them. "Which will be delivered once we leave this camp tonight. I do caution you, however, that when you write your messages, the clandestine nature of this mission must be maintained. All letters will be screened. Only those satisfying my censure will be dispatched by messenger."

Plotnikov stopped again. The room had remained in dead silence. He folded the letter, quickly stuffing it into his tunic, and summarized: "With that, I shall leave. Official paper is available from the quartermaster. Write messages to your family, if you so desire. But I remind you, letters must be completed by seventeen-hundred hours tonight. We shall leave here thirty minutes after."

Plotnikov made one brief survey of the crowd, then tugged down on his tunic and stiffly stalked through the middle of the room. He thrust the door open and exited. The slamming behind him sent a ghostly echo through the silent room.

"I don't believe this," Voldemars grumbled to himself as he stood.

"When you've been with the army as long as I have, old friend, you'll get used to it," Gunars solemnly added with a long face. He placed his hand on Voldemars' shoulder and peered into his filmed green eyes. Without uttering a word, Gunars told him about the years of sudden changes and disappointments he could expect. He shared with him the pain of love forever lost because of the demands the Cavalry placed on his life. He let him know that he grew to question whether his time in the service was worth the number of disappointments along the way.

Voldemars' reverie was interrupted by a movement in front. Plotnikov raised his hand and signaled the brigade to stop. He methodically surveyed a clear area upwind of the bog, then silently ordered his aide to scout the edge of the forest at the north and south ends. Upon their return, the commander ordered the brigade to strike camp.

"Six months," Voldemars spat, disgusted as he sat on the soggy ground outside his tent. Surrounded by the muffled howls from wolves on the prowl and whispered chatter from the files of small pup tents, he played with his hands, methodically cracking his knuckles until each had snapped at least once. Each crack, though, only rekindled his anger at the Russian Command and the way they'd used him.

"This will all be over in six months, and then I'll be back with Otilija. I can survive six months," he consoled himself, closing his eyes. He tried to defuse his rage, but it continued to seethe. His stomach knotted as he remembered what few cryptic words he was allowed to send to her. He picked up a thin, dead stick and angrily snapped in with one hand.

"Are you really that nervous, Voldemars?" Gunars muttered as he crouched down next to Voldemars and picked at some of the ground pine.

"Christ, Gunars, you scared the hell out of me," Voldemars expelled a lung full of air.

"Didn't mean to." Gunars shrugged. His face was covered with a wide cynical smile. He hung his head and let his honey colored locks flop over his stiff collar.

"Hell, I don't know if I'm nervous, upset, or just down right angry."

"Doesn't matter. Just pick one and deal with it."

"Maybe I should just be satisfied that even though I'm Latvian, the Russian command regards me one of the elite."

Voldemars picked a ground pine and twirled it between his fingers. He opened his hand, let it drop into his open palm, then formed a fist over it. An icy shiver then suddenly ran down his spine. His thoughts about Otilija vanished. A queer restlessness toying with his psyche quickly filled the void.

"Something else is bothering you, isn't it?" Gunars probed. He sat down next to Voldemars and stared up at the starless, soupy sky. An owl whooed in the distance, then fell silent amidst the marsh's creaking frogs.

"You know, I've had a strange feeling just in the last hour. A feeling like...well, like the feeling you get when a cold breeze sweeps across your back after you've been working in the sun for a while."

"Oh, I know that feeling all too well." Gunars nodded. His lips tightened into a crooked grin.

"But this one is much colder. Almost chilling," Voldemars added, absently.

"That, my friend, is 'No Man's Land'. After a few campaigns, it's a feeling you'll come to know as a friend. Sometimes a very valuable friend."

Voldemars cocked his head, suddenly intrigued. Gunars chuckled softly then threw his sprig of moss toward the peeping symphony of frogs.

"It's your senses warning you that things may not be what they seem."

Voldemars stared at Gunars as a cloud of moldy leaf odor insulted his nose. He pinched his nostrils together.

"Do you believe in spirits?" Gunars asked. A gleam sparkled in his eyes, turned charcoal in the dim light. His face seemed gray and gaunt.

"Spirits?"

"You know. The dead. Ancestors looking out for you? You've got to have something like that in your culture."

"The Livi."

"Well, 'No Man's Land' then is the Livi warning you to beware."

"Beware of what?"

"Just to beware."

"Maybe it's that I've never been on a mission like this before?" Voldemars rationalized.

"Or perhaps your Livi is telling you what I realized a few months back," Gunars' eyes hollowed. "With all the political posturing in the cities, and with all the armies gathering at the fronts like herds of reindeer in rut, there's no doubt in my mind. It is inevitable. The war we've all been trying to avoid? It is inevitable."

Voldemars tried to logically work through the details while Gunars remained silent.

"But won't the size of our army alone keep anyone from starting it? Isn't that why we're here to keep anything from happening?"

Gunars clearly remained consumed in his thoughts, absently staring out into the night. Voldemars felt his body flush as a sulfury garlic smell slipped through his collar. He grew restive each second Gunars did not respond.

"Even if they do try us, we'll surely be victorious. Our size alone is twice what anyone else in Europe can muster. We'd obviously win any war."

Gunars did not even flinch.

"We will win, don't you think?" Voldemars prodded.

"I wouldn't be so sure, my friend," Gunars finally acknowledged. He brought his hand to his chin and started rubbing. "I've had this no man's land feeling for some time now, too, and it bothers me that

I can't resolve why. Maybe it's the tension in Europe. And in Russia. Hell, it's everywhere."

Gunars sighed heavily as he grabbed another handful of ground pine. He tightly squeezed his fist closed. The forest sounds lulled. Even the whispers from the other soldiers petered out.

"I hate to admit this," Gunars started again, his voice wavering with concern. "But I sense that for some reason, the events of the next five years, events where we may only be pawns in the grand scheme of things, will surely shape not only Europe, but the world for years to come. In some countries, it'll be for the better. In others, for the worse."

"And us?"

"Who knows," Gunars shrugged and closed his eyes. He snorted a forced laugh, then added, "Maybe we should talk to the gypsies."

"Gypsies?"

"In these parts, traveling gypsies meander around in their covered wagons and tell of things to come."

"Can you believe them?" Voldemars asked, curious.

An owl's loud screech announced the culmination of his successful hunt. The swamp fell silent momentarily before two frogs tentatively started their croaking again.

"Other men who have come this way say that they speak the truth most of the time," Gunars tone grew despondent.

"Have you?"

"Have I what?"

"Talked to the gypsies?" Voldemars whispered.

"A few times."

"And?"

Gunars turned his head toward Voldemars. With a subdued, breathy voice he admitted, "All any of them say is that rivers of blood will stream through the fields."

"Whose blood?" Voldemars leaned closer.

"They never say." Gunars peered past Voldemars and into the woods with glassy eyes. Silence ominously ruled in the forest and marsh.

Voldemars nodded his head, clearly understanding he had much more to think about now.

❉   ❉   ❉

Hours later, prone in his tent, Voldemars peered out his open flap and watched the fine mist thicken the already dense fog as if the night's stew simmered. Each time he closed his eyes, trying to get some sleep, the faces of the Russian soldiers appeared, comrades he'd have to trust, sneering at him as if he didn't belong with them. They were quickly replaced by Plotnikov's gaunt, stolid face, wryly smiling as he read his six month sentence. His face faded, replaced by each of the soldier's blank, aghast expressions when they first peered out over the bleak, fog-shrouded landscape.

"Six months," he grumbled as he scooted deeper into his tent, closing the flap behind him. I can survive six months, he thought, closing his eyes.

Nordeki, Outside of Riga

17 May 1912

*E*nfolded by a quiet, misty morning, Otilija sat in her father's chair on the porch, where she'd slept for most of the damp spring night. She hadn't moved since evening, when her friend and local gossip, Drina Spruniks told her about a regiment of cavalry which she had heard was being shipped out. All through that evening, and into the night, she hoped and prayed that Voldemars was not with them. But after the sun dipped below the horizon and twilight slipped away into the fog-shrouded night, she realized that Voldemars must have been.

Otilija startled when a young boy riding up the street stopped in front of her house and dropped his bicycle. He tugged down on his tunic, then slipped a brown sachel that was riding on his back around in front of him. His uniform was curiously similar to Voldemars, but missing much of the insignia. The young boy yanked down on his cloth cap, then marched toward her.

"Good day Madam. I have a message for Otilija Vechi. Are you this person?"

Otilija stared at the boy's steely blue eyes, then nodded slightly. The boy reached into his sachel and pulled out a handful of letters. Quickly flipping through the thin envelopes, he stopped mid-way through the pile and snapped hold of one. He pulled it out, then quickly replaced the pile into the sachel.

"Where is this from?" Otilija asked.

"I am not sure. Even if I did know, I would probably not be able to tell you."

"Then it is clearly a military letter then?"

"Anyone can tell that by the seal," the boy mumbled as he pushed the letter toward Otilija. She remained in her perch. "Well, are you going to take this or do I just leave it here?"

Otilija thought for a moment. She glanced down to the envelope. It was definitely Voldemars' handwriting. Of that, she had no doubt.

"Just leave it there," Otilija mumbled, then sat back in the chair. The messenger snapped closed his sachel, smartly pivoted, and headed back for his bicycle.

"Did a regiment leave last night?" she called out. The boy stopped in his tracks and quickly glanced back at Otilija.

"I don't know."

"That's what everyone is saying you know. Everyone is saying that a regiment of Cavalry left last night."

"Even if I knew, I couldn't tell you," the boy restated, then quickly turned back.

Otilija realized he was not about to get any information from the boy. She reached down and picked up the letter. She looked at it intently again, but instead of ripping it open, she wavered between revealing its secret and just throwing it away.

Other than he's gone, what else could it say? She stared at it catatonically. Unable to hold back the tears welling in her tired eyes, she let them spill down her cheeks and drip onto her trembling hands. Physically exhausted and emotionally drained, she set the tear-spotted letter down beside her, drew her blanket up around her neck, then leaned back and closed her eyes. Her body succumbed quickly to her need, and she slipped into a deep sleep.

❦   ❦   ❦

The front door slammed, startling Otilija awake. As she opened her eyes, her sister Augustine scooted past, dress flying up behind her. She ran down the steps and toward the road, but then suddenly froze and looked back at the porch.

"Did you sleep there all night?" A quizzical expression wrinkled her face for a moment, but was quickly replaced by one of enlightenment. "I'm never getting married if that's what happens when you have a fight."

She spun around and disappeared behind the olive green hedge, before Otilija could think of a response. Alone again on the porch, she glanced over to the small table where her father kept his pipe and tobacco. She picked up the small carved pipe by the bowl, then turned it slowly in her hand to inspect every centimeter of it. When she got to the bowl, she brought it to her nose and inhaled deeply.

She loved the aroma of pipe tobacco. Ever since she was a little girl, she snuck out behind this special chair just to catch a brief whiff of the rich smoke that lingered for hours after Poppa sat here and smoked. Carefully, she set the pipe back down on the small carved table, then noticed the letter she'd dropped there.

"You were right, Momma. It wasn't the last time," she said aloud. Otilija sighed bitterly and reached for the envelope. She ripped open the end, tearing a sliver of the letter off in the process, then extracted the letter and dropped the envelope in her lap. A quick glance at the letter confirmed the author. Voldemars.

"I shouldn't even give you the courtesy of reading this, you know. Do you know what you did to me? Do you even care?" She realized yelling at a letter from a man probably hundreds of kilometers away was futile. After a huge sigh, she read.

16 May 1912

My dearest Otilija,

By the time you receive this letter, I'm afraid that I'll already be on my way to wherever it is they're sending us. I hope you'll find it in your heart to forgive me for being wrong when I said you'd be by my side wherever I go if we get married now, but it was out of my control. Maybe I should have done as you said and thought a little longer about what you wanted instead of what I wanted.

Mostly, I beg of you to believe me. This sudden reassignment was as much a surprise to me as it is to you. If I'd known this type of thing could happen, I'd never have asked you to change our plans. I hope you believe me. I didn't expect this kind of assignment at this time.

I've been informed that I won't be able to send letters from where I'll be stationed. I can only hope that the memories of the days we spent together will keep you, as it does me, hoping that this mission will end soon, and that once again, I'll find myself in your arms.

I love you with all of my heart, and I hope that you believe me when I say that things will get better once the tensions in the political arena have been diffused.

Until then, my love,
I remain, yours, forever,

Voldemars

Otilija briefly looked up to the morning sky, wondering why this was happening to her. It hurt. Everything about the situation hurt.

And she was alone, like she was before they were married. Almost nothing had changed. Almost. She felt queasy but didn't know why. Her mother was convinced she was with child, but she felt it was too soon to tell. But if she was, she realized she would probably have to bear the child alone, while Voldemars was off somewhere with the army.

Something her mother had said to her years ago when she didn't understand why she was the one that bad things were happening came back to her. It was her fate, and now it was her fate to bear this child alone. There was something she was to learn from this which God would reveal to her in due time. But that didn't help make the pain any less. It still hurt.

She sighed, then dropped the letter in her lap, buried her face in her hands and wept.

Telmeni Farm, Vidzeme Province, Latvia

18 May 1912

J anis Vechi folded his hands over the carved handle of his pitch-fork, leaned his wispy frame forward, and perused his farm's wind-swept, budding rye fields. Grain extended forever, dipping and rising like an open sea along the rolling terrain. Resting quietly below and to the west of the land's contours, spread the placid, sapphire cover of Bauzis, a natural reservoir and fish supply. Across the water and nestled among freshly scented spruce and birches along the far bank, liepa trees swayed, teeming with tiny sallow clusters of winter-green scented blossoms amidst glossy, heart-shaped leaves. In all his travels he had never before seen any tree like the liepa except in Latvia.

Telmeni, he mused, recalling the first time he'd walked this land. Forty-five years ago, the old Lettish word that meant 'in The Father's hand' immediately came to his mind. And nothing over the forty years it belonged to him had made him think any differently.

A rumble in the distance broke his reverie. He turned to the noise and noticed a line of towering, dark gray clouds lumbering in from the north-east. White billows extended outward like thick steam from a doused fire. Of all the cloud patterns he's seen over the years, this one was the rarest.

It certainly meant rain, he thought. He sniffed at the breeze blowing in and sensed a touch of moisture, but not much. The storm might hold off for a day. Two at the most. He scanned the balance of the sky and spotted another dense band of angry, swelling storm clouds sweeping in from the south and west. When those two meet, there will be alot of crashing and banging up there.

The combination meant only one thing to him. Rough weather. Enough to cause damage.

His stomach growled. He quickly glanced around to check that he had done everything he'd needed to do for the morning. Satisfied, he quickly planned out the balance of his day, then carefully slung the pitchfork over his narrow, square shoulders. Slowly at first but then quickly breaking into a strong jaunt, he took long, steady strides and headed for his house.

He stopped for a moment at the porch and surveyed the storm clouds again. This time he saw more than just storm clouds. They were images. Armies marching into battle. Battle lines converging. And in the lines were faces. One line was filled with the angry grimaces of the German Huns. The other were proud, young boys of the Russian Army. One of the faces looked particularly like Voldemars.

Shaking the thoughts from his head, he propped his hay fork against the house, turned away from the clouds, and sauntered into the kitchen.

The door slammed behind him. It echoed, but quickly died out and left the house still. It wasn't just the kitchen that was abandoned, but the whole house. Dead, empty silence seemed to resonate off the plank walls. It had been this quiet every morning since he sent Romans, his youngest son, to Moscow. He remembered agonizing over that decision for weeks. He wished he could have another choice, but there was none. And when he left, the last of his four sons were gone. Four different sons, four different stories. And now the house was empty.

First Edwards left to start his own life. Then Augusts chose to teach in Moscow. Then Voldemars. That left him no choice with Romans.

He wished one of his sons would have stayed with him. Romans, though, wasn't the right one. For Romans' own good, and his own piece of mind, Romans had to leave. Otherwise the army would conscript Romans away from him and Kristine. The possibility that he'd lose another son to the Czar was something which he simply couldn't bear.

He unbuttoned his shirt part way as he shuffled to the table. Plopping into his chair, he leaned back, let his arms drop limply to his sides, then noisily released a sigh.

"Kristine?" he called out.

No answer.

"Kristine? Are you in here?" he called out louder, but still received no reply.

Must be out at the hen-house, he concluded. Slowly, he raised his arms, then rested his elbows on the arms of his chair. As if in prayer, he squeezed his palms together and pressed his lips into his fingers. His eyelids slid closed. The moisture inside them immediately soothed his tired eyes. For forty years he stayed ahead of the exhaustion which farming and raising four sons caused. Now, though, it seemed that every minute he cheated on his sleep had finally caught up with him. And was taking its due, with interest.

Stopping, though, was something he realized he couldn't do now. Passing the farm on to one of his sons was fading from his list of options. All four of them were gone, and there was no one left. Of all of them, Voldemars fit the farmer's mold the best. His wide, strong shoulders, large hands, and strength were precisely the features needed to work the rocky, rolling hills of Vidzeme. Contrasting most of the other muscular boys he knew, Voldemars was also intelligent. He retained everything he'd explained to him down to the tiniest detail. Janis felt he should be the next 'Telmenu Saimnieks,' and he wished that he would've felt the same way.

But it wasn't the way Voldemars to him he had felt. That bothered him. Constantly.

The house remained still enough that he felt himself drifting into his memories. Like a recurring nightmare, the day Voldemars left Telmeni continuously returned.

"I have to go Poppa." Voldemars' words grew more cutting and clear, filled with adolescent obstinance as they had been eight years before. But it had been different now. It had been for real. He'd actually left.

"You know, as well as I, that mandatory service is inevitable," he proudly and defiantly said. "If I choose to go, however, instead of waiting for conscription, I'll have a choice. The choice of becoming cavalry."

His eyes had widened as if in awe at the thought. His chest raised and his voice remained proud. "Cavalry. Think of that, Poppa. Your son, a cavalry officer in the Czar's army."

Is that all that matters to you? He remembered thinking as he peered into those hazel-flecked eyes. There was nothing but a stolid determination mixed with youthful tenacity.

"Then will you come back after you've served your duty?" he asked icily.

Voldemars balked. Janis knew he'd decided on leaving more than a year ago, but for some reason, he'd never talked to him about it. He knew his long, dour expression wasn't helping Voldemars admit the painful truth.

"I really don't think so," Voldemars admitted, finally.

"And University? Have you changed your mind about school?" he asked.

"Oh, no Poppa. I will be going back to school," he said, then paused and stared toward the sky. "In Paris, though, instead of Riga.

I'm going to learn French. Live life as a Frenchman, live in Paris and teach there."

Voldemars had puffed out his chest like a proud cock in the chicken pen. Janis tried to hide his disappointment, but knew he did a poor job.

"Europe has so much to offer, Poppa. You'll see. I'll make you proud of me, Poppa."

"And what of Telmeni. You know Edwards will most likely not come back from Daugavpils." Janis had pleaded, groping for words that could sway his son's opinion. Voldemars had stood fast. His expression remained stiffly cold and determined. He'd hiked up his pack and started to turn away.

"Voldemars, listen to me. At least for a moment. We've worked hard together to mold this land into what it is now. It's one of the best farms in all of Vidzeme. We did that together. If no one is here to continue what we've done—"

"I know Poppa, but I don't think I'm really cut out to be a farmer," Voldemars waved his hands in front of him. "I want to learn. I want to use my mind. I want to be my own man, not a ward of a simple farm in the countryside."

The words stung. Especially the word simple. Janis sucked in a deep breath and tried to quench the searing wound he felt burning in his chest.

"There is only one Telmenu Saimnieks, Poppa. And that is you."

"But, I'm growing old and weak, Voldemars. You can see that! Someone needs to take the land when I can no longer farm."

Voldemars remained stone faced and silent.

"And your Momma…Kristine. Have you talked with her?" Janis changed his tact, hoping Voldemars' closeness with his mother would stir something more than his coldness.

"Yes, I have talked to Momma," Voldemars emphatically answered.

"You know that your moving away will break her heart."

"She understands. She respects the fact that I've made my decision to go to the city."

There is nothing I can do to change your mind, is there? Janis thought as he peered into his son's eyes, wondering how much of his distress showed on his face. Eighteen years wasn't long enough for you to grow a bond to this land? What was it that I did wrong to have you turn your back on me like this? What have I done so wrong?

A small smile, the expression which always etched Janis' face when he realized he had been outwitted in debate, twitched at his mouth, but then quivered and drooped into a frown. He dropped his head and sighed, regained his composure, then reached out and grasped his son's shoulders. Tears blurred his vision as he pulled him close for one last strong, traditional embrace.

"Then I can do nothing but wish you well, son."

Defeat seared his heart as he watched his son turn away and start down the long dirt road which led toward Cesis. He couldn't hold back the tears any longer. Refusing to let his eyes blink for even a second, he'd stared at Voldemars as he walked away, wanting to savor every bit of this last glance.

Janis startled when he heard the kitchen door creak open.

"Oh, I'm sorry, Janis. I didn't mean to wake you," Kristine said quietly.

Through bleary eyes, he saw his wife thoughtfully close the door he'd so carelessly let slam when he entered. She drifted into the house with a fluid grace most women saved for a ballroom, carrying a reed basket in the bend of her elbow.

"I know how much you enjoy your morning naps," she added with a smile that beamed cherubic and youthful, although she was only five years younger than he. Slipping past, she sauntered to the crackling wood stove.

"Oh, I wasn't sleeping," he lied, yawning and stretching his arms above his head. "I was just thinking of how quiet the house has been since the boys left."

"Again? Come now, Janis. You've been doing that for years." She tittered, then placed her favorite black iron skillet onto the stove. "Romans left almost three years ago now. And Voldemars left five years before that."

She sliced eight thick strands from a well-marbled chunk of smoked ham, then gently laid them into the pan. Immediately, the strips sizzled and popped. She wiped her hands off on the towel draped over her plain, full-length green dress.

"Would you like some tea, dear?" she asked. But without waiting for his answer, she headed to the cupboard and took down two small cups. She gently placed them next to the tarnished silver samovar, already steaming on the corner of the stove.

"Sure. I'd like some. Is there any of the spiced tea left?"

She wiped her hands on her apron, then walked back to the cupboard. Opening a small waxed paper bag, she quickly sniffed and checked the amount.

"Maybe a cup or two."

"With cardamom." He rubbed the stubbles on his pointed chin, and gazed toward the ceiling. "When I was out in the field, I thought I heard artillery again."

"Artillery? Why are you so possessed with listening for cannons? There is no war, Janis."

"I thought I heard artillery."

"Or were you just lamenting that Nicholas seems to be losing control?" Kristine added, a bit sarcastically. She filled a slotted tea spoon with the mix of spices and crumbled tea leaves, then snapped it together and gently placed it into her husband's cup. After carefully pouring steaming water from the samovar, she balanced the cup on a saucer and delivered it to Janis.

"Now, don't be impatient this time. You know it's weak if you drink it hastily." She lovingly scolded him, waving her finger. "Let it steep at least a few minutes before you start drinking it."

He reached out and took hold of the cup, then stared up at her grayish-blue eyes.

"It's really Voldemars, again, isn't it, Janis?" Kristine sat down next to him and placed her hand on his arm.

He nodded and set the cup on the table.

"There is not much we can do for him...other than pray for his safety," she assuaged.

"The least he could do is write," he humphed. "Romans and Augusts write from Moscow. Edwards writes, and he's still close enough to come home often. Why can't he write? Even just a brief note to let us know he's all right?"

She didn't answer. He turned his head toward the window and pensively stared out to the fields. "I guess I just can't help but wonder that perhaps if I was a little less gruff with him, he might still—"

"The bacon!" Kristine gasped. She jumped up and raced to the stove. Furiously she waved at the smoke billowing from the skillet while spearing the bacon with a small fork. She dangled the charred bacon over a plate next to the stove, then laid out the stiff, sizzling strips.

"Well, you do like your bacon a little crisp, don't you Janis?" she chuckled. Still waving at the swirl of aromatic smoke with one hand, she poured some of the drippings into a metal bowl.

"Do you think I was too hard on him? Do you think that's why he was so stubborn? Do you think that's why he's not writing?"

Kristine quietly continued with her cooking. She dropped a pat of lard on the skillet before cracking eggs on the edge of the metal bowl. She slid them into the skillet and they began to crackle.

"No, but I know someone just as bull-headed as he is," she finally responded. She turned and grinned wryly at her husband.

He gazed catatonically out the window, unresponsive.

"He'll be back, Janis," she offered. Slicing two pieces of black sourdough rye off a loaf, she tipped her head seeming to revel in the warm pungency emanating out of the center. She lathered the tops with butter, drizzled a line of honey on top, then set them on the edge of the stove to warm them up. "In due time, he'll be back. Telmeni is in his blood, Janis. Didn't you see that in his eyes. That's why I felt there was no need to argue."

She removed the eggs from the pan and placed them next to the bacon. She added the bread to the fare, then brought the plate to the table and set it down in front of Janis.

"My word, Janis, you're still brooding," she said as she sat down. "This isn't like you."

He thought for a moment, then looked down to his plate. He picked up a slice of the bread and absently swept up his egg yolk and remaining bacon shards. He lifted his cup and sipped noisily at the hot tea, jerking back as the hot fluid singed his lips.

"Oh, it's nothing," he mumbled, then silently finished his breakfast.

After breakfast, while Kristine tended to the dishes, Janis stepped out onto the porch for his customary smoke and second cup of tea. He plopped in his chair, and as if cued, Oskars Ziemels appeared in the rye fields. He strutted through the grass, lips pursed as he whistled away. When he finally looked up, Janis knew he'd seen him. He waved, smiled, and hastened his pace toward the farmhouse.

"Morning, Janis. Any news?" Oskars started as Janis lit a match. Janis sucked rhythmically while he held the match over his pipe. When puffs of smoke finally escaped his lips, he flipped his wrist and snapped out the little flame. He drew in deeply, then held the smoke for a moment before he exhaled a thick, aromatic cloud toward Oskars.

"I've received some interesting news from Romans," Janis teased.

"Moscow? What's in Moscow that could be so interesting? Hell, the only thing I've heard from there has been bread riots and mass arrests." Oskars chuckled as he pulled out his own curved pipe and grabbed Janis' tobacco bag.

"I was thinking, Oskars. Say that Nicholas falls—"

"But what about Moscow?" Oskars interrupted, packing down the bowl of tobacco.

A sly grin crept onto Janis' face, revealing his toothy grip on his pipe. "If Nicholas falls, what consequences could you imagine?"

Oskars lit his pipe, sucked in deeply, then let out a cloud of his own. He stared into the sky and rubbed his chin, then turned back to Janis with a quizzical expression.

"The obvious result would be some sort of provisional government I'd guess. Who knows."

"Or?"

"Or the Bolsheviks take over. Or the Germans roll in. I don't see your point."

"In any case, all eyes will be on that government," Janis explained. "No one would really be interested in, say a small country starting a separatist movement—".

"Are you saying that if Nicholas falls, that would be the best time to make our move?"

Oskars saw a smile grow wide on Janis' face.

"My friend, if the timing is correct, we could be part of history," Janis dreamily spoke. His eyes were glazed as they peered out over his rye fields. "The fall of the Czar could give us the opportunity we've been waiting ten years for. We could be the beginning of the Republic of Latvia."

Oskars grinned as his eyes smiled, and gleamed with the same sparkle that twinkled in Janis'.

Masurian Lakes, At the Polish-German Border

13 September 1912

*V*oldemars languished over starting another day in seclusion, awake at dawn, thinking only how to muddle through another day of meaningless and fruitless incursions into Prussian territory. In the four months they had been camped at the border, he had been on at least fifty scouting parties into the heart of Prussia and found no evidence of what Plotnikov had warned they would find. The only life across the border was bland and harmless. Old men tended their fields, swine rooted in the parched meadows and dried out swamps, and peasants begged them for handouts from their well-stocked packs.

He stumbled out of his musty tent and shuffled in his unlaced boots to a smoldering campfire where three other soldiers sat disheveled and quiet. The lack of rain and relentless summer heat had so parched the area that just his scuffling was enough to stir a cloud of dust behind him.

"Morning," he grumbled, joining his comrades. Each man in turn glanced up with glassy eyes, nodded an obligatory acknowledgement at his arrival, then drifted back into themselves.

"Has Gunars been by?" Voldemars asked as he rummaged in the pile of metal cups. He grabbed one, then habitually rubbed the inside clean with his shirt.

"We're going south today," Ahmed droned. His dark, Middle-Eastern complexion stood out among the blanched white Nordic faces. "Not far enough south, though," he added with a chuckle.

"I see." Voldemars dipped the cup into an open pot of steaming water, then took out his dwindling private stash of tea leaves. He sprinkled in a pinch and swirled carelessly.

"How can you drink hot tea in this weather?" Pavel grumbled, throwing a handful of sticks onto the fire. His demeanor had soured quickly, and had grown worse with each fruitless scouting party.

"Habit, I guess," Voldemars answered and sat down. He brought the liquid to his face and let the steam bathe his face. Even on hot days, he enjoyed the soothing swirls on his skin.

"We have our orders," Gunars announced, loud and sarcastic as he joined the group.

Pavel threw another handful of twigs into the dying fire. "Will we need to record number of chickens for Plotnikov this time?"

"Resources. Even chickens can be considered as food resources," Gunars corrected.

"These hikes in the woods are pointless wastes of time," Pavel countered. "We can't do anything, so what's the point."

Gunars ignored Pavel. "We will head south toward Tannenberg. Be prepared to leave on the hour." He turned away from the group and headed for his tent.

"You heard the commander," Ahmed said, despondently. He stood up and brushed off his lap. "We leave in twenty minutes—"

"This is stupid. I'm not going to look for more fucking chickens," Pavel replied.

"Resources," Ahmed insisted.

"Chickens!"

"We have our orders," Voldemars jumped in, trying to quell the argument.

"Well, the orders are stupid, and I am not going." Pavel debated. "If you want to waste another day tromping through this God-for-saken hell-hole, go right ahead. I've made my decision and I am not going!"

"Insubordination is punishable by—"

"Who are you to quote rules, Vechi?" Pavel vaulted to his feet and confronted Voldemars face-to-face. Voldemars felt his heart pump harder and faster with each foul-smelling breath Pavel exhaled into his face. "This isn't your army. You are here because we invited you here. If your people had any spine—"

Gunars appeared out of nowhere and grabbed Pavel by the shoulders, yanking him away from Voldemars. Clamping his hands onto Pavel's shoulders, he turned him smartly and shook him.

"This is one army, and you will do as I order you to. I said to be ready on the hour, and I expect you to carry out that order." Gunars' eyes bulged from his flushed face. His stiff-lipped frown punctuated his displeasure. "Did I make myself clear?"

Pavel swatted Gunars' arms away and stepped back. He remained defiantly at attention, nostrils flared and chest heaving.

"I will be there," he grumbled. As he turned and stormed off to his tent, he glowered at Voldemars.

"If we do go to war, we will never win with men like him," Gunars mumbled under his breath.

"Then let's hope we don't go to war," Voldemars added as he walked by, headed to his tent.

Gunars stopped the reconnaissance party at the edge of a partly dried swamp, already reeking in the sweltering morning sun. The gagging odor like a pall, forcing everyone to turn away to catch a breath. The solitary occasional grunt of a bullfrog echoed in the silence of the swamp.

Voldemars wiped the sweat from his forehead with his sleeve, then squinted and surveyed across the water. The slight incline to the summer scorched land ended in a barren crest, dotted with wind twisted and half-dead oaks. A pair of ravens circled effortlessly around a swirl of rising smoke beyond the mound.

He turned back to Gunars who had already dismounted. Gunars unbuttoned his coat and reached into a pocket. He extracted a topographical map and crouched down. He unfolded it, then laid it out on the ground. After a brief study, he glanced up and pointed to a ridge on the map.

"This is the target area. Plotnikov wants a survey of this portion of the line. If we span the hill, we should be able to get a good look at what is going on over there."

"What do we expect to see?" Voldemars asked.

"Chickens," Pavel grumbled.

Gunars glared at him briefly, then chose to ignore the comment.

"There are reports that the Germans are using the cover of this ridge to stage a supply line. If these reports are true, then we should see armament here unlike we've seen in the north. If they are not true—"

"What do you think we'll see?" Ahmed asked.

"Same as we've seen before. Nothing." Pavel said.

Gunars closed his eyes and hung his head as he pursed his lips.

Voldemars turned to Ahmed. "Have you talked to the gypsies?"

Ahmed's eyes grew as wide as saucers. Voldemars had his answer.

"Let's just hope they are wrong," Gunars was openly disturbed. He scooped up his map then clumsily folded it and stashed it in his pocket. "It will be easier if we cross in single file," he added, then started toward the water.

One after the other, the soldiers slogged into the knee deep water, splitting the floating, bubble-filled green scum as they crossed.

Gunars emerged on the other side first, followed by Voldemars and Ahmed. As the last three soldiers emerged from the swamp, the scouting party spread out and moved toward the ridge.

Voldemars' boots squished under his feet as he started up the incline. His mind drifted, thinking how much more pleasant this would be if he were back at Telmeni, barefoot, walking through the glen with Otilija. Instead he was here, scaling some ridge in Poland, in wet boots, looking for some alleged buildup of enemy forces that no one had found for months.

This whole expedition has been a waste of time, he thought. There were no heroics to be shown in these swamps. There was no battle to fight. No quarry to chase and defeat. He was just a menial scout here, wasting time with a brigade full of malcontents.

Nor was there any sign of the danger Plotnikov have warned them about. There was no reason why officer's wives had to be left home. Pavel was right. There was nothing secret about chickens, pigs and beggars. That was the way it was all over Eastern Europe. The wives could have come. They wouldn't have been in any danger, nor would they have been in the way. In fact, this would have been much better if the wives were here. It would be a break from this daily monotony.

And what do I tell Otilija why she couldn't come? How am I going to be able to explain I was put out in the woods to spy on chickens? Is she even going to believe—

Gunars hit Voldemars in the shoulder hard enough to send him to the ground. When Voldemars looked up, he noticed that he was less than a meter from the ridge.

Gunars cracked a weak smile, then nodded his head toward the ridge. He dropped into a prone position and pulled his binoculars from his satchel, then wormed to the crest. Voldemars followed suit and snaked up behind him until he was able to look over himself.

Voldemars swallowed hard. The entire countryside was criss-crossed with trenches that stretched on for kilometers. He couldn't remember ever seeing such an elaborate excavation before. At each

sandbagged crest, barbed wire ran in what looked like a massive spider's web, waiting for unwary prey to fall into the trap.

He rolled over, scrambled through his pack for his binoculars,
then dug his elbows into the soft ground and scanned the sprawling
field. There were hundreds of boxes piled high. They looked like
photographs he had seen of the pyramids in Egypt. What seemed
like a whole battalion of gray-uniformed sentries patrolled the
mountains of armament. Behind the shells were rows and rows of
cannons and wagons full of more shells. In the open fields further
back, thousands of gray-clad German foot soldiers impressively ran
through offensive drills, leapfrogging in lines as if they were advanc-
ing a battle line.

"Hell-bent on war," Voldemars gasped.

"I've been in battles before, but I've never seen numbers like this,"
Gunars replied under his breath. "Remember everything you can.
When we get back to camp, we need to detail a report of everything
for Plotnikov."

Voldemars quickly glanced down the line to the others and read
the surprise in their faces as well. Even Pavel remained glued on the
trench.

"This has been here all along," he noted. Gunars nodded silently.

The grim reality of what was now in front of him stung Voldemars. As a cold chill swept over his now sweat dampened nape, he
realized he may not be going home after six months. What the gypsies said haunted him as his mind reeled thinking of how he was
going to explain to Otilija that he was not coming home.

Near Riga

3 October 1912

*A*s his calf-length coat flapped at his thighs, Otomars Braze crouched forward, lifted into his half seat, and moved in unison with his chestnut stallion. He whipped his mount into an even faster gallop, then tightly gripped the reins in his large, vice-like hands. His red scarf snapped wildly behind him, trailing like a scarlet ribbon.

Tumultuous strains of Tchaikovsky's 1812 Overture resounded through his head as the wind whistled by his ears and whisked back his fine amber hair. Burying his face into his mount's wind-swept mane, he pressed deep enough into the horse's bulging neck muscles that coarse hairs scraped against his large, round face. He squinted, trying to protect his steel-blue eyes from the buffeting, oncoming air, but streams of tears still dribbled down his cheeks, evaporating quickly into two salty trails on his face.

He turned his head just enough to catch a glance back, and spotted his brother, Oswalds, on his bay colored Arabian unwavering in their diligent pursuit. Otomars cupped his hand around his mouth to ensure his words would drift back through the wake of the kicked up leaves and dust.

"You won't beat me this time, little brother!" He reached down, opened his hand, then slapped his horse's flank. "Com'on, boy! Faster!"

"Little brother, ha!" Oswalds coaxed his stallion's strides to widen even further to close the gap. "I was born only fifteen minutes after you. And it's the only fifteen minutes in my life that I've ever been behind you!

"Com'on!" He snapped his reins. His mount instantly responded, quickly closing the lead. Once caught up, he turned his head enough to flash a wide, victorious grin at Otomars.

Neck-and-neck, the pair galloped along the dusty road as it bent sharply down and left, toward a bleached white birch lined glen. Oswalds leaned into the turn, toward Otomars, close enough that his hair snapped at his brother's ballooned pants. Beneath them, hooves pounded with a stampede-like rhythm, exploding each time they pummeled the hard, dirt road.

The road straightened. Oswalds shifted back close to his mount's neck and pressed his face against the dancing mane. Urged on by another gentle snap of the reins, his horse surged ahead.

Success! Oswalds gloated privately, then turned his head just long enough to flash another grin at his brother.

"You're as slow as a turtle, Otomars. Too much bread?" he goaded.

Otomars menacingly bared his teeth and grumbled with his usual low guttural humph, but the sound was swallowed by pounding hooves.

"That's it, isn't it? You're spending too much time eating instead of practicing your riding, Otomars! Or is it just your inflated ego that's slowing you down!" Oswalds badgered, pulling away.

The pair fiercely raced through the rows of white birch, then plunged though a pile of dried catkins, stirring them up like a brown, dusty cloud. As the chaff settled behind them, cool shade transformed into bright sun. In front of them, like a medieval story book scene, the skeleton of an old Teutonic castle rose out of the swamps, low sun burnt brush, and sprawling amber fields. Its round, brownstone turrets, fragmented at the top from centuries of weathering, stood as sentries on each corner. Bright red ivy blanketed the lower half of one of the pillars, and completely shrouded the south-ernmost.

Otomars surged ahead of Oswalds as they thundered through a narrow road splitting a summer dried swamp. Blackbirds squawked as they scattered from the dried reeds, startled by the racing horse-men.

Before the dust cloud in their wake settled, a gray flecked, white horse majestically vaulted over the sun-baked brush like a Lippizan stallion, then landed in the center of the road. With only a second's hesitation, the red-cloaked horseman's mount turned and exploded into a blindingly fast gallop toward the racing brothers. The steed's remarkably long strides churned up the road so rapidly that the mys-terious horseman drew even with the two brothers within seconds. He turned his scarf hidden face toward them, obviously to flash a grin, then effortlessly raced by, leaving only the sight of his long trail-ing white scarf flapping in tandem with his scarlet cloak.

Startled by the sudden appearance of the rider, Otomars and Oswalds awed at the passing horse's rippling muscles. The powerful animal continued its astounding pace as it distanced itself from them. The horse moved with such speed that it stayed one full stride ahead of its own dusty wake.

The rider himself was no less amazing, obviously highly skilled to manage deft maneuvers at such speed. His body movements so per-fectly matched every motion of the gray-speckled mount that they looked to be a mythical centaur.

"You'll never keep up with the Cossacks riding like that!" The voice drifted back as the rogue rider vanished where the road crested then sank behind the castle. Only the echo of his mount's hooves hammering across a planked bridge remained.

Oswalds and Otomars maintained their pursuit, following in the settling dust trail left in the hussar's wake. They pounded across an old wooden drawbridge, then veered left and skirted the west side of the castle. As the road vanished and blended into the castle's idyllic green courtyard, the brothers quickly pulled up on their reins. The horses stammered to an abrupt stop in the pasture.

Across the field, three willows draped their delicate green and yellow branches in a babbling, clear water stream. Underneath the sweeps, the already dismounted rider arrogantly posed under the trees, arms and legs crossed as he leaned against his horse. Unwrapped from his face, his scarf rested across his chest.

"Voldemars?" Otomars was stunned.

"And who were you expecting?" Voldemars grinned and tipped his head slightly. He twirled his thin, blonde mustache between the fingers of his right hand.

"Where the hell did you come from?" Otomars briefly studied the physique of the animal, still awed at what the horse had accomplished.

"And where did you get him?" Oswalds asked.

"That really makes no difference, does it?"

"But what a ride…."

"And believe it or not, I've got one even better than him back with my regiment."

"And the Russians didn't get it?" Oswalds asked, closely inspecting the horse.

"It takes a keen eye to spot a good horse amidst all the cannon fodder the military tries to pass off to us. But it does help to bribe the quartermaster."

Voldemars turned back to his horse and fished into his saddlebag for a moment.

"And it helps to have good friends," he announced as he pulled out a tall, clear bottle.

The brothers eyes opened wide before grins split their faces.

"Stolichnaya. The best from Petersburg," Voldemars said, reading from the label. "Had to pay some extra bribe money for this one."

"You know, when you jumped out of the brush, you scared the living hell right out of me." Otomars admitted as he hopped off and secured his mount to the willow tree.

"For a moment, I thought I'd seen Lacplesis," Oswalds admitted.

"Who knows, with a little of this, you may still see him." Voldemars glowed, pushing out his chest.

"But I didn't think Lacplesis was so short." Otomars chuckled.

Voldemars' expression quickly soured. Oswalds covered his face to stifle his laughter.

"Did you ever think that my height may actually be an advantage on a horse, Otomars? After all, have you ever seen a tall Cossack?"

"Touche," Oswalds noted, jabbing his finger at his brother like a rapier.

Otomars pruned his lips.

Holding the bottle high in the air like a prize, Voldemars took five paces toward the stream, then threw himself prone onto a thick stand of green sedge grass. Oswalds and Otomars followed suit, then rolled onto their backs, unbuttoned their olive green tunics half-way and sucked in the crisp autumn air.

"So, Otomars, what's the home guard doing in Petersburg?" Voldemars asked as he uncorked the bottle.

"Nothing. Drills, marching, and mucking stalls. Just like we're in school or something," Otomars admitted.

Voldemars lifted the bottle to his lips, sipped quickly, then gasped.

"Whoa." Voldemars waved his hand in front of his mouth then passed the bottle to Oswalds. "Gunars got some good stuff!"

"Don't get me wrong, though," Otomars quickly added after a brief hesitation. "The Dragoons surely have their hands full, and I'm content not to have anything to do with that mess."

"Oh?" Voldemars leaned back on his hands.

"Tension in the city is thick." Otomars maintained a close watch on his brother and the bottle. "And I really don't think its anything specific."

"Oh, no? I think it is. It's Nicholas." Oswalds spouted, gasping for breath after a hard gulp. "He's why everyone's so damned restless."

"What I meant was that there are so many things to get riled up about, Oswalds." Otomars humphed. He whacked his brother's shoulder, then swiped the bottle from his hand. "Hell, it could be the impending war, the strikes, or just everything in general."

"I think it's just that it's fashionable now a days to be against something," Oswalds mumbled, wiping his lips with his sleeve.

This is what I'm missing while I'm at the front, Voldemars thought, maintaining a safe distance from the conversation.

"Factory workers clamor about money and rights, and since no one listens to them, they strike," Oswalds continued. "Then Nicholas, in all his wisdom, sends in the Dragoons to restore order, has the Okhrana arrest half of them on some trumped up charge, and order is restored. But with the jails full, there is no place to send them."

"And that's about the only thing the Duma and Nicholas agree on. With everything else, they're at each other's throats." Otomars interrupted as he passed the bottle back to Voldemars. "Christ, it seems that the Bolsheviks are the only ones not raising a ruckus, but I'm sure it's only a matter of time before they start something again."

"If you ask me, I think they're just sitting in the wings, waiting for the government to fall apart, and then—"

"Bolsheviks?" Voldemars eyes popped open. "Aren't they outlawed? Haven't the Okhrana arrested all of them?"

"Everyone's an outlaw in Petersburg now. The Okhrana just can't keep up," Otomars said, his head bobbing.

Voldemars carefully brought the vodka to his pursed lips, then let the fluid seep past his lips and further numb his tongue.

"They're like rats, you know," Oswalds added with a sneer, "breeding in the squalor. I really wonder how long it'll be before they all get together and take over the Duma."

"I can't believe even Russians could be so blind as to not see what kind of crap those anarchists are peddling," Voldemars said, swallowing so quickly he started to gasp. He handed the liquor to Oswalds.

"Bread for the poor. Power to the people's soviet." Oswalds mocked.

"If you ask me, it sounds more like another damned religion than a political philosophy." Voldemars finished while Oswalds chuckled.

"You may have a point there Voldemars," Otomars said, pensively. "After all, religion has been a tremendous motivator in history."

"The Mohammedans are proof of that," Oswalds sniped, waving the bottle in front of him.

Otomars rescued the vodka from his half-drunk brother before it could be dropped.

"They'll fight to the death for their Allah and not even get paid for it."

"But if Poppa's right," Otomars' stopped abruptly to bury his chin into his chest and burp, "we might not have to worry about what happens in Russia," he finished sloppily.

"Huh?" Voldemars snapped his head around.

Otomars smirked, then held the half empty bottle in the air as if celebrating.

"My God, Voldemars, haven't you heard? The Latvian deputies to the Duma have set the stage for separation. All they need now is—"

"Separation? That's crazy," Voldemars interrupted. "Don't they remember what happened in 1905?"

"Of course they do. That's why they think they can get away with it this time," Otomars stated nonchalantly.

"But don't they realize what Nicholas will do. They don't call him 'Bloody Nicholas' for nothing."

"The deputies think they can do it this time—"

"And Nicholas will surely make them martyrs for the cause."

"Poppa thinks this is true. And if he feels that way, I am certain something's already been started," Otomars said, wiping his lips with his forearm.

"Guaranteed," Oswalds chimed in.

Voldemars could not believe what he heard. He tried to concentrate through his drunkenness, but his head only spun faster. He tried to weave through the fuzzy distinctions between reality and fantasy. A free Latvia, he thought. A free Latvia in my lifetime? Freedom from the Czar? Our own country?

"Enough of this home guard babble. What about the real war?" Oswalds asked.

"Tell me, oh great warrior Voldemars Vechi," Otomars' tongue flopped loosely as his slurred words interrupted Voldemars' soul searching. "What do you think? What are the prospects for a glorious war?"

As if that one question drained him, Otomars rolled onto his side to the amusement of his brother. He then propped his head up with his arm and stared glassy-eyed at his brother-in-law.

"You're at the front. What do you hear?" Oswalds leered at Voldemars.

"How did you know?" Voldemars snapped defensively. "I'm not suppose to say anything about where we are or what we're doing. Command has ordered…my orders are…it's still a military secret."

"Oh Christ, Voldemars. Do we look like commoners?" Otomars badgered.

"We're in the same damn military that you are, you know," Oswalds injected. "They can't keep everything from us."

Otomars swiped the bottle from Voldemars' hand, then gulped the last mouthful. He winced as it slid down his throat. "We hear rumors about what's happening. All you'd be doing is confirming or denying their truth."

Voldemars remained defensively quiet. If word of this gets out, I'll never get that promotion they promised me, he mulled.

"Com'on, Voldemars. We're your brothers, now."

"What the hell," he abdicated. Hunching over, he secretively peered around as if concerned that he was being watched. Waving his finger, he urged the brothers to scoot in closer, like schoolboys gossiping about a girl from class.

"There's no direct evidence of war starting soon, but we've seen armaments, heavy armaments, flowing like water toward the fronts. From both sides. The Germans are digging so many trenches that they must have cities underground or something. Barbed wire is stretched everywhere like spider webs. The sheer volume is mind-boggling. And that was just in Poland. I've heard that it's even worse on the Western Front. Everybody up there is saying that it's only a matter of time before war breaks out. One stupid move—"

"When? A month…a year…."

"A year, maybe two."

"And where do we fit in? I mean, I really don't think that anyone is stupid enough to try attacking us?" Otomars badgered.

"Our strength is in numbers, not tactics. You've seen how the Russians run things." Voldemars solemnly noted. "The Germans, on the other hand—"

"Oh, we've seen what the Huns have done before." Oswalds sneered, then appeared to drop into deeper thought. "They may just be crazy enough to try it."

"But what is still an unknown is what Nicholas and his cousin, Kaiser Willy have talked about behind closed doors."

"Half of our history was under the rule of those bastards."

"Maybe that's why he married Alexandra—to keep the Huns out of Mother Russia."

Oswalds playfully started to chant "Huns, Huns, Huns," as he swept his hand around like an orchestra leader, marking time with marching feet.

"I agree." Voldemars noted in a resigned tone. "If there's a war, you can be sure the Germans will play a major part in it, if not start it out right."

Voldemars stood up. His knees started wobbling, but he retained his stand with spread out legs. "I don't know about you, boys, but

I've got a wife who's expecting me home. I've been gone for five months, and my last day of leave should be spent doing things I can't do over the next six months."

Oswalds feigned vomiting while Otomars tied to suck out the last drops of vodka from the empty bottle.

"Like a visit to the steam house for a nice, hot bath, and an enjoyable evening with a beautiful woman."

"Beautiful woman? I thought you were married to my sister." Oswalds' boyish giggle drew a swipe from his brother. Otomars missed, though, and his arm swung full circle and slapped his own shoulder.

"Ah, dear Oswalds," Voldemars started with a chivalrous retort. "Growing up with Otilija has blinded you to all she has to offer."

"Touche," Otomars snipped back at his drunken brother.

Staggering toward his horse, Voldemars stiffened to maintain some semblance of composure, although he managed only to look more like an awkward toy soldier stumbling along on rubbery legs. When he reached his mount, he fell into the secured reins, then groped to regain his balance. Fumbling at first, he freed the leather straps with his numb hands.

Otomars and Oswalds broke into loud, disrespectful laughter as they watched Voldemars floundering against his horse. Each time he failed to gain his mount, the boys guffawed harder and louder. Finally succeeding, Voldemars turned the horse around with much less precision than he arrived, then wormed into a sloppy mount, waved and headed back toward the city.

An hour later, sickly looking and slouched markedly to his right in his saddle, Voldemars stared at the Braze house through bleary, blood-shot eyes. His head felt like it was about to explode. His mouth felt like damp flax and an acerbic, stomach juice taste gurgled in his throat. He tried to remember how he'd made it here, but not a single thought registered. Keeping one hand on the horse to prevent losing his already tenuous balance, he slipped toward the ground.

When his boots hit the ground hard, the sudden stop immediately stirred vertigo. He weakly leaned into his horse, closed his eyes and laid his head on his mount's flank, willing his dizziness away. As his nausea subsided, he carefully took the reins, stumbled toward the fence, and tied his mount to the rail.

Now if I just slip onto the porch and catch some sleep before she gets home, he thought as he cautiously tip-toed through the gate. But when he turned around and saw Otilija standing perfectly still, hands planted firmly on her hips, he froze.

Oh, shit! Otilija's image blurred as he jerked backward, but there was no mistaking her sour mood. He immediately stiffened, pulling down sharply on his tunic in a confident display. Concentrating on walking a straight line, he tried to clear his head with steady deep breaths, but the breathing seemed only to make everything spin faster and make him list more.

"My word, Voldemars. You're drunk." Otilija scolded as he reached the steps.

"You can say that again," he mumbled under his breath. He looked up to her and sheepishly grinned, trying to stop his weaving. His body, though felt like it kept swaying.

"Why?"

"Why what?"

"Why did you have to go and get drunk?"

His head pulsed and ached as each word formed in his throat then passed his furry feeling tongue.

"Oh come now, Otilija. It's not like I was out whoring in the city. I was just having a few drinks with your brothers. At the castle."

"I still don't like it. Why couldn't you meet my brothers here?"

The wind in my hair, the horse at my beckon command, the sense of freedom—

"At least that way I wouldn't worry about you falling off your horse and hurting yourself. You know nobody travels out that way any more."

Hurting myself? Me? Are you serious?

The pounding in his head grew unbearably stronger. He tried to focus on her words, in the case she asked him a question, but his concentration was scrambled and just made him more queasy.

"What is it about the army, anyway? Even Otomars and Oswalds seem to be drinking all the time now. They never used to drink at all." Otilija's face had grown cherry red.

His ears rang so much he raised his open hand, pleading for Otilija to stop her shrill castigation. He lowered his head and slowly weaved it right to left.

"I'm sorry, Otilija. I can't take any more of this," he said as soon as Otilija stopped for a breath. Careful not to stir up his vertigo, he slowly turned and swaggered back to his horse. With each step he felt her wide, glazed eyes burrow deeper into his back. Past the gate, he grasped his horse's reins, then tried to concentrate on the poorly tied knot. His muddled head, blurred vision, and numb, fumbling hands though, had no coordination.

Turning his head, he gazed at Otilija. "Uh, do you think, uh, you could help me with this? I can't seem to get this knot—"

"Help you? No. I will not help you."

Voldemars turned back to the knot and pawed at the leathers with his numb fingers.

"Not only have you wasted half of your leave out drinking with my brothers, I'd bet you'll be sick tonight and tomorrow. I thought we might be able to spend some time together. I hoped you'd be a little more thoughtful." Otilija stomped off into the house and slammed the door.

"Damn, I really messed that up," Voldemars muttered through a deep sigh, then concentrated on the tether. When he finally loosened the knot, he longingly glanced back at the porch.

I guess I'll spend the rest of my leave alone at Gunars' beach house on the Jurmala. Damn, I wish she'd understand.

Voldemars repeatedly hoisted his rubbery legs onto his horse's flank, failing to gain his mount until finally succeeding on his fifth try. Worming into his saddle, he slowly turned the horse, and headed toward Gunars' beach house at Jurmala.

❧   ❧   ❧

Under a black but brightly speckled starry sky, Voldemars sat alone on the open porch of the beach house, staring out beyond the fine, white sandy beach. The bay seemed to be covered with a rippling, deep sapphire cover, which shushed as each of its waves washed onto the shore. As if it were like the grains of sand on the beach, his head felt as if it were being cleansed with each pulse.

A gentle, salt-tainted breeze weaved in off the bay and warmed the air enough so that he felt comfortable with his shirt sleeves rolled up. He felt foolish concerning the way he'd acted. Even embarrassed with what Otilija called his seemingly boyish selfishness. But there was little he could do now.

"Life on the front is hell, why can't she understand that," he muttered. "Not knowing if you're even coming back from a penetration, not knowing if you'll ever see your loved ones again. Christ, maybe I just expect too much from her."

His eyes burned and his eyelids grew heavy. Instead of fighting his exhaustion any longer, he just laid back and let the shushing of the waves washing ashore lull him to sleep.

"I guess I really can't expect her to understand what it's like up there."

Voldemars shivered when he felt a feather-soft stroking on his bare forearm. Half-asleep, he simply relaxed and let the soothing touch ease away the tension.

He startled when it finally registered what the stroking was. His eyes popped open. He sprung up from his chair. Through bleary eyes, he saw Otilija silently standing in front of him, slowly pulling back her hand. Her face shimmered with a bright bluish hue as the moon's light glanced off her cheeks.

"I'm sorry for what I said, Voldemars," she swallowed hard. "I talked to Otomars. I think I understand why you needed the time to unwind like you did."

Voldemars squinted. He clearly saw Otilija's tear streaked face. He reached up and gently wiped her rounded cheeks clear of the tears.

"Otomars talked to you?"

"Yes, Otomars. Like the big brother is supposed to, he explained why. I guess I just wanted to spend more time with you before you left, because, well, lately, I've just been feeling so lonely." Otilija let a smile wrinkle her lips.

"I guess I didn't realize that."

"I'm sorry for being so selfish, Voldemars."

He smiled without saying another word. Just the movement of his face muscles sent his head spinning again.

Good vodka, he thought, peering into Otilija's wistfully gazing eyes. He reached over and gently placed his hand on Otilija's slightly bulging stomach.

"Any kicking, yet?"

"No, nothing," Otilija sighed as she sat down on the porch. He watched her head jerk back as she sniffled, trying to hold back her weeping. "I'm worried, Voldemars."

"Worried?"

"Momma says I should be feeling something by now."

"Maybe, he's a thinker…like his father."

"Oh? His father?"

"Yes, his father," Voldemars playfully bantered. Otilija tried to hide her grin, but it slipped out anyway.

"First, how do you know it's a he? And second, I know his father and he is not what I'd consider the quiet, studious type. After all, he's gallivanting all over creation instead of teaching. Like he said he was going to."

"In another year, when my duty to the Czar is over, you'll see," Voldemars spoke introspectively, yet carefully, feeling the alcohol still toying with his thoughts. "I'm only doing what I have to do, Otilija. And for now, that's the service."

Voldemars reached over and offered open hands to Otilija. She rested hers in his open palms, and smiled.

"You do believe I'm not planning on being a career soldier, don't you?"

Otilija remained silent, tipped her head slightly and grinned with a skeptical expression. Moonlight glinted in her eyes, reflecting like stars in them. Voldemars felt spellbound as her small, thin-lipped grin dimpled her cheeks, melting away his lingering hangover. He couldn't help but remember the way she appeared the first evening they'd spent together at this house six months before.

"Can I interest you in a drink, perhaps a little French wine? I'm sure Gunars has a bottle in here somewhere."

"You're going to drink more?" Otilija's eyes widened.

"Oh, no, I've had enough for one day. I just thought you might like—"

Otilija melted into Voldemars arms, stopping him in mid-sentence. She giggled as she wormed herself onto his lap.

"I don't need anything right now…except you," Otilija whispered, nuzzling closer. She briefly rubbed noses with Voldemars, then passed her lips over his and softly kissed them. Her arms wrapped around his square shoulders as she buried her head into his neck.

Voldemars drew in a full breath through her mist dampened hair. He closed his eyes and let the fragrance of her perfume tingle inside his nose. It was a delicate fragrance like the early summer lilacs at Telmeni that always soothed him. He combed his fingers through her wavy hair, then brought a lock close enough to entangle his mustache.

In his chest, his heart started to beat faster and stronger. He felt his breath shorten. Succumbing to his desire, he slipped his right arm under his Otilija's knees.

She giggled briefly, then gazed into the fire dancing in his eyes. Groaning, he unleashed one powerful display of strength, lifting her, then carried her into the house.

Riga

25 November 1912

*C*urled into a ball and writhing in pain, Otilija startled awake by a sudden jabbing at her stomach. She sucked in deep, steady breaths, one after another, trying to ease through the pains, but the searing sharpness ripped at her mercilessly. Her breaths grew choppy and shallow as she worked harder and harder to grasp control, but the feeling of a knife was turning inside of her only strengthened.

Just breathe. Breathe normal, she remembered, trying to concentrate on what would help. She sat up and focused more intensely, but her breaths grew even choppier and shallower. Like the waves of an angry, storm-driven surf, the pains intensified. Underneath her, the bed squeaked, complaining with the motion of her panting. Sweat beaded profusely on her brow, then stung as it dribbled into her eyes. Fear sparked panic as she realized her self-control was slipping away. Her chest felt like a belt had been drawn so tight that not even a mouthful of air could seep in. Gasping, she froze, eyes clenched shut.

Like a suddenly answered prayer, the stabbing relented. She sucked in a chest full of air, then released it as slow as her trembling muscles would allow. Control. Control was back in her grasp. She breathed easier, finally able to calmly draw in through her nose.

She winced from her own odor, the same revolting scent she emanated after a hot, steamy night. But this seemed stronger and more acrid. Lifting the bed sheet, she wiped her brow, then bunched it up and cleaned the tears from her cheeks and eyes.

"Oh, my God," she gasped, struck by a sudden revelation as strong as the pain that had awaken her.

"Momma! Momma!" she yelled as loud as her cottony mouth and parched throat allowed.

Doroteja rushed into the room, battling to push her arms through the sleeves of her housecoat.

"Otilija, what's wrong?"

"My baby! Momma! My baby! Something's happening to my baby!" Otilija screamed. Thrusts of pain returned as sharp as needles in her stomach.

"It's too early for the baby, Otilija. Are you—"

"Momma! Look!" Otilija pulled the sheets back and revealed the brownish stain she was sitting in.

"Oh, my God," Doroteja gasped, covering her mouth with her open hands. She spun around and started out, but ran into Andrejs, still half-asleep.

Somebody has to save my baby!" Otilija sobbed.

"Get the doctor, Andrejs. And something to drink. Something cold," Doroteja ordered, then rushed to her quivering daughter's bedside.

Andrejs stood dumbfounded, mouth agape, and eyes darting between Doroteja and Otilija.

"Now!" Doroteja barked, glancing back at her husband.

As if suddenly splashed with cold water, Andrejs shivered, then shuffled his feet and hurried out of the room.

"Something is wrong, Momma. I can feel it. Something is terribly wrong," Otilija mumbled. Her eyes peered at her mother, wide and frightened.

"Calm down, mazulis. You'll be all right. Poppa is going for the doctor now. He'll be here soon." Doroteja comforted with firm gentleness. "Dear God, help me," she then whispered frantically to herself.

"Momma, I'm scared," Otilija's voice quavered.

"Everything will be all right, dear," Doroteja answered firmly as she wedged a pillow between Otilija's trembling thighs. She drew the sheets back over her daughter, then draped the corners around her shoulders. Out of breath and sobbing hysterically, Otilija melted into her mother's bosom.

At the edge of the doorway, awaken by her sister's crying, Augustine peered around the corner. Quietly, she watched her mother and sister embrace as tears welled in her saucered eyes.

"Momma, my baby," Otilija whimpered, but stopped abruptly as another contraction rushed in. "Oh." Her voice faded as her face contorted grotesquely.

"I know dear," Doroteja comforted, rubbing Otilija's back.

"No, Momma. It's coming. I can't hold it."

"It just feels that way—"

"No! My baby is coming!" Otilija screamed. Her faced wrenched as her entire body stiffened.

"Try to hold back, Otilija. Poppa went for the doctor," Doroteja's voice cracked an octave as she lifted the covers.

"I can't!" Otilija screamed. Overwhelmed, she reflexively lifted her knees, ripped the pillow out and spread her legs.

"Dear Lord, please help me," Doroteja mumbled as she saw a head begin to crest. "Andrejs! Come quickly!"

Heavy footfalls clomped through the hallway. Augustine scurried for cover inside the room behind a corner chair. Just as she hunkered down behind the dowels of the chair back, her father stepped into the room.

"Doroteja, here's some raspberry leaf tea. From the icebox. That's what you want, isn't it?" he asked nervously, appearing with a full cup balanced in his hand.

"Yes," her voice registered surprise. He always seemed so aloof before when she prepared her mother's special female remedies. "And water. I need some clean water. And towels."

"My God, what's happening?" Otilija mumbled, fighting to hide the terror that made her legs quiver and stomach churn.

Doroteja took the cup of tea from Andrejs with two hands as if she were afraid she'd spill it and set it down on the floor.

"Hurry, Andrejs. Get the doctor. The baby's coming."

Andrejs started to back out of the room, but when he turned to leave, he bumped the chair behind where Augustine was sitting cross-legged. She was clearly so completely engrossed in what Otilija was experiencing that she did not even look up to her father. Andrejs reached over the chair back and gently touched her shoulder.

"Oh." she gasped as she jumped. "I'm sorry, Poppa. I just couldn't sleep."

"No, no mazulis. It's fine you are here. Why don't you go and hold Otilija's hand. She needs to know you are here." Andrejs calmly said.

Augustine gawked at her father, not expecting him to be so calm and understanding. She untwined her legs and stood up, then sheepishly shuffled to her sister's bedside.

Doroteja startled at first when Augustine slipped in beside her, but then nodded and urged her to come closer. Augustine reached for Otilija's hand, carefully slipping her open palm onto her sister's. Otilija glanced at her sister, flashed a weak, trembling grin, then snapped her head back toward Doroteja.

"Oh, Momma," she cried as tears streamed down her face. Her jaw quivered, hanging open as she panted through her mouth.

"I'm sorry." Augustine jumped back and quickly withdrew her hand.

"No, no dear. It's all right," Doroteja assured, grabbing her arm. She pulled her back to Otilija and placed her hand into her sister's trembling palm.

Andrejs reappeared at the door, carrying a bucket of water with one hand and a pile of clean, folded towels in the other. He shuffled to his wife's side, then set the towels and water down. As he sat down next to Otilija, he caressed her quivering head.

Otilija arched her back as she grasped her father's arm, clamping her fingers closed hard. Her nails sunk so deep in his skin that blood oozed from the marks.

"The baby is coming, Andrejs. There's no way to stop it." Doroteja's words grew frantic again. "Where is the doctor?"

"He said he is coming as quickly as he can," he said, then peered at his daughter. "Hold on, Otilija. Just a little longer. The doctor will—"

Otilija screamed.

"It's not waiting. The head's half way out now. We've got to do something." Doroteja snapped.

Can you? Andrejs asked with his eyes.

Doroteja sucked in a deep breath. She squeezed her eyelids together as she threw her head back. She noisily expelled the lung full of air, then looked back down at her writhing daughter.

"Yes. Stay down there." Doroteja ordered. "Augustine. Get me a towel…no, two."

Augustine immediately grabbed two towels and tossed them to her mother. She stood, as if waiting for another order as her mother quickly dipped one towel into the water. Doroteja wiped her hands clean, then dipped the second towel into the water. Without wringing it out, she slipped it under Otilija's spread legs.

Otilija screamed again. The tiny blood smeared head slid further out.

"Another towel." Doroteja ordered.

Augustine immediately complied, quickly soaking the towel before handing it to her mother. Taking the dripping linen, Doroteja draped it over Otilija's legs.

"Andrejs, help me turn her. I have to get her on the edge." Doroteja swung her hands in a circle.

Andrejs slipped his arms under Otilija's shoulders. Doroteja and Augustine wrapped their arms around each leg. Under Doroteja's lead, they nudged Otilija to the edge of the bed.

Otilija groaned, then dropped her jaw open again and wailed with an ear-piercing scream.

"Okay, now. Push down, now, Otilija. Push down," Doroteja ordered as gruffly as a drill sergeant.

Otilija sucked in a deep breath and pushed. Her pruned face flushed, then turned various crimson shades. Veins pulsed on her temples. Her clenched eyes dripped tears. She screamed again, louder and longer than before.

"Again. Push again," Doroteja ordered directly into her daughter's face.

As Otilija sucked in a breath for another push, Doroteja glanced back at Otilija's legs. The peeking head pulsed further out than before, then started slipping back in.

"Now. Push."

With a spurting gush, a tiny, blood smeared, head slopped out into Doroteja's waiting hands. A flood of brown stained fluid poured out of her daughter and splashed onto the floor next to the bed. Otilija exhaled with an loud, agonized groan, then started to quiver uncontrollably.

Andrejs draped a sheet over Otilija and held it in place with his arm, then wrapped it around her shoulders. Augustine sheepishly squeezed in closer. She craned her neck to grab a peek at the baby, then held her breath as she saw the tiny head in her mother's hands.

The baby's pale, ashen skin seemed transparent. Her mother stroked the baby's head, but it remained limp in her hands.

Augustine felt a pit grow in her stomach, sensing something was wrong, but afraid to ask. The change in her mother's face from joy to a cold, sober, emotionless gaze confirmed her fears. Her blood drained rapidly from her face, and she felt vomit gurgle in her throat.

"Once more, Otilija. Push once more," Doroteja stiffly ordered.

Otilija groaned as she squeezed her eyes closed, then 'ughed' as she pushed, weeping. Augustine watched as the baby's shoulders slid through the opening. As the rest of the baby slipped out, a thick, jelled clump of dark, bloody mucous followed.

Doroteja stopped for a moment as she glanced down at the steaming infant in her hands. Her lip quivered as tears welled up in her eyes, then dropped onto the still body. She sighed, shook her head, and with a pained expression on her face, bit her lip, and methodically wrapped the baby with a clean, dry towel.

Andrejs' eyes showed he understood the disappointment in her face.

"Is it a boy, Momma?" Otilija asked in a partly happy voice which quivered with exhaustion as it barely escaped her mouth. Her brown eyes sat deeply in her pale, washed out face.

"Voldemars said it would be a boy, you know," she added.

Doroteja dutifully wiped most of the blood and mucous off the baby's head with a damp washcloth. She flipped the edge of the towel over the sallow face, then slowly glanced up at her daughter.

"It doesn't matter, Otilija. She's dead." Doroteja said bluntly.

Otilija's face drooped as tears instantly flowed from her eyes. She felt everything crash in around her. She wanted this baby. It would be the only thing of Voldemars' that she knew would always be with her. It had to be alive. It just had to.

"I want her anyway," she insisted, stiffening her lips and opening her arms. "Please, let me hold her," she whispered through sobs.

Doroteja carefully handed her the bundled baby, then gently wedged it into the crook of her daughter's arm. Otilija laid still for a moment, staring at the ceiling. She sighed heavily, then drew the baby to her face and gently lifted the towel's edge.

As a flood of tears gushed from her eyes and ran down her cheeks, Otilija carefully picked at the film which remained on the baby's tiny face. She methodically inspected the stiff baby, worming her fingers in between the limp arms at her sides. She sighed again, then slowly lifted her head. With an pale, drawn expression etched onto her lips, she stared at her mother with hollow eyes.

"Why? Why my baby?" she whispered.

Doroteja was silent.

❦   ❦   ❦

Drained from continuously sobbing for three days, Otilija finally felt as if she had spilled every drop of her soul onto the musty bed sheets. She knew she had to get on with living, but she vowed never to forget what she had and how quickly it was ripped from her womb. She knew there'd always be an emptiness now whenever she saw anyone else's baby. That was her fate, and for some reason, she believed she was chosen to endure it. There was something she was to learn from this, and someday, God would reveal what it was.

But for now, she understood that she simply had to accept it. Slowly at first, she slipped her stiff legs out of her bed and set her feet onto the floor. Stiltedly, she scuffed to her bureau by the window, then eased down to her chair and blew out a noisy sigh. The hard chair hurt the small clotted rips bulging from between her legs, but she gritted her teeth and focused outside the window.

The crisp autumn morning had warmed past freezing, melting the frost off the freshly bitten grass. Sparkling rainbows glimmered on the broader leaves as the sunlight refracted through the melted frost. Geese honked with a mourning tone as they flew past the house in a low formation on their way south. Underneath the oaks near the house, squirrels scurried through the stiff brush, collecting acorns to store away for the winter.

Otilija sighed noisily as she picked up the long slender pen. She absently nibbled on the end, all the while thinking of how to start her letter to Voldemars. But each time she dipped her pen into the ink-well, her thoughts evaporated. After pondering for an hour, she realized that even if she did figure out what she wanted to say, she had no place to send the letter. He'd never told her where he was going, other than near the front.

"But he has to know," she mumbled, chewing even more frantically on her pen. Finally, she had an idea. She dipped her pen point into the inkwell, then started the letter to her brother.

28 October 1912

My dearest brother,

Three days ago, the baby girl that I had carried for Voldemars was born dead. I have had a most difficult time reconciling the loss, but I believe I've finally accepted that sometimes this experience is inevitable. I am sure you understand that I need to tell Voldemars about this, but I have no way of sending word directly to him. I was hoping that you may be able to find a way through your superiors, so you can explain the situation, and ensure that this news can be delivered to him.

I know how much he was looking forward to seeing his new baby when he came home, and I am concerned that he may not take the news well if he arrives uninformed. I realize how difficult getting a letter to Voldemars must be, but at least you have a better chance than I would of dealing with the military. This is very important to me, and I'm sure you'll do what you can. If I know you as well as I think I do, I know you will be able to get this message to Voldemars.

Your loving sister,

Otilija

Riga

19 June 1914

*A*ndrejs slammed the door closed as he walked into his house, then noisily exhaled as he shuffled right through the parlor and into the kitchen. He blew out again, exasperated, as he plopped into his chair at the table, then let his muscles melt between the arms of his seat.

Doroteja needed no other clue why her husband was home early. As she headed for the cupboard, she quickly wiped her hands on the damp towel slipped into the tie of her apron. She pulled down two cups and a tea stained cloth bag, then quickly prepared drinks for them both. Before he could release another heavy, labored sigh, she placed the steaming tea in front of him, then settled into her seat across from him at the table.

"You're home early, Andrejs. Another strike?" she asked, rhetorically.

"More complaints, more grumbling. The economy is so bad you'd think they'd be thankful that they even still have jobs." He grunted. He leaned over the steaming cup and let the swirls meander around his face.

"Why don't you stay just once and talk with them. They'd listen to you, wouldn't they?"

"And condone this childish behavior? No. I refuse to even be seen with them."

"But don't you agree with what they are trying to say?"

"Of course, but—"

"Then why don't you try?"

"There's more than just the worker's end of it," he leaned forward. A skeptical look crossed his face. "There are some politics going on there that I'd rather not talk about right now."

A knock at the front door startled him silent.

"Now who could that be?" A puzzled expression grew on his face as he stared at the door. He slowly pushed himself away from the table, then moved toward the door as Doroteja shuffled to the parlor window and peeked outside.

"It's a messenger, Andrejs." Her voice noted concern as the door rattled with complaint as an even more urgent knocking hammered on the outside.

Doroteja watched the uniformed boy nervously sway from side to side as he waited for someone to come to the door. His wide, blue-gray eyes darted back and forth as he scanned the road beyond the fenced yard. His cap sat squarely on his closely cropped hair as he fidgeted with the stack of letters in his hand. Just as the boy stepped toward the door to knock again, Andrejs opened the door and spooked the young man.

"Good afternoon, young man?" He lifted his eyebrows and sternly frowned at the boy, then tried to hide his chuckle with the boy's reaction. "Do you have something for me?"

"Uh, yes. I have something for, uh," The boy paused, then took a breath and glanced down at the envelopes in his hand. He peeled the top one off the pile and presented it to Andrejs.

"These telegrams are for Fricis and Vilis Braze."

Andrejs instantly chilled and glowered at the boy. His lips squeezed together nervously as his welcoming, open hands curled into fists.

"Thank you, they are my sons," he quickly mumbled and swiped the envelopes from the boy's hand. Without looking at the letters, he stuffed them into his shirt pocket, then peered at the boy, fervently chewing on his quivering lower lip until he left. He gently closed the door, turned, and walked stiffly back to the kitchen. He thudded into his seat, threw the letters to the table, then slammed his fists so hard that the cups rattled on their saucers.

"Damn it all," he suddenly erupted. His face blanched before he buried it into his folded arms.

"Good, Lord, Andrejs, what is it?" Doroteja hurried back into the kitchen.

He lifted his head just enough to be able to stare at his wife through the glistening film growing over his eyes.

"This is Nicholas' doing," he said with a morbidly dry voice. "The good Lord has nothing to do with this."

"What are you talking about, Andrejs?"

"The letters. I don't have to open them to know what they say. Just look at the seal."

Doroteja tentatively slid her hand over to the top letter and flipped it over, revealing the Czar's official army seal.

"I don't understand, how can they? They can't have all of our sons. How can they?"

"It's going to be war, Doroteja, that's why. That bastard Nicholas is going to war."

"But there's been no formal declaration of war has there?" She slipped her finger under the flap of the envelope, opened it, then started reading.

"No, there hasn't. But that has never stopped bloody Nicholas in the past. Port Arthur wasn't declared a war. Crimea wasn't—"

"The message says mobilization, Andrejs," she interrupted. "There is no mention of war here."

"Mobilization, practice, drills. They can call it what they will, that doesn't change things. I know what this means. I can feel it."

"But Otomars' letter last month seemed so upbeat. He didn't say anything about war. In fact, he said he—"

"He's blinded by his boyish feeling of immortality. He can't see what Nicholas' filthy game is. The bastard is off to start a war. A damned, bloody war. A war to take everyone's mind off the troubles in Russia."

Andrejs vaulted up from his chair then paced around the kitchen like a caged bear, all the while slamming his fisted right hand into his open left palm. His face has blushed so red that his hair looked white in comparison.

"They're headed for war, Doroteja. I can feel it in my bones. All of our boys are going to war for the Czar. The damned, blood-thirsty Czar."

"Andrejs, please remember what the physician told you. You shouldn't get so angry—"

"Oh, no. This has been planned for some time," Andrejs continued in a fuming tantrum. He waved his finger scoldingly as he squinted one eye closed. "Why do you think that Oswalds and Otomars were transferred to the front? There's nothing for soldiers to do in Petersburg other than guard grain houses from starving people."

"Andrejs, you need to—"

"But in Poland. Yes, in Poland, there is land to win." He enfolded his hands within each other and hunched over them like a devious, plotting villain. "Land from the Germans, land from the Austrians, and land from the old Duchy itself."

"Andrejs!" Doroteja grabbed her husband's arms and seemed to muster all her might to shake him out of his fury.

His eyes had widened so far that his blue eyes were completely surrounded by red-streaked white. His arms had clenched so tightly that they quivered.

"And since there are soldiers from every side in that God forsaken wasteland, there will be war."

"If there's war, Andrejs, then so be it. There's nothing we can do about that, now. All we can do is pray for our sons' safety!" Doroteja yelled.

Andrejs fell silent. His whole body trembled as he stood at attention. Doroteja slipped her hand around his forearm.

"Come have your tea, Andrejs. It will make you feel better," she whispered softly.

"Damn you, Nicholas," Andrejs mumbled under his breath as he let Doroteja escort him back to the table. "Damn you all the way to hell."

Drums beat slowly in the distance, gradually growing louder and faster as the sun drew closer to the horizon. One faint bagpipe joined the instrument call as the traditional bonfires of Jani came to life. Kokles twanged through their wooden bellies as fingers danced over their tightened strings, joining the pagan symphony for the solstice while more people gathered around the growing fire. Spoken words moved from their monotones to more melodic tunes of the ritual as flames lapped at an indigo sky.

"I don't care, Fricis," Vilis spouted as he strutted along the stone laden pathway toward the bonfire, intent on not missing any of the revelry. "I am not going to let this damned conscription ruin my Jani."

"Damn it. See what your fretting has done?" Fricis punched his brother when he heard voices begin to sing the dainas louder and in more earnestly. "Now we've missed the lighting of the ring of fire."

Vilis punched back, then quickened his pace. "Even if you do meet someone, you won't be able to spend the night with her," Fricis taunted as he passed. "The letter said we have to report by—"

"Listen carefully." Vilis grabbed his brother's arm and twisted it so that he had to submit and turn back to him. "Right now, I don't care. I don't even want to think about it."

Vilis released him, then began to strut toward the fire again. Fricis caught up to him, and bounced next to him like a playful puppy.

"But we have to."

"Shut up."

"Didn't you hear Poppa?"

"I don't want to think about it."

"We are a breath away from war! If someone—"

Vilis stopped and grabbed his brother again. He shook him hard twice, then yanked him into his face. His eyes flamed with anger.

"We'll have enough time to think about the hell we're walking into tomorrow. For now, I want to just forget about it and enjoy what little freedom I have left. If you want to lament about it, go home and leave me alone, all right?"

Fricis swallowed hard. His eyes grew wide and worried. After a moment of silence, he sighed and nodded.

"You're right," he mumbled.

Vilis let him go.

"We should enjoy this while we can."

"Ligo!" Reserved laughter followed the half-sung, half yelled word ending one verse of the folk song. Fricis and Vilis stopped in their tracks as they crested the hill and heard the gathering slip into another song. They looked down to the fire ring in time to see a figure dash toward the orange flames. With an acrobat's grace, he spread his legs front to back and leapt over the orange flames to the pleasure of the crowd.

Fricis glanced at his brother. An impish twitch sprouted on his face, then blossomed to a full grin. He nodded toward the fire, then punched his brother square on the shoulder before bolting. Vilis reflexively grabbed his shoulder, then watched his brother head toward the crowd for a moment before striking up chase himself.

Fricis slipped into the line for the fire jump as he joined the gathering, out of breath. He leaned over and sucked in a lung full of the smoky cloud that hovered in the midst of the field. After a second, he craned his neck and watched his friend Sandis break into a mad dash toward the fire. Centimeters before the fire ring, he crouched.

"Ligo!" the crowd cheered as he vaulted the lapping flames, then landed on the other side of the fire unscathed. The crowd immediately started another verse as Sandis stumbled a few steps forward and fell into the waiting arms of two very attractive girls.

"If I can get just one like that I'll be happy," Fricis mumbled. He glanced down at his feet and rocked back and forth as he waited for the verse to be finished. When the familiar final words rose from the crowd, he coiled himself up then took off. The orange flames seemed to grow huge as he headed toward them. He felt the heat start to build as he neared.

"Ligo!"

Fricis closed his eyes tightly, not wanting to see the flames spanking his legs as he flew over them. Crouching into a ball, he bent his knees, then pushed off with all the spring his legs could muster. He spread his legs out to his sides in a well practiced pike, like the Russian fire dancers he had seen years ago. Heat lapped at his butt as he touched his boots with his fingertips.

The crowd gasped at his leap. He heard every voice over the crackling fire. He grinned for a second, but then he hit the ground feet first. He crumbled into a ball and tumbled forward, as if trying to salvage some hint of grace with his recovery.

The crowd chuckled at his demise, but only briefly before they broke into the next verse of the festive daina.

"Damn!" he groused. He tucked into a head roll, then sprung to his feet, keeping his eyes tightly closed.

My dreams should be answered! He opened his eyes.

"What the hell are you doing here?"

"Catching my clumsy older brother," Augustine smirked, as she pushed Fricis back into a standing position.

"Does Momma know you…."

"Momma told me to come here and keep an eye on you."

Fricis looked over her shoulder and saw Vilis crouched behind her, laughing and pointing at him with one hand while he held his stomach with his other.

"I'll get you for this," Fricis vowed. His feet slipped on the damp ground at first, but then caught traction and he took off in pursuit. He chased his brother once around the circle before the pair turned and headed back up the hill. Closing the gap quickly, Fricis left his feet and tackled Vilis as he reached the crest. The two boys wrestled for a few minutes before rolling on their backs, giggling at themselves.

Fricis suddenly stopped laughing and sat up. He sensed a sudden change in the mood below. He looked down at the fire ring and saw that the crowd had oddly and rapidly thinned. The dainas took on a more somber tone.

"Do you think we'll ever see another Jani?" Fricis felt guilt twinge at his gut.

Vilis immediately stopped his chuckling. Sobriety doured his expression.

"I don't know, Fricis. But maybe you are right. We should enjoy this one while we can."

❀   ❀   ❀

Under a low, thick, weeping cloud cover, morning arrived as a cold, raw day. Andrejs, Doroteja, and Augustine joined the crowd who had already converged near the Central Train Station. Some of those assembled held flowers, while others proudly held small, tricolored Russian flags.

As Augustine and Doroteja moved into the crowd, Andrejs noticed an old man milling near the entrance to the flower shop.

"I'll be there in a minute," he nudged Doroteja on toward the crowd, then nodding toward Elmars, his old acquaintance from the factory. As his wife and daughter sifted into the crowd, he shuffled over to him.

"Don't like what I feel," the old man grumbled. He passed his long, thin fingers through his thinning gray hair.

"What is it that you feel, Elmars?"

Elmars noisily forced up a large mucous glob from his throat and spit it onto the ground.

"They want war. They want a damned war." He contorted his wrinkled, sunburned face as a faint thumping drum beat punctured the air's thickness.

The thumps grew louder and closer. Clopping hooves on the cobblestone joined in, followed by pounding, boot covered feet. The mass fell silent. Necks stretched, poking heads into the alley of people, each peering through the mass in an effort to see the first soldier appear from behind the buildings.

"Listen to them, Andrejs. Listen to them as the boys come by." Elmars shook his head and coughed up another glob of phlegm.

As the first row of perfectly dressed soldiers suddenly appeared, the crowd's quiet anticipation was quickly replaced by a buzzed excitement, then blossomed into a frenzied anticipation. Cheers spilled from the mass, swelling as the first rows of soldiers passed.

"Those are our boys in Russian uniforms, Andrejs. There's just something wrong with that," Elmars glanced down to his bowed legs, then shuffled his feet. "You know Nicholas is doing this because he can't keep control over his empire…sending our boys into war so he can create a sense of nationalism to him."

Andrejs remained silent and listened to the crowd, which seemed to grow more delighted by the first rows of soldiers thrusting their brown polished rifles forward as if they were commencing a charge. At each barrel tip, a four-edged bayonet poked menacingly, gleaming with a thin film of moisture.

The crowd then erupted with cheers as hundreds of red carnations flew through the air and dropped at the feet of the marching regiments.

"See what I mean?" Elmars noted with disgust in his voice. His crooked finger pointed accusingly at the people massed at the street.

Andrejs felt compelled to look for his boys as the Twenty-Third regiment marched by. Rows of battle greens stepped by with long, proud strides. Each double column row was flanked by handsomely decorated officers with polished sabers gripped in their white gloved hands. Majestic purple tassels brushed over the hilts, swaying in unison with marching men. Next to each officer, the flag-bearer hoisted a stiffly flapping Russian tricolor, completely unfurled to reveal the two-headed, black imperial eagle emblazoned on its field.

"If we get it, old friend, do you think it will be quick?" Andrejs whispered loud enough so that only Elmars could have heard him.

"This isn't the time for a war, Andrejs, I'm sure you're quite aware of that. Look at what's happening in Petersburg. Riots, people starving. Those damn Bolsheviks on the loose."

Elmars voice faded as he turned away from the crowd.

"I know it's not the time for war. But if it comes, will it be quick?" Andrejs insisted again.

"No, Andrejs. If we have war, Nicholas will lose this one. He'll lose this one just like he's lost the others. Crimea, Port Arthur. Nothing's changed, you know," the old man rambled.

Andrejs continued listening closely to Elmars. It seemed uncanny, but he always seemed to be right. Even if his views were different from the majority.

"And my boys? Do you think they'll come home?" Andrejs wondered if he really wanted to know the answer.

Elmars' eyes had grown wide and seemed to be lost in a skyward gaze. "Fighting is different now, Andrejs. There are too many machines. Aeroplanes. Armored motor cars. Machine guns. I've seen the damned things. They're hellishly frightening. This time, it won't be the same kind of war we're used to—"

"Will my boys come home, Elmars?" Andrejs cut him off.

"And I don't think the Czar or his staff realize that," Elmars continued catatonically. "Like all the wars before, in their eyes, the boys are expendable. That's the only strength Nicholas has, you know. Numbers."

Elmars turned toward the parade and noticed that the last regiment had passed and the crowd had spilled into the street behind them. He then shifted his gaze into Andrejs face, blinked his eyelids once, then let a tear roll down his weathered face.

"If there is a God, we all need to pray, Andrejs." He patted Andrejs' shoulder twice, then turned and shuffled away from the crowd.

❦   ❦   ❦

A week after Fricis and Vilis were shipped west toward the Polish border, Voldemars stood on his train's boarding dock, peering at his own reflection in the darkened window of a passenger car. He adjusted his cap to set squarely on his head, then snapped down on his new olive green uniform tunic. He toyed with his thin, waxed handlebar mustache, twisting the ends to keep the tips erect.

Colonel Voldemars Vechi. Brigade leader, he mused, smug with the promotion he had received with his orders.

"I don't think I've ever seen you acting so pompous," Gunars said as he chuckled at how Voldemars primped at his reflection.

He smartly about-faced, then clapped his boot heels together.

"Gunars. I thought you'd be on your way to the Polish front."

"I may still be going there, but for now, I'm taking advantage of my old age."

"Forty?"

"Old enough to get out before the bullets fly."

Voldemars swallowed hard. It never occurred to him that there might be a war. In his mind, this was just another mobilization to some other corner of Europe for reconnaissance. After thinking for another moment, reading Gunars deep blue eyes, he concluded it was just more of Gunars' cynicism.

"So, old friend, what do you think?"

"I think the Huns would be fools to get into a scrap with you." Gunars laughed aloud as he slapped Voldemars between his shoulder blades. Voldemars leaned over and cupped his hand over his mouth and Gunars' ear.

"I know these gold epaulets look good on me, but I really think you should have taken this promotion."

"I wouldn't dream of standing in your way, Voldemars. Besides, I've had enough fighting for my lifetime. It's time I move aside for you young bucks."

Gunars winked as the train peeped impatiently three times. Voldemars stared at his deep set eyes and searched for the right words to express how he felt. This man was the reason for his promotion, and he knew it. He'd learned so much from Gunars, and he was also sure that it was his recommendation that clinched him the honor of a cavalry command in Samsonov's Eighth Army.

He placed his hands onto Gunars squared shoulders, then wrestled him in close for a traditional hug of friendship. He held his mentor for a moment, then let him push away to arm's length.

"Thank you, Gunars. This promotion means so much to me, and I'm sure it does to Otilija as well."

"Don't be so sure about that," Gunars nodded with a weak smile, then nodded up to the train.

Voldemars glanced up and saw Otilija resting her face against the window pane. Her face was long and her eyes were searching.

"It's just that she's never been away from home." Voldemars passed her look off absently. "It'll be good for her to be on her own instead of in her parent's nest."

"You may be an excellent soldier, my friend, but you still have much to learn about life," Gunars mumbled as he shook his head. "And women."

Clomping boots charging down the planks of the dock drew both men's attention.

"You'd better be going," Gunars said as he saw the officer in charge of the train hustling other straggling soldiers onto the train.

"And don't be another Plotnikov," he waved his finger in his face.

"He was a real son of a bitch, wasn't he?" Voldemars laughed out loud as he placed his boot on the first step.

"If those bastards start something, you be sure to take them out."

"Don't worry about me, old man," he said sarcastically. "If they start something, you can be sure I'll be in Willy's back yard before he knows it."

The both of them chuckled loudly, then parted, Voldemars onto the train, and Gunars down the dock, headed back into the city.

Voldemars strutted down the aisle, then stood at his seat next to Otilija. She turned toward him, weakly smiled, then turned back toward the window again. Voldemars quietly sat down next to her, and waited for the train to leave.

Announcing its departure with another three successive peeps, the train billowed out a wide cloud of stale odored steam from its iron belly. The engine lurched ahead, then slowly chugged away from the station and gained speed, leaving Riga behind.

"Doesn't it seem odd to you that we are headed east and everyone else is headed west?" Otilija innocently asked after fifteen minutes of silence.

"South," Voldemars corrected. "We are actually headed south."

"South, west, does it really matter? It still is heading away from where everyone else is going, isn't it?" She blankly stared out the window as the train's wheels clacked rhythmically.

"The front stretches the width of Europe—"

"Why did my brothers go to Poland, Voldemars. Why?"

Voldemars swallowed hard. After he had seen with his own eyes what the Germans had brought to the Polish border, he knew why so many soldiers were needed there.

"You were in Poland before, weren't you?"

He nodded.

She turned back to her husband with a soft glance, her eyes begging for a good answer. "What was there that needs so many soldiers?"

The truth wasn't what he thought Otilija wanted to hear. "I think it's obvious, Otilija." He couldn't think of anything else to say.

"Oh, Voldemars, please don't mention war," Otilija's voice trembled. "The politicians will work out this mess rather than let it be decided on the battlefield, won't they."

"I really don't think there is much hope for that at this point."

Otilija's eyes revealed a sincere and deep fear. Her face was etched with a concern he'd never seen before. Even the look he thought was the anxiety of leaving did not look as scared as she looked now.

"Just pray that it will be short."

"Then if it will help, I'll pray," she mumbled and turned back toward the window.

Odessa, Southern Russia

9 July 1914

Sweltering in the hellish combination of a heavy cotton uniform and Odessa's oppressive, thick air, Voldemars accepted that this steamy summer heat was something that would be forever seared into his memory. Each additional day they remained grew even more unbearable than the last. Evenings served no better fare, emitting a thicker dose of humidity, lingering clouds of stale body odor with but a feeble reprieve from the heat.

The days of quasi-mobilization, as Command called it, plodded at a snail's pace, filled only with boredom and rumors. The officer's wives were again left behind, in a safe zone near Astrakhan, some hundreds of kilometers away. Voldemars wondered if there was some plot by Command to keep him and Otilija separated.

As the sun rose, hope of an order to move out sparked speculation, but by noon it was dashed. By evening, the long, miserable day was logged as another wasted twenty-four hours.

After a week of tossing in his cot every night for hours trying to get some sleep, futilely battling against the stagnant air, Voldemars took to escaping the oven-like barracks with long strolls by the port. Along the emerald colored water, inadequate but at least existent breezes swept in, diluting the syrupy air enough to be barely tolerable. The fine, white sand beaches stretched on for kilometers, while the sea shushed onto the shore with a soothingly rhythmic flow, bathing every grain with a lazy rinse.

The ninth of July marked two weeks in Odessa's purgatory. That evening, he ambled along his favorite stretch of the shore, gaining respite from frustration brought on by the incessant waiting. Nearly a kilometer behind him, sometimes it felt even more, the bustling port, muffled by distance, continued yeomanly undaunted, sweltering in the relentless tropical heat, consuming an endless tonnage of incoming supplies.

Voldemars really didn't care about that, though. What was important was simply that the air was tolerable, and he could walk without the relentless exertion needed during the day. After an hour of meditation on the sand, sanity crept back in like a cautious cat on an evening hunt, wary not to be seen for fear of being whisked away. His uniform no longer clung to him like the damp, scratchy wool it was and lost most of its musty odor.

As he turned away from the beach and headed back to the barracks, he spotted a woman sitting alone on a bench, gazing out over the calm water, seemingly lost within her own thoughts.

Her alluring beauty caught his attention first. Her delicately proportioned nose ended sharply above her thin lips. Her face was a shade pale but seemed appropriately coupled with her apparent sadness. What starkly stood out, though, was that considering the warmth of the evening, she seemed oddly overdressed with her long overcoat draped over her narrow shoulders. Where it fell limply below the bench, her crossed legs peeked out. Voldemars could not help but stare, awed into a frozen silence.

In the back of his mind, like the irritation of a mosquito, heinous echoes of lower ranked infantrymen's chortling boasts stirred to life, bragging of their seamy, stolen conquests during their night-time carousing. An immediate chivalrous concern germinated, then surged to life, overpowering his fascination with her beauty.

She turned suddenly and caught his gaze. She startled as their eyes met, then fidgeted for a moment before she returned a warm, friendly grin. Dimples gently creased her face at the corners of her mouth as she briefly let her grin widen. Her melancholy quickly returned as her expression faded back to glum, and her eyes reverted to a distant gaze.

Perhaps I can help, Voldemars thought, tugging down sharply on his tunic. He brushed the sand off his trousers. Silently, he approached with a gallant swagger to his step. He stopped at her side, then courteously lifted his hat.

"Excuse me, Madam? Are you alone?" He slipped his hat under his arm.

She tipped her head and looked up with her stunningly wide brown eyes.

"A woman of your attract—, uh," he caught himself, then quickly recovered. "I really do not think you should be out alone this late."

"Yes, I know," she responded in a reserved and quiet tone. Her eyes wandered briefly about his uniform until they fixed on his rank insignia.

"What I meant to say was—"

"I believe I understand your intentions Colonel, however, I do not believe you fully understand."

Voldemars raised his eyebrows quizzically.

"When I go home, I am truly alone. Here, I am not. The sea accompanies me, and the stars and the moon when the sky is clear."

The woman stopped her explanation to take a deep breath. She stifled a sob, placing her delicate hand over her mouth. "Oh, it really doesn't matter," she said and sighed. "Here the night is blissful, like it was before the war. Before Momma…."

She stopped again and hung her head. Confused by her parable, Voldemars searched for something quick and profound to say, but failed when he noticed tears welling in her eyes. Sympathy blossomed in his heart.

"I'm sorry. I didn't mean to bring up such painful memories," he assuaged. "May I?" he politely asked, pointing to the bench.

The woman nodded. He sat beside her, then started nervously fondling the stiff brim on his hat.

"I was just concerned for your safety. I've heard stories, you know, of carousing soldiers," he said.

Voldemars stopped, sensing eyes peering directly at him. With a quick glance, he confirmed his feeling. What little breeze there was carried hints of her delicately sweet perfume. He felt his face flush as his lips quivered into a crooked, tiny smile.

"Oh? I didn't know." She coyly raising her eyebrows and tipped her head. "Maybe I've been fortunate, then. None of them have ever bothered me."

"And I—" Voldemars stopped and swallowed hard.

"Thank you for your concern."

"Well, when I saw you, sitting here alone—"

"You were afraid some immoral soldier would whisk me away and take advantage of me?" She smirked and shifted her eyes to Voldemars with a side ward glance.

He blushed more as sweat beaded up on his forehead. Onion tainted perspiration wafted up from his collar.

"How do I know that you aren't just another one of those immoral soldiers you wish to protect me from?" she asked.

Speechless, he just gazed at her, transfixed by her oval eyes. When she slipped into a coy smile, he felt his face grow hot.

"Would you grant me the honor of walking you home?" He stood and politely offered his arm to her.

She tilted her head and gazed upwards at him. He felt their eyes engage and lock. They passed queries without words. He tried to read her thoughts, but everything about her remained veiled. She finally stood up and carefully pulled her unbuttoned coat together. Holding it in place with one hand, she cautiously slipped her free hand into the crook of Voldemars' offered arm.

"Since I don't know where you live," he began, remaining in place, ready to lead but somewhat embarrassed. "I'm sorry, nor do I know your name."

"My name is Maria," she said softly. "And I can show you."

Arm-in-arm, the pair headed back toward the city. For five blocks, Voldemars remained silent. Something about her felt comfortable, but he could not place it. Was it that his stiff, military-style pacing was strangely in rhythm with Maria's graceful strides? Or was it that this was the first woman that had come this close to him since he left Astrakhan?

"Will you be here long, Colonel?" Maria asked, breaking the silence, then tittered. "I'm sorry. Nor do I know your name."

"Please pardon my poor manners. I am Voldemars Vechi."

"Colonel Voldemars Vechi," Maria repeated, rolling the name over her tongue. She glanced up at him, squinting as she drank in his features. "That's a different sounding name. What part of Russia are you from?"

"Some people call it Latvia. Some call it Livonia, but not if you are Latvian, mind you," he added with a chuckle. "Whatever you wish to call it, it's—"

"It's near Riga," she finished for him.

Voldemars snapped his head around and stared at Maria's smirking face.

"You know where Latvia is?" he said.

"I know a little about geography. My Poppa, God rest his soul, insisted that I learn."

"And to be completely honest," he said, returning to her first question, adding a sarcastic bite to his words, "I am not sure how long I will be here. My battalion has no orders. I would have to say that my stay depends on how long Nicholas decides to hold off starting his war."

"I fear, then, that it will not be long," she said somberly.

"Why do you say that?"

Maria stopped and glanced up to Voldemars. She tipped her head and raised her eyebrows.

"You are interested in my opinion?" she asked.

"Why should that surprise you? I am interested in anyone's opinion about this damned mess we seem hell bent to be hurling ourselves into."

"Oh?" Maria tilted her head as her face blushed lightly. "You must excuse me, Colonel Vechi."

"Voldemars. Please call me Voldemars. Even my men do not formally address me."

She recoiled again. "I find that as interesting as you asking what I think about things. I did not expect that from anyone, especially when that person is an officer."

She looked down at her feet, shuffled them for a moment, then glanced back up at Voldemars, as if again asking permission to speak. He nodded.

"If you insist," she said.

"Please. Tell me."

"I sense that Nicholas is a paranoid and frightened man. I believe he is grasping for anything that he can use to show he is strong and in control. The only way I see him accomplishing that is by sending Russians into battle. Thousands of Russians. And only to face—"

She stopped and glanced back down at her feet. Her head jerked as she sniffed, holding back tears. Without thinking, Voldemars placed his arm around her shoulders. She melted into his chest. He absently combed his fingers through her hair. A sensual mix of salt and her perfumed hair stirred up from her scalp and tingled in his nose.

"I fear, though, that blood shed, both Russian and the enemy's, will be spilled only to vainly satiate his hunger for glory and acceptance," she said.

Maria's opinion surprised Voldemars, not so much that it was different than his, but that it was frighteningly similar to the Gypsies' premonitions he heard so frequently in Poland. He tried to push the thought from his mind, but it lingered. Silently, they turned and headed down a street lined with closely packed apartment houses.

As they continued down the narrow, gas lit street, Maria's hands gripped tighter on his arm. Centuries of must baked onto the walls by the hot summers oozed from the bricks and lingered in the street like a fog.

"Would you come in for some tea, Voldemars?" she asked as they stopped at a wooden stoop. She stared up into his eyes and offered her open hands.

He looked up at the apartment building for a moment, then shifted his glance back to Maria. Her wide, sultry brown eyes danced as he laid his sweat dampened palms onto hers.

He wondered if she was merely being polite as he peered deeper into her eyes. He knew that women, especially beautiful women, were his greatest vulnerability. Not being able to say no was his greatest fault. Her closeness invigorated him. The military was cold and passionless. His heart ached for warmth and softness, things only a woman could offer.

Then Otilija slipped into his mind.

"Did I say something wrong?" Maria's amiable voice broke into his thoughts.

"I'm sorry, yes. That would be fine. I'd like to stay for some tea."

Voldemars' eyes sparkled as he again offered his arm. She wormed her arm into the spot between his arm and body, and they went inside.

While Maria prepared the tea in the kitchen, Voldemars sat on a small sofa in her quaint living room. He tried to maintain thoughts of Otilija foremost in his mind, hoping it would keep his will strong. But when Maria emerged from the kitchen, carrying a silver tray which held a steaming pot and two small cups, weakness reared. Her coat was gone. Voldemars could not help but notice her snug black dress, and how well it complimented her petite figure. He felt his eyes fixed on her every movement.

Maria stopped in front of him, tipped her head, and smiled. Carefully balancing the tray, she set it down on the table, then poured water into the cups and sat next to Voldemars. Without letting the tea steep, he picked up his cup with both hands, then peered into it and watched the tea stain the water with orange swirls. Steam wisped about his face as he brought the cup to his lips, but Maria's perfume penetrated through the mist, luring Voldemars for a closer, more pleasurable sample.

He glanced up, and through the steam from her cup, her alluring eyes penetrated into his soul. Her thin, quivering grin blossomed into a sensuously warm smile. Otilija's image faded away as desire conquered Voldemars' thoughts. Suddenly, Otilija was gone, and Maria, gently stroking her hair with her delicate hand remained, real and close enough to touch.

Tannenberg, East Prussia

27 August 1914

*K*nowing that he'd face a third day of battering by the German artillery, Vilis Braze found sleeping in the mornings impossible. Even worse than the ongoing battle, the week long absence of food rations made the front unbearable. Instead of fighting with his growling stomach for another fifteen minutes of rest, he climbed out of the musty smelling trench. When he reached the soft muddy crest edge, he pushed his loosely fitting cap back off his forehead and rested as he surveyed the wasteland in front of him.

He gazed out over the sandy bogs where his group had been pinned down by relentless German attacks. He pulled himself the rest of the way out of the trench, then slogged to the shattered remains of a tree stump, and sat on the frayed wood. He scanned beyond the swamp, watching the dawning sky mellow the dark bleakness of the cloudless night. A pall of misty, eerie fog danced and swayed over the bogs, wafting in the nauseating combination of burnt flesh, gunpowder and decayed matter from the bog. Crippled remains of oaks crawled up from the marshy ground, spreading what remained of their once majestically wide reaching boughs.

He hadn't seen sunlight for what seemed a week. He prayed that the pervasive cloud cover would clear today, at least enough so that sunlight could start to dry out his mildewed uniform. What he saw, though, made him realize that this day would be just as gray, dank and miserable as the last three.

"Eah!" Vilis screamed as he felt a hand touch his shoulder. He spun around and crouched defensively, ready to take on the perpetrator. But when he saw his brother's face grinning at his skittish response, his panic subsided as quickly as it snapped into place.

"Christ, Fricis, you scared the living hell right out of me," Vilis gasped, calming himself with deep breaths. He stood and brushed his pants clean of the stump's water-logged splinters.

"Couldn't you at least have said something to let me know you were there?"

Fricis chuckled as he shook his head. "What, like 'boo' and miss the fun of watching you piss your pants? No, I don't think so."

Vilis plopped back down on the stump and resumed his gaze into the dawning sky. He turned his head back to Fricis. "So, what do you think? Are we in over our heads?"

"After the last couple of days, I really don't know," Fricis admitted.

"Well, so much for the quick retreat of the Huns. I guess Command completely fucked up on calculating their fighting will."

Fricis humphed loud enough that his echo carried into the swamp. "Miscalculated? I'd say they didn't know a Goddamned thing about the Germans…or for that matter, even our damned Army, by the way things are going. Christ, Vilis, we've got no food, not enough ammunition to even consider an attack, and…."

Fricis stopped long enough to furtively scan the area to ensure no one was listening to him.

"And these sorry excuses we've got for officers and soldiers. Hell, if I were an officer, I'd be more worried about my own men turning on me than the Germans."

"I know. Vitolds told me about a Colonel in the Fifteenth getting shot by his own men. Don't those fuckin' Russians realize we're in the same Goddamned army?"

Fricis stared blankly into the bogs, thinking he had seen something. He squinted and looked again, but saw nothing.

"Sometimes I wonder if we'll ever get home," Vilis' tone grew morbid.

"We'll get home, Vilis," Fricis assuaged, setting his hand on his brother's shivering shoulder. "And it may be sooner than you think."

"Huh?" Vilis spun and stared at Fricis.

"Lieutenant Murnieks and I were talking last night. He said that somebody in the Duma is trying to put together a completely Latvian division."

Vilis' eyes grew wide and hopeful. "Vitolds said something about that, too. Do you think it'll really happen?"

"God, I hope so. At least it'd be a little more palatable than living with these damn Russians. You know, sometimes I wonder how they even survived all these years with the way they fumble even simple orders."

"And if this is the heart of the Russian Army, it's a wonder they could have even made a single conquest."

A muffled rumble echoed in the distance. Vilis' face paled while Fricis' smile congealed with a locked open jaw. He gazed skyward and scanned until he saw a wispy trail of white smoke arc toward the bog.

"Jesus, did you see that?" Fricis gasped, watching the sky for more smoke trails.

In the distance the rumbling continued.

"We'd better get back to the—"

Suddenly, a salvo exploded next to them with a blinding light.

"Shit!" Vilis scrambled back to the safety of his trench. Fricis froze momentarily, trembling violently, then gathering his wits and hastily chased his brother.

The sky suddenly split open, releasing hell. Shells exploded overhead, the ground shivering with their concussions. Huge sections of the bog erupted, spitting foul smelling sand and partly decayed logs into the air. Screams and curses wailed out from deep in the trenches. Half-dressed bodies scurried to the openings. Bleary, wide eyes glared at the spectacle, while hands blanched as they clutched for dear life, sinking into the muddy crests.

Vilis reached his trench, then leapt into the hole just as a shrill hiss ended with a violent shudder immediately behind him. He curled into a ball near his half-empty pack as sand and splinters rained onto his head.

A sudden rush of air startled him for a moment. Confused, he listened more closely until all that was left was a continuous ringing.

"My ears! My God, my ears!" he screamed. He felt the vibration in his throat but couldn't hear himself. He popped his head up and peered from behind his pack, just as a spew of mud sprayed over the trench opening.

A body slipped over the crest of his trench, then slid down the embankment. It caught on a rock, flopped over, and stopped. Vilis gagged as he saw his brother's blood-smeared face etched into a contorted grimace. A bone fragment hung from his shoulder where his arm should have been. Mud-clumped blood oozed into a puddle in the rain saturated trench.

Vilis felt a prickly tingle under his cap. He glanced up and shuddered uncontrollably, seeing that only ten other soldiers remained in the long, narrow trench where more than one hundred had been sleeping just minutes before. Each of them cowered with their arms crossed and heads tucked close to their knees. Littering the bowels of the pit, canteens dribbled clear liquid onto abandoned bed rolls and backs. A wafting vodka odor competed with the pungent stench of urine, smoke, and blood.

"Those bastards deserted! They left without even trying to fight!" Vilis scoffed.

Above the trench he heard wailing above the shrill of incoming artillery. Explosions again trembled the ground. Metal balls rained into the trench, pinging off of scattered mess kits and canteens.

The dawning sky he had witnessed only a few moments before darkened quickly as a choking pall of soot-tainted smoke poured in over the crest and down the embankment. Vilis buried his head into his pack. The hell seemed to linger for hours until the earthen rain subsided and the ground stopped quivering.

He slowly lifted his head and looked around his trench. The ten soldiers that had been cowering with him had all been buried by the embankment which had once protected them. Not able to hear, he couldn't tell if they still screamed for help or had already died. A sudden sense of loneliness strangled him.

Concerned now only with salvaging his own life, Vilis abandoned his pack and struggled up the embankment. As his weary hands gripped the edge, he pulled himself up and peered at the pallor which lingered over the battlefield.

He sensed he had to run, but with the explosions seemingly all around him, he grew confused with which direction to go. The urge intensified until it finally overwhelmed him. He scrambled to his feet and started running in the direction he remembered the others went. The muddy ground was suddenly replaced by the sandy, mucky bog he remembered seeing that morning. He felt his boots filling with water. His feet squished as he slogged through the marsh. Through the blinding artillery and salvos trembling the ground under his feet, he sensed horses' hooves growing closer. Vilis froze, suddenly realizing he was headed in the wrong direction.

His head snapped side to side, from the Germans to his abandoned trench. His food-starved body complained. His drained, weary legs ached. His head spun in circles, reeling with disjointed thoughts of flight. Finally, he collapsed and fell face first into the marsh.

He breathed heavily out of his mouth. Water gurgled around his face as he struggled to pull it out of the foul-smelling, sandy peat. Soaked and exhausted, Vilis rested on all fours, trying to slow his frantic panting. Catching his breath, he lifted his head and gasped.

"A fuckin' Hun!" he said, breathlessly.

With his stained teeth bared in a sinister looking grin, a German soldier stood ankle deep in the marsh, glowering at Vilis. The soldier extracted his saber and held it momentarily above his head.

Helplessly stuck and too tired to struggle, Vilis muttered, "Dear God," as the metal blurred.

He felt his chest grow warm. He tried to scream, but only blood dribbled past his lips. As the same cold, prickly ring he felt around his head returned, he realized it did not matter if he cried out. No one would hear, and if anyone did, he would probably be German. Vilis' breathing slowed. The gruesome smile of the Hun expanded and faded.

❧   ❧   ❧

At dawn on the 29th, Captain Otomars Braze, in temporary command of the Fifteenth Mounted Brigade, impatiently waited at the edge of a mist-laden birch forest for the daily orders from command. He sat high in his saddle, as pompous and proud as a medieval knight receiving laurels after claiming victory in battle. After a brief wait, through the marsh's hovering, dense fog, and even through the muffled rumbles of artillery exploding in the distance, he heard hooves slogging through the sandy ground. Otomars trained his view at the edge of the misty pall, searching for the messenger. Finally, a horsemen pierced the mist.

"He must be a Cossack," Otomars mumbled as the hussar deftly broke his weave and headed directly for him.

The Cossacks' lavender calf-length coat flapped up behind the horse's pumping flanks. His gray pile wool cap was tilted forward to prevent its being blown off.

As the horseman drew closer, Otomars recognized the antics as that of Ivan, the messenger that had sent all his letters. An envelope flapped in the horseman's face as it dangled from his clenched jaw.

Ivan once told Otomars he carried messages that way because he wanted to feel the wind whistle through the spaces in his teeth.

Otomars' horse started pounding his hooves, obviously agitated.

"Steady, boy," Otomars muttered to his horse and cinched up on the reins as the horse started to rear and paw at the air.

When Ivan was within one hundred yards, the Cossack snatched the letter from his mouth and swung his left leg over the galloping horse's back. Otomars rolled his eyes as he watched the daredevil performance.

"Steady, boy," Otomars said, as his horse shifted his weight nervously from side to side.

The Cossack headed directly for Otomars' mount at break-neck speed. As the distance closed to ten yards, the Cossack thrust his legs into the air and swung them within inches of the ground. The short rider's ballooned pants flapped next to his horses flank as the animal reared its head, then stopped within inches of Otomars, splattering mud onto Otomars' boots.

Ivan guffawed as he dropped to the ground.

"Command sends regrets," Ivan mumbled, revealing a cynical grin.

He bowed and handed the message to Otomars, then popped up quickly.

"I will wait until you assemble your brigade and assist your so called cavalry regiment in their—"

"Our what?" Otomars bellowed.

"Those are orders to retreat. I know that much," Ivan spit back, disrespectfully. "Every other brigade is retreating. Casualties are heavy. So that must be your order to chicken out."

"How do you know? These letters are supposed to be for commanding officers only!"

"Listen, nib, I don't really care what's in your letters. I was told to escort you and your band of schoolboys past the Huns. I would take that as your command doesn't feel your horsemanship is good enough to get you back out of this hell-hole."

Ivan swaggered as he inspected Otomars' mount. He grabbed at the horse's throat and stared directly into his eyes and grinned.

"Fine horse you got here. Can't understand why he's being wasted on you brats."

"We are officers, Cossack! And we know more about the Germans than you do!"

"Then why is command telling you that you have to retreat?"

Ivan remained silent, politely waiting for Otomars to answer.

"Hell, you know as much about the Germans as you do about horses," Ivan taunted when Otomars didn't answer. "And the way you asses ride, it's clear you know nothing about horses!" Ivan guffawed as he remounted his horse. "That's why your command is paying me to get your asses home. Go ahead, read the letter. I'll wait for that, but not much longer."

Otomars did not know what to believe, other than his overwhelming desire to beat the Cossack senseless. He stifled his urge, though, realizing that if the Cossack was right, he had to mobilize his men quickly. He ripped open the message and started reading.

By order of Second Army General Samsonov,
Otomars Braze has been granted a field promotion to Major and is placed in command of the Fifteenth Cavalry Brigade. I regret that your first duty as commander is a general retreat to Willenberg.

"Son of a bitch!" Otomars said.

"Told you so, nib," Ivan said, smiling devilishly.

Otomars looked down at Ivan, who simply glared at him with a wry grin etched onto his face.

"Follow me. The camp is this way," Otomars humphed as he turned and snapped his reins. His mount reared, spun around, and broke into a full gallop. Ivan yelled happily, whipping his mount to an immediate gallop of its own. He quickly caught up with Otomars, and even weaving through the trees of the German lowlands, maintained pace.

The Fifteenth Regiment, officially under the command of Otomars, broke camp quickly and started their hasty retreat, following Ivan through the fog shrouded swamps. Oswalds caught up with his brother and silently maintained pace beside him for a few hundred meters.

"So, the promotion is official?" Oswalds asked.

Otomars glanced over and smiled. He then acknowledged with a nod, but nothing more.

Ivan abruptly stopped and raised his hand to signal the rest of the brigade. Otomars directed his men to circle Ivan.

"I've only been through this swamp once or twice before, but what I remember is that it has very few pathways on which we can travel," Ivan said when they had gathered. "I know the Huns have surrounded the bog, but they're afraid to wander in. I'll lead you through the safest causeway, but you need to follow me in single file if you wish to come out alive."

Otomars read acknowledgement in all of his men's eyes. He glanced at Ivan and nodded. Immediately, Ivan yanked on his reins and snapped his mount into an instant gallop.

Following Ivan and Otomars, the brigade complied quickly, forming an orderly file, maintaining their speed as they slogged onto the causeway.

Halfway across, the swamp exploded with the rattling of machine guns. Otomars turned abruptly and watched his men begin falling and splashing helplessly into the murky water. Oswalds' groan next to him turned Otomars' stomach, as bullets whizzed by his face. He turned and watched as his brother's face paled and froze, etched with a terrified, silent scream. Oswalds' body then slipped limply from his saddle.

"Ivan!" Otomars screamed. As he did, he felt hot lead pelt his body as if knives had been thrust through him. His horse stumbled, throwing him forward and onto the causeway. Otomars flopped over on his back but stiffened as he saw the body of his horse falling directly at him. He tried to move, but when the full weight of the horse pinned him, he heard a sickening crack in his chest. Then there was more machine gun fire rattling around him like a swirling wind. Muffled screams of his men pierced his ears, followed by splashing into the bog. The voices faded. Otomars felt himself grow colder, and his vision faded to darkness.

❧   ❧   ❧

A month later, Andrejs Braze sat alone on the porch of his house. He stared at the few yellow liepa and scarlet oak leaves which still precariously hung from otherwise naked branches. Warm breezes which traveled in from the bay nudged at the few remaining splashes of color, and finally succeeded in urging the last few from their perches. Andrejs sipped his hot orange tea, inhaled a nose full of the honey-sweetened aroma, then placed the cup next to him.

Beside the cup rested a letter which he had received earlier in the day. He looked at it for a moment, then picked it up and inspected the official seal of the Russian army. He was sure he knew what it said, since Elmars had told him about the debacle the at Tannenberg. With the war about to enter its third month, Elmars' fateful words at the mobilization parade rang loud and clear in Andrejs' mind. He had accepted the fact that by chance alone one of his sons must have been killed in the fighting.

He remembered how Otomars and Oswalds always tried to fool their friends into thinking each was the other. In growing up, they were inseparable. They always seemed to share the same interests and have the same goals. When he had talked to other parents of twins, they shared similar stories. But for Andrejs, his twin boys, both officers, would always be special.

He then thought of Fricis, his next oldest son, who was always so interested in politics. If the draft had not taken him away, Andrejs imagined Fricis would have gone to Riga University and become one of Latvia's deputies to the Duma. He chuckled as he remembered Fricis saying it wasn't the Russian government he would be a part of, it was going to be the free Latvian government.

Then Andrejs thought of Vilis, his youngest son, always the follower. Whatever Fricis wanted to do, Vilis was right behind him, begging to be a part of his big brother's world. Andrejs closed his eyes and hoped it wasn't Vilis. He was too young to die. But Andrejs convinced himself that the loss of one of them was inevitable.

He sighed deeply and decided he had delayed the inevitable long enough. Andrejs pried his fingers underneath the envelope's flap and broke the official seal. With measured motions, he unfolded the letter, then inhaled deeply again before he started reading.

"A perfect score! I don't think I've ever received one before!" Augustine beamed, rechecking her exam paper. She continued congratulating herself as she took three steps, skipped a couple more, then ran a few steps, unable to restrain her joy. She varied her speed all the way home as she swung her head happily from side to side. When she turned onto her street, she dashed up to the privet hedge and peered through the leaves, looking for her father. Spotting him on the porch in his chair, just where he always sat, she surmised he was waiting to hear the results of the test. Even if it was cold and snowy, he would be waiting for her. She had grown used to his ritual.

Augustine sprinted along the yellow-leafed hedgerow, then sharply turned up the pathway to the house.

"Poppa, I'm home!" she yelled, waving the paper above her head.

He did not respond, but she figured he was just asleep. As she drew closer, she saw a letter laying on the porch.

Augustine guessed it was another boring letter from Katerina about that farmer she was working for in Russia. For such an educated girl, she certainly led a boring life, Augustine chuckled.

As she reached the steps, she noticed that her father's face looked more pale than usual. She immediately stopped, then tipped her head and inspected him more closely.

Maybe he's just real tired, Augustine thought. He had been up quite a bit lately, complaining about not being able to breathe.

Augustine snuck up the steps, not wanting to wake her father, then stooped over to retrieve the letter. Curious as to what it said, she turned it over. The double headed eagle immediately caught her attention. In the minute that it took her to read the letter, she felt life drain from her heart. She dropped her hand, then stared at her father.

"Oh my God! Poppa!" she screamed.

She fell into her father's open arms and nuzzled her face against his stubbled cheeks. When his cold, clammy skin touched hers, she shuddered.

"Poppa?"

"Augustine, what is it? Why are you screaming so much?" Doroteja asked as she swung open the door.

She looked down at her husband, slumped in his chair, with Augustine draped over him weeping. She drew her open hands to her mouth and gasped. Tears immediately streamed down her cheeks.

"Momma, the letter," Augustine said, pointing to the paper that had fallen to the floor.

Doroteja stooped, picked up the letter, and then wiped her eyes. As she started to read, her eyes grew wide. Rivulets of tears trailed down her face, spotting the letter. She staggered back, then tried to hold herself upright against the house. Her knees buckled. She slumped down to her haunches, then buried her head in her lap.

Augustine left her father and dropped next to her mother.

The Carpathian Mountains, Austria-Hungary

6 May 1915

*P*eering through a veil of condensed breath spewing from his mount's nostrils, Voldemars stood at silent attention and surveyed the Carpathian Mountain Range. Compared to all the other mountains he had ever seen, this one was bland and unimpressive. Sparse evergreens spotted the snow streaked lower elevations, then abruptly ceased at a line drawn like a border between the trees and the mountains' barren, rocky, and white capped peaks. They stood less than half the size of the Urals and just as minor in comparison to the Caucasus.

Nonetheless, the Carpathians were daunting enough. They stood a bitter, vivid reminder of failure. His failure. This modest mountain range, its narrow, snow-filled passes, deceptively rugged terrain, and protective crannies, had stymied him. They thwarted the successful completion of his brigade's mission. One which he thought would surely have brought an early conclusion to the war. And if not the entire war, at least this theater.

Voldemars watched the lethargically rolling fog sink and expose a concealed rocky pass at the northern fringe of the mountains. He studied it, trying to recall if he had seen it before. The pass was protected, a perfect approach.

"That's what we should have done, Uguns," he mumbled to his horse. "We should have circled around and approached through there. Christ, why didn't I see that before?"

He spit in protest. A stale odor slipped past his nose. It reminded him of the decaying peat bogs he slogged through in Poland.

Pensive, Voldemars watched the dank, gloomy dawn fade into a gray, dismal morning. He twirled one end of his waxed, thin mustache into a curl and imagined how different things would have been if he had not failed.

A loud, sinister cackle in the distance broke the solitude and drew his attention to the naked, mangled branches hanging over the ravine. Not more than one hundred meters away, at the farthest end of a crooked perch, sat a huge, black raven, fiendishly surveying the landscape like a leering vulture in search of carrion. As it turned toward him, Voldemars wondered if that cursed bird was laughing at his failure as well. It arrogantly hopped out to the end of the branch, then spread its wings and launched into the misty sky. Sinking at first, it caught an updraft, then rose and started a wide, swooping circle above the trees.

The faint pounding of hooves challenged the morning's stillness and drew Voldemars' attention from the ravine. Uguns snorted, releasing a steaming cloud, then shook his head. Droplets of dew collected on his muzzle sprayed in a cloud around his head.

"Easy boy," Voldemars said, patting his mount's thick, chestnut neck. He recognized the trebled rhythm of a horse's canter thudding repeatedly through the ground. "It's just Renegade. Oleg's probably getting impatient again."

Uguns twisted his ears until they cupped to the rear. In a clockwise pattern, he anxiously shifted his weight on his legs. His eyes, though, remained fixed forward on the Carpathians.

Voldemars turned, squinted, and studied the single charge as it approached. The long, narrow, white stripe on its black head, running the full distance from his eyes to his nose, uniquely distinctive of Renegade, confirmed his suspicion.

Captain Oleg Stativsky slowed his charge to an easy trot. His smooth-skinned, cleanly shaven, boyish-looking face grew clear.

"Wonderful morning, wouldn't you say Voldemars?" he announced as he drew closer.

"Yes, a fine morning!" Sarcasm oozed through Voldemars' wry grin.

Oleg turned Renegade perpendicular to Uguns and whoaed his horse. He let the animal prance for a moment before he sighed with an exasperated tone.

"Tell me, Voldemars, are you holding out on us? Do you have a order hidden somewhere or has Command forgotten that we exist out here?"

Voldemars smirked, remaining silent. He shook his head and glanced back over the ravine.

"Patience, Oleg."

"Are we supposed to just sit here and rot until the Huns come pouring over the hills?" Oleg twitched his blonde eyebrows, mere wisps of hair perched above his wide, blue eyes.

"Even after a year, I still can't convince you of the virtues of patience in battle, can I?"

"Christ, they can't expect us to wait months for an order!"

Oleg's face pruned. He swung a foot over his horse's back and dismounted, folding the reins over in his hand. He strutted toward Voldemars, horse in tow. He stopped ten meters from the precipice and studied the far side of the ravine.

"Look at that! Nothing but unprotected pathways leading out of this trench."

"There is a pass over there." Voldemars pointed to the break in the mountains he had discovered.

Oleg turned back and huffed. "Wouldn't you at least like to know what the hell we're waiting for? We've been sitting here forever with no word. Not even a message about how the rest of the war is going. Don't you find that strange?"

"Not quite forever." Voldemars hid his disappointment with a sage-like, sobered voice. "We took Przemysl in March, then lost at Gorlice the following week. That means we've been here only a month."

Just the sound of that fateful battle at Gorlice knotted Voldemars' gut as much as the loss itself.

"Well, it sure as hell feels like forever in this God forsaken hole!" Oleg stared deep into the rolling fog bank.

"If I just didn't lose that last battle—" Voldemars grumbled sourly.

"Oh, no you don't, Voldemars," Oleg quickly interrupted. He grabbed hold of Voldemars' pants and yanked for attention. "You didn't lose that battle! You didn't get the support Command promised you would. But that's beside the point. Gorlice isn't what's been eating at me. It's all this damn standing still. Damn it, we're cavalry! Cavalry means horses. Horses are made to move. In my mind, it logically follows then that we should be moving."

"Maybe that is it, then. We haven't received any new orders because Command has lost faith in my leadership."

"One loss?" Oleg tugged again at his commander's pants. "No, Voldemars. One loss is not going to ruin the reputation you've built as one of the Czar's most successful cavalry leaders."

Voldemars raised his eyebrows and shot a cold stare at Oleg.

"Even General Brusilov knows of Voldemars Vechi, the brash, intelligent, and most importantly, successful Latvian colonel in an army exclusively commanded by Russians," Oleg continued. "Hell, I remember Brusilov's face when he came to Przemysl after we won, and that was after a string of victories as long as your arm. Victories which you commanded! Gorlice wasn't all your fault, and I won't stand back and let you feel sorry for yourself because you lost one lousy battle!"

Voldemars stood silent. The agony of Gorlice still nagged him like an open, festering wound that refused to heal.

Oleg quietly stood next to his commander, obviously disgusted he could not talk Voldemars out of his self-induced purgatory. He studied the mountains for a moment, then turned and peered directly into Voldemars' eyes.

"Don't you ever wonder what's over there? You know, what the Huns are plotting?"

"Yes," Voldemars responded.

"Isn't this foolish waiting just irritating the hell out of you?"

"Christ, Oleg, my hands are tied!" Voldemars tried to quench the impulse driven fire in Oleg's eyes by sending an exasperated grimace at him.

"But don't you think we should do something?"

"If anyone is there, riding into that pass like a bunch of brainless Cossacks would surely get us killed."

"Sitting around here is going to kill me as well. And the rest of this brigade."

"Patience, Oleg, patience," Voldemars said calmly. "Something will break from Command soon enough."

"I certainly hope so," Oleg sighed loudly as he shook his head. "My ass is so sore from sitting on it for so long that I feel like I'm picking at bedsores!"

And you think I'm enjoying this? Voldemars thought as he watched Oleg fluidly remount Renegade.

"I'll head back to the encampment and wait for any late breaking news from Command," Oleg said as he turned his horse sharply around. "That is, of course, if I don't die of old age first!" He chuckled, then snapped his reins. Renegade immediately broke into a full sprint, spraying mud divots in his wake.

"I wish he wouldn't do that. If we don't get any orders now, I'm not going to be able to stop wondering what might be back there,"

Voldemars muttered as he watched Oleg and Renegade disappear into the mist.

Uguns moved his ears stiffly forward, toward the northern edge of the mountains.

"Well, what do you think, ol' boy. What's back there?"

Voldemars surveyed the area for himself, peering at the narrow pass now clearly visible through the thinning mist. The thought of leading his regiment into the valley and surprising the enemy sparked to life.

"Those damn Huns are back there!"

He sighed deeply. He imagined his regiment charging through the pass and breaking through, like he should have done before.

But he had standing orders. No advances without Command's concurrence. The image of sudden victory faded. He sighed as he reached into the pocket of his knee length, field overcoat. Fumbling through his depleted supply of crumbled sugar cubes, he pulled one out then held it under Uguns' muzzle. The animal's pinkish nostrils flared as he sniffed the treat, then protruded his lips and deftly drew the morsel into his mouth. Voldemars gently stroked the coarse, matted mane with his other hand.

"Atta boy," Voldemars muttered, stroking his mount's long, black mane.

Uguns had the same fire in his eyes that Voldemars remembered had mesmerized him when he was selecting his horse. He was set on a white Arabian when he arrived, but Uguns was so much a horse that it was worth forgoing that long lived desire.

Uguns had looked up at him as if he read his thoughts. Their eyes met; his large, protruding orbs looked like rounded chunks of fine, high grade coal. His muscles were well defined, and his blood vessels pulsed slowly, strongly. His ribs were thick, laddered, and curved gently, encasing a wide thorax.

When Voldemars had approached him for the first time, he stopped centimeters away and peered into his eyes. As reflections danced on the mirror-like surface, he could see a fire burning within. It was then he knew he would be Uguns, the old Lettish word for fire.

Uguns jumped and broke Voldemars' reverie. He twisted his ears back. Voldemars turned his head and listened as well. Again, pounding hooves hammered in the distance.

Voldemars studied the approaching horses. He immediately recognized Renegade as one of the two. The other had brown and white markings which made it look as if it were wearing a hood. At full gallop, he could see it was at least three hands taller than Renegade. That had to be Titan, and there was only one officer in his brigade who needed a beast the size of Titan, Alexiev.

Voldemars slipped his boot into one stirrup, mounted Uguns, then turned him to face the oncoming horsemen. The approaching hussars slowed their charge, letting their mounts break down to a more leisurely pace.

I wonder how many Austrians surrendered merely at the sight of that monster, Voldemars mused, inspecting the massive horseman accompanying Oleg. Alexiev had to have been at least two meters tall and weighed no less than one hundred twenty-five kilograms. As he coaxed Uguns toward his men, Voldemars noticed a letter flapping in Oleg's hand.

He nudged Uguns to move a bit faster. Instantly the horse responded, breaking into an arrogant canter.

"It's a message from command, sir!" Oleg yelled, waving the communique in his outstretched hand. His smile was so taught Voldemars thought his face was going to split open.

"After three months on the front, you would think they would have set up wireless by now!" Voldemars grumbled as he snatched the message from Oleg's hand. "Well, what's in it?"

"Orders," Oleg said quickly.

"Your perception or knowledge?" Voldemars' said harshly.

"Perception, sir. I didn't read it."

"Then why did you drag Alexiev along?"

Voldemars scowled as he carefully ripped the end open and puffed at the torn edge. When the envelope popped open, he extracted the communique, then glared icily at Oleg before reading the message. Alexiev slipped a small, but still perceptible grin.

"I was concerned you might think I wrote it myself," Oleg said.

"You're right!" Voldemars said, nodding.

He flashed a wry grin at Alexiev, who remained stolidly still, peering at Voldemars through his large eyes, which bulged out below his heavy black eyebrows. Hidden behind a dark shadow of beard growth and a thick, black mustache, his face looked stern and cold, but that seemed to be perpetual for him.

Voldemars glanced back to the message and started to read. His face paled instantly. A cold sweat soaked the brim of his cap as his eyes bulged. He nervously chewed on the inside of his pursed lips.

"Our wait is over," Oleg whispered to Alexiev.

"Colonel?" Alexiev queried.

"Well, tell us the news! What do they say?" Oleg prodded, a bit of hesitation in his voice. He took a deep breath and closed his eyes as Voldemars cleared his throat.

"Second of May 1915, from his Majesty's Military Command, General Alexii Brusilov, Eighth Army." Voldemars sucked in a deep breath to regain his composure. He noisily exhaled, and while hidden behind a cloud of condensed breath, continued.

"On this day, the Central Powers of Germany and Austro-Hungary have commenced a mass offensive at Gorlice. Casualties have been heavy. A general retreat for all his majesty's forces is being ordered. The Kaiser's forces have...."

Voldemars fell silent. He dropped his hand to his side as his face had blanched as white as the hairs at the twisted tips of his mustache. His lip chewing grew more fervent.

Oleg nudged his mount closer to Voldemars. "Colonel...?"

"Gorlice! Damn, I should have taken it!" Voldemars suddenly felt a cold chill shiver through his spine. Instantly he perked up, trying to place the sensation. Everything became frighteningly clear.

"No man's land! Oleg, we've got to get the hell out of here!"

All three horses grew restless as a chorus of muffled thuds echoed up from the valley. Voldemars saw the streaking shells first as they crested the precipice. Faint whistles warbled overhead as the shells peaked in their trajectory, then turned and headed back toward the ground.

"Damn!" Oleg yelled, yanking back on Renegade's reins. The horse reared, pivoted, then broke into a frenzied gallop as soon as his front legs touched the ground.

Muffled thumps behind them punctuated the morning stillness as the shells landed. Small explosions discharged. A yellowish-green cloud swirled out from each cartridge.

"Gas!" Voldemars gasped. He reached down for his mask and froze, realizing he had left it back in the regiment's bivouac.

"Gas! Alexiev, get out of here!" he yelled as he spurred Uguns.

Alexiev dug his heels into Titan's flanks, and the steed sprang into action, headed toward the spreading fog now hissing out of the cracked open canisters.

Oleg plunged into the cloud first, followed by Alexiev. Voldemars trailed, slipping into the blinding cloud just as his comrades' wake closed. He leaned into Uguns' neck, trying vainly to hold his breath through the choking, burning mist. The gas seeped into his nostrils, then burned as it scraped his throat. He tasted blood on his tongue, as his eyes felt as if they were being singed by hot pokers.

Voldemars jerked forward as Uguns suddenly tensed up. His nose rammed his horse's neck, stinging as the hairs scraped his skin. Uguns slowed a bit, then grew tentative. As he regained his mount, Voldemars felt his horse drop into an uneven gait.

"Com'on, boy, move!" He slapped frantically at Uguns' hindquarter. "We've got to get out of here!"

Voldemars suddenly felt airborne. Uguns stumbled, then collapsed. Time seemed to stop as he felt nothing around him but air. He flailed, then braced himself for impact. He hit, chest first. Air exploded out through his mouth as he crumbled into a ball. Reflexively, he inhaled.

Voldemars screamed. His chest radiated with pinpricks like he had just swallowed a hand full of burdocks. The stings seared through his lungs and throat.

Breathe shallow, he reminded himself. He tried to collect himself, but he could not stifle his heavy panting. Prone and helpless, lucid thought faded quickly. Confusion and stupor slipped in as the gas grew more chokingly acrid than Alexiev's Russian cigarettes. The hot stinging crept up from his chest and singed mercilessly at his mouth and throat. His lips felt scorched, as if on fire. Reflexively, he spit gobs of mucus just to keep his breathing passages clear.

Mustard gas, he thought. Deadly, thick mustard gas. He remembered what Command had said about how quickly this gas would reduce a soldier to a bleeding mass. Have to move. His thoughts grew disjointed as he tried pushing himself up. As he struggled to his knees, he gasped for a breath of fresh air, but there was only pungent, stinging, ubiquitous smoke. Breathing grew impossible. Voldemars felt more suffocated with each shortened breath. He tried opening his eyes, but the gas singed his membranes. Every movement shot pain through his whole body, but he knew he had to try to escape.

He reached into his coat and ripped out the pocket. Holding his breath, he shifted to his knees, then fumbled at his pants. He freed two of the buttons, then slipped the cloth through the opening. The gas insidiously crept in and stung at his genitals. Voldemars strained his aching stomach muscles and forced a squirt of urine onto the rag. Then again and again. He finally felt damp warmth seep onto his hand. He struggled to extract the rag, then rung it out and draped it over his nose and mouth.

Voldemars cupped his hand over his nose, forcing a fit over the bridge. Slowly at first, he inhaled, vividly remembering how violently he vomited during the training drill. He swallowed hard to stifle his gagging, but he couldn't hold his reflex at bay. His stomach and chest spasmed. Vomit surged through his throat. Voldemars lifted the rag from his face just as the spew ejected from his mouth. He spit twice, then covered his face again with the rag.

Voldemars listened closely, groping for direction through the swirling yellowish-green smoke. The hissing canisters had stopped, but so had the slamming of hooves into the ground. He wondered if the others had escaped, or fallen victim to the choking death.

He sucked in through the cloth, and the stinging in his mouth and chest subsided. Two more deliberate breaths. Better. Another. His stomach muscles relaxed as much as the stinging pain allowed.

He listened again. The distance was silent. No one was coming to take him. That was clear. Or to save him. That was clear as well.

Still holding the cloth tightly against his face, Voldemars gathered his rubbery legs underneath him and stood up. He stumbled forward, then stopped, realizing he had no idea which direction to go. He spun around, cracked open his eyes, and tried to find anything that looked familiar.

Nothing. Just yellowish-green smoke swirling around him, thicker than an early spring fog in Riga. He felt his chest tighten. Panic danced through his thoughts.

He stood still again and heard labored breathing. And it was close.

With stilted steps, he moved. After stumbling three times, he bumped into a large mass. His eyes burning and useless, he reached out and touched it. Coarse matted hair. He moved his hand up.

"Uguns! You're up! Good boy!" Voldemars' breath rasped sharply in his throat.

He felt his way up and around the horse until he found smooth leather. He fumbled along the saddle.

He found the straps and followed them down until he touched a cold, steel stirrup. With his hand quivering uncontrollably, Voldemars steadied the foothold, then sucked in a deep breath though his rag and held it as he reached up and grabbed the pommel. Mustering all his might, he lifted his leg and slipped his foot into the hole. That effort alone exhausted him. He strained again, lifting himself off the ground. He wormed his other leg up Uguns' loin and tried to clear his back. Failing at first, his foot slipped, but he buried the toe of his boot between two of the horse's protruding ribs.

Uguns remained perfectly still, unwavering until he let Voldemars' weight drop into the saddle. He rested his head on Uguns' neck, then held on as tightly as his weakened condition allowed. Uguns started a labored, limping pace. With each step, Uguns' lungs gurgled. His wheezing grew louder and more labored.

"Just a little farther, ol' boy," Voldemars' said over his swollen tongue and past his stinging lips.

He took a quick breath through the cloth, then tried to cover Uguns' nostrils, but the horse snorted and violently shook his head.

The cloud thinned, and Voldemars felt a slight breeze tussle at his hair. He gasped taking in a deep breath. Cleaner air mixed with the stinging gas that remained trapped deep in his lungs. He winced but forced himself to keep breathing. After a few breaths, the needling sensation subsided. The air seemed to have cleared.

"Camp," Voldemars muttered through a coughing spell.

He reached down and locked his hands over Uguns' throat latch. Obediently, Uguns continued his plodding. Voldemars felt his head clear a bit, but nausea wrenched at his stomach. His eyelids slid over his stinging eyes, cooling them with what little moisture still oozed out of his tear ducts.

Suddenly, Uguns stopped. Voldemars felt the animal's muscles spasm as he tried to stifle his snorting and coughing. Voldemars then gagged on a soft, salty clump of mucous which had worked its way up his throat. He hacked and let the lump fall to the ground.

"We'll rest here, old boy," he whispered into his horse's ear.

Exhausted, he slid off Uguns' back. When his body dropped onto the mushy, ground pine, his knees buckled. He fell face first into the ground cover.

Voldemars' body ached. The stinging in his eyes continued, even though the needles in his lungs had subsided. His head spun. He tried to inhale deeply, but his chest spasmed and stifled his attempt. His breaths grew shorter, too short to keep thinking. His lungs felt as if they were filled with fluid. His eyes burned mercilessly.

He looked up around him and saw what seemed spires of gray rock face surrounding him like a fortress. Wisps of yellowish gas drifted by above the tops of the jagged rocks. Closer to him, a mat of lichens clung to the rocks, then melded into the soft looking grass and mushy ground pine.

He scanned the enclosure his horse had plodded into. One entrance, a small crack separated them from the outside world and this small hideaway Uguns had discovered.

The ground muffled a sudden thud next to him. Voldemars rolled his head, then squinted.

"Uguns!" he cried.

Uguns laid next to him, helplessly twitching. A blurry maroon puddle pooled near his half-open muzzle. The horse wheezed and struggled for each shallow breath, then would hack, snort, and choke. More blood-streaked, viscous fluid dribbled from between his bared teeth.

Voldemars dragged himself toward his horse, his closest companion for two years. He reached out and touched one of Uguns' front pasterns, but quickly pulled his hand back when a bone sliver pricked his palm.

"Son of a bitch!" He pulled himself closer, then wrapped his arm around Uguns' chest, laying his head on the animal. His coat reeked of the putrid smelling gas.

"If I had my pistol, I'd give you peace, old friend."

Voldemars' thoughts grew hazier as his vision blurred again, then faded to a flat, undefined gray. Every muscle in his body hurt.

Uguns' chest stopped jerking and his wheezing ceased. Voldemars felt helpless, unable to even comfort his horse. Dizzy, nauseous, and broken-willed, Voldemars closed his eyes and slipped into unconsciousness.

❧   ❧   ❧

With his rifle slung crosswise on his back, Oleg led his compliment of six officers to the area where the gas had landed. An unnatural frown was etched onto his wind battered face as he nervously bobbed in his saddle, scanning the area for any evidence that Voldemars may be nearby.

"Whoa, boy," he said, suddenly pulling back on his reins.

As Renegade's legs pounded into the ground, slowing his forward motion, Oleg raised his white gloved hand. When he stopped, he pulled Renegade around and faced his oncoming brigade. In turn, each rider slowed, then assembled in a circle around Oleg.

"Peotr, Ahmed, head north, toward Galacia," Oleg barked as Renegade shifted his weight between his front legs. "And be wary of an ambush. We don't know how far the Huns have closed in since they gassed the area."

"Encounters?" Peotr said, expressionless.

Oleg chewed his lip for a moment, then adjusted his mount. "Avoid engagement," he answered in a grave tone. "We have to accept that if Voldemars has been captured, there's nothing we can do."

"Yes, sir!" Peotr snapped his right hand into an open-palmed salute.

In unison, he and Ahmed tugged their reins, pivoted their mounts, then bolted off to the north.

"Vladimir, Kamil, head west," Oleg said. "You shouldn't have any problems, but don't let your guard down. We weren't expecting anything this morning either." He snapped his head right, and his eyes met Alexiev's.

"You double back and search east," Oleg said. "I want to be sure we didn't miss any place where Voldemars might have crawled into. Evgeny, you and I will head back to the ridge."

Evgeny furtively glanced down to his saddlebag and peeked inside. Obviously finding what he was looking for, he patted his bag twice, then looked back up to Oleg with wide eyes and nodded.

"Let's go!" Oleg yanked at Renegade's reins and buried his boots in his mount's ribs.

Renegade instantly responded, leaving Evgeny still turning his horse around.

In the short time it took Evgeny to catch up, Oleg spotted the rock formation he barely avoided running into during his mad dash away from the gas. He pulled up, stopping a safe distance away, just as a strange anxiety quivered through his spine. He craned his neck, trying to see past the break in the rocks, studying the tactical position they offered.

Evgeny, though, galloped past him without stopping, headed directly for the opening.

"Evgeny, wait! It might be a trap!" Oleg called.

Immediately, Evgeny pulled up, turned, and circled back.

"I'll give you cover from over there," Oleg whispered as Evgeny stopped next to him. "Let me secure my position, then you move ahead."

Evgeny nodded enough to twitch his blonde locks from under his cap, then turned back toward the rocks. Oleg nudged Renegade ahead to a strategically positioned station near the opening, then slipped his rifle off his shoulder. Fidgeting until he acquired a comfortable stance, he flagged Evgeny, then focused on the opening.

With a cautious silence and a determination etched into his boyish looking face, Evgeny drew his saber. Holding it stiffly at his side, he applied gentle pressure from his heels, nudging his mount toward the rocks.

Oleg felt his pulse quicken. Breathing deeply and deliberately, he maintained his rifle level to the ground, ready to react at the first sign of trouble. His chest thumped as his heartbeat quickened. Blood surges swelled his neck enough to make his collar feel like it was choking him.

Renegade twitched, shifting between his left and right legs. Oleg soothed him by stroking his neck, then brought his arm back into position. He bit his lip and tempered his nervousness, just as Voldemars had always cautioned him to do.

"No Man's Land," he gasped.

A prickle raced across his neck as Evgeny slipped between the rocks and disappeared. His heart jumped to double-time. His breathing shallowed. His muscles twitched and tightened, growing more stiff as each second passed that Evgeny was out of his sight.

Don't tense up! Rely on your instincts! Oleg heard Voldemars' words echo in his head.

Ten seconds, then I'm going in after him, Oleg thought, growing nervous.

"Five," he said.

"Six, seven…" He prepared to scramble to his feet and charge in.

"Eight. Nine…"

"Captain!" Evgeny's high-pitched voice called out from behind the rocks.

Oleg froze. His finger twitched on the rifle's trigger.

"Captain! I found the Colonel!" Evgeny's voice jumped a pitch.

Oleg's heart fluttered. Immediately, he slung his rifle back over his shoulder and stood up in his stirrups. He snapped his reins and directed Renegade in a wide turn, intending to enter the pass at full gallop. As his mount broke his circle, Oleg drew his saber and pointed it forward, prepared for anything.

When he passed the rocks, he pulled up and stopped. The stench of blood and sulfur slapped his face. There was a faint yellowish-green tint to the rocks, like the choking pollen blooms from birches. Oleg waved a hand and surveyed inside. Evgeny crouched next to a prone Voldemars, his horse nervously pacing at his side. Oleg spurred Renegade and raced in close, then pulled up on his reins. He kept his left lead taught, forcing Renegade into a tight pirouette. Taking a careful look around as his horse turned, Oleg ensured no one else was laying in wait for an ambush. Seeing none, he turned back to Evgeny.

"He needs help. He's bad," Evgeny said, not taking his focus off of Voldemars.

Oleg did not hear him. Next to Voldemars, Uguns lay dead, his legs locked in place as if he was still in full gallop. A jelled pool of blood and mucous spread out on the ground under his open mouth. Open, oozing sores covered his eyes and nostrils.

Oleg gagged. Forcefully swallowing, he turned away and quelled his reflex.

"Captain! We need to get the commander back to camp," Evgeny said.

Shaking his head, Oleg broke his focus and looked down to Voldemars. He gasped as he slipped off his horse. He stumbled toward his friend, dropping his saber. "Has he been shot?"

"I don't think so. It's gas," Evgeny answered quickly, running his hands over Voldemars' stiff body.

Oleg dropped to his knees next to Evgeny. He could not keep himself from staring at the blood which streaked from the side of Voldemars' open mouth, feeding a phlegm pool beneath it. His pale, yellow complexion enticed a surge of vomit to dribble up Oleg's throat, but he stiffened and held it back.

"His lungs sound full, could be blood," Evgeny said. "His throat's raspy. Breathing shallow. It's definitely gas, but it's not like the others I've seen. All this blood—"

"He's alive, damn it! That's all that matters now!" Oleg suddenly felt a surge of energy. He didn't know much about gas, but he knew had to do something. As he scrambled to Voldemars' feet, Evgeny shifted toward his head, crouched down, and slipped his hands under Voldemars' shoulders. Oleg grabbed hold of Voldemars' mud covered field boots. In unison, the pair lifted their fallen commander and started toward Renegade, but he had moved.

Oleg and Evgeny froze when they saw Renegade poking at Uguns with his snout. With slow, deliberate nudges, he pushed at the dead horse's still chest, then moved a step back. He rocked his head back and forth, then pawed at the ground.

Urgency egged the soldiers on. They carried Voldemars to Renegade and hoisted his limp body onto the horse's back. Oleg vaulted into the saddle, while Evgeny whistled for his mount.

"How bad is it?" Oleg asked as he turned to his charge.

Evgeny turned and peered at Voldemars with his small, dark eyes, and paused for a moment before answering. "I think he'll make it, Captain."

"But?" Oleg said, sensing tentativeness in Evgeny's words.

"But he'll need prompt medical attention." Evgeny dropped his head and looked down at his boots.

"What is it you're not telling me?"

"Captain, the only gas I've ever seen was chlorine, and chlorine can't do this much damage. The stuff he got hit with is something worse. Much worse."

"Will he live?" Oleg demanded.

"You saw the lesions and blistered lips. And his face, that color, it's like mustard. I've never seen that before, either."

"Will he live?" Oleg insisted.

For a moment, Evgeny stood silent. Finally, he glanced at Voldemars and dropped his head.

"I just don't know."

Reality chilled Oleg, sending a shiver through his entire body. He glared at Voldemars' slumped body and for a moment imagined becoming the brigade leader. It turned his stomach, but it was the way things worked.

"Let's go!" he ordered, and the pair headed back to the encampment.

❧   ❧   ❧

"Head out for the message post," Oleg ordered as he and Evgeny rode into the bivouac. "Request—"

He stopped as he heard hooves in a full gallop. Glancing up, he looked toward the sound.

"It's a scout!" Evgeny said, pointing.

"Don't leave yet. I want to see what he's got. He might even be able to help us."

Oleg watched the rider close in on them. As the scout neared, he pulled up on his reins and slowed his mount.

"Are you the commanding officer?" he asked.

"I am now," Oleg icily answered.

Amazed at the youthful appearance of the rider, he gawked, realizing the boy could not have been more than fourteen.

Fear suddenly blossomed on the boy's face as he caught a glimpse of Voldemars' body slumped in front of Oleg. "Gas?" The boy's voice trembled.

"Yes. Listen, can you—"

"How close are they?" the scout interrupted. He quickly handed an official letter to Oleg.

"Just over the ridge, I guess. Get us some help. We need a wagon for transport."

"I don't know what I can do. I'll try, but—"

"But what?" Oleg blurted, incensed. He straightened and pushed out his chest, hoping to intimidate the boy.

Cowering, the boy pulled his horse back. His eyes darted between Evgeny and Oleg for a moment as his jaw dropped open in silence.

"The whole army's in retreat, sir," the scout finally uttered, shrugging his shoulders. "I don't know if I can get anything to come back here."

The words stunned Oleg. Wasting no more time, the scout pivoted and whipped his horse into a full gallop, headed back from where he came.

"Wait!" Oleg yelled, but the boy hurried off without hesitation.

"Retreat?" Evgeny gasped. "Why would Command order a retreat?"

Oleg shrugged, confounded as well.

"Christ, we've held this area for more than a month. It's as secure as if it were in Mother Russia itself!" Evgeny protested as Oleg opened the envelope and stared at the letter.

"Fourth May 1915," he read aloud. "General Alexii Brusilov, Eighth Army. Heavy losses at Gorlice have forced Command to direct that in order to preserve his Majesty's arms, all troops are to retreat to the lines held prior to our offensive at the start of this year. The entire Eighth Army will regroup in Tarnopol for redeployment.

"All cavalry divisions not necessary for defensive posture will be withdrawn to Russia and remain as reserve forces."

He stopped reading and dropped his hand to his side. He glanced up to the gray cloud cover as his face first paled, then blushed.

"Damn Command!" he spit out in rage.

Evgeny's eyes glazed over as he grew stone faced and silent. Oleg simply shook his head.

Thunderous pounding drew Oleg's attention back to the encampment. As he looked up he saw Alexiev and Titan galloping at full speed toward them. When Alexiev himself came into view, Oleg noticed his toothy grin.

"You found the Colonel?" Alexiev's words and smile evaporated when he saw his commander's condition.

"He's alive, but he needs attention," Oleg said.

The huge Russian's grim stare melted into a relieved smile, revealing wide spaces between his peg-like teeth. "If they didn't kill him, he'll live," Alexiev confidently chuckled.

"Command says," Oleg paused, then looked back at the letter and finished catatonically, "we're to withdraw to Tarnopol."

"Tarnopol?" Alexiev's loud, bass voice boomed disparagingly. "That's two hundred kilometers behind the front! Do those idiots realize what they're ordering?"

"We have our orders!" Oleg insisted. He quickly glanced at Voldemars. "Our first duty, though, is to Voldemars. We need to get him to an aid station quickly."

Even before Oleg finished, Alexiev dismounted with a wide sweep of his leg over Titan. As soon as his huge boots stomped onto the ground, he strutted to Renegade, slipped his hands under Voldemars' shoulders, then grinned widely at Oleg. Effortlessly, he lifted Voldemars and slung him over his shoulder, releasing a grunt for effect, then carried his fallen leader to the collection of small pup tents. Careful not to jostle him, he set Voldemars down on bedding Evgeny had hurriedly pulled out.

"Colonel?" Alexiev prodded, hovering over Voldemars. His eyes were wide and seemed distant. He placed his huge hands onto Voldemars' shoulders and gently shook him.

Voldemars' eyes fluttered, then slowly cracked open. Oleg rushed over and dropped to his knees.

"Alexiev! His eyes!" Oleg gasped. He felt queasiness blossom in his sour stomach as he watched Voldemars struggle to keep his eyelids off his hideously opaque eyes.

"Evgeny says it's not chlorine," Oleg muttered to Alexiev.

"It is not. Chlorine doesn't do this much damage," Alexiev said in a hushed tone.

"Oleg," Voldemars' raspy, soft voice was not much louder than a whisper. He winced as he spoke.

Oleg leaned close enough, he thought, so that Voldemars could distinguish his face, and forced a smile.

"Don't tell Otilija," Voldemars breathed. "I don't want her to know. It would be too much—"

Voldemars stiffened, then quivered for a few seconds. Evgeny quickly threw a blanket over him.

"I'll wait to tell her when she has to know," Oleg assured.

Voldemars feebly smiled and extended his trembling hand toward Oleg.

"Uguns, did he?" Voldemars winced again, then coughed and turned his head. Loose, blood-streaked mucous drained from his cracked mouth. He weakly spit twice.

Oleg glanced up at Evgeny. He closed his eyes and nodded.

"He's dead," Oleg admitted.

Voldemars' ashen face grew long. He pursed his bleeding, blistered lips, then struggled to inhale deeply. "He saved my life. He came back for me," Voldemars shook his head and closed his eyes.

"Command has ordered a general retreat," Oleg started, but stopped when Voldemars' eyes popped open. His glare was penetrating as he remained silent for a moment.

"I guess the mail is slow around here," Voldemars said as he cracked a wry looking smile. "When was that one dated?"

"Fourth of May."

"Only a two day delay. This morning it was four," Voldemars responded, but as he tried to grin, he winced horribly. He closed his eyes and let his head roll limply onto its side. "I guess that means they're getting better."

"When is that damn wagon going to get here?" Oleg impatiently blurted as he stood up. "Evgeny, make him comfortable! I'm going out to assemble the regiment.

"And tell them Command has ordered a damned retreat," he mumbled. Disgusted, he strutted toward Renegade. In one fluid motion, he hoisted himself, grabbed the leathers, and snapped them

Astrakhan, Southern Russia

7 May 1915

O tilija noticed Emilia sitting alone on a concrete bench overlooking the Caspian Sea, staring out over the water with her piercing, crystal blue eyes. Under her curly, coal black hair, her eyes gave her a mystical appearance which fascinated Otilija since the day they had met.

"Has Kamil written?" Otilija asked innocently as she sat next to Emilia. She slipped her hand across the back side of her plain blue dress as she sat down. Immediately, the cold morning dampness left on the bench seeped through her dress and chilled her thighs.

"No," Emilia curtly replied without turning, continuing to stare out over the calm water.

Otilija recoiled. It was so unlike Emilia to be terse. Usually she had so much to say that Otilija found herself walking away before she finished talking.

Otilija adjusted the pins in her bunned hair as she studied Emilia. Something was obviously bothering Emilia, and it was her duty to help her. Assumed or otherwise, she was the leader of all the officer's wives, like Voldemars was to each of the soldiers. She was the one to provide counsel if they were upset. She was the one to keep everyone mutually cordial, a task made especially difficult by their diverse backgrounds.

"It has been more than two months since his last letter," Emilia suddenly blurted. "He wrote they were going into another battle, and since then, nothing." She stopped as abruptly as she started, then sighed.

Otilija sensed a hint of concern through her typical formality. She brushed down the wide white collar and slipped open a couple of the small pearl like buttons at her throat.

"Well, I have just not heard from him."

"I am sure he's all right, Emilia," she said with a bit of a smile. "You remember that letter I received from Voldemars last month, don't you? He assured me the whole regiment was unharmed."

Emilia remained icily silent.

"Kamil will write soon, I'm sure," Otilija assuaged.

"I would certainly like to believe you, but I know Kamil too well. He does not write much, nor often."

"But Voldemars does," Otilija said cautiously, not wanting to sound like she was boasting. "And I promise, I will tell—"

"And I know men!" Emilia exploded in a bitter tone. She turned toward Otilija and glared with wide, accusing eyes. "Men are very conniving and deceitful. Even if something did happen to Kamil, I know they would band together and hide it from us! That is just the way they are. I know it, and so do you!"

"That's not true, Emilia. Voldemars has always been open and truthful with me."

"Then you are either gullible or naive."

"No, I know him!"

Otilija stared back at Emilia with a fiery stare of her own. Emilia's eyes melted from the adamant gaze to one more deeply reticent and unsettled. Obviously uncomfortable, she pulled her trembling, tightly clenched fists in close to her side.

"I am sure he would write me. Especially if something happened to any of his men," Otilija added, more subdued.

"I am sorry I doubted your husband," Emilia said. "But, sometimes I just feel…" She dropped her head and a tear rolled down her cheek. She sniffed twice and swung her head back. "Perhaps it is just that it is so difficult to adjust to all these changes."

Otilija placed her arm around Emilia, then pulled her close enough that her pungent perfume wafted into her nose.

"I promise, Emilia. I will let you know when Voldemars writes."

"It is just so difficult! Look at us! We are all so different. They bring us here and throw us together in this compound hundreds of kilometers from our families. Then they send our husbands off to war, and we are left here to lament. No contact with them, no contact with our families! What do they expect us to do?"

"We do have something in common," Otilija said. "All of our husbands are—"

"It is not just that," Emilia interrupted. "I am used to Kamil not writing now." Her face suddenly paled as her expression grew stern. Her whole body began to quiver as she inhaled deeply.

"What truly concerns me is that I have not heard from Momma since that Command officer slipped and told us that Turks invaded Batum!"

A sudden, frightening chill shot through Otilija's neck and down her back. Emilia's eyes had opened so wide that they bulged from their sockets.

"I do not sleep well at night. I keep having nightmares about my sister," Emilia said.

She dropped her head and began to weep. Otilija felt her shoulders tremble.

"I see…I see my sister being carried away," Emilia continued, her voice quivering as she sucked in short breaths between sobs. "And dirty faced soldiers leering at her, having their way, taunting her, violating her!"

As Emilia purged her soul, Otilija felt her own suppressed memories lurk forward and stir to life. She saw her mother's shaky hand as she stared with disbelief at the letter that told of the deaths of her four brothers at Tannenberg. Poppa's face shimmered in the fore-front, frozen in a death grip, his heart too weak to take the news. A chill quivered under Otilija's skin as she realized that her mother and Augustine were now alone in Riga, and she had not heard from them either.

Had the Germans invaded and Command was not telling them? Was there some reason she should not believe her own sister was in danger?

Otilija shook off her own fears and stiffened her quivering lip.

"Then I see my mother, laying helpless, beaten and bleeding on the floor, calling my name!" Emilia's volume swelled while her pitch heightened a shrill octave. Her terror-filled eyes were wide and afire.

Otilija swallowed hard and quelled her own angst. "Maybe they escaped."

"Escaped? Escape from them?" Emilia said quickly. "They are Mohammedans, you know. They have no mercy. They don't hold the same virtues as we Christians do."

"You don't know that."

"Oh, yes I do! I lived with them in Armenia. They always thought we were inferior to them. They thought we were meant to be their slaves. Even their—"

"That's not true," Otilija vaulted to her feet. "They may be differ-ent than us, but their virtues are the same as ours!"

"Our virtues?" Emilia's face flushed a deep scarlet as she sprung to her feet. She faced Otilija and waved her finger accusingly.

"You have no right to speak of our virtues! You people were the ones that invaded my homeland ten years ago! With God witnessing every unconscionable act, I remember how you Russians brutalized thousands of us in the name of that damned Czar of yours! The church was corrupt, you claimed. Hah! You robbed the church. Then you tried to rob our spirit!"

"How dare you? How dare you?" Otilija seethed.

"And when you failed, you paid the Cossacks to finish off your dirty work!" Emilia raged on, pacing back and forth like a caged lioness. She stopped with only a breath's distance between her and Otilija and crossed her hands over her bosom. "Hundreds and thousands of them rode in like a raging tide! How the blood filled the streets! That will never fade in my mind or any Armenian's mind. Do you hear me? Never will we ever forget your brutality!"

"How dare you accuse me with what the Russians did!" Otilija stiffened, struggling to hold back from slapping Emilia. She spun around and started to walk away, but then stopped and turned back.

"I am not Russian, Emilia! I am Latvian. We have suffered the same brutality that you cry about. We have been run over by Cossacks. We have been mutilated by Nicholas' Dragoons. Not a single city in Latvia has been spared his blood thirst!"

Otilija felt herself tremble as her glare iced over. She spun around and strutted off toward the beach, insanely furious. She stomped across the sand and splashed into the cool sea water without stopping to remove her shoes. Slogging until she was ankle deep in gentle waves, she finally stopped, crossed her arms tightly over her chest, and gazed out at the rippling blue water.

"Do you know why Otilija is acting so oddly?" a voice quietly asked Emilia while she glared at Otilija in the water.

Emilia glanced over her shoulder and noticed Natalya Stativsky shuffling toward her. She threw her a pruned, sour expression.

"She is sulking," Emilia spat. "She is so damned naive about world affairs. Christ, if all those Letts are as ignorant as she is, I do not understand how her husband could have reached command rank!"

"Oh?" Natalya asked, appearing more curious than surprised. "And why do you think Otilija is naive?"

"Oh, come now, Natalya. She had no idea what the Turks did to us. All Armenians suffered greatly."

"And you think her people have not suffered under Nicholas? Do you really think no other people but yours have suffered under Nicholas? I think you are being a little too cold and self-consumed."

Emilia vaulted to her feet. "Self-consumed? Cold? No, I do not think so! I just opened her eyes a bit to reality."

Natalya stepped back, unprepared to deal with Emilia's anger.

"She has no concept of what the real world is like! She has not gone through the same things we have!" Emilia ranted.

"Are you sure?"

"Yes!"

"Have you ever taken the time to just sit and talk with—"

"Just look at her! Look at the way she carries herself. She prances around here like some princess or something. That tells me she has obviously had an easy life. She has not had to work for what she has. She has no dirt under her fingernails! I would even venture that her wants have never gone unfulfilled."

"Then I would say that you don't know Otilija well," Natalya said.

"I should expect you to say something like that. You are her best friend here. You and her never have to worry about whether or not your husbands are coming back. They are the commanders! I believe all of us know commanders let their men face the brunt of the fighting while they sit back and watch!"

Natalya took a deep breath.

"Do you know what she said? Of all the naive things to believe," Emilia fumed. "She says the men would not keep information from us."

"That's enough, Emilia!" Natalya stomped toward her, grabbed her shoulders, and forced Emilia to look at her.

"You don't know Otilija or Voldemars or Oleg as well as you think you do! And if you had spent some time talking with her instead of avoiding her, you would have found out some of the things about that woman that I know!"

"Like what? What in her pampered life could have possibly disturbed her?"

"All of her brothers were killed at Tannenberg! All four of them!"

Emilia recoiled, stunned. She mouthed the word four in her surprise.

"And then her father, who for your information was a common laborer in Riga, died after hearing the news," Natalya said.

Emilia's face softened as she glanced over her shoulder at Otilija, who was still sauntering in the water.

"And what has Otilija been doing ever since we were all dropped off in this God-forsaken place? She has been trying to befriend you and every one of us. She has been trying to provide us the moral support we all needed while our husbands were off at the front, regardless of how upset she has been!"

Emilia flushed, obviously embarrassed. She stared out at Otilija, then tipped her head and started to cry.

"If you had spent any time with her, you would have come to know a very warm person who has suffered as much as any of us. As for being naive, her only fault is that she is simply trying to be sympathetic to all of us."

Emilia started to step toward the water catatonically, as if in a daze. Stopping short of the frothing edge, she gazed out at Otilija, still standing alone, ankle deep in the water.

"I am sorry, Otilija." Emilia's voice quivered as she forced the words out.

Otilija immediately turned and peered at Emilia.

"I do not know why I said what I did. Maybe I am just too tired to think clearly."

Otilija looked down at her dress soaked up to her knees. She tried to hold back her titter, but it escaped as she trudged out of the water.

Emilia, meanwhile waited at the water's edge, covering her mouth to hide her own giggling. Tears began streaming down her cheeks.

"Dear Emilia."

Otilija stumbled and almost fell in, but caught herself. She chuckled as she stepped out of the water. Her shoes squished as she approached Emilia, who stepped back to keep Otilija at arms' length.

"Natalya told me about your brothers," Emilia admitted, hanging her head. "I never knew."

"Natalya?" Otilija said, sounding startled. She immediately looked up to the bench and saw Natalya waving, grinning widely, and pointing to her limp, soaked dress.

"My word, we must be quite a sight!" Otilija giggled and waved back to Natalya.

"You must be chilled," Emilia said. "Perhaps we should go back to the compound for some hot tea," Emilia noted, staring at Otilija's dress.

Otilija looked down, then glanced back up to Emilia. She nodded, then without another spoken word, they sauntered back to the compound.

Odessa, Southern Russia

16 July 1915

"Time to wake up, Voldemars!" a warm, feminine voice sang as Voldemars felt his shoulder being jostled.

He rolled onto his back and slowly cracked opened his eyes. Darkness. Nothing but darkness. He had not seen a single thing since he had arrived. Even when the bandages were taken off, he saw nothing. He didn't know whether he should be angry or just complacent with his loss.

"I need you to sit up. It's time to change your bandage," the woman said.

He recognized the voice as Lize's, the nurse who tended him exclusively, so much so that he wondered if there were any other nurses in the hospital. They had already talked so much that he felt he knew her. At times, Voldemars imagined what she looked like, piecing together her soft skin, firm hands, and melodious voice. He wished he could have seen her, but she never left the bandage off long enough for him to recognize anything but blurred flesh and white.

Firm hands edged down between the bed and his shoulder blades. Her palms, warm and supple, emanated a soft comfort, so much that he wormed his back around and leaned into them.

"Ugh!" Her voice instantly turned raspy and gruff as she pushed against his back fruitlessly. "Are you going to help me, or do I have to lift you by myself?"

"Do I really have to?" Voldemars said.

"Yes, you do!" Lize's voice grew aggravated.

Voldemars drew in a lung full of the antiseptic tainted air, then strained his stomach muscles. He groaned and started to sit up. Lize's hands pressed into his back, slipping down for more leverage as he rose.

A bolt of pain suddenly ripped through Voldemars' chest. His stomach felt as if it was being torn away. His chest spasmed. He gasped but could not catch his breath. A thick mass crept into his throat, then lodged in his windpipe. He tried to breathe again. Nothing. He tried to exhale. Still nothing. Panicked, he flailed his arms, gagging and choking.

He flailed time and time again to move the mucous plug. The warm hands left his back. Voldemars opened his mouth to scream, but nothing came out.

An open hand thumped between his shoulder blades, vaulting him forward. The jarring hit jolted the mucous plug onto his tongue. He sucked in a quick gasp of air, then hacked until the bitter tasting mucous oozed into his mouth.

Voldemars waved his arms in front of him and grunted until a hand grabbed his wrist and pulled it down. He wrapped his fingers around the neck of a spittoon, clumsily brought it to his mouth, and quickly dispensed of the fetid glob.

"Are you all right?" Lize asked softly.

"Yeah," Voldemars slipped out with his breath. "I'll manage." He wet his lips, then cringed, tasting the even more bitter cream lathered on his open sores.

"I guess it just caught me by surprise today," he whispered between coughs.

Lize sighed. "I should say so. You even had me worried."

He extended the spittoon out in front of him and waited until Lise took it. As she did, her hand brushed his. Soft, yet firm.

"Well, let's get started on your bandage," she said.

He propped his arms on the bed behind him, then leaned back into them. Lifting his head, as if he would be looking at the ceiling, he waited. A tug came, then another. He turned his head, thinking it would help.

"No, keep it straight," Lize said.

He stiffened. Another tug and it released.

Voldemars felt the bandage pull away from his head. He sensed the circular motion of Lise's hands as she unwrapped the gauze. As if he were being set free bit by excruciatingly slow bit, he felt the pressure on his face diminish. On each revolution, he sensed her getting ever so closer to him, until finally, skin touched his nose.

He inhaled perfume. It was sweet and delicate. Lize circled again. This time it was stronger.

Pastel blue and red hued stock, which Voldemars' father planted in the corner of his potato field appeared. That was the aroma on Lise's neck-stock. A slight breeze toyed with the blossoms, tossing the bunched heads from one side to another. Nothing but darkness again. He grew angry.

"Couldn't you just wash this crap out of my eyes and leave the damn bandage off?" Voldemars demanded.

"No," Lize said curtly, continuing her work.

"Christ, it's been almost two months! If that crap hasn't helped by now, it never will."

"And when did you become an expert on these medicines?"

Voldemars pursed his lips and humphed.

"Give it some time. These medicines almost work miracles, considering what we used ten years ago," Lize said.

"Then why am I still laying in a hospital ward two months after getting gassed?"

"I said almost."

"If these medicines are so miraculous, I should be healed by now!"

"You won't be healed in a couple of days or a couple of months." Lise's voice grew brusque. "This is going to take some time. The problem, my dear boy, is that even though these medicines are better, they are just barely keeping ahead of all the toys you soldiers dream up to maim each other with!"

"I'm a soldier, and I'm supposed to fight. That's what I get paid for," Voldemars joked, sensing Lize's voice growing agitated. "And it doesn't matter what the enemy—"

"Did you ever think that maybe if you were a little more careful at the front, like thinking things out before jumping head-long into battles, you might not be here now?"

Lize unraveled the last layer of the bandage. Thick gauze patches slipped away from Voldemars' eyes and fell to his chest.

He squeezed his eyelids closed.

"But that really doesn't matter anymore since there won't be any more fighting for you," Lize muttered. "Why don't you just relax and let me do my job!"

Voldemars snapped his neck in her direction.

"Now blink," she ordered.

He complied.

"What did you mean by that?" Voldemars wished he could read her expression, but all that was in front of him was a blur. A chill walked up his spine. "You mean just me? You're saying that I won't be going back? That is what you mean, isn't it?"

"Shut up and blink!" she demanded.

He squeezed his eyelids shut, then batted them twice. The crusted layer over his eyes melted, then oozed to the corners, congealing into squishy blobs. Reflexively, he reached to pick at them.

"Don't do that!" She grabbed his hands before they made their mark. "Just keep blinking! That'll clean them out enough!"

He complied. His eyes burned and ached as if he had been out on an all night binge. All Voldemars wanted to do was flush them with cool, fresh water.

"Blink!" Lize said again.

The burning dulled a little more each time he slid his eyelids closed. The aching subsided until it grew tolerable enough to keep them open. With his eyelids fully open, he tried to focus. A cloudy yellow haze and blurred images.

"Damn!" Voldemars shouted.

"Use your fingers and prop them open while I flush," Lize said as she took his hands and placed them on his forehead above his eyes.

While he fumbled to pull his eyelids up, she eased his head back. Cold metal touched his neck under his ear.

"This may feel a little cold, so don't jump."

Voldemars waited. Cold water lanced his eyes. He flinched, but Lise's hand behind his head kept him from recoiling. He concentrated on keeping his eyes open, imagining a soft spring rain washing away the ointment. He saw ripples rinse by. The burning eased. The muscles in his face relaxed. His perpetual wince seemed to dribble away with the water, down his cheek, pinging into the metal basin.

The rinse stopped. The last trickles of water dripped into the basin. Voldemars could smell the stinging sulfur emanate from the slurry as the soothing rinse eased away the burning. His face relaxed as the water dribbled down his cheeks and splashed into the catch basin.

"Here's a towel." He felt Lize place a warm cloth over his face. "Now pat them dry. Don't rub or wipe, just pat. I'll be back in a few minutes."

Voldemars did exactly as she ordered, pressing the towel against his eye sockets as he listened carefully to Lize's footsteps cross the room.

"I'm glad they don't let women in the cavalry," he mumbled, dabbing the last of the soothing moisture from his eyes. When he was done, he lowered the towel and looked.

He craved for the sight of anything, even the nauseating view of the hospital ward. He stared forward. Shimmering against dingy white walls, haloed images danced like ghosts in a breeze. His focus sharpened.

"I can see!" Voldemars whispered, unable to restrain his sudden relief. He widened his eyes to survey the room. Finally, images came clear enough to discern. Casualties. There must have been hundreds of them lining each wall two deep. He swept the room, drinking in every detail. The men laid in their cots at various stages of recovery. Some restlessly tossed, thrashing in search of missing limbs. Others lay as still as death, blankly staring at the peeling, water-stained ceiling, while blackened, cauterized, holes gaped in their heads. The balance was like Voldemars, scanning the room quietly through opaque eyes, seeing little.

It didn't matter where he was when he could not see. For all Voldemars cared, he could have been in Paris or Saint Petersburg or even Berlin. Now, though, it was suddenly important. His curiosity blossomed. Between the narrow alley between the beds and cots, he identified several nurses dressed in white and gray gowns. He knew one of them had to be Lize, and even knowing her precise motions, he was baffled as to which one was her. For what he was now plotting, it did not matter. The only thing that did was that none of them saw what he was about to do.

Stealthily, Voldemars slipped his legs over the side of his bed. They limply dangled at first, but he slid closer to the floor until his feet touched. He eased his weight onto his feet, the cold floor pressing harder into the naked bottoms. It felt good. Even sharp rocks would have felt better than the bland sensation of his bed sheets.

Once all his weight was shifted, Voldemars pushed up from the bed and stood. His knees felt feeble, but they held. Wavering a bit, he gained his balance, then stumbled clumsily, lunging for the support of each bed rail as he stiffly shuffled toward the window. Shifting from the support of one bed after another, he closed in on his target until success was an arms' length away. He clamped onto the sill and pulled himself to the window.

Voldemars drank in everything the outside world offered. Even the sting of the bright sunlight was a cherishable vision after two months of seeing nothing but opaque bandages and thick, yellow films. He squinted to ward off the growing yellow and brown halos quivering like gelatin around each image. Searching for anything familiar, his eyes wandered past the blurred escarpments along the waterfront to the soothing sight of the lazily rolling, green tinged water.

He vaguely remembered Lize telling him where they were a number of times, but now he simply could not remember where she said this place was.

He finally remembered. Odessa. The landmarks were clear but it looked different. It was lazy. It was not the same bustling supply port he remembered.

"Colonel Vechi! What the hell are you doing?" Lize's shrill scream pierced his ears.

"Oh, shit!" Startled, Voldemars spun about. He swallowed hard as he stood face-to-face with an obviously angry Lize.

"Maria!" he breathlessly gasped. Hauntingly vivid memories flooded his mind.

Images of his short but steamy affair with Maria cascaded like a log rolling down a hill. Every detail of her figure stood in front of him, her face, her body, her voice. He quivered violently. Reality returned in the face of the woman in white now glaring angrily at him. But, he could not shake the thought of Maria. With the exception of her deep red hair, Lize was Maria.

"No, I'm Lize!"

Voldemars froze, unable to distinguish between reality and his imagination. His face drooped, waning into a slack-jawed stupor.

"And as far as you should be concerned now, sir, a Lize who is very mad!" Her face flushed, matching the fiery color of her hair. In one swift motion, she grasped Voldemars' arm and pulled him stumbling along behind her.

"You damn soldiers! Not a one of you know how to follow orders. I'm warning you once and for all, I'll tie you down if I have to!" she threatened as they reached the side of the bed.

Obediently, he dropped into his bed, exhausted from the walk. As he rolled over to his back, he was attacked by her icy scowl. With a handful of wraps, she pulled an end off and drew it out in a line.

"This should keep you in place for a while," she said as she placed the gauze over his eyes.

Without fighting, Voldemars let her place the gauze over his eyes and complete a first pass around his head. Only slivers of yellow slipped through the edges. The ensuing layers darkened his view even more, until complete darkness returned. With nothing else to see, he closed his eyes and dropped his head into the thin, rank pillow.

"The next time you feel like walking, please ask me. I'll help, you know." Lize's words slipped out in whispers next to his ear. Her voice had mellowed, buoyed by a gentle concern. Just like Maria's.

"I'll remember that," Voldemars said.

"Good."

"Is this Odessa?"

"I thought you already knew that?" Her voice was suddenly more distant.

"Please, come back Lize. I need to know." Voldemars felt his arm twitch with a nervous tick.

"I've told you several times."

"Well, is it?" he asked again, more insistently.

"My God, yes, Voldemars. This is Odessa."

"But, where are the ships? When I looked out the window, there were none!"

"Lize?" he said when she didn't answer.

He reached out, but there was only emptiness. He suddenly felt cold and alone, even though he knew the room was full of soldiers.

Even just mulling over the name of Odessa conjured a paradox of vividly etched memories. The city by the sea. The city where his regiment stopped on their way to the front where so many soldiers won their first conquest. The city where he met an enigmatic woman called Maria.

Encapsulated in his darkness, her image appeared as brightly and clearly as the first day Voldemars saw her. Wavy strands of auburn streaked black hair caressed her face. Her alluring, steel blue eyes, her broad, delicate nose, and her thick, delicious lips.

He fought off sleep as Maria's image lingered in his mind, but fatigue quickly made inroads.

The word Odessa alone seemed magical. He felt himself drift away, even as Maria's image lingered. Drawing in steady, deep breaths, he grew more relaxed with each lung full of air. His body felt numb. His mind, though, remained active, peeling off the months until he was drawn back to the summer he had spent in Odessa.

Captain Oleg Stativsky strutted pompously into the hospital as if he were a victorious commander returning from battle. He brushed off the ribbons on his dress uniform and prepared for a ward of soldiers to sit up, smile, and salute him as he stepped into the ward. But as the door closed behind him, the stale, nauseatingly heavy antiseptic odor choked him. He opened his eyes and immediately cringed, unprepared for the sight of a ward full of invalid soldiers unable to even acknowledge his authority. The hollow, bereft stares coldly faced Oleg, dotted by empty eyes and slack jawed mouths. Their uniforms were bandages, custom tailored to each of their unique needs of a missing limb or gaping wound. Most of the men were unresponsive, without so much as a twitched attempt to acknowledge his presence. Others just turned away, as if ashamed they were in beds and cots while Oleg easily stood over them.

He forced a hard swallow to keep from vomiting and quickly shied away from the gazes. He collected himself, then searched the ward quickly, not letting his eyes rest for more than a second, trying to avoid any contact with the living corpses. When he spotted a red-haired nurse reviewing a disheveled note pad, Oleg sighed, then tugged down on his tunic and shuffled toward her.

"Pardon me," he mumbled, stopping two steps behind her. "I was wondering—"

Oleg stopped when she did not respond. He cleared his throat forcefully, but she remained engrossed in the papers clenched tightly in her hands.

"Excuse me," Oleg repeated, this time much louder. "Could I briefly disturb you for some information?"

The woman spun around, apparently surprised. She caught her breath, then briefly inspected Oleg's uniform before returning her eyes to his face.

"Can I help you, Captain?" she said, her voice more cold than gracious.

"Could you be so helpful as to tell me where I may find Colonel Voldemars Vechi?"

"Yes, I could," she bluntly replied, then returned to her notes and slowly ambled away.

Oleg frowned, unsure what to make of the nurse's strange behavior. He waited for a moment, thinking that she would respond shortly, but when she continued to walk away, he grew impatient.

"Uh, excuse me?" he asked after taking a few steps to catch up to her. "I don't believe I heard you. Where may I find Voldemars Vechi?"

"Why?" She fired back.

A hostile frown etched her face as she glared at him with cold eyes. Oleg recoiled but held his ground.

"What do you want him for?" she demanded, slapping the clipboard against her dress.

Stunned, Oleg perched his eyebrows.

"Never mind, it's obvious why you want him," she blurted before Oleg had a chance to respond. Her eyes were iced with anger. She propped her hands firmly on her hips and squeezed her eyes shut. Her pursed lips punctuated her glowering frown.

"I would like—"

"You would like to drag him back to the front before he's ready! Well, what if I told you he's not ready to leave?" the nurse demanded.

"Wait a minute!" Oleg raised open hands in a conciliatory gesture. "I am from Colonel Vechi's regiment! He is my commander and I am his best friend!"

"Hmph!" She grunted.

"In fact, I made sure he got here." Oleg frowned himself, puffing out his chest a bit. "Believe me, Madam, taking him back to the front is the last thing I would want to do. What I am here to do is to bring him the news that our regiment has retreated and we are here in Odessa."

The woman's face blushed as her jaw dropped. Her icy expression waned as her mouth melted into a tiny, twitching grin.

"Retreat?" She whispered, her voice cracking. "I am truly sorry, Colonel. I did not mean to—"

"Captain," Oleg corrected with a grin. "I do understand your reticence."

"You must admit that Command has a reputation—"

He raised his hand, cutting her off.

"Colonel Vechi?" Oleg asserted, removing his cap and slipping it under his arm.

"You will find him in there."

"Thank you," Oleg said, then started to walk by her.

"But he's sleeping," she added meekly.

"I will only be a minute with him," he assured, then tipped his head and smiled.

He headed directly for the threshold leading into the room the nurse had indicated, but as he slipped through, he was stunned, aghast at an even bleaker sight. Stagnant, oppressively hot, even thicker antiseptic tainted air slapped his face while wafts of acrid, stale blood wormed into his nostrils. Oleg swallowed hard.

Rows of beds lined the walls two deep, every one holding a shell of a man, either wrapped with bloodstained gauze or covered with black, cauterized holes. At the far end was a row of small, yellowed windows that let in a pitiful fraction of the day's bright sunlight. Oleg searched the beds one by one until he fixed on a figure quietly sleeping among the wooden-eyed stares.

"Captain?" a hushed voice from behind said.

Oleg quickly turned his head and realized the nurse had followed him into the ward and was now standing next to him. A perplexed look twisted her face.

"Do you know who Maria is?" she asked.

"Maria?" Oleg rubbed his chin.

Her eyes touched Voldemars silently and her lips twitched as if about to mumble something.

"Why do you ask?" Oleg said.

"He's been babbling the name as if…well, it just seemed strange that he called me Maria at one point."

Oleg remained baffled.

"Maybe it's nothing," she mumbled. She bowed her head, turned, and headed back to tend to the other patients.

Oleg shuffled toward Voldemars and stopped at the foot of his bed. He stared at the emaciated frame that helplessly laid in front of him. It lacked any semblance to the enviable physique he remembered. Spit dribbled from Voldemars' open jaw. His ashen face and dark rings under his eyes appeared ghostly. The yellow stained wrap laying next to his pillow made Oleg uneasy, but he assumed that being in this place, it must have been fine.

"You look much better than the last time I saw you, old friend, but I know that's not saying much. To be honest, I did not think you would make it," Oleg whispered.

Voldemars' eyes twitched feebly, as if he heard him.

"I wrote to your father and told him about your encounter. I hope you don't mind that I asked him to reconsider taking you back, to let you become 'Telmenu Saimnieks', if I remember your phrase correctly."

Oleg stepped closer, moving to the side of the bed and Voldemars' head. He gently placed his hand on Voldemars' chest to be sure he was still breathing.

"Now all I need to do is convince you that you want to."

Voldemars suddenly stirred and Oleg jerked his hand back.

"Lize? Is that you, Lize?" Voldemars' scratchy voice slipped by his pasty lips.

"No, it's Oleg. It's your old friend, Oleg," he said softly.

"Oleg Mikailovich?" Voldemars reached out with his hand and weakly flailed.

"Yes, sir, Colonel," Oleg said as he grabbed Voldemars' hand and gripped it tight.

"Ah, Oleg. It's good to see you." Voldemars' lips twitched into a brief smirk. "Well, hear you. It has been sometime, hasn't it?"

"Yes, it has."

Voldemars adjusted into a sitting position, as if startled. His face twisted into a puzzled look as he released Oleg's hand.

"Why are you here? Did you resign your commission? Were you injured?" Voldemars' voice grew more emphatic with each question.

"No, Voldemars. Nothing like that. I am fine, and nor would I just leave after all they've put me through! I'll be damned if they try to get away without giving me my due!" Oleg chuckled.

"Then why are you here?"

"Don't you remember the last message from Command?"

Only a blank expression replaced Voldemars' confused look. "What message?"

"Command ordered a retreat."

"Retreat?"

"Christ, Voldemars, don't you remember?"

"No. I don't remember any retreat. When?" Voldemars' hands groped.

"The original retreat order was when you…" Oleg cringed, swallowing hard, "when you got gassed."

Oleg stopped to read Voldemars' expression. It was blank and emotionless.

"Then we received orders to retreat to Tarnopol," Oleg said.

Again, no response.

"And just yesterday, we were withdrawn to Odessa. Christ, at this rate, we should take Astrakhan in two more days!" Oleg could not help but laugh.

"Why would Command do something foolish like retreat?" Voldemars said, his voice growing angry.

"I don't really know. All I can do is guess."

"Are we losing?"

"I don't know," Oleg said.

"Nicholas!"

"I think he has become concerned by what he sees at home. No, I think he's more frightened."

"Frightened about what?"

Oleg grew concerned as he watched Voldemars' cheeks flush.

He furtively glanced about the dingy room to be sure no one was listening, then leaned close to Voldemars' ear.

"I think Nicholas has lost control," he started in a whisper. "The Duma badgers him daily to stop the war, claiming it is destroying Mother Russia. The streets are filled with riots, and the people are clamoring for his abdication!"

Voldemars' color grew fallow again. "Maria!" he suddenly blurted. Oleg jumped back. "Who is Maria?"

Voldemars grew agitated, then started thrashing, trying to get out of his bed. "Maria said this was going to happen!" he insisted in a rambling, distant voice. "Almost a year ago, she said the same thing!"

"Are you going mad?" Oleg mumbled.

"She said that Nicholas—"

"Voldemars! Who the hell is Maria?" Oleg insisted, growing more confused.

"I met...spent some time with...we..." Voldemars sputtered, then stopped. He ceased thrashing and laid still. Oleg felt he must have been reeling about something, but for the life of him, he could not figure it out.

Oleg leaned over and placed his hand on Voldemars' shoulder, then squeezed gently. "I need to know who this Maria is you keep talking about," he said, speaking directly and slowly into Voldemars' ear.

Obviously attempting to gain composure, Voldemars sucked in a deep breath, then began chewing fervently on the inside of his lip. Oleg knew he had ventured into a secret Voldemars had kept from everyone, even him. He must have had a reason, but this one, was now blatantly eating at him. And as his friend, it was his obligation to help.

Oleg's voice grew insistent as he asked, "Who is this Maria you keep talking about?"

Voldemars drew in a deep breath and sighed. His hands fidgeted, then started a wringing motion. "When we stopped here last summer, during the mobilization," he started in a slow, deliberate whisper, "I met a woman. Her name was Maria. We got to know each other. Very well."

"So?" Oleg shrugged.

"This was not just a friendship."

"So?"

"Don't you remember how I ranted and raved, warning all of you what not to do!" Voldemars blushed as he took another deep breath. "Well, I screwed up! I got involved with a local girl."

"So?" Oleg said again.

"So! This is not some foot soldier here, you know!" Voldemars' tone grew louder. His hands flailed for emphasis. "I did exactly what I expected, exactly what I ordered everyone else in the regiment to avoid. I disobeyed my own orders."

"You are human, you know! You can't expect—"

"I could very well have gotten her into trouble, and I violated a trust that I had with my wife," Voldemars rambled.

"Listen to me!" Oleg clamped more firmly on his commander's shoulder, wanting to shake him, but choosing not to. "You can't be perfect! What you did was a simple error in judgment. A completely understandable error. Don't you think you should allow yourself a mistake now and then?"

Oleg let his words seep in through Voldemars' bandages. But as he watched him, there was nothing but slow, deliberate breathing.

"Christ, Voldemars! That was over a year ago! Just let her go and stop punishing yourself!"

Voldemars remained pensive and silent.

"Help me find her, Oleg. Then I can put this whole thing behind me," Voldemars blurted.

"Are you sure you—"

"I can see well enough to find my way to her apartment. She lives a short walk from the port."

"Lived," Oleg soberly corrected.

"And I saw this morning that we are not that far away from there," Voldemars said. He lurched toward Oleg, his yellow ringed eyes bulging grotesquely from his face. "What do you mean by that?"

"When you looked at the port, what exactly did you see?"

Voldemars tipped his head and thought for a moment. "Mostly buildings, and I saw the port. No ships, though. But we're probably too far away."

"Those buildings you saw, did you notice what condition they were in?"

"No."

"You didn't notice their condition?" Oleg repeated.

"What are you trying to say," Voldemars said, his voice growing desperate.

"The port was leveled by the Turks two weeks after we left for the front!" Oleg stoically noted. "Nothing survived. The only thing left was this hospital. My, God, Voldemars, didn't you notice that all you saw were skeletons?"

Voldemars' mouth fell agape. He bowed his head, then brought his hand to his chin and fervently rubbed the bristles sticking out of his pasty skin.

"We must go there. I need to see for myself. We must go!" Voldemars insisted, stumbling out of his bed. He started to search for his clothes. "Well, are you going to help me, or am I doing this by myself?"

Oleg feigned a surrender, then sighed loudly. "All right. Let me find you some clothes, and we'll go. You wait here and I'll be right back. I'll go talk to the doctor."

"No! No doctors!" Voldemars quickly grabbed Oleg's arm. "You know they won't let me go!"

"Then maybe you shouldn't."

"I have to! I have to go. You do understand, don't you?" Voldemars grabbed Oleg by the shoulders and glared at him through his opaque eyes.

"But if you can't go out—"

"I've got to know what happened to her!" Voldemars' voice teetered on yelling. He pleaded with Oleg with his eyes, begging him to comply.

"I see," Oleg said as Voldemars' feeble grip attempted to squeeze into his shoulders. Conciliatory, he nudged his commander back into the bed. "Why don't you sit down and relax. I'll get you a uniform."

"No doctors." Voldemars dug his fingertips into Oleg's uniform as hard as he could.

"I promise. No doctors."

"Then, I'll wait," Voldemars quietly said.

❦   ❦   ❦

Voldemars waited until Oleg was gone, then stood up and wandered to the window. He stared out over the city and tried to focus on the buildings, straining to see the shells that Oleg talked about, but the images were still too blurry. He had to believe Oleg, he had never lied to him before. Disconsolate, he shuffled back and plopped his down onto the stale smelling cot.

Voldemars slammed his fist into his pillow. How could they bomb a city? Thousands of innocent people, not soldiers, just people. There was nothing to gain.

Oleg surprised Voldemars, returning almost as soon as he disappeared. He lay a uniform on the bed, then dropped a pair of boots to the floor. Dried, yellow dirt flaked off in a faint cloud. A shiver raced through Voldemars' spine.

"Christ, it's mine! Why the hell didn't they burn it?"

"I don't know," Oleg meekly answered, as he picked up the shirt and started unfolding it. "But supplies are critically low, even uniforms. Maybe they figured the gas would kill anything on it."

"I can dress myself," Voldemars insisted, grabbing the uniform. "I have to learn to live with this."

"Fine," Oleg replied, releasing the shirt. He added, "The doctor says—"

"You bastard! We agreed, no doctors!" Voldemars exploded. He vaulted to his feet and threw the shirt onto the bunk. As he glared at Oleg, he felt a hundred pairs of eyes turn his way.

"It's all right, Voldemars!" Oleg said, his eyes wide. "He said some fresh air might do you some good. I had to explain why I needed the uniform."

"But we agreed."

"He said you can go out, but only under supervision, at least until your vision clears up."

"If it ever does," Voldemars grumbled as he snapped up the uniform. He draped it over his shoulders. Instantly, his skin itched like a nest of ants crawled over him. His nose twitched, insulted by the faint, pungent odor of gas still trapped in the fabric. He sniffed, then quickly covered up as he sneezed violently.

Within minutes, Voldemars was dressed. With Oleg leading the way, they stepped out onto the street beside the hospital under an ominous, thickening cloud cover. Voldemars glanced down at his crumpled uniform, once tightly fitting, but now hanging loosely over his withered body. Oleg took his hand and placed it on Voldemars' shoulder.

"I'm not blind, damn it! I can still see." Voldemars pulled his hand back. He frowned at Oleg, and to prove his point, stepped in front of him and started with a stilted gait toward the port.

"I was just trying to help," Oleg assuaged, catching up to Voldemars. "I've already walked through the port. I don't think you will like what's there."

Voldemars harumphed and continued silently in the direction of the port, scanning left and right with each step. The closer he drew to it, the more intense the devastation became. Even through his blurred vision, he recognized many of the empty brick carcasses. Where he remembered ships had docked and unloaded tons upon tons of material remained only building shells and rubble. With each additional step, his heart sank deeper into his chest.

Maybe she left before it all happened. She knew what was to happen to Nicholas. She must have seen this coming.

"It's about a kilometer from here. This way." Voldemars pointed north when he recognized a building's familiar stone foundation.

"I'm sorry," Oleg said. "I don't think you'll find what you're looking for down there."

"No, it's just down this next street!" Voldemars insisted through gasping pants. "I remember that corner."

"You won't like what you're going to see, my friend," Oleg whispered.

Physically, Voldemars felt exhausted. Emotionally, he was drained. Nevertheless, he persevered, determined to seek out Maria's destiny. He turned onto a street that had been completely leveled and immediately stopped.

Open mouthed, he peered at a pile of brick and stone rubble. He felt his legs wobble, but he staggered forward anyway. His face grew long and subdued. Stumbling twice, he dropped to his knees at the exact spot Maria had invited him into her apartment on that fateful night.

"How could they? How could they?" Voldemars mumbled catatonically. Slowly at first, then more frantically, he dug through the rubble with his bare hands, cursing the Turks with each brick he removed.

"Voldemars, I'm sorry. I tried to warn you there was nothing left here." Oleg shuffled toward his old friend, stopped next to him, then gently placed his hand on Voldemars' quivering shoulder.

"This is all that's left," Oleg said.

Voldemars stopped his digging long enough to glance up at Oleg. Tears welled in his eyes before they streaked down his gaunt cheeks. He sighed deeply, then turned back to the rubble.

"I'll find her. If I have to stay here for a year, I'll find her!" Voldemars insisted, his voice filled with reckless determination.

"Let her go. This happened a year ago. She's gone, one way or another."

"She can't be dead! She can't be!" Voldemars dug more furiously.

"Christ, Voldemars, you're not going to find her here!"

Voldemars continued burrowing through the shattered bricks and mortar shards. Oleg grabbed him by the shoulders and yanked him out of the rubble.

"Just accept the fact that you'll never find her! If she's dead, she's been dead for a year! If she left, you're not going to find out where she went!"

"I can't accept that!" Voldemars insisted, pulling away from Oleg and back to the pile of crumbled rock.

"For Christ sakes, Voldemars, there's nothing here! Think about Otilija! You have a wife to return to! You can't just let her think you died at the front."

Voldemars stopped and glared at Oleg. His frantic breathing slowed as Oleg's words finally struck a familiar chord.

"Let Maria go," Oleg said. "You've got to continue on with your own life and let her go!" His tone mellowed. A sincere smile emerged from his quivering lips as he reached out with open hands to help Voldemars stand.

"I've never been able to let go," Voldemars said quietly.

"Don't destroy yourself over this. There's nothing you can do here."

Fatigue etched Voldemars' face as he dropped his head and stared at his dirt covered hands. A tear fell into his dust-covered palm and quivered for a moment before it was sucked up the dry mortar. He closed his eyes, then looked up to Oleg.

"You've got your whole life ahead of you," Oleg added.

"And what do I tell Otilija? How can I face her after this?"

"Otilija doesn't have to know," Oleg said reservedly. "No one does. You know I won't say anything."

Voldemars peered at Oleg, realizing he had to trust him with this secret now.

"Listen to me," Oleg said. "I can see how you must have felt about Maria, but don't make it any harder on yourself. It was something just between you and her. Keep it that way."

"I'll remember that," Voldemars said, wiping a tear that had dribbled onto his still swollen cheek. "I'll remember that for a long time, old friend."

Astrakhan, Southern Russia

22 August 1915

"*I* don't understand how you can live with yourself," Natalya mumbled, peering through Irina Kolov's window and watching her wispy shadow skitter around. "The army gave you food and a home, and now you go out to preach revolution against the very fiber of your existence?"

Natalya wondered if Irina was so consumed by her mission to convert the masses that perhaps she had lost her touch with reality. She then caught herself, realizing that if anyone heard her, they may think she had lost her senses. She closed her eyes and turned away, then pulled out Oleg's latest letter.

"I wonder if Vladimir is like she is," she muttered as she unfolded the thin, onion skin paper. She settled into the bench, prepared to savor every word. Delving into her mind, she imagined Oleg sitting on a stump in the woods, reading to her in his soft, melodic voice as he penned the words.

∽

12 June 1915

My dearest Natalya,

I hope this letter finds you in good health and good spirits. So many things have happened since the last time I was able to write that I find it perplexing to find a place to begin. Perhaps the most important item I have to mention is that my arms may not need to be yearning for your warmth much longer. Do not worry, my love, for I am in good health, as is everyone else. The other details as to why I am coming home are unimportant. What matters is that fifteen, or is it sixteen months, hell, it doesn't matter, for however long it has been, finally, we will be close soon.

I do have some disturbing news concerning my commander and close friend, Voldemars Vechi. In May, Voldemars fell victim to a terrible gas attack. He was alive when we found him, but he did not look well. His horse died from the gas, and each day I grow more concerned that Voldemars may not survive. We were able to get him to hospital, but since then, we have received no word about his condition, other than I have been placed temporarily in command. If Voldemars is improving, he may be transported home shortly. And if that is so, I am unsure of how Otilija will respond to him. Perhaps if you could

"I know what's in there," someone whispered sinisterly.

Natalya snapped her head around and saw Irina standing behind her, waving a folded letter of her own.

"I know what happened to Voldemars!" Irina said again.

Natalya glared at Irina's drawn face. Her evil, deep set eyes sent a chill to her bones.

"Your husband took my Vladimir's rightful rank as second in command. Vladimir should be in command now!" Irina hissed her words from behind clenched teeth.

"That is no concern of ours, Irina. That decision is Command's. We are not the ones—"

"Your Command!" Irina interrupted with a bitterness and malevolence that seemed to ice the air. "If the army was run the way it should be, instead of the way that simpering Nicholas runs it, the leader should have been a Muscovite right from the start! This is Russia's army, not Latvia's, Ukraine's, or any other of your lesser peoples!"

Irina sat down next to Natalya, then stiffened her back arrogantly. Natalya knew Irina had her trapped right where she wanted her.

"Please," Natalya begged. "I need your help. I know we come from different lives, and we have quite different philosophies. That is something we will never change."

Irina tilted her head and glared at Natalya, obviously confused by her sudden openness. Her eyes quickly narrowed to suspicious slits.

"What is it that you want from me?" she asked bluntly.

Natalya drew in a deep breath, and hoped that for once, she and Irina could talk frankly.

"What do you know about Voldemars' condition?"

"Vladimir says he was gassed and could very well be close to death, if he's not dead already," Irina answered coldly.

"It doesn't matter to me what happens between Oleg and Vladimir as far as rank and position goes. What does concern me, though, is Otilija. I am very close with her."

Natalya swallowed hard, realizing how tenuous would be the friendship she was trying to sow. "I need time to think of how to tell her. Please, Irina. I need you to be silent. At least until I can tell Otilija myself."

Irina's icy silence frightened Natalya. She tried to peer through Irina's frosted eyes and read her thoughts, but her veil was impenetrable. She glowered at Natalya for a lingering moment, then shifted to her feet. Natalya hoped that befriending Irina was not a mistake, even if it was just for this one time, but she felt she had no choice.

Irina drew in a deep breath, then stood and stiffly took a few steps toward her quarters. When she stopped and turned back, the stony expression etched on her face immediately worried Natalya.

"I have no real hatred for you or Otilija. But you, and I mean all of you, irritate me so with your arrogance." Irina's bent finger waved menacingly at Natalya. Her eyes had closed even further, now only peeking out above the dark circles under them.

"You wish a deal?" Irina said. "Fine. These are my terms, Stativsky. As long as that bourgeois Lett doesn't incite me, I will not reveal our little secret."

Natalya sighed.

"But the first time she digs under my skin too far with her crap about Voldemars or Latvia or whatever righteous cause she feels so compelled to infect me with, I will use anything I can to inflict a wound as deep as I can make it!" With that said, Irina spun and haughtily walked back to her quarters.

"You bitch," Natalya muttered under her breath as she watched Irina strut onto her steps and into her quarters.

Stunned, Natalya felt sapped. She wanted to scream. She wanted to run after Irina and bludgeon her with her own sense of righteousness. But in her heart she knew that would be as foolish as expecting Irina to understand why this information needed to be handled so delicately.

"Good afternoon, Natalya!" a melodic voice said.

Natalya nervously folded up her letter, then clamped it tightly in her hand. She looked up and saw Emilia walking in her direction. She sighed, relieved it was not Otilija.

"Is that a letter I see in your hand?" Emilia asked.

"This? Oh, no! It's just an old letter from Oleg. I enjoy rereading them. It lifts my spirits a little on these bleak looking days." Natalya hoped her suddenly flushed face would not reveal her secret.

"Oh, I do know what you mean! I get so depressed when the sun does not come out. Perhaps I should take to reading Kamil's old letters?" Emilia smiled as she sat next to Natalya, then looked out toward the beach as if searching.

"Have you seen Otilija today?"

"No, why do you ask?" Natalya grew suddenly self-conscious. She snuck a glance at her hand to ensure the letter had not unfolded. Suddenly paranoid, she quickly stuffed it away in her dress.

"We were going to walk along the beach this afternoon, but when I went to her apartment, she was not there. I can not imagine where she might have gone," Emilia babbled in a puzzled tone. She craned her neck, looking back toward Otilija's quarters, then sighed loudly.

Natalya did not hear a word Emilia had said. Instead, she grew more woven in her own thoughts, wondering what she should do with the news Oleg had sent. Otilija was such a good friend. Her most intimate thoughts were shared with her.

"Good afternoon!" a cheery voice announced.

Natalya plunged her hand into the pocket in her dress and stuffed the letter as deep as she could.

"Oh, Otilija!" Emilia said. "There you are! Where have you been? I've been worried sick about you!" she squealed, springing up from the bench and wrapping her arms around Otilija.

"I'm sorry. I just needed some time alone. I don't know why, but I was thinking about my brothers. It has been a year since they were killed at Tannenberg. For some reason, they came to mind."

Natalya swallowed hard. Flushed with a sense of guilt, she pushed at the letter again. "Emilia was just telling me that you two were going to walk on the beach," She mustered in a feeble cheeriness as she nervously gripped the letter.

"Yes, we were. Would you care to join us?" Otilija offered, then quickly glanced at Emilia, whose smile confirmed she did not mind. "We'd enjoy your company."

"I don't know," Natalya balked. "I'm not really prepared to walk on the sand."

"Oh, nonsense! We don't own sand shoes either, Natalya," Otilija said, giggling, coaxing Emilia to a chuckle as well. "We simply take our shoes off and let the sand slip between our toes! Don't tell me you haven't walked on the beach before?"

"It is usually too cold where I come from to walk on the beach." Natalya grinned weakly, then frantically searched for another reason to decline.

"Come on, Natalya, it's fun! It will make you feel like a school girl again!" Emilia tilted her head and offered her hands.

"All right," Natalya conceded.

She lifted one hand, keeping the other firmly clenched on the letter, and let Emilia help her up. Stiffly upright, she smiled more sincerely, then habitually brushed her dress.

As the three women walked toward the beach, Natalya glanced back toward Irina's barracks and gasped, realizing she was staring out her window, watching their every move. The thin drapes quickly snapped shut.

"Have you heard anything from Voldemars, Otilija?" Natalya heard Emilia ask innocently.

Natalya snapped her head around and blushed as she plunged her hand into her dress and fished until she felt the letter. A wave of relief settled her jitters.

"No, I haven't heard from him for some time now," Otilija admitted as she leaned over to removed her shoes. Her tone was obviously depressed. "He usually writes once a month, but I haven't received anything since…well, since July. Of course, that would have been an April letter."

Natalya swallowed hard as she quickly removed her shoes, sensing hinted apprehension in Otilija's voice.

"Once a month! I would be fortunate if Kamil wrote more than once a year!"

"I think that may be what is bothering me," Otilija noted, kicking into the sand with her toes. She stopped and swirled designs with her big toe, as if in deep thought. "Voldemars enjoys writing so much that when his letters are late, I start thinking something may have happened to him."

Natalya gulped as she fumbled to grasp the letter tighter. She carefully watched Otilija's expression waver between sadness and apprehension before a tentative smile crept onto her face. Her quivering lips, though, revealed her suppressed trepidation.

Perhaps when we're alone, Natalya thought.

"Has Oleg written?"

Natalya jumped as Emilia's words seemed to broadside her.

"No," Natalya blurted defensively. Fleeting panic burned her face red with embarrassment.

"I mean more recently than that letter?" Emilia pointed to Natalya's hidden hand.

"Oh, no. I have not heard from Oleg." Natalya glanced at Otilija, but instantly shifted her focus when she caught Otilija's eyes looking at her. "Recently," she quickly added.

"That's surprising. I thought Oleg wrote as often as Voldemars did?" Otilija asked innocently. "I was hoping that if Oleg had written, we would at least know that they are all right." Otilija turned to Emilia and muttered, "I must admit, though, I grow more worried as days pass without a letter."

Natalya remained silent. She felt her growing self-conscious make her exceedingly uncomfortable. She had never been secretive with Oleg's letters before, but this one was different. It had to be. At least for now. She stopped and let Otilija and Emilia forge ahead to a safe distance.

"I'm sorry, Otilija," Natalya said when they turned back to her. "I guess I am feeling a bit fatigued."

"You do look a little peaked. Are you sure you are all right?" Otilija asked, tipping her head.

Even though Natalya read something more in Otilija's expression, the question seemed innocent enough. Natalya simply nodded and turned back toward the compound.

She stopped at the bench, then sat down while she put her shoes back on. She looked up and watched Otilija and Emilia playfully dance in and out of the water as it washed upon the shore.

How am I going to tell you about Voldemars? The thought ate at Natalya as she she watched Otilija's expression blossom as she danced with the energy of a teenager.

Natalya stood and pensively sauntered back to her barracks. As she sat on her porch, she extracted the letter, then furtively surveyed the area to be sure no one was watching her. Skimming rapidly through the words, she found where she had left off, then thought of Oleg again, sitting on a stump in the woods reading to her.

Southern Russia

15 September 1915

O leg glanced out the corner of his eye at Voldemars and watched his head bob forward and back in rhythm with the train's rocking. He reached over and waved his hand in front of his face. Voldemars did not move.

"Good. I've got something to take care of," Oleg mumbled under his breath.

He slipped out of his seat, careful not to jostle Voldemars, then stood upright in the aisle, holding onto the seat back. He tugged down on his tunic, then strutted toward the rear of the car, stopping at the last seat.

"We have something to talk about, Kolov," Oleg whispered in a tone as biting as a winter's wind. He glowered at Captain Vladimir Kolov, now his second in command.

"We have nothing to talk about, Stativsky," Vladimir hissed back through clenched, yellowed teeth. He tipped his head and glared at Oleg for a moment with a blank, non-committal stare, then fired an angry frown.

"Come with me. We'll talk outside. That is an order." Oleg ordered with an icy glare of his own. Without waiting for Vladimir's response, he stepped to the rattling rear door, unlatched the handle, and exited.

As the door closed behind him, a cool breeze mussed through his tawny hair. It was a clean breeze, one that smelled as fresh as the rolling fields from his small Ukrainian village in the fall. He consumed a lung full and held it in as long as he could, savoring every bit of the grain scent. Leaning over the rail, Oleg watched the wide gauge Russian tracks weave back toward Tzaritsin, now two hours behind them.

Reality crept back into his thoughts. He had a task to perform, one that had been eating at him ever since he had taken command. Closing his eyes, Oleg mulled over what he had to say until he heard the door unlatch behind him. He sucked in a deep breath, stiffened to attention, then spun around with a perfect about-face.

Vladimir stood stiff-backed in front of the door, narrowed his eyes into slits, and with stone-faced defiance, glared into Oleg's eyes. A contorted, wry looking grin eked out on his thin, pale lips. He took two measured steps toward the rail, then tilted his head and cockily peered back at Oleg.

"What the hell did you think you were going to accomplish?" Oleg tried to keep his voice back in his throat so it would remain deep and forceful. His vocal cords were tense, and his voice cracked with a squeaky tone.

"With what?" Kolov sneered.

"Your incessant defiance of every one of my orders."

"Your orders are foolish."

"They are still orders."

"If you were competent, I would abide by them. But since you are not, I have no reason to follow them."

"Your insubordination put half the brigade into danger at the front. And then you ignored my request not to write anything to the wives about Voldemars."

"Who cares?"

"The whole brigade cares."

"That's horse shit. What's the big deal with a letter to my wife?" Vladimir shrugged his shoulders as his grin blossomed into a devilish smile. "I simply told her what was happening to us. I didn't feel there was anything sensitive about what happened to Vechi."

"Well, I did! What the wives should be told is more than just a matter of sensitivity, it's also a matter of correctness. We had no idea what happened to him. It was all conjecture! We didn't even know if he was alive for three months!"

Oleg stopped to catch his breath. Vladimir remained stone-faced, glaring back at Oleg.

"Christ, Kolov, don't you realize what women do when they get information from the front?"

"I can trust my wife."

"That's not the point!" Oleg shouted. "Did you consider that Otilija would not be getting letters all of the sudden?"

"What I write to my wife is my business."

"That order was to protect Otilija," Oleg's voice cracked as he interrupted.

Vladimir cackled. "Besides, I revealed no military secrets, not that anyone would care to spy on this disgrace you and Nicholas call an army!"

"The fact remains that you continue to willfully disobey direct orders from me, your commanding officer! You were specifically ordered not to—"

"I don't recognize you as my commanding officer!" Vladimir exploded. He waved his finger in Oleg's face. "I told you the day Vechi was gassed that this command was due me! In fact, this command was due me even before that fucking Lett was reassigned to this brigade! I was the ranking Russian in the regiment, not him, and definitely not you!"

Vladimir's eyes grew to wide, white ringed-circles while his face flushed deep red. Oleg grew even more indignant with Vladimir's insubordination.

"I did not make that decision," he said. "Command recognized me as the first officer in line even before we left Astrakhan, and it was my duty to obey that!" Oleg's voice squeaked like an adolescent. "And any soldier's duty, regardless of rank, regardless of whose army, is to obey your commanding officer."

"Ha! You have no right being an officer, much less a commanding officer, Stativsky! You are just a little smart-assed, squeaky-voiced Ukrainian Cossack!"

Oleg felt his veins bulge in his neck as he bit his lip hard enough to draw blood.

"Why don't you just back off and leave me alone!" Vladimir's face twisted grotesquely. "Why don't you just leave this army to Russians and go back to your pogroms, slaughtering innocent civilians like your cowardly kind are still doing for that bastard Nicholas!"

Oleg exploded, backhanding Vladimir across his chin. Vladimir staggered, but grabbed the rail and remained upright. He gathered his wobbly legs under him as he faced Oleg again. His eyes bulged with anger etching deeper furrows into his face.

"Consider yourself under arrest, Kolov!" Oleg pointed his finger directly in Vladimir's face, inches from his nose, and mustered all the restraint he could. "I am charging you with insubordination, in that you have incessantly disobeyed orders from a superior officer, and—"

"Fuck you, Stativsky! Do you hear me? Fuck you and this charade you call an army!" Vladimir fumed as he ripped the bars from his shoulders. Glaring into Oleg's eyes, he shook the insignia in his hand for a moment, then threw them over the rail where they fell limply into the passing meadow.

"I'll have you shot, Kolov!"

"Look at my sleeve, Stativsky! I'm nothing to you now. I am not yours! As far as you're concerned, I'm just a civilian! I'm just one of those innocent civilians that you and your stinking, rotten, drunkard kind chase down and slaughter like animals!"

Vladimir's eyes frosted over as they bulged from their sockets with a crazed glare. Lunging at Oleg, he slapped his hands onto his tunic, then clamped the collar tight and pulled him into his face.

"Let me tell you something, Stativsky. All of this shit isn't going to matter soon, anyway. This circus you call an empire will fall to the Bolsheviks, and in very short order, I might add."

"You're mad, Kolov!"

"And then I'll have you arrested as an enemy of the government, you fucking little Cossack!" Vladimir hissed menacingly, punctuating his words by spitting into Oleg's face. With one hard thrust, he then shoved Oleg toward the rail and released his grip. "Do you hear me? You are the insubordinate!"

Oleg groaned as his back slammed into the rail, buckling him over backward. As he recoiled, Oleg covered his sidearm with his hand, cursing under his breath while he considered executing Vladimir. He would be within his rights as a commanding officer.

But it was not his way. Oleg seethed as he clutched his anger, then chambered a bitter glare and fired.

Vladimir suddenly turned ashen. His eyes darted from one side of the train to the other, then once again he scowled at Oleg. His hands gripped the rail, and then in one deft motion, he vaulted the car's railing. Oleg scrambled to the rail and watched as Vladimir fell to the ground and curled into a rolling ball alongside of the train. His boots dug into the ground, he vaulted to his feet, then turned back toward the train.

"Fuck you and your army, Stativsky!" Vladimir screamed as he defiantly waved his fists.

"Thank you, Kolov, for making my job easier," Oleg mumbled as he brushed himself off.

Turning back to the door, he jiggled the latch and let himself back into the stale smelling car. As he closed the door behind him, he sucked in a deep breath, then released it slowly and sauntered back to his seat.

Oleg plopped down onto the hard bench. He caught a glimpse of Voldemars and released another deep sigh before melting into his seat.

After collecting himself, Oleg let his focus drift out the window to the passing sun-scorched fields. As the lingering image of Vladimir's angry face and shaking fists faded from his thoughts, the fields of dried grasses enticed a welcome, comforting image of home. The grasses magically transformed into the swaying brown reeds along the Prypyat Marshes. Flitting blackbirds jumped from one stalk to another, trilling with each movement.

Oleg leaned back, closed his eyes, and let his mind drift aimlessly to his past. He saw his father, withered into an emaciated skeleton of his once stout physique, rocking in his favorite chair, calmly accepting his own death. Oleg recalled how long and hard he cried when he found him dead in that chair. Momma came out from the house and comforted him, easing the grief, softly assuring him that it was what Poppa wanted.

Everything went black. Oleg startled, realizing he had dozed, then cracked his eyes open and rolled his head back. There was Voldemars, slouched sideways, wedged between his seat and the window, clothes draped over his body in crumpled bunches. Just like Oleg's father, his sickly, emaciated stick figure rocked like a child's rag doll. His jaw hung slack, a trail of drool dribbling from an open corner of his cracked lips.

Feeling sorry for what remained of his old commander, Oleg retrieved his knapsack, fished for a pen and his small writing pad, then started scratching a letter to Voldemars' father.

15 September 1915

Mr. Vechi:

Again, this is Oleg Stativsky writing on behalf of your son, Voldemars. He is slowly recovering from his encounter with the Hun's gas, however, he has been greatly weakened by his hospital stay. His lungs have cleared a bit, but it is obvious from his coughing that there was some damage. His eyes have healed some, but they are not as sharp as they were when I first met him.

Voldemars has told me much about Telmeni and Latvia. Through him, I have seen why he loves his homeland so much. He often explained how much he enjoyed growing up in the hills of Latvia, and how much he loved you and his mother. I understand that he may have left on less than cordial terms, and that he has neglected writing to you for some time, but I think there is something about my friend Voldemars which you should know.

He has always spoken of you in the highest regard. Though he may not have said it, he loves Telmeni and yearns to return.

Knowing this, I would ask you to help your son and my friend, Voldemars. I would hope that whatever the digressions you and he had experienced could be forgiven. I think you can convince him now that Telmeni is his future. I believe that for his own health, living at Telmeni would be much better than the constant turmoil that promises to be the rule in Europe. Although I am not a scholar when it comes to politics, I do not see peace coming to Europe for some time.

For Voldemars' and Otilija's sake, please find it within your heart to forgive him, and ask him to come back to Telmeni. I am sure his attitude has changed just in these past few months.

I pray that Riga and Latvia have not been subjected to the debacle which is presently ripping the heart and soul from Europe. I also hope that this war will come to a final and swift conclusion for the better of mankind.

Sincerely,

Captain Oleg Stativsky

Oleg folded the paper into thirds and carefully slipped it into an envelope. He started to casually slip it into his jacket pocket, but then quickly stuffed it in when he noticed Voldemars moving. With the letter safely tucked away, Oleg turned to him.

Voldemars rolled his head, then stretched his jaw forward, as if groping out of hibernation. His eyelids fluttered, then cracked open enough for Oleg to see his cloudy eyes.

"Welcome back, Voldemars," Oleg said jokingly.

Voldemars' lips parted enough to reveal his yellowed teeth, then turned up at the corners into a weak smile. "So, old friend, where are we?" Voldemars scratchy, morning-like voice passed through his lips. "How much have I missed?"

"We passed through Tzaritsin a few hours back," Oleg said, then realized how stiff his response was. "We should be arriving in Astrakhan in about another hour or so. It may even still be light."

"Astrakhan," Voldemars said, his voice distant. His eyes cracked open a bit more. "Damn, that sounds good."

"Anyplace away from the front sounds good right about now."

"You know, Oleg, I was just thinking of how nice it would be to sip a nice cup of Turkish spice tea on a sandy beach."

"Concerned about nothing other than getting overheated in the sun," Oleg finished for him, holding back a chuckle.

Voldemars weakly coughed twice.

"That would be nice, wouldn't it?" Oleg said.

Voldemars lazily rolled his head toward the window. His eyes glazed over, enfolded by the sun, now hovering like a swirling orange and red hemisphere above the horizon. Solemnly, it started a mushroom of pastels through the cloud cover as it set behind the Volga plateau.

"Tell me, what exactly is going on at the front?" Voldemars asked.

"It's not important," Oleg answered.

Voldemars remained still for only a moment before turning back to Oleg. He opened his eyes wide and glared at Oleg with a ghostly expression.

"I would like to know. They kept me pretty much uninformed while I was in hospital."

"We're retreating. Oh, excuse me, the official word is redeploying. But I guess that's obvious since we wouldn't be here otherwise."

"Are we winning?" Voldemars' words grew harsher each time he spoke.

"Nicholas has personally taken command of the front line forces," Oleg said. "That's probably—"

"Nicholas?" Voldemars snapped his head around. His face contorted, blatantly puzzled. "Nicholas Romanov? At the front? What the hell is he doing there?"

"I don't know."

"He doesn't know anything about tactics! He's already proven that in China!"

"I am only telling you what I know."

"He can't even manage Dragoons that he hand-picked! How the hell does he expect to manage undisciplined troops at the front?"

"I honestly don't know," Oleg soberly replied.

"And with an enemy breathing down his neck to boot?" Voldemars finally stopped.

"I can only hope that we don't lose too badly," Oleg conceded with a shrug.

"If that isn't an invitation to the Bolsheviks, nothing is!"

"That's probably not far from the truth. I've heard reports they're gaining strength and numbers, even though Nicholas has outlawed them." Oleg's exasperation was clear. He hung his head and realized he could not hide the truth from Voldemars any longer. He sighed deeply, then added, "Hell, they've even penetrated our own ranks."

"Kolov," Voldemars whispered with surety in his voice.

Surprised but relieved, Oleg affirmed his suspicion with a nod.

"You know, even before we left Astrakhan the first time, I suspected as much, but I never had any real proof," Voldemars said.

"He deserted." Defeat oozed from Oleg's tone.

Voldemars nodded as a blank stare crusted his face. His mouth turned down as he rolled his head back toward the window. "I guess that's just their way, old friend," he added, disconsolate, as a monotonous landscape of field after field passed by the window.

❧   ❧   ❧

Trading nervous grins and titters, each of the cavalry officer's wives waited on the wooden planked platform, pacing when they could no longer sit, and sitting when their feet swelled too much from their pacing. Clouds of sweet, seductive aromas hovered around each young woman like individual scented auras, clashing openly to be the most noticed. A blanket of color from bright new dresses purchased from smiling, peg-toothed hawkers swayed through the station like a breeze blown field of wildflowers.

Standing next to Otilija, Natalya nervously rubbed her hands together as she fidgeted with minute long sentiments cycling from exuberance to anxiety ever since Oleg wired that the regiment was finally coming home. The emotional flux kept her restless all night, ebullient that Oleg would soon be there, but then troubled that she had yet to find a way to tell Otilija what had happened to Voldemars. Even Irina had kept her promise, right until she had left suddenly a day ago.

But now, somehow, she had to disperse with the terrible secret she had held so well. It was her responsibility. If she did not, Otilija would be shocked at the sight of Voldemars, even more so if she found out that Oleg had forewarned her. She sighed heavily as she watched Otilija fondle a postcard Voldemars had sent when the regiment first arrived in Odessa more than a year ago. She remembered that picture as one where he appeared dashing and strong, and most likely nothing like what he looked like now.

"Otilija," Natalya said. Her voice cracked.

Otilija's eyes shifted and warmly gazed at her. Natalya swallowed hard.

"Before the train arrives, I need to tell you something," Natalya whispered, hoping not to alarm her.

Otilija's eyes grew wide as she looked up from the postcard to Natalya. Her face paled with a sudden rush of terror.

"You know something, don't you. Oleg told you something terrible when he wired," Otilija said, her voice trembling.

Natalya felt paralyzed. She tried to eke out the words, but nothing except a wisp of stale air passed her throat.

"What's wrong with Voldemars?" Otilija said in a high-pitched tone.

"Do you remember a few months back, the letter I said was an old one?"

"Something happened to him! Something happened to Voldemars, didn't it?"

"Yes."

Natalya watched Otilija's expression grow stolid.

"Why didn't you tell me?" Otilija demanded.

"I'm sorry. I didn't know how. I don't know how to tell you now."

"What happened to Voldemars?" Otilija calmly demanded.

"He was hurt."

Otilija gasped, then covered her mouth with her hands. She started shaking her head.

"He's been recovering in a hospital in Odessa," Natalya said. "He's been there for three months. That's why he didn't write."

"Then he's not coming on this train, is he?"

Otilija's expression grew long and disconsolate. Natalya felt her soul shrink down though her legs and out her toes.

"No," Natalya said, but then quickly blurted, "I mean, yes, he's coming. Oleg said he rejoined the regiment in Odessa, but he was—"

"Then he's alive!"

"Oleg said he was hurt in a gas attack," Natalya blurted, then immediately felt guilt stab her in the chest.

Otilija gasped loud enough to be heard by anyone nearby. In her eyes, Natalya read every thought she had in the past weeks, thinking of how devastated Voldemars must be. Gas. Burned flesh. Blindness. Grotesque disfigurements left in the wake of carved out, rotted tissue.

Otilija sighed deeply as she stared back at the postcard. A tear trickled down her cheek and spotted the photograph.

"But he will be all right?" she quietly asked.

"Oleg says he will."

Natalya wrapped her arm around Otilija just as a train whistle sounded in the distance. When Otilija tipped her head just enough for Natalya to read her pain, she felt terribly empty.

❧   ❧   ❧

When the large, black steel wheels screeched to a stop, hidden amidst a thick white and gray billowing steam blanket, the mass on the platform coalesced near each car door. Windows dropped open. Heads popped out, faces clean-shaven and hair freshly cropped. Hands reached out as if searching for a soft hand or brief stroke through long, silky hair. Smiles beamed between the deck and the train. Shouts and screams filled the air.

Doors finally slid open. Anxious, fidgety feet twitched on the planks as the first of the returning army stepped off the train. Then, through the lingering steam clouds, more and more olive covered bodies plunged into the sea of brightly colored, flowing dresses.

As each car emptied, Otilija and Natalya shuffled to the next one, anxiously awaiting a familiar face. Finally, as they waited at the last car, Oleg emerged, assisting Voldemars down the steps and onto the platform. Wobbly-legged and feeble looking, Voldemars stood erect, jutting his jaw forward. His eyes scanned the crowd, thinning quickly by twos.

Suddenly a flash of yellow dashed by him and collided with Oleg with a wheeze and a squeak. Together, he and Natalya swung around as if dancing on the ballroom floor.

"Voldemars?" a soft, reserved voice said.

He turned his head and let his eyes rest on Otilija, her open hands stretched out to him, stiltedly moving closer. He complied, lifting his weak arms until he could grasp her soft hands in his. Otilija stopped in front of Voldemars.

"I'm all right," he whispered.

Otilija's hands slid over his bony arms and wrapped around his neck. The weight pulled him forward, but firmly planting his feet, he recovered his balance.

"I'll need some time to get my strength back, but I'm all right," he whispered into her ear.

With her arms gripping as tightly as he could tolerate, he felt Otilija jerk as she wept on his shoulder.

Telmeni

23 September 1915

A refreshing autumn breeze, lightly scented with the aroma of mature rye, tossed Janis' thinning hair as he relaxed in his favorite chair on Telmeni's wide, open porch. He rubbed his stubbled chin and gazed out over the rolling, tawny sea of mature grain. It was ready to be cut and baled for the winter, but he wasn't. Now he just wanted to rest his thinning frame in his favorite chair.

Absently, he reached over and picked up his tin of fine Turkish tobacco, set it on his lap, then wedged it between his legs. He popped it open with his large, burly hands, then reached over to his hand carved end table for his pipe.

There it was, right next to the pipe, as bold and obtrusive as it had been since it arrived. Janis felt frozen for a moment. His round, hazel eyes fixed on the cream colored paper and strange looking writing. He felt his fingers twitch until they fondled the bowl of his pipe. Picking it up, he turned away from the table, then dipped his pipe into the tin.

Honking geese flying in formation, melodically punctuating their yearly migration, caught his attention as he tamped the mound tightly into place. He glanced up and watched the graceful, long-necked birds wave their wings as they turned and faded to the south. Slipping the mouthpiece between his small, tobacco-stained teeth,

Janis sucked a mouthful of the flavor over his tongue, then covered the canister and placed it back on the table.

It caught his eye again. Next to the tin, resting precisely where he had dropped it that morning, was an official military letter, addressed to him in Cyrillic. His hand fondled the small, silver vial of matches as the letters commanded his attention, as crudely as any Russian he had ever known. Fleetingly, he thought of what it might say, but instead he grabbed his matches, turned away, and hunkered over his pipe. With one stroke, the match head burst into a pungent sulfur flame. He held the flicker over his bowl and sucked repeatedly with short draws through the well-chewed mouthpiece. A smooth blend of air and rich smoke bathed his mouth, sending a tingling stream though his temples as the tobacco glowed to life. Finally, he released a thin, blue stream of smoke over the match, extinguishing the flame, and leaving the stick smoldering with its own twisting wisp of white.

As he placed the matches back onto the table, the letter again caught his eye. This time, the black print demanded his attention. He tried to imagine anything other than what he felt was an inevitable announcement of Voldemars' death, but his mind concluded nothing more. There was only one way of finding out what message sat inside that official envelope.

"I guess now's the time," he mumbled as he drew in another mouthful of the smooth, sweet tasting smoke. Reaching over, he laid his fingers on the embossed, imperial, double-headed eagle, then pulled the letter toward him and picked it up. He carefully turned it over, wormed his finger into the fold, and with short, firm jerks, ripped open the envelope. Janis pulled out the letter, inhaled deeply, then closed his eyes and leaned back. Tears, prompted by anxiety, welled in his eyes as a nervous tic developed in his crooked frown. He sighed loudly, then carefully opened the page, using delicate movements as if he was unpacking a crystal goblet.

1 June 1915

Dear Mr. Janis Vechi,

I am Captain Oleg Stativsky, of his Majesty's Cavalry. I am writing to you on behalf of your son, Voldemars. It is with deepest regrets that I need to write this letter.

Janis dropped the letter, convinced he knew what was to follow. He drew in a quick breath through his pipe and held the smoke in his throat, letting the acrid essence scrape his tongue until he could tolerate it no further. With a slow, controlled release, smoke slipped through his pruned lips until not even a wisp remained. Janis then sighed again, prepared to return his attention to the letter.

During a scouting mission in the Carpathians, Voldemars was felled by a German gas attack. He survived, although his lungs and eyes were injured.

"Nicholas, you bastard! You bloody bastard!" Janis dropped the letter on the table, unable to read any further. He vaulted to his feet, fuming. With long, determined strides, he stomped off the porch and toward his tool barn. He yanked his long bladed scythe from the wall, slung it over his shoulder, then stormed off into the swaying rye fields. Partway in, Janis began whacking at the tall, drying grass, all the while cursing Nicholas.

"Janis!" Someone called from a distance.

Janis recognized the voice but ignored the call. He knew it was Oskars Ziemels. And Oskars always came from the same direction, along the bank of the lake, between the two large oaks, through the potatoes, and the along the field. He walked that path so many times that the grass no longer grew where he traveled.

With even more determination, Janis hacked at the rye, gritting his teeth to muster ever stronger swipes.

"Have you heard the news, Janis? Nicholas has taken control of the army." Oskars tone oozed wry cynicism as he slowed to a walk and tried to catch his breath.

Janis stopped in mid stroke and glanced back at Oskars. His reddish, rounded face, wisps of black hair, and hauntingly thin frame made him look like a scarecrow with a ripe apple stuck on its shoulders. Janis squinted, unable to tell whether he was surprised or confused.

"Who the hell had it before?" Janis asked.

"No, no. At the front! Nicholas has assumed field control of the army. The news was posted in Riga this morning."

"Nicholas has done what?"

"I couldn't believe it myself when I heard it."

"Spineless Nicholas? You have to be joking!" Janis said sardonically.

"It's true!"

"Why did the field marshals ever agree to that? Don't they realize what they've done?"

Oskars shrugged his pointed shoulders, while an impish grin formed on his mouth.

"Do you really think I'm going to believe that bull?" Janis shook his head and frowned, then spit insultingly as he moved to taller grass.

"It's not bull, Janis—"

"Listen, Oskars!" Janis turned and glowered at him. His face registered his patience had been tested. "I'm going to cut. I don't have time for jokes or your convoluted riddles."

"But, it's true. I didn't believe it myself at first, but that is the official word, directly from the Russian government!"

Janis stared skeptically at Oskars.

"All right, I'll listen," Janis conceded when he read sincerity in Oskars' eyes. "But, I am going to cut. The field needs it. I need it. So, if you want to talk, go grab the rake and help me. I need someone to sweep the chaff away."

Without another word, Oskars spun around and hustled back to the barn. Janis returned to his task, hacking into the rye as he mulled the strange news. He raised the gleaming blade high over his head, then cocked it before he angrily whooshed it down and effortlessly sliced through the stalks. With each pass he grew even more disturbed.

"A waste!" Janis grumbled, remembering the letter he had just read. Another swipe and three additional meters of rye lay severed before him. "What the hell does Nicholas think he's doing? Has he gone mad?"

Another swoosh. Three more meters cut.

"What the hell is he going to do up there?"

"He's at the front, Janis," Oskars said in a squeaky voice.

Janis stopped his stroke before he cut another swathe.

Oskars inched closer, babbling as if he had never left to get the rake. "Nicholas left Petersburg two days ago by train. My sources have witnesses that have seen him there."

"The front? Why?" Janis glared at Oskars, fire and disbelief raging in his eyes. He adjusted his hand on the curved grip, then lifted and twirled the scythe's sharp blade skyward. As he steadied the handle with his other hand, he swung deep, swooshing it through the hip-deep amber grass.

"There must be some political reason for it," Oskars offered, following Janis and dutifully scratching up the cut rye into piles.

"Is he trying to create the same disorder up there that he has plagued all of Russia with? What the hell is wrong with this damn country anyway?" Janis grumbled as he lifted the blade again. Sunlight glimmered off the sharpened steel for less than a second before he plunged it back into the grass.

"If you want my opinion, as far as I'm concerned, the bastard can take a bullet. Right in the head. And I really don't care whose!" Janis blurted as he stopped his harvest for a brief rest. He crossed his arms on the handle, then rested his chin on his sweat-dampened forearms.

"Oh?" Oskars recoiled.

"That bastard's responsible!" Janis shouted with anger, then fell silent. He stared out into the southern sky, his sober expression emphasized by hollow, deep-set eyes locked in a wistful gaze. A tear escaped and ran down his wrinkled cheek. He then sighed, shook his head, and returned to his work with much less vigor than before.

"Responsible for what?" Oskars said, sounding concerned.

"He's responsible for every one of the thousands of lives wasted at the front! He's the only one obsessed with this damn war, a pointless war that's bound to keep going until Mother Russia bleeds dry!"

Janis stopped, stood straight, and glared at Oskars. His eyes grew as wide as his breathing verged on panting. "And for what? Give me one good reason for this insanity! Russia is in total chaos! Who knows who's in control!"

"Exactly the point, Janis!" Oskars peered into Janis' eyes, a devious grin on his face. "Think about what this all of this means. Nicholas going to the front could be just the situation we need. The break, Janis! We could make the break from Russia and no one will try to stop us. We have now what we didn't have in 1905."

Janis cocked his head and squinted as a furrow sunk in his forehead. "What are you babbling about?"

"Latvia, Janis! Independence! Freedom!"

Janis froze, captured by Oskars' rambling. Suddenly it all made sense. Nicholas gone, the Duma without direction, restlessness in Russia preoccupying the Dragoons.

"My God, you're right!" he said. "You are absolutely right! If the separatists take initiative now, the bastard won't know what to do, nor will the Duma. If he wants to save his dynasty, for the good of Russia, he'll have to let us go."

Janis' euphoria was short-lived. He stared off into the south and watched the smoldering front again stain the autumns' blue sky with sooty, black spew.

"But, what about them," he mumbled, nodding to the west. "How will they respond?"

"I don't think it really matters what the Germans do," Oskars said. "It's what we do that will make the difference. If we can break away from Russia, even just long enough to breathe freely, other countries will surely recognize our valiant struggle!"

"I don't know," Janis mumbled.

"And when they do," Oskars continued, undaunted, "they'll come to our aid!"

"Are you mad? Every time someone's empire has crumbled, the Huns have rushed in like a band of hungry scavengers. What happened when the Swedes fell, and the Lits, and—"

"It's a chance we have to take, Janis."

Oskars dropped the rake and grabbed Janis by the shoulders.

"And what about the Huns?" Janis asked. "We would be giving them exactly what they need to rebuild, a welcomed respite from a two front war!"

"But it's our future!"

"We failed ten years ago," Janis said.

"Because we weren't together!" Oskars countered. "The sentiment in Riga is strong now. Much stronger than it was back then. Even better, the political situation is favorable. Nicholas is hated by everyone!"

"And when did you become an expert on politics?" Janis demanded.

"I'm not an expert, Janis, you know that! Let's just say I've been educated by some very influential people," Oskars added smugly.

"Not the damn Bolsheviks!"

"God, no! We've got nothing to do with the Bolsheviks."

"We?" Janis stared at Oskars through squinted eyes.

"The separatists."

"How many?"

"I'm not really sure, honestly," Oskars said. "With the Okhrana running around, no one speaks openly."

"Who?" Janis peered over his shoulder, suddenly paranoid at the mere mention of the Okhrana. "Who's heading this up?"

"Zanis, Rostislavs. I've talked with Ivars as well. I'm really not sure who's heading it up."

Janis was immediately impressed. Zanis and Rostislavs were close friends of his, and he knew how influential Ivars was in local politics. It was the revelation he needed.

"Then I think it's time we find out!"

Janis slung his scythe over his shoulder, then turned and wrapped his free arm around Oskars. Together they headed back to the farmhouse.

Telmeni

17 October 1915

"You're a fool, Janis!" Rudolphs said as he brought his stein to his mouth. Thickset and arrogant looking, Rudolphs hardly looked like a farmer, but he did manage to breed the finest herd of milkers in all of Vidzeme. "Why would you want to be associated with separatists, no less join them?"

"If your son had suffered under Nicholas' futile army, you would understand how I feel now," Janis mumbled under his breath. He squirmed in his chair and pensively puffed on his pipe, while Rudolphs gulped another mouthful of Janis' homemade kvass.

"There comes a time when we all need to assess what we have, compared to what we want," Janis responded behind a cloud of lingering smoke. "And I personally think that now is the time we should consider independence from Russia."

"Independence?" Rudolphs bellowed with a deep belly-laugh so loud the porch shook. "Think about what you're saying, Janis! Aren't we independent enough out here?"

"But real independence."

"Christ, the government doesn't even bother us!"

"Except to steal our children."

"Even the Okhrana leaves us alone! We live our lives day to day, without anyone sticking their nose in to tell us what to do," Rudolphs rambled without hearing Janis. "Hell, sometimes I wonder if they even care what we do out here! I think you're fooling yourself. Independence from Russia won't buy us anything, except a government closer to home."

Rudolphs slammed his mug onto the small table next to his chair, sending his red cheeks jiggling. As he devilishly grinned at his host, he waved his thick, short finger.

"And that could be a hell of a lot worse than what we have now!" He burst into another guffaw before he belched loudly. "This kvass is fine!" he added before bellowing another laugh.

"I don't think I agree with you," Janis rebutted.

"Christ, you are modest, Janis!"

"I mean independence."

"And perhaps a bit misled—"

"We should be allowed to decide our own fate, instead of letting a Duma hundreds of miles away decide it for us," Janis said.

"And a Duma in Riga is going to listen to us farmers out in Vidzeme?" Rudolphs turned soberly grim. "No, I don't think so. Hell, I don't know what you put into this kvass, but it's surely scrambling your head," he finished with a chuckle.

"You must at least agree that we deserve the right to defend ourselves?" Janis said.

"Defend ourselves? Why would we want to do that when the Russian army is the biggest army on the continent. What better defense is there?"

"If this army is so goddamned powerful, why are the Germans just outside of Riga?" Janis fired back. "And over the past hundred years, how many times has Latvia fallen to invaders, even with this all powerful army protecting us?"

Rudolphs froze, hidden behind the stein quivering so precariously close to his gaping mouth that the foamy brew filmed his lips. Slowly, he lowered the mug to the table, licked the foam from his lip, and squirmed in his chair. He leaned forward, then craned his wide neck to force his head forward.

"Do you know what the Okhrana will do to you if they find out you are a separatist?" he asked in a hushed tone.

"I believe I do," Janis stated proudly. "And I'm willing to take the chance of being caught in order to see a free and independent Latvia."

Rudolphs slid back in his chair, straightened, then cocked his head. His eyes darted up and down as if inspecting Janis for the first time.

"What was it?" Rudolphs asked. "What happened to you to make you act so righteous and patriotic?"

Janis pursed his lips and glared back at Rudolphs. He was right. He had only recently changed his belief about independence. He closed his eyes and thought for a moment, debating whether he should reveal the reason.

"Voldemars," he said softly.

Rudolphs immediately blanched. "I'm sorry, Janis. I hadn't heard."

"He was injured, but at the rate the mail gets through, he very well may have died by now."

❈   ❈   ❈

Janis startled awake as a hand set on his shoulder. Rudolphs' image evaporated. Janis shook his head, opened his eyes and looked up at the blurry image.

"Oskars," he sighed. The dream of how foolish he was to reveal his feelings still lingered.

"Are you ready to go?" Oskars asked quietly.

"Hmm." Janis shook his head again, trying to clear his thoughts. "I must have fallen asleep."

"Second thoughts?" Oskars pried as Janis gingerly rose from his chair.

"No," Janis lied as he shook his head again. "Just tired I guess. I'll get the wagon ready."

❦   ❦   ❦

With his small supply cart hitched to his largest draft horse, Janis steered along the winding, dusty road toward Cesis. Oskars sat quietly beside him, looking out into the fields and trees as if a young boy on his first trip to the city. Janis himself sensed anticipation prickle at his skin, reminding him that this journey was also his first. He had never been involved in politics before, much less revolutionary matters. This would be his first party meeting. Politics was best left to the lawyers and the statesmen, he always thought, not men of the earth like him and Oskars.

But there comes a time in the course of human events, he had once read, that even common men need to become part of the process, not just acted upon by others.

It was clear in his mind that he was indeed doing the right thing. Even so, there were still plenty of reasons for anxiety. What he was doing was illegal, even if the prohibition was placed on him by a Russian decree. People were being arrested for their involvement, and knowing that, Oskars' feeble assurance that only separatists would be there did little to quell Janis' fears.

He glanced at Oskars, unusually silent since they had left Telmeni. He could not remember a time when Oskars was quiet for minutes, much less the hour they had been on the road. He seemed to have been completely consumed with everything around them, and that alone tightened the grip in Janis' chest. Instead of starting a conversation that he knew Oskars would feel obligated to finish, though, Janis turned and stared forward again. Assuaged by his horse's rhythmic clopping on the hard-packed, amber pathway, he let himself become enfolded by the scenery and consumed in his own thoughts.

In the cart's wake along the road, brown leaves took flight and circled lazily, then settled back down, blanketing the dusty, rutted road. Boughs in full autumn panorama, in every conceivable shade between gold and brown, swayed in the breeze, waltzing with the mingling winds. Their leaves twitched, until one by one they jostled free from their perches and fell in a rainbow of color aimlessly sauntering to the ground. Spreading oaks draped in fiery scarlet highlighted the rolling hills, while liepas quivered in their yellow coats. Like sentries behind the brilliant colors, earthy green toned pines swayed, scratching against the sky's blue crispness.

Janis conjured an image of what he expected to see in Cesis, having only what he had read of party politics to gauge his thoughts. A vague impression of a large house nestled in the center of the city appeared, and he and Oskars stood in open mouthed amazement at the threshold of a large, smoke-filled meeting room. In the center of the unbreathable thickness, gathered as if around a large, round altar, fat, well-dressed men haggled minutia, billowed heavy cigar smoke from between tobacco stained teeth.

"I forgot to tell you that Rostislavs said the party was meeting in the old castle outside of Cesis," Oskars said, his voice cracking. Janis' image immediately metamorphosed into the stately gathering hall he remembered inside the majestic, sprawling old castle.

"I know where that is, Oskars," Janis mumbled. When he turned and glanced at Oskars, he shivered. His partner's bulging, fish-eyed stare sparked an odd tingling up his back like a wood spider creeping across a log.

"Christ, what's that look for? This is only a meeting, isn't it?" he added with hesitation. The tingling grew more insistent.

"Yes."

Oskars' blunt reply made the tingling grow even worse.

"Christ, Oskars, you're scaring the living hell right out of me. I've never seen you so quiet." Janis felt compelled to squeeze some conversation from him.

Oskars' head snapped from one side to the other, responding to any movement which twitched a branch or rustled some grass. "Just a feeling. I guess I really don't know who to trust anymore," Oskars answered.

"What are you trying to say?" Janis swallowed hard. The hairs on his neck stood on end.

"I know the separatists are taking precautions, but how do we really know that the Okhrana won't have...you know, anyone there? I've heard they've done that before. Somehow, they get into these secret meetings, then a week later, someone disappears."

Janis squirmed in his seat and gently nudged his horse along. A knot wrenched tightly in his stomach as his paranoia grew stronger. He even started craning his neck to peek behind brush hedges along the road as they passed.

"Ivars was arrested last night, you know," Oskars said.

"Ivars?"

"Of anyone, I wouldn't expect him to be caught. He was very careful."

"You have to admit Ivars does have a way of irritating just about everyone. My guess is that someone got upset with him and turned him in." Janis tried to laugh off his growing fear, but it remained chokingly strong.

"I think it was a spy! I'm sorry, Janis, but with the way everybody is mixed up with everyone else around here, you can never tell who's Bolshevik, who's Okhrana, and who's just a loyal Latvian looking for freedom. Everybody looks the same!"

"Then maybe the real answer is simply don't trust anyone," Janis mumbled as he pulled on the reins to turn left and onto a shortcut which he remembered led to the castle. His horse complied and pulled the wagon onto a seldom used pathway covered with summer scorched, matted grass.

"That's what Ivars said the last time I saw him, too," Oskars noted.

After a quick right turn back onto the main road, Janis slowed his horse enough to give him a good view of the brownstone castle. Framed by a stand of dead, craggy trees, the seven hundred year old castle appeared as if out of a Rainis' fable. Its weather beaten corner turrets stood twice as tall as the long, brownstone walls. Flame red ivy waved weakly as it clung like a cloak over each turret wall. Behind the southernmost turret, the sun hid, but its rays streamed out brightly around and above the castle's ancient walls.

Suddenly lost in the memory of reciting passages of folklore to Voldemars when he was young, Janis slowed his horse even more to drink in all the castle had to offer.

"What was that?" Oskars suddenly jumped and turned around.

Janis snapped back to reality. He spun his head around to look where Oskars was pointing.

"What was what?" Janis asked, seeing nothing.

"I saw something move. Up there!"

Janis focused on the brush, but still saw nothing. "Are you sure you aren't imagining—"

"There!" Oskars yelled, pointing to a boy who suddenly ran out in front of them.

Standing not more than twenty meters away, he outstretched his hand like a traffic officer. His tunic was a naked, badge-stripped, pitifully tattered Russian infantry field jacket, hanging so loosely on the boy's slender frame that he appeared to be poorly masquerading as a soldier. His baggy trousers abruptly ended at ragged cuffs midway between his knees and bare, filthy feet.

"Christ, Oskars, it's just a boy!" Janis said. He immediately stopped his horse with two firm jerks on the reins.

Darting toward them, the youth charged the cart with rabbit-like quickness. He assumed a position next to Oskars and pantomimed aiming a rifle at his chest. His determined scowl seemed almost playful as he peered up at his captives.

"Brivibas!" he whispered, then grinned innocently as he turned his ear toward Oskars.

"Now, that's something the Okhrana would never suspect," Janis mumbled under his cupped hand, holding back a chuckle.

"Brivibas?"

"No, a boy that age as a sentry!" Janis said.

The boy frowned at Janis, then more forcefully repeated, "Brivibas!"

Oskars leaned closer to the boy and cupped his hands around his mouth. "Sveiki, brali! Oskars, Oskars Ziemels and Janis Vechi of Valmiera," he whispered back, then flashed a quick grin.

"I remember those names!" The boy smiled widely, then turned toward the castle and whistled twice. "I am Aleksandrs Baronovs! Rostislavs sent me! I will lead you to the castle," he proudly announced, turning back to the travelers.

From out of the brush, another barefoot boy rushed out and stood at attention. As his eyes closely inspected Janis and Oskars, Aleksandrs leaned over and whispered in his ear. The boy nodded, then whispered something back to Aleksandrs.

"Ja!" Aleksandrs noted, sending the boy back into the brush. As soon as he was gone, Aleksandrs deftly hopped up on the cart and snapped the reins from Janis' hands.

"I've been in Cesis before, young man," Janis patronized, yanking back on the reins. "And I know how to get to the castle from here. You don't need to help me."

"But without me, Rostislavs says you don't come in. Nobody comes in without one of us." Aleksandrs' smug grin grew wide, almost connecting his large ears.

Janis looked at Oskars, shrugged his shoulders, smiled, then surrendered the reins to the boy.

"All right, you win. Lead on!"

"Poppa says we're going to be free, Mr. Vechi!" Aleksandrs spouted as he snapped the leather and the wagon lurched forward. "Poppa says that we're going to reconquer and defend Latvia! That's what Goldmanis said, too, you know. I read that decree."

"Aleksandrs, how old are you?" Janis slipped in when the boy stopped chattering.

"Fourteen. I'll be fifteen next year. Then I am going to be part of the Strelnieks."

"Fourteen? No, I'd say you're only twelve, thirteen at best," Janis wryly interrupted.

Aleksandrs swallowed hard. Janis reckoned he was right.

"But I'm old for my age! Don't you think I can pass for fourteen now?"

"Does your Poppa know exactly what you're doing?" Oskars asked, clearing his throat.

"Of course. He's here! He's part of the party from Riga!" Aleksandrs crowed as he pulled hard on the leathers, turning the horse right.

"But the castle is to the left. I can see it through the trees," Janis said, reflexively reaching for the reins.

"I know. The sentries will escort you in." Aleksandrs deflected Janis' hands and stopped the horse. "I'll take your wagon down this road and tie it up. Rostislavs wants the horses spread out so the Okhrana won't suspect a meeting is going on here."

"All right, but careful now. Just nudge him. He's a very responsive horse!" Janis cautioned as he stepped down from the cart.

Aleksandrs smiled and nodded. As two older sentries converged on Janis and Oskars, he coaxed the horse forward.

"I still can't believe he's doing this," Janis noted as the sentries inspected his identification card.

"It's the only way we can keep him out of the meeting," one of the sentries grumbled while the other chuckled under his breath.

"Everything is in order. This way," he noted, then silently escorted Janis and Oskars to the south side of the castle.

"The meeting is in there." The older guard pointed to the open, arched entrance, then turned and left Janis and Oskars standing at the opening. Almost immediately, a crusty looking old man appeared in the archway and weakly waved. His frame was as wiry as the rest of them. His long face was deeply furrowed and blanched white.

"Rostislavs!" Oskars' voice jumped an octave. "Damn, it's good to see you again!" Oskars grabbed his wretched looking friend and wrapped his arms around him tightly.

"They got Ivars," he whispered into Rostislavs' ear.

The man pulled back and solemnly shook his head. His droopy eyes explained everything he felt.

"This is Janis Vechi. My neighbor and good friend," Oskars offered.

"Glad to meet you, Janis. Oskars has told me much about you." A short-lived grin revealed Rostislavs' peg-like teeth, but his lips quickly closed again as his expression turned sober. "I'm glad you both could make it, but we've got to hurry! The meeting is about to begin."

Janis and Oskars quickly followed Rostislavs into the darkness, and in sequence, they plunged into a dank, narrow hallway. Two steps into the darkness, the rank odor of animal feces lingered and insulted Janis' nostrils. The three men hustled through the pallor, holding their breath to keep from vomiting.

At the end of the hallway, Rostislavs leaned on a massive oak door, forcing it to slowly creak open. A thin cloud of smoke escaped, riding the light which grew brighter as the door swung open. Janis craned his neck and squinted to see through the thick haze, hovering like a curtain at the entrance. Inside the buzzing room, a crowd of over two hundred people lingered, submerged in the blue cloud. The scene was just as he imagined, except the people were all commoners; thin, dressed in work clothes, and smoking nothing but hand rolled cigarettes.

"Come." Rostislavs waved his hand, signaling to Janis and Oskars to enter as he plunged into the haze. "Ulmanis is about to address us."

"Ulmanis!" Oskars gasped.

Ulmanis, Janis thought as he followed Oskars and Rostislavs into the room. Karlis Ulmanis, the man reputed to be the most intelligent man in all of Latvia.

Janis remembered a lecture Ulmanis had given at Rubene where he explained the concepts of American specialty farming. Janis was so excited when he left the meeting that as soon as he arrived back at Telmeni, he started building the windmill Ulmanis had described.

Suddenly realizing Oskars had slipped into the crowd while he remembered the lecture, Janis shook his head and strutted quickly to catch up to him.

"Friends," a booming, faceless voice announced from behind the bluish pall.

Instantly, the entire room silenced.

"That's him," Rostislavs muttered.

"My friends!" Ulmanis continued with his characteristically deep voice. "We're on the verge of the most historically significant event of all of our lives!"

The speaker paused and scanned the room. The pall of smoke thinned, letting Janis see the enigma he knew as Ulmanis. His large, square face, topped with tufted, sandy brown hair, ended with a deep cleft splitting his strongly jutting chin. Under his furrowed brow, alluring, friendly eyes simply asked for respect. His sturdy frame, combined with seemingly choreographed hand gestures commanded unwavering attention. As he opened his hands to the audience, he drew them in with a firm but friendly demeanor.

"You and I are the honorable delegates which from herein will be the union of our provinces, Kurzeme, Vidzeme, and Latgale. I submit to you that the Latvian nation, just as any other nation, has the right to complete and unhindered self-determination. Latvia must not be divided any longer. It must be an autonomous, democratic unit, free from the chains of Russia!"

The entire assembly was mesmerized while Ulmanis' echo reso-nated off the ancient walls of the castle. His heavy eyebrows danced expressively over his fiery eyes.

"Russia and the Czar are troubled, and this turmoil leaves us pre-cariously at the mercy of an invader. German troops have already invaded Kurzeme and now threaten Riga. Goldmanis' bold actions in the Duma have given us the right to a Strelnieks so that we may defend our homeland. It is my belief that the time has come for us to break away from the devastating monarchical rule of Nicholas!"

The entire assembly erupted with loud approval as Ulmanis force-fully pounded his hand into his fist. He grinned, then tried to con-tinue, but the cheers drowned out his words. After a brief pause, he held his hands in the air. Instantly obedient, the crowd's noise dwin-dled to hushed murmurs.

"I envision that here will be the second coming of a great democ-racy. In the United States, from the roots of the people rose the Republican Party. And so shall the Latvian Farmers Union in our united state of Latvia, but we must start methodically and slowly. Elections shall be held, laws shall be passed, we will seek out diplo-matic friends, and then we will bring our new republic into the twenties, free of the bindings of Russian or German rule!"

The crowd again exploded with a raucous approval. Ulmanis stepped back and basked in their revelry, allowing the applause to continue for what seemed ten minutes before finally attempting to hush them again.

"Our symbol," Ulmanis started in again as the crowd settled. "Our symbol, my friends, will represent our strength in unity. Our prov-inces will each be represented by a single gold star, like each of the states in the American flag. Our joined three stars shall be the sym-bol of our new country. Rally under the Latvian colors! Onward to liberty!"

Applause again erupted from the crowd as everyone vaulted to their feet. Ulmanis stepped back and let them chant "Brivibas" over and over. His characteristic wide mouthed smile beamed on his face as he turned the traditional Latvian tri-striped flag behind him.

While the frenzied crowd continued their chant of liberty, Janis collapsed to his chair. Smoke seemed to swirl about his head, and blurred images moved in blobs before him. Slowly the image came into focus, and he recognized one as little Voldemars playing Lacple-sis in the woods and fields around Telmeni.

"When you were a boy, Voldemars," Janis mumbled, "you enjoyed our heritage. I know what was and still is in your heart. You wanted to fight for Latvia, not the Czar!"

The boy had looked up to him with bright eyes and a wisp of a smile. Pride was visible on his face as he had listened intently to Janis.

"So for you, I will take my place alongside this movement and do all I can to help the fight for a free Latvia. For you, my son, we will become a free nation!"

Janis wished he had the felt this same way before, and had told his son. He thought he may have understood Voldemars better, like he did now.

Astrakhan, Southern Russia

30 June 1916

*E*xhausted from a countless procession of fitful nights, Oleg sauntered with a pensive, short-stepped gait in the light of a haze-
shrouded moon. Summer had arrived with hellish vengeance, with
air so heavy it felt like he was breathing steam. As sweat beaded on
his forehead, running in rivulets down his unshaven face, he picked
at his saturated and clammy uniform where it stuck to his skin. He
knew he smelled, but without another uniform to change into, he
had no choice but to tolerate the musty, damp wool.

Oleg paced the shoreline, hoping the cooling night breeze would
not succumb to the swelter, but it too had given up and let the searing heat dominate. He stopped and sighed heavily. He tried to suck
in enough of the humid air to satiate his lungs, but his chest failed
him. Turning toward the sea, he peered out and watched the reflection of the moon shimmer on the glass-like surface. The wavering
image hypnotized him, coaxing his aching, heavy eyelids closed. He
dropped to his knees and expelled a lung full of air, then hung his
head on his chest. Dampness seeped through his trousers, then
pooled in the pockets his knees made in the sand.

The coolness wicked tension from Oleg's body, as if the pools
offered an escape route. As the calm, rhythmic shushing of the water
washing onto the shore, it soothed him and carried him back to his
childhood, to a time when his father brought him to the Black Sea

for holiday. Oleg remembered how he played for hours on the white sands, charging in and out of the water, then rolling in the sand until his skin glistened with grit.

Leaning back, he kicked out his legs and sank his buttocks onto the beach. He opened his eyes, grasped his boots and struggled them off, freeing his feet from their leathery purgatory. He let his toes dance in the air for a moment, then pushed himself up, and slogged out into the warm, foaming water until his ankles were submerged. With the sea lapping at his legs, he gazed out over the water and fell mesmerized by the moon's blurred reflection.

"You were right, Poppa," Oleg mumbled, feeling the water seep the strain from his muscles. He closed his eyes again and tried to escape in his mind, but his angst kept him prisoner as it buzzed about with tenacity.

"Can't sleep either?" a voice said from the darkness.

Startled, Oleg spun around to the sound, splashing up the water as he did. He squinted and recognized the long, loping strides of the approaching figure.

"Too damn hot," he mumbled. Feeling a bit embarrassed, he sloshed out of the water and met Voldemars on the shore. Hiding his face, he looked around for his boots. Then he glanced up into Voldemars' eyes.

"Looks to me like it's more than just the heat," Voldemars noted matter-of-factly before gazing out over the water.

Oleg thought for a moment about lying and keeping his misery to himself as he sat in the sand to slip on his boots. He toyed with telling Voldemars it was really just the heat that was bothering him. Not the floundering war, or Natalya's baby, or even that he felt uncomfortable with the field command of the troops, especially while Voldemars was present and capable of second guessing everything he did, even if he didn't.

"I don't know," Oleg started soberly, "sometimes I really don't know what's bothering me anymore."

Voldemars offered his hand. Oleg clasped it and let him help him up from the sand. As he stood up, while Voldemars' firm grip seemed to squeeze the blood from his fingers, Oleg felt eyes piercing through to his soul. He knew he had to say something.

"Brusilov's offensive," he blurted with a disapproving tone. Oleg turned away and emphatically tried to jam his foot deeper into his boot, but only succeeded in burying his heel in the sand.

"Did I hear you right?" Voldemars perched his eyebrows and tilted his head toward Oleg. "Or am I missing something? I thought after a year in retreat you would jump at the chance of getting back."

"It's not so much the return to fighting." He stopped short of admitting what he really felt.

Oleg stared at Voldemars' eyes, noticing for the first time that some spark had returned to them. His physique had returned somewhat, although it was nothing of the well developed specimen that he had been before the gas laid him up.

It's that Command still has not acknowledged you are ready to return to duty, Oleg thought, peering deep into Voldemars' eyes. Unless they do, it's my responsibility to lead the regiment, and I don't know if I'm quite ready.

"Christ, Oleg, here's your chance at a real command!" Voldemars said.

"Hell, I don't know. Sometimes I think it's the war. Sometimes I wonder if it's the damned Bolsheviks, then other times—"

"Natalya?" Voldemars prodded.

"I don't know." Oleg shrugged.

"Do you want a little advice?"

"Even if I said no, you'd probably give it to me anyway," Oleg mumbled.

Voldemars grinned and looked back out to the water. "Concern yourself only with the things you can do something about," he said. His eyes glazed over. "With the war, what will happen, will happen. And with Nicholas leading the troops, it may be best to stay back.

The Bolsheviks—I don't think they're anything to worry about. My guess is that their saber rattling won't amount to anything but another failed coup, if they even get that far. As for Natalya, well, women are an enigma which I don't think any man has ever figured out."

"Maybe it is Natalya, you know, the baby and all. She's doing fine, and I don't have any reason to believe anything is wrong. I just have this burning in my gut, all knotted up and twisted, kind of like that no man's land you always talked about."

Oleg bowed his head, shuffling his feet thoughtfully. He dug a small trench in the sand and watched the water seep into it. "Christ, I don't know. Maybe I am starting to think that bringing a child into all this swirling hell isn't such a good idea."

"A little late to think of that now, Oleg," Voldemars dryly said.

Oleg offered no response. He scratched the stubble on his chin as he continued a catatonic gaze out over the water. "What happens to us if Brusilov's offensive keeps making headway?" he finally turned and asked in a hushed voice. "Do you think we'll get sent back?"

"We're one of the best offensive units in the Southern Army."

"I just don't know if I can do it, Voldemars." Oleg sighed heavily as his eyes wandered back toward the compound.

"I know you can. I've seen you in action, and I know that."

"No, you don't understand." Oleg sighed again. He turned back to Voldemars and peered into his eyes. His glare was frosted and determined. "I just don't know if I can go back there without at least seeing my baby."

Voldemars was immediately silent, obviously moved by Oleg's words.

"I just don't," Oleg stopped suddenly when he saw an odd looking figure running toward them. "Oh my God!"

Voldemars spun around.

"Oleg, come quick! It's Natalya!" Otilija yelled as she ran toward the men with her open robe flapping wildly behind her.

Oleg froze. His eyes grew grotesquely wide and his head snapped back to Otilija. Slow at first, his feet dug into the sand, then sprayed grains behind him as they scrambled him off toward the barracks.

"What's wrong?" Voldemars asked as he ran toward her through the soft, shifting sand. "What's wrong with Natalya?"

"She's having the baby!" Otilija gasped for air. "Natalya's having the baby!"

"She's supposed to have a baby, isn't she?"

"It's much too early, Voldemars! I can see pain in her eyes. It's the same as when—"

Otilija covered her face as she burst into a hysterical sob. Voldemars collected himself as he stared at his wife. His eyes glazed as he looked at his hands. Stiffly, he inched toward her, then placed his hands on her quivering shoulders. For a moment, he froze.

Reflexively, he squeezed his hands on her shoulders and pulled her erect. Underneath the film of tears, her eyes screamed out loudly.

"I'm sorry I wasn't there," he whispered, but the words never escaped his lips.

"I sent Katya for a doctor," Otilija uttered between sobs. "She would know if there are any nearby."

"You didn't leave Natalya alone, did you?"

"God, no! Emilia is with her."

Without another word, they turned and headed back. As they reached the barracks, Otilija stopped and stared at Katya and Emilia weeping on the outside steps, consoling each other with arms wrapped around each other. With stiff, measured steps, Otilija parted from her husband and moved closer.

Katya looked up, her eyes swollen, red, and bereft.

"She doesn't look good," Emilia mumbled, then sniffled.

She jumped when Natalya's agonizing scream wailed through an open window. Otilija's eyes withered as her knees buckled. Voldemars caught her and guided her to a place beside Katya.

Natalya screamed again. Then again. Obviously disturbed, Otilija shuddered, then collapsed, melting into Katya's arms.

An hour passed. Natalya's screaming faded to pleading, then dissipated to moaning whimpers. Another hour passed in disconsolate and uncomfortably tense silence, broken only by scuffing feet, Oleg's high pitched, cracking mumbles, and Natalya's sobbing moans. Then silence reigned.

Dim yellow light poured out into the steamy night as the barracks' door slowly cracked open. Clutching the doorjamb, Oleg appeared at the threshold, glassy-eyed and wan. He stumbled as he stepped onto the porch, but caught his balance and remained erect. Stiffly and stiltedly, he shuffled by the women without saying a word, passed Voldemars without even a glance, and headed in the direction of the beach.

Voldemars watched Oleg disappear into the mist, then looked back inside the open door. Noticing the doctor scuffling around inside, he started to step by Otilija, but she reached up, asking with her eyes for him to take her with him. He drew her close, then gingerly stepped inside.

"What…what happened," he stuttered. His knees trembled as he looked about the room.

"I did all I could," the doctor said in a cold, matter-of-fact, monotone voice. "There was nothing more I could do."

Voldemars immediately fixed on the partially dried blood splattered on the front of the doctor's white shirt.

"What do you mean?" he said.

Otilija pressed deeper into his shoulder as she stifled sobs. Behind them, he heard Katya's and Emilia's weeping explode into frantic crying.

"They're both dead," Otilija said coldly. "They're both dead, aren't they?"

The doctor nodded. "The infant died weeks ago," he mumbled as he methodically wiped his bloody hands on a white towel. "Then she tore before I could get the body all the way out. The bleeding was just too much to stop. I just couldn't stop it."

Otilija covered her mouth with her hands as she heard Katya and Emilia gasp, then cry louder.

"Go find Oleg. You need to help him," Otilija said, startling him.

He shook his head to be sure he heard her correctly. Voldemars locked eyes with her and saw a strength in the steel blue that peered back at him. He knew she was a strong willed woman, but this was more than just will. It was courage.

"I'll be all right," she said, stiffening her lips and nodding.

Without a word, he agreed and hurried off to console his friend.

❧   ❧   ❧

At the precise spot on the beach where he had seen him earlier that night, Voldemars found Oleg, standing at attention, gazing out over the barely creased water. He calmly shuffled up to him, then laid his hand on his shoulder. Oleg remained perfectly still.

"I'm sorry, Oleg. I don't know what else I can say," Voldemars offered.

"Nothing," Oleg said curtly. His pruned lips trembled slightly, his eyes wandered out toward the water and grew vacant. He sighed deeply, expelling a breath noisily.

Voldemars raked his mind for the right thing to say. He tried to remember how ripped apart he felt when his own son had died, but the words he wanted to hear escaped him. He did remember that he wanted to hear something.

"I guess there's no reason for me to stay here now. I might as well volunteer for Brusilov's damned offensive!" Oleg said.

"I know how much you loved Natalya."

Voldemars swallowed his words when Oleg snapped his head and glared into his eyes.

"You aren't the right person to be talking to me now, especially not about what Natalya meant to me!" Oleg's words oozed venom.

His eyes seared deeply into Voldemars' soul, then ripped every bit of regret for his affair with Maria. He turned away and sauntered farther down the beach, leaving Voldemars alone.

❦   ❦   ❦

A torrential rainstorm rumbled through two days later and broke the sweltering heat. The heavy rain washed away the stale, lingering odor from perspiration soaked linens and left the air dry and clean in its wake. Gentle breezes ushered in a more pleasant aroma, a mix of sweet and delicately pungent perfumes wafting out of blooming poppy fields.

Voldemars wandered past the poppies and let the scent intoxicate him. He hadn't been treated to such a heady aroma since his days in Riga. The battle fronts he had lived in for four years had deteriorated to mud filled swamps that smelled like run over latrine pits. Rotted, decayed flesh was the only respite from the putridity. But here, Astrakhan, was an oasis of sight and smell.

He didn't believe Oleg would have carried through on his threat to return to the army, but not seeing him in two days worried Voldemars. He felt guilty that even though he was Oleg's closest friend, he was not there in his greatest time of need. He had to do something, so he started a search for him. At first he thought he might have simply hidden away somewhere to be alone. Inside and outside the compound, he asked everyone he saw at least twice if they had seen Oleg, but no one offered anything. Voldemars considered contacting command to see if he had headed off to the front, but he quickly realized that the army, in its convoluted way, would consider his absence desertion, especially since he was still the commanding officer.

Exhausted and depressed from a futile day of searching, Voldemars returned to his quarters as evening fell. Shuffling inside, he collapsed on his cot and tried to sleep. Even the cooler, more comfortable night did not soothe his worries. Exasperated after an hour of tossing, he sat up in his bed and pulled on his boots.

"Where are you going?" Otilija asked as she sat up and placed her hand on his back.

"To take a walk. Maybe it'll help me sleep."

"It's not your fault, you know."

Voldemars was silent for a moment. He let her words penetrate but felt that she was wrong. Oleg was always there when he needed some solace. Now, as if he had turned his back on him, he felt like he had betrayed the friendship they had nurtured at the front. He hiked up his boots, then grabbed his tunic and draped it over his shoulders.

"Maybe being alone for a few days is just his way of dealing with grief," Otilija said. "Everyone has their own way, Voldemars. Even you!" Her eyes were wide and emanated understanding.

Voldemars reached over, cupped his hand behind her head, and stared into her wide eyes. He returned a knowing glance before standing up.

"I can't help but think he needs someone to talk to. He's done so much for me. At the front, we were so close that—" Voldemars stopped, catching himself before he revealed his digression. "He was there for me at the hospital, when I needed someone. If he needs me now, and I know he does, I have to find him. I owe it to him."

"Then go find him," Otilija said softly as he walked out of the barracks.

Voldemars continued out the door, then stiltedly walked out of the compound. All the way to the quiet, shushing beach, he tried to remember any place he had not looked, but none came to mind. He reached the exact spot where he and Oleg had argued and sat down in the warm sand. He dug his heels into the fine grains, propped his elbows on his knees, and gazed out over the water.

Thoughts cascaded through his mind as the waves washed upon the shore. He remembered how he had felt when he finally accepted that Maria was dead, but then realized how much different that must have been from what Oleg was feeling. He tried to imagine how he might have felt if Otilija had died when his child was born. A shiver shot through his spine as he recalled how devastating enough his baby's death was.

"Mind if I join you," a hushed voice said through the darkness.

"Oleg!" Voldemars spun and stood but saw nothing.

He opened his eyes wider and stared into the darkness until finally, within arms-length, Oleg appeared. Relief surged through Voldemars' veins.

"How are things?" Oleg's mouth hinted a weak smile. He lifted his arms, then rested his open hands on Voldemars' shoulders.

"Where the hell have you been?"

"I guess I need to apologize for being such an ass," Oleg offered humbly.

"I can't say that it wasn't deserved."

"I can. I'm sorry, old friend."

Voldemars inspected Oleg, his head bowed as if he was a boy being punished. He then started an infectious chuckle which sparked a giggle from Oleg as well.

"Well then, tell me, where the hell have you been? Christ, I was starting to wonder if you ran off for the front!"

"The front?" Oleg laughed, then turned and walked toward the water. He stopped short of the creeping sea, then stood silently and gazed out over the rippling black cover. "You really want to know?"

"Yes, tell me. I searched everywhere. Twice! And I still couldn't find you."

Oleg bowed his head. He slowly turned back to Voldemars with a straight, serious expression. "I went someplace I haven't been in ten years. I went to church and I prayed. And you know, now I realize how ridiculous that was."

"For two days?"

"I didn't expect to end up there, I just did," Oleg rambled, his eyes vacantly prophetic. "After all the pushing my father did, making me go to church and bare my soul, I vowed I would never go back. But there I was! Just like I was a little boy again, twenty years ago, head bowed, hands folded, and in such a stupor that I didn't even know what to say. Hell, I don't even remember why I went there."

"If it made you feel better, why question the motive. It served the purpose, didn't it?"

Oleg turned his head. Puzzlement contorted his face. "And now I am talking about going to church to another atheist! Isn't that supreme irony!"

Oleg slipped out a loud belly laugh. Voldemars could not contain his either, and he guffawed so loud the echo resonated back over the water.

"But I did come to accept that nothing will bring her back." Oleg suddenly grew serious. "And as I think about what you were trying to tell me, I understand, perhaps there is a future for my Ukraine."

Oleg stopped for a deep breath. He shuffled his feet, then gazed back at Voldemars.

"I listened," Oleg said. "For once I listened closely to the people. I heard everything about how much turmoil there is in Russia, and I heard from some friends exactly what you had intended to say. The movement is not dead. It's regrouping!"

"And I remember an old friend telling me once to let go of the past once you've grieved," Voldemars added.

Oleg smiled. "You must have some intelligent friends."

"I do, and I'm damn lucky I still have them."

Telmeni

16 October 1916

*J*anis coaxed his rocker into motion and pulled a tattered envelope from his coat pocket. He puffed quickly through his pipe
and let a series of smoke rings rise up over his head as he looked out
over his wilted, frostbitten fields. The streaks of white ice crystals
appeared beautifully painted on each leaf and stalk of grass. Everywhere the bright morning sun had crept, swirling steam clouds
wisped toward the sky like slender white snakes.

He glanced back at the letter in his hand. Romans' characteristically squared and precisely formed Cyrillic script addressed the envelope simply with 'Mr. Janis Vechi, Telmeni, Valmiera, Vidzeme.' The
corners were dog-eared and worn through in spots. Janis toyed with
the corners and wondered how many other jacket pockets this letter
had to have been stuffed into. Flipping up the collars on his coat, he
wormed deeper into his chair and slipped his finger through one of
the worn through places. Once open, he pulled out the letter, opened
it, and started reading.

∿

12 Sept 1916

Dearest Momma and Poppa,

I hope the method by which this letter was delivered did not disturb you. I have grown suspicious of the authorities and was concerned this letter would not get through, so I took extra precautions to ensure that it would get to you. The Bolshevik movement seemingly grows in strength by the day, and I have heard that all regular mail is read before it even leaves Moscow. Ever since the Bolsheviks uncovered and thwarted the Okhrana's covert plans for mass arrests, the police distrust everyone, especially non-Russians like myself and Augusts.

The mood in Moscow is as gray and dismal as the early winter sky, apprehensive of what is to come. Thousands gather daily, protesting against Nicholas, his failing ministry, and the poor effort in the war. In so many of these crowds, people carry banners on posts-blood-red banners with slogans like 'bread, peace, and brotherhood.'

The people call these gatherings peaceful strikes, but it seems they always grow controversial and escalate into horrible, violent riots when the officials get involved. Dragoons and cold-blooded Cossacks charge through them with sabers unsheathed, uncaring if they slice them to pieces or if their horses trample the life out of them. In the aftermath, hundreds of broken and bleeding bodies are carted off in wagons, lumped four and five high as if they were nothing more than sacks of potatoes. In the snow covered streets, rivers connect lakes of blood, gruesome reminders that law and order have deteriorated into what seems nothing more than anarchy.

I must apologize for the vile images I have portrayed here, but I feel that you need to know precisely what is going on here to understand how I feel.

Cannons rumbling in the distance shattered the morning's peacefulness and drew Janis' attention south. He squinted and peered as far as the clarity of the morning allowed and saw faint wisps of black smoke weave skyward from the horizon. The image was punctuated by a tremor which shuddered the house.

"They've been at it for five days now," he mumbled to himself. "I hope the Latvian regiments can hold them off until Ulmanis can get some reinforcements."

Kristine burst through the door, stumbling onto the porch as the door slammed against the side of the house. With her bulging eyes fixed on the rising smoke, she nervously wiped her hands on a kitchen towel.

"They're getting closer, aren't they?" she said, a tremble in her voice. "The ground shakes more, don't you think? Those guns seem so much louder today."

"It's just the crispness of the morning. Sound carries much farther than usual in this weather."

"Then how far away are they?" she muttered, her nervous fidgeting growing worse. She edged closer to her husband, not taking her eyes off the horizon.

"We'll be safe for another month, maybe a bit longer." Janis puffed through his pipe pensively and let a series of smoke rings rise over his head. The rich aroma of the smoke hid the reek rising from the quickly defrosting plants.

"Maybe we should consider moving up north. Edwards says that we can stay with him in—"

"No!" Janis interrupted sternly. "We will not be forced from Telmeni! Not by the Russians! Not by the Germans! Not by anybody! This is our home, Kristine, and that it will remain."

Appearing shocked by her husband's sudden outburst, Kristine stared agape at his blushed face. His draws on the pipe increased, leaving a growing cloud over the porch. His eyes grew cold and adamant. Stifling tears, she inhaled deeply, nodded, then turned and shuffled back into the house without uttering another word.

Janis glanced back at the smoke rising up in the distance and drew repeatedly on his pipe. But when nothing but a cold, acrid taste filled his mouth, he took the pipe out and stared at the bowl. Discovering what his mouth and tongue had already told him, he simply shrugged and slipped the mouthpiece back between his teeth and glanced down at Romans' letter.

The handwriting where he had left off grew unusually sloppy. Janis read on.

I must apologize for the vile images I have portrayed here, but I feel that you need to know precisely what is going on here to understand how I feel. I don't know how much longer Augusts and I will be able to stay in Moscow. Life itself becomes more difficult by the day with all the tension in the streets. I am finding it impossible to even go out to school without being accosted by some Bolshevik soliciting his propaganda or badgering me to join in their protests. Sometimes, even the students protest, leaving the classes empty except for the few of us who are here to learn. Then there is no school at all, and once canceled, we have to fend for ourselves to get through the picket lines and get home.

As you can tell by what I've written so far, the health of Russia as a country is as poor as a city plagued with typhus. Talk about a violent takeover continues in the streets, challenged by Dragoons on a daily basis. Kerensky has all but taken over the Duma, sometimes it seems he rules the country as well. I have heard Nicholas is at the front, and Czarina Alexandra has lost control, as well as any respect. Some queer monk named Rasputin seems to have her spellbound. She is not strong enough, nor it seems wise enough to control the Duma, the ministry, and this odd man she claims to be her personal messenger from God.

I have heard some reports which indicate there are many casualties at all of our battle fronts, but with all the strikes going on, obtaining good information is virtually impossible. I pray that Voldemars has written and let you know that at least he has been spared the bludgeoning it seems this war continues to inflict...

Janis dropped the letter into his lap and sighed deeply. He knew what was happening with Romans, Edwards, and Augusts. But he had not received a single word from either Voldemars or Oleg since Oleg's letter a year ago. Tears welled in Janis' eyes as he wondered why.

The resistance movement had no news from that part of the world. The official word was that the war against Germany was proceeding well, but the unofficial news carried back was that the effort was failing miserably. The rumors ranked desertions in greater numbers than casualties.

Maybe I should be pleased that I haven't received any official word, Janis mused. At least I know that means he is probably still alive.

"Morning, Janis!"

Janis gasped, startled by Oskars as he clomped up the steps.

"Have you ever seen such a clear day? I don't think I've ever seen the sky so blue," Oskars said.

"Christ, you scared the life out of me!" Janis squeezed the words out as a sudden twinge in his chest sent a tingling quiver through his right shoulder. A painful pricking tingled in his hand, growing more like needles by the second. He slacked his jaw and struggled to suck in air, but it seemed he could not draw in enough to satiate his urge. Panicked, he forcefully expelled what remained in his chest, then rolled his eyes and tried again. Just a wheeze. The stabbing in his chest grew excruciating. The more he pulled in, the more it hurt.

"Janis, are you all right?" he heard Oskars say, but felt helpless to answer.

He felt Oskars' hands shaking his shoulders, but he remained limp.

"Damn it, Janis, say something!"

He felt frozen. Nothing moved. His arms were as limp and weak. His feet felt like they were nailed to the porch. He wanted to call out, but no sound emerged. He could feel his mouth groping and his eyes rolling, but his chest felt as if it were strapped in place, too tight to breathe, too stiff to exhale.

Suddenly, as quickly as it had hit, the tremor subsided. Janis threw his head back and breathed in as deeply as he could. His jaw wide, he pulled even when the air stopped coming in, hoping for just one more wisp to relieve the gasping feeling.

Satiation trickled down his head and through his chest. He drew in another lung full of air. The stabbing pain subsided to just a stitch.

"Voldemars! Jesus, I've got to get Kristine," he heard Oskars squeak.

"No!" Janis thrust his hand out and clamped onto Oskars wrist. His hand still tingled, but nothing like it had before. "Don't get her. I'll be all right. It's just a twinge."

"Talk about scaring the life out of somebody!" Oskars exhaled explosively.

"I've had it before," Janis mumbled. "I probably just overworked myself this morning."

"Hell, for a minute you looked like a damned ghost!" Oskars' voice still trembled. His wide eyes remained fixed on Janis, as he grabbed a chair and dragged it across the wooden planks. He sat down, plunged his hand into his coat, and after fumbling for a minute, pulled out a crumpled pack.

"Cigarette?" he offered.

Janis eked out a brief, weak smile, then declined with a wave. He reached over to his stool and offered a small box of matches to Oskars. After worming a hand rolled cigarette into the corner of his mouth, Oskars took the matches and quickly lit the knotted end. After sucking in a full breath, he leaned back and blew out a blue cloud which hung right above his head.

"Are you sure you're all right?" Oskars asked.

"I'm fine," Janis said softly, finally starting to breath easier. "So, tell me, what news do you bring? I can't believe you just happened to be taking a walk in this direction."

"It's that obvious?" Oskars tipped his head and chuckled. "I guess I'd never survive an Okhrana interrogation if I can't even hide anything from you!"

"No, I'd say you wouldn't." Janis grinned. "Something tells me you've been to Riga."

Oskars sucked on his cigarette, then released a stream into the air. His eyes widened and fell into a doleful stare aimed at the sky.

"Yes, I went last week. It's really quite disheartening."

"I've seen the sky filled with smoke so much that I wondered if it's even still there."

"It's not the same Riga you would remember, Janis. Even with the threat of the war spilling into the city, protesters still fill the streets."

"Where are they?" Janis asked. "I've heard them pounding away daily. Hell, sometimes it seems they're just over the ridge!"

"The Huns are close enough to smell them."

Janis dropped his head and shook it slowly.

"The Okhrana is so paranoid that even speaking German in Riga will get you arrested," Oskars said. "That's if you survive the beating the townspeople will give you!"

"That's not surprising. We're at war with Germany, you know." Janis leaned back and noticed wisps of smoke rising from Riga's direction.

"They're not getting any closer, believe it or not. It seems we're holding them off on the other side of the Daugava." Oskars coughed two thin clouds, then cleared his throat. "God knows how we're doing it, but we are!"

A rumble in the distance interrupted Oskars. They both looked up and watched the smoke rise from the ground like a filthy blanket.

"Did you hear Goldmanis got the Duma to relent?" Oskars said. "Our own provisional government has been given permission to form several Latvian regiments."

"From what? Hasn't every Latvian boy been conscripted into Nicholas' brigades?"

Janis suddenly realized what Oskars had said. Latvian regiments. Hope twitched in his heart that Voldemars had been reassigned.

"Do you remember Aleksandrs?" Oskars asked.

Janis nodded and rolled his eyes, still evaluating the possibility of Voldemars coming home.

"I swear some of those faces I saw marching off to battle couldn't have been much older than him. But by some miracle, they're doing it. They're actually holding off the Germans!"

"For how long?"

Oskars looked out to the horizon. His eyes glassed over. "Who knows. All we can do is hope it's long enough."

Moscow, Russia
16 March 1917

$\mathcal{R}$omans turned up his coat collar and cinched it closed over his white silk ascot, trying to keep the bitter air from slipping behind his scarf and stinging his bare neck. He bowed his head and used his wide-brimmed hat to fend off the damp wind. The knifing chill, though, continued to seep through his overcoat and bite at his exposed skin. The whole winter had been like this, Romans thought. So bitter and so unbearably cold that he wondered how any of the people had survived the winter in the streets.

Stiltedly he walked along the sidewalk with a cautiously measured pace, wary of anyone who peered his way. This bloodless revolution, he thought, at least as compared to what he read about the French Revolution, had driven Moscow and the rest of Russia into lawless anarchy. The provisional government plodded along in their creation of post-Czarist Russia, factories continued to sit idle, and schools remained closed. The human toll, the already block long bread lines, continued to grow, while unsavory packs of society's dregs wandered freely and ruled the streets.

Romans realized what he was experiencing could be the most significant historical event of modern times. He was witnessing a great experiment in modern societal change. Every fabric of the old paternalistic culture of Czarist Russia was ripped away, as if that action alone was to make things better for everyone. The result, though, was a country left in tatters and a government mired in lethargy. Endless debates languished as thousands of people fell to the bottom of society within months. With the jobless and homeless populous growing and becoming more and more helpless by the day, central control of the country's direction ground to a halt, leaving the people aimless.

At the moment, though, he did not care. He was a scientist, and the only effect he felt was that his education had ground to a halt.

"Long live the revolution!" a voice bellowed out from over one of what seemed hundreds of soot-belching, burning barrels.

"All power to the Soviet!" crowed another of the dirt-smudged faces, part of the huddle around the barrels.

"Don't you see what infection your revolution has given you?" Romans mumbled, angry that the revolt had disrupted his life so drastically.

As he hastened his steady pace, hoping to prevent being accosted, Romans fleetingly studied the collection of ornery people on the street. He knew pack dogs were unpredictable, and so similar seemed the street people to them that he imagined seeing dog-like features on their faces. But he also saw an eerie emotional paradox which seemed to etch forced smiles onto long and worried faces. Wide, hopeful eyes were glazed and frozen into endless stares. The collective, impetuous rocking from side to side seemed more appropriate for an asylum than the freedom of public streets. The red tattered scarf tied onto their sleeves seemed worn more in fear of not being a part of the crowd than pride in their spontaneous revolution.

The sudden clattering of a single worn, oil-starved engine startled Romans as it turned onto the road. He jumped off the road, concerned that the driver had been preserved by vodka. As the truck approach, weaving from curb to curb, torn, blood-red pennants propped up on each fender flapped as wildly as the pervasive fanaticism throughout the past month. Finally, the truck chattered by, leaving a spewed legacy of blue, oily smoke from its tailpipe.

"Fools!" Romans mumbled, shaking his head. "They're all fools!"

"It's silk, isn't it?"

Romans froze, startled by the gentle female voice. Immediately, he was captured by the allure of the woman's red hair. As she fondled his ascot, letting the fabric slip through her fingers, her blatantly suggestive motions captured his attention.

"It is silk!" Her green eyes widened and danced as she ran her fingers over the white ascot again.

She wrapped her arm around Romans, then let her hand slip over the satiny smooth cloth again.

"Would you like some company, young man? I'm Marina, and I think I could do a little something for you, if you have a little something for me!" she said while she stroked the ascot.

Romans flushed. Despite the biting wind, he felt hot. He glanced down and saw Marina's ample breasts pushing up into the opening in her coat. Temptation trickled through his veins at first, then seemed to rush rampant as he entertained the thought of being with her.

"How much?" he said, catching a whiff of her perfume, a heavy lavender aroma, obviously enough to linger even in the stiff wind.

"What do you have?" she coyly replied, then winked. Her smile blossomed as her hand slipped off the ascot, then stroked Romans' wind-burned cheek.

"I only have a couple of rubles," Romans said, and felt his legs quiver. "But if that's enough, I'd be—"

"That's enough," Marina interrupted, then latched tightly onto Romans' arm. "I've got a room down the street. I share it with Olga, but if we get there before she does, its ours!"

Romans felt his blood rush through his veins as her free hand slipped off his face and ran down his coat. She smiled invitingly as she let her fingers walk across his trousers, hesitating long enough for Romans to feel his erection grow. He urged her on toward the room. Obediently, she complied.

Once they stepped into the doorway and out of the wind, Romans recoiled, suddenly smacked by the stench of stale, smoke filled air, tainted by urine. Marina quivered, as if shaking off the chill, then leered at Romans as she muscled the heavy door closed against the howling wind. Taking his hand, she led him down the narrow hallway over creaking floorboards and stopped at the last door. She turned to Romans, then fished out her keys from between her breasts. Jingling the keys together, she unlocked all three locks on the door, then pushed it open.

Romans peeked inside and quickly scanned the room. A tiny, worn, faded sofa rested against one wall, and an unmade bed covered the other. On the end table next to the bed was an open book, which even at this distance, he could instantly identify as a textbook. He jumped as Marina closed and locked the door behind them.

Intrigued, Romans shuffled across the room for a closer look. As he neared he saw cut away diagrams of plants and a hybrid cross table.

Romans turned around with the intent of asking about the book, but startled when he saw that Marina had slipped open her full-length coat and posed invitingly for him, virtually naked. Her breasts stood out, her nipples erect.

"You look surprised," she said in a soft, sultry voice. As she slowly strutted toward him, she exaggerated a swing with her hips.

Romans glanced at the book, then back to Marina. His jaw dropped open as he tired to reconcile what was in front of him.

"What's the matter? You've never seen a woman?"

"Uh, no, I mean yes. I have. It's just," he stuttered, then pointed to the book. "I'm kind of surprised at the book. You're studying biology, I mean botany?" he finally blurted. He could not help but stare at Marina's pointed nipples.

"Why does that surprise you?" she asked as she rubbed against him.

She stepped back and unbuttoned his coat, then swept her hands under the fabric and over his shoulders. Romans felt the cold air hit his neck and arms as his coat fell to the floor.

"It doesn't." He tried to collect his thoughts, turning back to the book. "It's just that you're a whore, I mean a prostitute."

Marina instantly stopped her advance and grew cold.

"Oh? You didn't think whores could do anything but fuck? Is that it?" She dropped to the bed, facing Romans and leaned back, pushing her breasts forward. "Do you think I'm doing this because I want to?"

Romans stood frozen, gaping at Marina's half-naked body. He glanced toward the book, then back to her, now more surprised than aroused. Unable to think of anything to say, he remained silently gawking.

"Listen, mister," she said bluntly, leaning forward. She crossed her arms, covering her breasts, and sighed loudly.

"I don't have any money," she said, glaring at Romans. "All I have is this room, some clothes, and what you see in front of you." Her fiery glare could have melted all the ice on the streets. Her lips pursed tightly as she crossed her legs.

"Do you think I enjoy being a slut?" she asked, leaving Romans with the impression she was waiting for an answer.

"Well, if you do, you're sadly mistaken!" she continued. "I'm only doing what I have to do to survive! You rich bastards can buy anything you want, but those of us who don't have any money, well, let's just say we barter what we can. If I can get two rubles for a quick one, well, I'll take it!"

"But the book?" Romans finally blurted.

"I've always liked botany, and when this damn revolution is over, I'm going back to University! That is, if it's still there," Marina snipped. She hopped up from the bed and walked past Romans without so much as a glance. She picked up her coat, then wrapped it around her goose-bumped flesh. "Listen, this isn't going to work right now."

"What about your parents? Do they know you're—"

"They're dead." Marina sternly crossed her arms in front of her. "Listen, I said this isn't going to work, so why don't you just get the hell out of here, and we'll call it even, all right?"

She stomped over to the door and unlocked it. As she did, Romans rummaged through his pockets and took out all of his money and threw it on the bed.

"I don't want your fucking money! I just told you that!"

"You need it more than I do," Romans said.

He picked his coat up and put it on. He walked up to Marina, then cupped his hand under her chin and stared at her.

"I don't know why such a beautiful woman has been dealt such a pitiful fate," he whispered, then stepped into the hallway.

He turned for one last glance before plunging into the street, and as he did, he noticed Marina's small but sincere smile. He stopped for a moment, debating whether he should go back to Marina, but then realized he had done what he had to do. Smug that his morals had remained stronger than his urges, he let the door slam behind him and headed out to the street with a hastened pace.

Instantly, Romans grew nervous. He noticed the line of burning barrels crowded with shivering people. Each of them seemed to be staring at him with disapproving glances, but he feigned them off, knowing they were mistaken. He quickly strutted past them, then turned and headed along a side street he always used as a short-cut.

He had not traveled more than two blocks when a blur leapt at him from a dark alley. Air immediately wheezed out of Romans' chest as the body hit him broadside, then fell on top of him. He hit the ground hard and lay stunned for a moment, but then quickly scrambled to his hands and knees and looked up. Two surly looking, dirty faces leered at him. One was at least ten years older than he was, and the other, a boy even younger than Romans.

"Give me your money!" demanded the older man. He bared his teeth in a sinister grin.

"I don't have any money," Romans mumbled, starting to stand up.

"Fuckin' liar!" the man yelled.

He swung his foot at Romans' legs and cut them out from underneath him. Romans fell back to the icy sidewalk in a heap.

"All you fuckin' bastards have money!"

Before Romans could utter a word in his defense, the thief swung his foot again, this time catching Romans' ribs. As he felt air rush from his mouth, Romans winced, rolling to his side.

"I told you, I have no money!" Romans protested, lifting his head out of the urine stained snow. He opened his eyes and saw a worn boot sole only inches from his face and approaching fast. Before he could cover, the heel slammed into his head. He heard his nose crack. Searing, stinging pain shot through him as blood spurted and dribbled into his cupped hands.

Incapacitated by the pain, Romans rocked into a prone position and covered his face. He felt hands rummage through his pants and coat pockets. Instead of fighting, he stifled his urge to resist and let the muggers discover what he had told them all along.

"The fucker's broke!" he heard the older man's gravelly voice spit.

A foot kicked Romans' thigh hard.

"Take the fuckin' scarf, Ivan! I can at least get laid for that!" the older man cackled.

No sooner than he heard the old man's voice, Romans felt his ascot slice into his neck. Cold air stung at the wound, then rushed into the opening in his coat. Still resisting his compulsion to fight back, Romans remained on the frigid ground, hands over his nose, and waited for the thieves to leave.

When he heard the crunching footsteps move off and fade, headed back toward the city, he peeked up and watched the backs of the two muggers turn and disappear.

"Bastards!" Romans mumbled as he pushed himself up to his knees. His head spun and throbbed wildly, twisting his stomach into painful nausea, but he knew he had to get some help as quickly as he could. He rose to his feet, and as his knees wobbled with wide swings, he stumbled into a lamp post and wrapped his arms around the cold metal. Gasping for air, he spat out a clump of blood, then rested his aching head against the soothing metal. Gingerly he touched his nose, which felt like it had been smashed and now covered half of his face. The bleeding had stopped, but blood crusted on his thin mustache pulled at the hairs.

Romans cinched up his coat as tightly as he could then, stumbling and weaving at first, started walking. Grimacing through the pain in his chest, he limped home.

❈   ❈   ❈

As Romans stumbled toward the porch he heard a door creak open.

"My word, Augusts! Look at him!" he heard Maria cry.

Romans glanced up and saw a blurry image scurry toward him just as he felt his legs buckle. He winced grotesquely as he fell to the steps in a lump.

A soft, warm body helped him up, then coddled him as she helped him into the house.

Romans felt warm air slap him in the face, instantly spurring lightheadedness. His head suddenly spun faster. He felt nausea knot his stomach. His legs buckled again. Through the corner of his eye, he noticed Augusts' blurry image approaching. He mustered as much strength as he could to stay upright but fell toward the floor before Augusts was close enough to catch him.

"Augusts, help me! I can't hold him!" Maria cried as she felt Romans slipping from her grip.

"Christ, look at him!" Augusts muttered, slipping his hands underneath Romans' armpits.

He lifted enough to get a good view of Romans' face, then inspected his wounds momentarily before carrying Romans to the sofa. With Maria's help, Augusts struggled with his limp brother and laid him on the cushions.

"His nose is broken," Augusts assessed, propping up his head. "I can't tell if anything else is though. Christ, is he a mess! Damn those bastards! Why the hell do they have to do this to an innocent boy!"

"I think you know why," Maria bluntly replied.

"But he's just a boy."

"And he's old enough to know better!" Maria waved her index finger in a scolding manner. "He may be your younger brother, but he's no longer that innocent boy you brought to Moscow. You know what the city is like."

"But that's no excuse."

"And he's been told what to wear and what not to wear!" Maria continued relentlessly. "He should know better than to boorishly walk the streets in such good looking clothes. You know what those people are like. They'll do what they need to do to survive!"

Augusts stopped cleaning dried blood from Romans' thin mustache, turned and stared at his wife. She looked as Russian as anyone. Her steely gray eyes were the softest feature of her stern looking face, and her body seemed more solidly proportioned than many men.

"You think they're right with what they're doing, don't you?" he said. "You condone this damned seething madness, taking from those who have more? Do you forget that these were the people that begged for this pitiful anarchy? These were the people that screamed for liberty, equality, and brotherhood! They abandoned their farms when the harvest needed to be taken in. They walked off their jobs. These are the people that took my job away from me. And now they scream that they're justified in taking anything they want, including a few rubles from an innocent boy, regardless of who they hurt? I'm sorry, Maria, but they got what they deserved!" He angrily glowered at Maria, but as Romans stirred, he redirected his attention.

Romans fluttered his swollen eyelids, then cracked open his eyes. Augusts' grimace melted into a grin for his brother. Romans winced as he tried to smile back.

"I guess I shouldn't have gone to school today," he muttered, raising his hand to cover his eyes.

"Maybe it was a good thing after all," Augusts said, sighing heavily. "Maybe it's what I needed to finally convince me it's time for us to go home."

Romans watched Maria come to Augusts' side and peer down into his swollen face. Tears welled in her eyes as her lips quivered into a brief smile.

"You're right," Maria said, her voice trembling. "There's nothing left here for us. We should go."

"Do you know—" Augusts began.

"If the trains are still running?" Maria interrupted. "I believe there's a train to Riga tonight. I'll go upstairs and pack our things."

Augusts nodded. Maria turned and headed for the stairs. He turned back to Romans and continued cleaning the blood from his fine mustache.

"I heard what she said, Augusts, and I agree with her," Romans mumbled through the washcloth. He spit out a clot of blood. "This isn't what the people expected when Nicholas abdicated."

"Oh?" Augusts recoiled. "And when did the scientist become interested in politics and society?"

"Today, I guess," Romans groaned as he sat up. His nose throbbed mercilessly as he talked, but he continued anyway. "I met someone who opened my eyes to the real state of affairs in this country."

"Am I safe in assuming he wasn't the same one that almost closed them?" Augusts quipped.

"In a matter of speaking, it was. I think what we perceive is much different than what the street people do."

"Perhaps."

"Christ, this aches! Do you think some tea would help?" Romans asked, hanging his head as he gently pressed each spot the thugs had hit him.

"It may," Augusts noted as he helped his brother from the sofa.

As they shuffled toward the kitchen, Romans staggered a bit but was still able to move on his own.

"What I sensed in the city was that everyone is just so consumed with what has happened, as if Nicholas' overthrow was a miracle of some sort."

Augusts helped Romans to the table, pulling out a chair for him to sit on while he prepared the tea.

"That may be true," Augusts noted as he clanged cups and saucers together. "But they also need to realize that history is rife with examples of how revolutions open the door for tyrants. The power obtained by single men after such a noble struggle tends to corrupt even the most well intentioned. If what I hear comes to bear, what we remember as Russia will be gone forever."

Augusts filled the cups from the samovar, then dropped the slotted tea spoons into the steaming water. Carefully balancing the cups, he shuffled across the floor and placed the tea in front of Romans.

"What have you heard?" Romans asked, tilting his head.

Augusts dropped a lump of poorly processed beet sugar into his cup and swirled the tea. He then leaned into the steam and whispered, "I hear Lenin is planning on returning to Russia."

"Lenin?" Romans' jaw dropped open. He felt his heart pound wildly in his chest. "Isn't he the Bolshevik that was exiled to Germany?"

Augusts somberly nodded.

"If he returns to power, what will happen to Voldemars if he's still in the army?"

"I don't want to know," Augusts said, his eyes glassy.

"Have you heard from Voldemars? Will he—" Romans trailed off.

"I think we have enough to worry about for our own lives," Augusts finally said. "I've never believed in miracles before, but if Voldemars is still in the army when Lenin returns, well, only God can help him."

Romans swallowed hard and let the steam filter through his blood caked nose.

Moscow
22 March 1917

"Christ, it's already March, and there isn't even a hint of spring," Augusts lamented as he trudged back from the center of Moscow, foiled again in his attempt to get any transportation out.

This winter in particular seemed endless. Although the days grew longer, the sun remained absent the whole week, hidden behind a persistent low, gray overcast layer of clouds. The bitter northerly winds continued battling with the damp wind, dusting the streets with icy snow which stung like hundreds of bees and seemed to grow more frigid by the day.

Three blocks from home, he noticed the dark, looted brick buildings where linen and china factories used to pour out products. They remained empty, silent, and as disheveled as if they had been the center of a destructive war. Broken down doors, half removed from their hinges, and broken windows, shattered by rocks thrown in hatred, stood as a reminder of the long winter of discontent.

From the side entrance of one factory, once used for a loading dock, two men emerged, furtively carrying two broken chairs. It was obvious that the seats were destined for cremation in one of the hundreds of barrels multiplying like smoldering mushrooms along Moscow's streets. The men startled, freezing when they spotted Augusts looking at them. But without an apparent second thought, they flashed sinister sneers and continued on with their thievery. Augusts simply turned away, shaking his head, and continued his journey home.

As he approached the porch, Maria rushed out to greet him with only a ragged sweater draped over her shoulders. He tried to hide his disappointment, but his eyes were too expressive. Her face withered from the joy of seeing him to sharing in his failure.

"I'm sorry, Maria. The Soviet controls the trains, and they aren't letting anyone without government association on them. I even tried to get us on a cattle car."

He threw his hands up in disgust. He hung his head, wrapped an arm around Maria, and walked her back into the house.

"How is Romans?" Augusts asked as he removed his scarf and coat.

"His swelling is down," she murmured, closing the door behind her. "He says he can finally breathe through his nose again."

"Well, that's good news at least. Could I have some tea?"

He sighed heavily as he dropped his coat on the sofa, then absently shuffled by her and headed into the kitchen. Maria dutifully followed, then moved to the steaming copper samovar.

"I don't think we have any fresh tea left, Augusts," Maria mumbled as she fished through the cabinet. "I think we have some old leaves, but I'm afraid it will be bitter."

"That's fine," Augusts sighed and fell into his chair.

Maria crumbled two very pale green leaves into a spoon, then snapped it closed and dropped it into the cup. She swirled the spoon as she brought the tea to the table, then placed the cup in the small spot exposed between Augusts' folded arms and chest. As he slowly wrapped his fingers around the cup, she sat down across from him.

"What do you think will happen to us?" she asked.

"I don't know. I wish I did," Augusts answered with a drone to his voice. He flared his nostrils and let the swirling wisps bathe his frozen membranes. The pungent odor stung his nostrils, but he was too tired to pull his head back.

"There's no food left," Maria lamented. Her eyes grew wide and expressive. "Here or in the city. Matilda says young children are dying, crying in want for even a tiny crust of stale bread."

Augusts' blue eyes glazed over. His mind recalled what he had seen just minutes ago; mothers weeping as they stood in endless food lines, rivulets of tears chapping crooked lines on their already raw cheeks. Misery and hunger seemingly took turns heinously etching pain onto their soiled faces. In their arms were motionless bundles, wrapped tightly as if being offered for some pagan ritual sacrifice. Augusts quivered, shaking free the gruesome, lingering image.

"We've got to go now. We can't wait any longer." Augusts suddenly vaulted up from his chair. "We'll go on foot if we have to, Maria, but we must go now!"

Without any emotion, Maria stood and nodded in agreement. Augusts watched her leave, then settled deep into his chair.

I hope I am correct, he thought. He sipped his tea and combed his mind for other alternatives, but he quickly realized there were none.

❧   ❧   ❧

An hour later, Augusts, Maria, and Romans plodded along the wide gauge train tracks, headed into a damp west wind. Bundled underneath worn, ragged coats, they carried small sacks containing what few of their more pleasant memories of their life in Moscow they could carry. As they reached the edge of the city, the landscape changed from disheveled, looted buildings to a cold, desolate tundra. By Augusts' estimation, they were at least a mile out of Moscow when he heard the distinct chugging of an approaching steam train.

While Romans and Maria turned to look, Augusts quickly scanned the brush along side the tracks.

"There!" he said, pointing to a thick growth. "We'll hide in there."

"Why do we have to hide?" Romans asked.

Augusts remained silent, and without even acknowledging Romans, continued to lead toward the brush.

"We haven't done anything wrong!" Romans insisted. "I think if we stay on the tracks, we may get them to slow down. We might even be able to convince them we're no threat and get a ride."

"Augusts means well, Romans," Maria explained softly while she urged him to follow. "There's no telling whether those running the train would or would not help us. It may seem strange, but the safest thing to do is to mistrust everyone."

Romans fell silent and instead of continuing to debate, followed Augusts and Maria toward the brush.

Augusts stopped at a small entrance which seemed to have been cut out at the base of the thicket. He searched around for a moment, then dropped to his stomach and crawled into the hole. Stiff, dead briars grabbed and tugged at his arms as he wormed into the hut. He reached the center and noticed that there was an area cleared enough for two men to comfortably sit down. The stale smell of old vodka was pervasive, but he saw no evidence of bottles.

Convinced it was safe, he crawled back out, then herded Maria and Romans into the hole. Huddled together for warmth, they quietly waited until the train slowly chugged by. To be sure no one would see them, Augusts listened closely for the last car to clack by, leaving silence. When the engine's noise faded to a dull rumble, he motioned for Maria and Romans to wait, then flopped to his stomach and crawled back outside.

When he poked his head out of the thicket, he heard a rifle bolt engage, loud enough that he knew it was next to him. Augusts froze, closed his eyes, and held his breath for what seemed minutes. Nothing. Cautiously, he tipped his head up, but a cold metal barrel bumped the top of his head. Swallowing hard, he opened his eyes and stared in front of him. A single pair of knee high valenki stood less than a foot from his face, close enough that he could smell the man's rancid, unwashed feet.

"Escaping from Moscow?" a gravelly voice asked.

Augusts remained stiff, not wanting to test the man's intentions. He breathed slowly and shallowly to be sure he would not move any closer to the ice-cold barrel.

"Not a wise thing to do," the man mumbled in a less threatening but still demeaning tone.

Augusts felt the barrel move off his head as the man cackled loudly.

"They got rail police, you know. Can't feed anyone in the city, but the bastards try to keep you from leaving. Makes no sense to me. How about you?"

"No, no sense," Augusts quickly mumbled. He breathed easier when the man's words seemed to be a little more affable.

"Mind if I come out and sit up?" Augusts asked submissively.

"Go ahead, but don't make any quick moves or I'll have to shoot you.

Augusts wiggled out, kneeled, and looked up. A wide set of yellowed teeth grinned widely at him. Behind them, a scraggly salt and pepper beard and smeared mud splotches covered his face. His head was covered with fur from a poorly skinned rabbit, and his coat, stolen from at least two wolves, was unskillfully sewn together.

"So, what you running from?" the man asked again.

"We, I just did not want to be seen by the train," Augusts said. Still wary, he kept his eyes trained on the man's weapon.

"We? You got more in there?" His grin grew wider.

Augusts realized his blunder. "My wife and brother. We're Latvians on our way—"

"Latvians? Oh! Foreigners then?" The man cackled loudly. "So, you mean to tell me the revolution caught you off guard, and now you're trying to sneak out and save your skins?"

Augusts swallowed hard. "In a manner of speaking, yes."

"Then, you got money, eh?" The old man's voice raised in pitch as he scratched his beard. "Hmm. Well, you used my house here while the train went by, so I'd say I'm due some rent!"

The man swooped his rifle toward Augusts and again pointed at his head.

"We don't have anything," Augusts protested.

"Hey, you two in there!" he yelled past Augusts, obviously unconvinced. "Come out here and give me your money!"

He stepped back, maintaining his bead on Augusts, who did not move a muscle. With a distrusting frown, the man glared at Augusts.

"I'm not going to be surprised, am I?"

"No," Augusts quietly said as Maria poked her head out. She craned her neck and sternly frowned at the dirty faced man. As soon as she moved out of the way, Romans followed, standing up as he squirmed out of the brush.

"Got in a fight, young man, eh? Who won?" The old man's eyes widened when he saw Romans' swollen face. He quickly switched his attention back to Augusts. "Looks to me here that you gotta know a few things, and I can see that you three aren't cut out to be wilderness types. Give me your money, and I'll give you a little advice about these parts."

Maria plunged her hand into her sack, took out five coins, and handed them to the man. He snapped his hand closed and brought the coins to his face.

"Now that's more like it!"

"It's all we have," Maria insisted, staring at the man with her stern gray eyes. "Now, as you were saying—" Maria stopped, keeping her eyes locked on the man's trigger finger.

"There's a farm about five miles down the rails." He lowered his gun and pointing west. "They've got some horses. I think you'll need them if you intend to get to where you want to go."

"Latvia," Maria politely said.

"Ah, yes, Latvia. Well, you won't make it without horses," the old man repeated, "not without freezing your asses off! Now get the hell out of here, or you'll never make it."

The man cackled again, shaking the coins in his half-closed fist. He waved the barrel of his rifle, motioning Romans to move away from his hideout's entrance. Once Romans stepped away, the old man plunged head first into the hole and disappeared.

From inside the brush, his gravely voice yelled, "I said get the hell out of here! I don't want no rail police catching me because I'm talking to foreigners! Get out! Get out or I'll kill all three of you!"

Augusts, Maria, and Romans immediately responded.

❦   ❦   ❦

After they had traveled uneventfully for what seemed all day, even though only three hours had passed, Augusts spotted a farm to the north of the tracks, just as the old man had said. The land surrounding the barns was mostly enclosed by split-rail fencing, but horses were distinctly missing. Nor did he see any signs of life in the main farmhouse.

Augusts debated if he should even go see if there were horses. Without money, he realized he would have to steal one. Augusts quickly dashed the thought, concerned he was beginning to justify his own immoral actions like the petty thieves he despised.

"Let's go. I don't see anything," he quickly mumbled. "With a little luck, we should be across the border in a week."

"That's forty miles a day!" Romans grumbled as he pursed his lips. "Do you think we can keep that up, especially since we have no food?"

Maria flashed a stern glare at Romans, but her face suddenly twisted into a horrified gawk. The men turned quickly and looked in the same direction. Romans froze. His mouth fell open. Augusts swallowed hard to keep from vomiting. But even his gagging did not break his macabre interest in what he saw.

On the west side of the barn, unseen until they passed, lay three horses. Two had been butchered mercilessly. Rivulets of blood stained the snow, trailing from half-frozen puddles under the dismembered flanks. At the third carcass, two men hunched over the still steaming flanks, hacking at the meat with bloody knifes, ripping out chunks with bare, dripping hands. So consumed with their deed, the men did not even notice they were being watched.

"My God, what has this world come to!" Maria gasped. She turned her head and walked on with a hastened pace. Romans and Augusts gaped silently for only a moment longer, then quickly caught up with Maria.

"We will need to kill for food as well, Maria." Romans bluntly noted after they had walked silently for ten minutes. "It's survival. We can't go for a week without food, you know."

"I understand survival, young man!" Maria snapped as she turned and glared at Romans. "I'm not so naive as to believe we will make it to Latvia without needing to kill. But I have never believed it's necessary to murder animals which can serve as more than just an easy meal."

"Maybe that was their last hope for food?" Romans said.

Maria continued walking. "And do they stop at the horses? If they can justify killing their own transportation for food, for survival, what next?"

"Dogs."

"And when they're gone, will they just as easily justify killing each other? I'm sorry, Romans, I can not accept what is going on here! This is nineteen-seventeen, not the Dark Ages! We left our barbarism when we created societies. Condoning those actions now, regardless of the circumstance, is tantamount to returning to barbarism!"

Outwitted, Romans grew stiff-lipped and silent. It was bad enough that he had been out debated. Worse was that he was beaten by a woman.

Telmeni

25 May 1917

*R*omans sat cross-legged at the shore of Lake Bauzis and threw a flat stone across the wind-rippled surface. When the stone lost speed, making smaller and smaller jumps, he tried to remember the physical principles which combined to explain what was happening. Instead, Romans only recalled that the skipping stone was the basis for an entire hour's lecture by his physics instructor in Moscow.

"Old Professor Makarov," he sighed.

He had always been so immaculately groomed: his white shirt had no wrinkles, even down to his puffy sleeves and gold cuff-links; his black bow-tie always perfectly tied below his trimmed salt-and-pepper goatee; his trousers always had a crisp crease down the front of each leg. The image of Professor Makarov faded as Romans realized that when the school closed, he had probably become just another one of the destitute people of Moscow.

"Mind if I join you?" an unfamiliar asked.

Pain shot through Romans' stomach as he flopped over and peered in the voice's direction. He cringed for a second, but immediately jumped to his feet when he saw what appeared to be an olive green battle style uniform.

"Hell, I didn't mean to frighten you! You could have stayed on the ground. After all, I'm no Bolshevik," the boy almost sang. With long strides he walked toward Romans and looked him square in the face.

"Sveiki! I'm Aleksandrs Baronovs," He extended his hand.

Romans tentatively reached out his hand, which Aleksandrs immediately grasped and pumped vigorously. The boy's face beamed with a broad, sincere smile.

"What happened to you? Got in a fight or something?" Aleksandrs cringed as he studied Romans' face.

"Yeah, you could say that. Should I know you?" Romans said, studying Aleksandrs' features closely. He forced a sincere but confused smile. "You will have to pardon me, but you have me at a great disadvantage."

"Oh, in a matter of speaking, yes, you do know me. I know your father, Janis, and he says I'm going to be one of the new Strelnieks, one of the new heroes of our free and unified Latvia!" Aleksandrs' enthusiasm flowed unbridled.

Romans inspected Aleksandrs from the top of his matted brown hair to the bottom of his ragged edged trousers and untied boots. His uniform was stripped of any insignia which would identify its source. Romans shook his head and laughed softly.

"People have tried it before. It didn't work," Romans mumbled.

"This time it will!"

"And what makes you think it'll be any different this time?" he wryly asked.

"This time, we're ready," Aleksandrs humphed. He plopped on his buttocks, pulled his gangling legs toward him, and removed his boots. He started unwrapping long, dirty cloth strips from his feet. "Our leaders are strong. Ulmanis and Goldmanis are paragons. They've already formed a united Congress which unanimously voted to form a united Latvia."

"And what did Russia and Trotsky's provisional government say about that?" Romans asked cynically.

"Russia's in such turmoil that they aren't even paying attention to what we're doing! Lenin's back, you know. I really don't think Trotsky's too interested in us with Lenin preaching anarchy to anyone who will listen. It's like the revolution never ended. But whoever wins out, it really doesn't matter. After all, when they do finally wake up and see what we've done, we'll have enough recruits in the militia to defend ourselves against anybody!"

Romans recoiled, taken by surprise with the boy's knowledge of events inside of Russia. He cocked his head and watched Aleksandrs unwrap his feet and then wade into the water until his ankles were submerged. While Aleksandrs sloshed water onto his legs and danced around with his big feet, Romans imagined him as just another of the thousands of battered, defeated, young Russian soldiers he had seen on his journey back to Latvia. He remembered the trains which flocked back into their tumultuous homeland, carrying men and boys exhausted from a war they could not win. Their wounds begged for attention, poorly bandaged, ill-treated, and festering with infection. He watched hundreds drop in their tracks, too exhausted and weak to go any further. Romans sighed, wondering if Aleksandrs could imagine how horrible war really was. After all, he was only sixteen, and had never seen what really happened at the war fronts.

Aleksandrs waded onto the shore and then walked up to and sat next to Romans again. After he wiped his feet clean, he began wrapping the dirty linen back around them.

"Goldmanis has already called back all the Latvians serving in the Russian army, you know," Aleksandrs said. "For the defense against the Germans. It will be a glorious day when we are finally victorious!"

"Goldmanis has done what?" Romans asked, not believing what he had heard.

"He's called back all the Latvians—"

Romans frantically vaulted to his feet, interrupting Aleksandrs, then scurried up the hill toward the rye fields, stumbling it seemed with every other step but never totally losing his balance. As he reached the top of the hill, he rested only long enough to catch his breath, then started running through the rye fields toward the house.

"Poppa! Poppa, wait!" he yelled when he spotted his father, then scrambled as fast as he could toward him.

Janis turned when he heard his son's cry, then squinted and searched around until he saw Romans heading toward him. He stabbed his spade into the road, crossed his arms, and leaned on the handle.

"Poppa!" Romans' voice sounded like a whisper through his heavy panting as he caught up to his father. He stumbled forward as he stopped, put his hands on his knees, and stooped over to catch his breath.

"Must be something big to have you so excited," Janis mumbled, looking down at his gasping son. "Well, what's got you riled up?"

Craning his neck, Romans tried to talk through his gasping, "A boy, Aleksandrs Baronovs, do you know him?"

"Aleksandrs? Ah, yes. He's one of the youngsters that are trying to get into Goldmanis' Strelnieks." Janis smiled. "He must have said something good to get you into such a tizzy!"

"He said Goldmanis called all the Latvian soldiers back!" Romans gasped. His eyes sparkled as he looked up at his father. "Voldemars is coming home, then. Is that right?"

Janis' smile collapsed. He sucked in a deep breath through his mouth, then snorted it out his nose. Without uttering a single word, he snapped at his shovel. Grasping the handle, he yanked it out of the ground and headed back toward the barns.

Romans' jaw dropped open, stunned by his father's response. He thought for a moment, then scrambled after him. Reaching out as he closed the gap, he touched his father's shoulder.

"What's wrong, Poppa? What did I say?" he gasped, trying to keep pace with Janis.

Janis stopped without turning around. For a moment, he remained at attention, then slowly turned and glowered angrily into his son's innocent looking face.

"I'm sorry, Romans. Two years ago," Janis' voice cracked as tears welled up in his eyes. "Two years ago, I received a letter from a Captain Oleg Stativsky, a member of Voldemars' brigade. The letter said—" Janis' voice escaped him for a moment. He drew in a deep breath and held it for a moment. "The letter said that Voldemars had been caught in a gas attack. Stativsky wasn't sure if Voldemars would survive. Since then, I haven't heard any word. I fear that he's already—I'm sorry, Romans. I'd rather not talk about this right now."

Janis bowed his head and covered his eyes. Romans extended his arms and gently gripped his fathers trembling shoulders, then tried to think of something to say. His mind remained blank.

"I'm sorry, Poppa. I didn't know," Romans finally mumbled, shrugging his shoulders.

Janis nodded once. "I know," he whispered.

He lifted his head, wiped the tears from his eyes, then looked directly at Romans. A small, trembling grin escaped his quivering lips. He sighed heavily, then put his arm around Romans, and together, the men sauntered back to the farmhouse.

Two days later, Telmeni was mercilessly pounded by a torrential mid-day rain. Worried that most of his freshly sprouted rye crop would be washed away, Janis sloshed out to the fields to check the run-off ditches he had hastily dug that morning. As rain poured off the wide brim of his hat in sheets, he watched the channeled, churning amber water tumble frantically through the ditches, then converge in a pathway heading down the hill toward the lake. Small pebbles stripped loose from the stony subsoil tumbled along the drainage stream, splashing and gurgling in protest.

Satisfied his crop was as safe as it could be, Janis turned and headed back to the farmhouse. As he crested the hill, he noticed a dark figure in a long coat slogging up the road. He stopped for a moment and monitored the man's progress, but when he grew chilled and realized that from this distance he would never be able to tell who it was, he decided to head back inside. After a few steps, though, the figure turned onto the pathway toward the farmhouse, and Janis reasoned it would be best to see who it was.

Plodding through the puddles, he intercepted the figure halfway to the farmhouse.

"Oskars! What in the world would bring you out on a day like this?" Janis said.

"I would say good morning, but I found something that doesn't make me feel too good right now."

"Christ, let's go inside and talk about it. This weather isn't fit to be out in."

Oskars nodded, and together the two men trodded their way toward the house. Kristine opened the door as the they stepped up on the porch and ushered them into the house.

"Oskars! What a surprise! Come in," she said, taking Janis' dripping hat and setting it aside.

She helped him remove his coat, then draped it over a chair she used for drying wet clothes.

"What's this news you have?" Janis asked as he sat to remove his boots.

"Maria! Draw another cup of tea. We have company!" Kristine yelled as she headed toward the kitchen.

"I really don't know if this is good news or bad," Oskars mumbled as he fished out a wet, folded paper from his coat pocket.

He handed it to Janis, then finished taking off his overcoat.

"Romans, would you get you Poppa some dry clothes and grab an extra pair of socks for Oskars!" Kristine called up the stairwell, then Janis heard his son's feet thumping across the upstairs floor.

"It's the Bolsheviks," Oskars said. "They're passing these out in Cesis. If I know them well enough, they're doing it in every other city as well."

"Bolsheviks! I thought we got rid of them?"

"Evidently not," Oskars grunted as he pulled off his boots.

Still in wet socks, the pair carefully walked through the house to the kitchen and settled at the table. As Janis positioned his nose over a steaming cup of tea, letting the vapors soothe his raw membranes, he carefully unfolded the paper, trying not to tear the soaked flimsy sheet. As he started to read silently, Romans clomped into the kitchen with trousers, a dry shirt, and two pairs of dry socks in his arms, and set them in the chair next to Janis. He curiously peeked at the flier over his father's shoulder and froze, his eyes growing wide.

"The provisional government of Russia has wrongly declared that Latvia should not be allowed to become a sovereign nation," Janis read aloud with a slow, deliberate tone. "Therefore, it is our belief and our duty to ensure that Latvia has the right to secede from post-Czarist Russia. We will lead the revolt to ensure the right to self-determination is preserved. Peasants should be rightfully delivered their land and—"

Janis read no further. His gaze slowly crept up and peered at Oskars. Romans' expression grew grim, then angered. Veins bulged from his temples and his face flushed.

"They can't do this here, too!," Romans shouted. "Poppa, you can't let them do this! They'll ruin Latvia like they've ruined Russia! I've seen what they caused. Bread lines, people out of jobs, universities closed. They preach anarchy. We have to stop them!"

"What is this? Where do they come off as the voice of the people? They're trying to undermine all we've done!" Janis slammed his fist to the table.

Romans jumped back, startled by his father's response.

"Nobody will buy this trash!" Janis declared.

"I certainly hope not," Oskars said despondently. "But you know how the Bolsheviks work. They're opportunists. If they find one way of weaseling into something, they do. Then they spread like the plague!"

"We got rid of them once," Janis noted.

"Yes, but somehow they've returned. And you know if they're able to get anything in the elections next month—"

"Then we have to be sure they don't get anything in the elections!" Janis emphatically stated.

"Latvians aren't foolish enough to believe the Bolsheviks, are they Poppa?" Romans asked.

"Most of us are aware of what the Bolsheviks are and what they intend to do," Oskars interjected with a straight face.

Janis sat back and stared at the ceiling, then rubbed his chin with his hand and looked back at Oskars.

"But there are some people who still believe they're the best hope for freedom from Russian rule," Janis mumbled, his voice laced with concern.

"Don't let them take over!" Romans protested. "They're liars! They're thieves! They only take from the people. I've seen what they did in Russia. I don't see how anyone can believe them."

Janis glanced back at Romans, and with a confident grin replied, "We will survive, Romans, and if I have anything to do with it, the Bolsheviks will not."

Southern Russia

27 May 1917

$\mathcal{E}$ vening arrived with a drizzling spring shower hovering like a depressing fog over the bivouac. Having already surrendered to being wet and miserable, Oleg paced in a circle around a hissing, smoldering fire, trying to stay warm under a hastily pitched tarp. The smoke was chokingly thick, but he felt the discomfort was worth tolerating to stay warm enough in the dankness to feel his hands.

He stopped for a moment and peered through the mist at the majestic, snow-capped Caucasus. For the last year, he had personally maintained vigilance on those mountains, especially in the morning hours when the Turks were noted to strike. He feared the Turks that lived beyond those mountains, unsure of what they knew of the crumbling Russian army, or of what they might attempt if they discovered the government was disintegrating. The recent news that Nicholas had abdicated and been arrested served only to make him more anxious.

He shifted his gaze to the west turning his back on the mountains, and allowed himself the rare luxury of drifting off into a wistful gaze. The tension around the encampment had grown so thick that the only way he felt he could keep his sanity was to daydream of his homeland. In his mind, sun-bathed wheat fields rolled like a sea of amber, coaxed into waves by gentle southerly breezes. Endless rows of massive, black and yellow sunflowers rose behind the grain spires, their heads bobbing gaily up and down, left to right.

Footsteps. He snapped back to reality when he heard slogging behind him. He covered his revolver with his shooting hand and spun, ready to fend off the intruder. He relaxed when he recognized Evgeny Bolinokov.

Am I still his captain? Oleg thought, watching Evgeny's boots squish through the muddy field. He wondered if there was even a cavalry left or if now he was an enemy of the government? Christ, how long is this provisional government going to keep me stranded out in this God forsaken swamp?

Evgeny stepped under the tarp and stopped. His pointed face looked even more mousy when it was drenched. He glanced down at his damp trousers and worn through boots, then looked back at Oleg and grimaced. He slipped a half smoked, hand rolled cigarette into his mouth.

"Damn rain. Soaks through everything! Can't even keep a fucking cigarette lit. Got a light?" he groused.

Oleg nodded toward the fire. Evgeny reached down and pulled out one of the glowing sticks. As he brought it close to his face, he closed his eyes, and seemed to bask in the warmth for a moment before lighting his cigarette. He released a ribbon of smoke, and stared at the blue-tinted cloud as it swirled past his face and stagnated around his soaked hair. Oleg chuckled and sniffed at the cloud, sampling the aroma of fine Turkish tobacco.

"How long?" Evgeny asked. His tone was somewhere between disgust and disheartened.

"I guess it depends on which how long you're referring to," Oleg said cynically.

"I think I know what you mean." Evgeny nodded. He sucked in another lung full of smoke and stepped closer to the fire. He expelled another disorderly cloud.

"Now that Rasputin is gone and Nicholas arrested, how long do you think it'll be before Russia itself falls into anarchy?"

"Or has it already?" Oleg's words oozed sarcasm.

"With what I've seen of Dumas past," Evgeny peered out toward the mountains. "I doubt those in the provisional government can keep control much longer. Russia needs a strong leader. Hell, even Nicholas would have offered more than these asses have."

"You sound concerned, Evgeny. Bolsheviks?"

"Bolsheviks? Maybe. Mensheviks, maybe. Christ, the whole kettle of viks is so messed up, I really don't think anyone knows who's who anymore. If I knew that, I guess I really don't know."

Evgeny stopped when Oleg held up his hand. They heard a pair of boots approaching. Both men covered their revolvers and crouched defensively.

"Christ, look at us," Oleg chortled, releasing his pistol. His lieutenant, Ahmed Hannoush, an olive-skinned, Middle-Eastern type, come into view. Evgeny and Oleg chuckled at their skittishness. Ahmed, with the silence of a sage, stopped next to the pair. He turned his head, nodded a cold but cordial hello, and gazed in the direction of the mountains.

"Homesick?" Evgeny prompted.

Oleg swallowed hard, wanting badly to make a joking comment about Ahmed not praying this morning because he couldn't see which direction was south. Ahmed's expression looked too serious to make any jokes.

"In a sense," Ahmed replied after a brief silence. He smiled weakly. "I'm concerned for what befalls my homeland in the demise of Russia.

"It's on all of our minds, Ahmed," Oleg mustered compassion.

"The Turks fester just across the border like an infection on the land," Ahmed continued without listening. "As you well know, they're untrustworthy souls. History confirms what I say is the truth."

Oleg tried to read Ahmed's calculating tone. If there was one thing he could count on, it was Ahmed's pure logic.

"We only have to look as far as Odessa. Even the Germans wouldn't do that!" Evgeny snorted.

Oleg silenced him with an icy stare.

"I fear that when they no longer feel they need to fear Russian resistance, they'll move into my Azerbaidzhan. It is that I fear, and for what they will do to my land and my people!"

"I understand," Oleg assuaged.

"Sometimes I wonder if we should wait for an order from Command, or just disband on our own and head home," Evgeny mumbled.

"That sentiment has crossed my mind, too. And more times than I care to remember," Oleg said somberly.

"I've already thought past that and I hope, Captain Oleg Stativsky, that you understand why I am doing what I am," Ahmed said, sheepishly recoiling. He opened his arms and embraced Evgeny with a traditional Russian hug, then moved to Oleg and did the same. He pulled away from Oleg slowly, then snapped to attention and glared into his eyes.

"I know as an officer that this may be considered desertion, but I beg you again to understand. As of today, I am leaving the army."

Oleg nodded.

"Katya and I are leaving for Baku tonight. A Persian trader I met at the market spared us two horses. For Katya's sake, I could not let the opportunity slip through my hands."

Oleg nodded again. Ahmed started to leave. Reserved and sincere, he said, "Whatever happens this side of the Caucasus, I pray Almighty Allah will be gentle to you both. And to Voldemars."

"And may God be with you, Ahmed," Evgeny noted as Ahmed turned and sloshed away, enveloped by the drizzle and fog.

❦   ❦   ❦

At sunrise on the following morning, Oleg stood at his outpost again—as he did every morning. The rain had saturated the compound and moved on, leaving canvas and leather musty, the air damp but clean. As he stared over the calm waters on the Caspian, the sun punched threads of light through a thin layer of clouds. He wasn't sure why he waited or what he was waiting for. He just waited, duty bound, feeling that eventually, some message had to come. Someone had to tell him who he was fighting for, or if in fact he was even still fighting.

"Damn. You were right, Voldemars." He chuckled, remembering how impatient he had been at the Carpathian front. *Maybe it's better that you were reassigned to Astrakhan. I probably would be making life miserable for you now.*

He started his habitual pace on the squishy, saturated ground until he heard the faint sound of horse's hooves slogging in the soaked fields. He twitched while he concentrated on the approaching horseman.

"Finally!" he sighed loudly. He recognized the Cossack. The rider's rounded, black pile cap bounced in synchrony with his horse's movement. His stringy long black beard rubbed his chest and a long, violet and red cloak, gaudily ornamented with gold and silver braiding flapped wildly behind him. The horseman slowed, but oddly, remained saddled as he pulled his horse to a stop.

"Are you Captain Oleg Stativsky?" The Cossack peered down.

"Yes," Oleg nodded. He kept his hand close to his weapon.

"In the name of the Russian Provisional Government, to which you now owe your allegiance, you are ordered to take this envelope." The rider's words were delivered officiously, yet his tone seemed cynical.

"But—?" Oleg let his hand slip from his pistol grip.

The Cossack pivoted his head and scanned, as if to ensure no one was near enough to hear him.

"Christ, Ivan. No one has been here for months. Tell me, what do you think is going on?"

Ivan leaned toward Oleg.

"If I were you, I'd be wary of anything which comes from the provisional government," he whispered through a sinister, yellow-toothed grin. "I hear Petersburg is in absolute chaos. The government is unstable at all levels. The politicians—" Ivan stopped just long enough to spit in disgust. "They don't know what the military is doing, nor does the military know what they are doing. Nobody trusts anybody anymore, and the people are rioting in the streets, taking anything they can find. I don't know what those orders say, but I'd say that in any case—"

"Is there deception here?" Oleg interrupted. He glanced quickly at the letter, and looked sternly back at Ivan.

"Like I said, I don't know. All I can offer is that if you are wise—"

The Cossack's face paled and he glanced back. His yellow teeth disappeared quickly behind pursed lips. Oleg turned and saw a band of ten other Cossacks approaching. Ivan grew nervous as his horse began to prance in place. Obviously not wanting to wait around to find out what they were after, Ivan leered at Oleg.

"You've got your orders, and what I think. I really don't care what you do!" He rushed the word, then whipped his horse's flank. With an instant burst of speed, his mount bolted and disappeared ahead of a trail of spattered mud.

Anxious that he was alone to face the oncoming hoard, Oleg covered his pistol and watched the Cossacks closely. Their charge in tight formation seemed obviously headed for him. Distinctive drunken whoops and hollers rose from the pack, and grew more raucous with each stride. But suddenly, like a flock of starlings changing direction, they turned south.

Oleg breathed a sigh of relief. He heard a bottle fall, shattering under the thundering hooves of the horses that followed. As they rode away, one wild, blood-curdling yell emanated. To him, more experienced than he cared to be with Ukrainian Cossacks, it meant only one thing.

"Another fucking pogrom! When will all this killing ever end?" He shook his head and watched the last of the hussars disappear beyond the horizon.

"If I were you, I'd be wary!" Ivan's voice echoed in his mind, making the hairs on his back stand on end. He stared at the envelope, debating for a moment not opening the letter. His conscience and curiosity overruled. He ripped open the envelope, pulled out the orders, and read, line by line, searching for any hidden message.

He sighed deeply. His gut told him there was something evil about the order, but the specific phrase that spurred that sense eluded him. He debated not telling the brigade about it.

"Duty!" The word rang in his head like a hammer on a chime. He had no choice and he headed back toward the encampment, convinced to fulfill his responsibility. But he would do it in his own way.

Assembling the brigade quickly, Oleg inspected each man personally, stopping in front of them to peer into their souls. He felt an understanding grow between each of them as he finished his round. Satisfied, he stepped back in front of them, pulled out the letter and snapped it open. He cleared his throat and sucked in a deep breath.

"By order of the Moscow Provisional Government," he started reading the order, word for word, in a grim monotone. "You and your brigade are ordered to assemble on the thirtieth of May, nineteen-seventeen, at eighteen hundred hours, at the port of Astrakhan. You will board a Russian transport ship, and travel north along the Volga, so that you may be redeployed in defense of Russia."

Oleg dropped the letter, looked up at the group and struggled over whether or not he should express his true feelings.

"Duty." Voldemars' words rung clear in his head. "We are soldiers and it is our duty to follow orders."

I have performed my duty and have delivered this order as required. Oleg swallowed hard and scanned the eyes of every one of the twenty men for which he was responsible.

"In my gut, I have reason to believe there is deception here. My personal advice to you, not as your commander, but as your friend, is to immediately disband. I will not see this as desertion, since we took no oath of allegiance to this government."

Dead silence was the only response.

🍁   🍁   🍁

In a quaint seaside bistro, Voldemars watched a single narrow candle flame flicker in each of Otilija's crescent shaped eyes. The shadow of her delicate nose darkened one cheek, while the other blushed. Her smile emanated placid contentment against the backdrop of the distant, still snow-covered Caucasus. Her amber hair was brushed back away from her smooth face and pinned behind her head so that it puffed out like an aura.

"I'm not at all sorry I missed the ship back to Astrakhan yesterday," Voldemars whispered. He smiled as he emptied a tiny spoonful of the Caspian Sea's finest caviar in his mouth, then reveled in the flavor as the sauce dribbled onto his tongue. He reached across the table, turned his palm up for Otilija and tried to engage her hand. She gracefully withdrew.

"I would much rather spend a quiet evening with my beautiful wife than to face those crazy Bolsheviks!"

"Let's not bring them into it, Voldemars." Her voice turned to ice as her eyes widened. "You know how their talk about revolution frightens me."

"It won't just go away overnight. We will have to face it sometime," he reasoned. "Try not to worry about it now. Things will clear up in a few months. I'm sure once—"

"Don't you understand?" She leaned over her folded hands, trying to keep her voice from carrying into the room. She scanned the room furtively. "You're not a hero to them! Your loyalty is to the czar. You know that, and they know that. You are an officer for the enemy's army now!"

"Otilija, please! We'll be all right. I promise." He reached over again, placed his hand over Otilija's, and squeezed. "We'll stay right here, or even better, slip down into Caucasia until all this Bolshevik saber rattling is over. I've got some friends here."

"But can you trust them?" Her eyes widened. The candle flame danced between them.

Voldemars raised his hand and waved his finger. "Don't worry. By the time the baby comes, the revolution if that's what they want to call it, will be over."

"But—"

"I've seen them. They're not fighting men. They're old and feeble. Incompetent. Their rifles are archaic, and half of them can't fire anyway!"

Her face remained taught with terror.

"Listen to me, please." he cocked his head. "When it's over we'll quietly—"

He glanced over Otilija's shoulder and saw a man standing at the entrance, waving at him. He squinted hard until he recognized the face.

"Son-of-a-bitch, it's Oleg! Excuse me, Otilija. Let me see what he wants." He tried to hide his sudden anxiety from her. He dabbed the corners of his mouth with his linen napkin and trying not to bring himself any undue attention, he pushed himself away and nuzzled Otilija. "I'll be back in a moment. Save some caviar for me, please?" Her response was cold and tense.

He stood up, brushed himself off, growing more curious with Oleg's urgency. He surveyed the room and walked toward him. As they met, they hugged and disappeared behind the draped entrance, escaping into the solitude of the night.

"Oleg! Christ, I never expected to see you here! I thought you were stationed in Groznyi?"

"I was when I was in the army. I, uh," Oleg hesitated.

"You resigned?"

Oleg nodded and bowed his head.

"Why?" Voldemars could not believe what he had heard. Oleg's face was deeply carved with an uncharacteristic pallor. "What's wrong? You look terrible! Have you seen a ghost?"

"Voldemars, the news is not good for any of us who are, or were in the cavalry." His voice squeaked and trembled as he spoke.

"Christ, Oleg. What is it?"

"The ship to Astrakhan? Remember the one that was supposed to take us up the Volga? You got the same order, didn't you?" Oleg nervously scanned around.

"I did, but I missed it. So what?" Voldemars flippantly responded and shrugged his shoulders. "What are they going to do, court-martial me for missing a damned boat? Hell, I'm not even in their army anymore. And it doesn't look like you made it."

"No, Voldemars. It's worse than that." Oleg's eyes, wide and filled with terror, punctuated his pasty complexion, grayed by the dim moonlight. His body quivered as he cowered and lowered his voice to a hushed whisper.

"Everyone on that boat was executed. We were supposed to be killed!"

"The Bolsheviks?" Voldemars gasped as his jaw slacked.

"From what I hear, the men were lined up against the rail, then shot. Every last one of them." Oleg closed his eyes, sucked in a deep breath, then released it slowly to regain his composure.

"Son-of-a-bitch!"

"We may be the only ones of the brigade that survived this purge."

Voldemars nervously chewed on his lower lip as he digested Oleg's news. He felt a rage begin to boil in his chest.

"Is this the way they're going to run the damned country? Shoot everyone? Even Nicholas—"

"I don't think Nicholas had any choice in the matter. Or any more," Oleg's tone remained reserved and composed. "The rumor is that he's been exiled with his family. Siberia. I figure they're already dead."

Voldemars stared catatonically at the moonlit sky, trying to absorb what this meant. His face remained long and expressionless.

"My God. Otilija." Voldemars gasped. His heart galloped into his throat.

"Oleg, we've got to hide! We've got to hide as best we can. Otilija's pregnant!"

"I know. I wanted you to know for Otilija's sake." Oleg's voice was tainted with a hopeless sounding drone. His head hung, and his face revealed his depressed, sincere concern.

Voldemars pursed and chewed on his lip, while ideas cascaded though his mind.

"We could all head back to Latvia!" Voldemars blurted without thinking. "Back through the Ukraine?"

"No. At least not now." Oleg mumbled. "I can't even go home and I'm Ukrainian. The Bolsheviks control Kiev, and with Kiev goes the Ukraine." His pain was obvious.

"Keep your hope, Oleg. We've seen worse in battle." Voldemars tried to rebuild his compatriot's morale. His attempt was futile and he grasped Oleg's shoulders again. "These soldiers of the Red Army are nothing. I've seen them, and they're a sorry lot!"

"I've got to go," Oleg uttered. He peered into Voldemars' eyes. "May God be with you, Otilija, and the baby." He grasped Voldemars, pulled, and embraced him tightly.

"Take care of yourself, Oleg Mikailovich Stativsky," Voldemars whispered. "If you can't live with the Bolsheviks, come to Latvia! I am sure we're far enough away from the Russians that they won't bother us.

Oleg snapped to attention, saluted smartly, then turned and walked away leaving Voldemars alone in the chilly evening. Taking a deep breath, Voldemars rubbed his pruned lips and watched his old friend disappear into the night. He went back inside the bistro.

As he ducked through the drapes, he stopped and gazed across the room. Otilija sat alone in the corner, bathed in flickering candlelight from the table, motionless.

How am I going to tell her? Voldemars thought as he strutted across the room. He placed his hands on her shoulders and leaned over to whisper in her ear. Otilija lay her head back into his shoulder, smiled, and closed her eyes. The fragrance of her sensuous Turkish perfume calmed his nerves. He closed his eyes and rested his face on her shoulder.

Tomorrow. I'll tell her tomorrow, he decided.

In the Caucasus

23 July 1917

*V*oldemars had been awake all night frantically pacing the well-worn floor planks like a caged animal. He vowed he was not going to miss the event, come hell or high water. This time, he was in total control. He had no other responsibilities. The army did not have him out at some remote corner of Europe, nor was he on his way away from Otilija. He was there. Right where he should be.

His feet bulged inside his worn boots, begging for freedom. Tingling pricked his legs, shooting shards through every muscle from his ankles to his hips. His back ached like he had been hauling timber all day, throbbing relentlessly each time his heel thumped the floor.

He stopped again at the heavy wool curtain separating the bedroom from the rest of the house. It was all that separated him from Otilija and her midwives. He leaned in, cupped his hand around his ear, then listened closely, undaunted by the rank odor of stale smoke trapped in the weave.

"Voldemars." A deep gravelly voice startled him, grating in his ears. He stiffened. His head snapped around and he peered toward the kitchen. Ivan Ivanovich, the master of the stanitza, leered at him from his throne at the head of the table. Five other pairs of wide, blood-shot eyes joined his in disapproving glares. As if he was holding court, he towered over his personal entourage of seedy looking men, directing their every move. He leaned back in his chair and demanded a refill of his shot glass.

"Why are you pacing so much? Come! Now is time for celebration!" Ivan grunted, lifting a half-empty vodka bottle toward the ceiling. A toothy grin split his full, red lips. An untamed black beard covered his face like a rug. But it was Ivan's crystal blue eyes, like beacons on an open sea, that were most intoxicating.

Voldemars tried to speak, but his dry, cottony mouth trapped the words before they could even pass his lips.

"Your Otilija will have baby!" Ivan grunted. "There is nothing you can do now!"

Deep, booming belly laughs burst from the Cossacks, accompanied by back-slapping, vulgar panting, and table banging. The noises ricocheted off the ceiling's low pine beams.

"Should think before the snake goes hunting." A guttural voice rose from the table, followed by another round of raucous laughter.

"Come. You drink with us, and you have big boy!" Ivan's voice boomed in a fatherly tone. He stopped his chortling long enough to wave Voldemars to the table. "Like Ivan!" he added, pounding his chest with the bottle.

"I really think I should be in there. With her," Voldemars answered, sheepishly pointing to the bedroom door.

"Bah! Foolishness!" Ivan exploded, vaulting to his feet. Another round of tavern-like laughter roared as he pointed his finger accusingly at Voldemars. "Delivering babies is woman's work! You don't see stallion next to nag when she's foaling, do you? Eh, Voldemars?"

"Custom," Voldemars slipped without thinking.

"Custom? Where do you get such strange custom?" Osipov chided in a creaky, chesty voice. "Terek custom is men celebrate with drink and friends! You are in Ivan's stanitza, so come!"

Osipov raised his right hand in a fist, then waved Voldemars toward the table. He was definitely the biggest of the bunch, looking more like an animal than a man. Voldemars shifted his glance to

Ivan, then to Sergei, then Osipov again. He had met the other three bearded men huddled around the table, but he was too tired to remember their names.

Ivan suddenly kicked out his chair and wobbled toward Voldemars. He draped his arm around Voldemars' shoulders, then gazed into his eyes and released a powerful alcohol stenched breath.

"Now, Voldemars. Three months ago, me and Osipov found you out in the woods wandering like some lost dog," Ivan's tone was condescending, but Voldemars knew every brash word from his mouth was purely sincere. "Wandering around with nothing but the clothes on your back and baby in Otilija's stomach."

He leaned toward the table, pushing Voldemars toward it. Voldemars clomped twice with his feet, resisting as best he could against Ivan's strength. Osipov stood, weaved across the floor and joined Ivan.

"Ivan and Osipov could have left you there." Ivan slurred his words as he tried to whisper. "You know, leave you for the Bolsheviks."

"Or the Don!" Osipov countered with a laugh and a sneer. "The undisciplined Don!"

"Or wolves—"

"Or Turks—" Whoops and hollers rose from the table.

"Or just shoot you and put you out of your misery right there. But no! Ivan said, something in that one there that seems familiar. Maybe—"

"Maybe there is Cossack in him, I said." Osipov continued the rapid-fire banter.

Cheers bellowed from the kitchen.

"So, I agreed with my friend, Osipov. After all, you thought you could escape the cursed Bolsheviks by yourself? That takes the courage of a Terek!"

Voldemars looked up to Ivan and read sincere friendship in his bleary eyes. He was right. There was only one reason he and Otilija could even be having a baby now, and that was him. As odd as it seemed to him, a Cossack; a brutal, savage Cossack, one of a band of vagabonds, he felt, had no worth but to serve themselves as violent profligates, and none other than the leader of the Tereks, a tribe renowned as the most brutal of all the Cossack bands, had the heart and compassion to spare his and his wife's life.

"So, Voldemars. You come drink with Ivan and Osipov, no?" Ivan punctuated his words with two hearty slaps on Voldemars' back, then grabbed Osipov and stumbled back to the table. He dropped square in his chair, grabbing the vodka bottle on his way down. Voldemars scratched at his three months worth of scraggly growth on his chin, grown more to help disguise his features than out of lack of means to shave it, and eked out a small grin.

"Ah!" Sergei announced it with a siren, pointing. As Ivan turned to look, he swept the bottle from Ivan's hand and tossed it to Voldemars.

He caught the flung bottle, more out of reflex than conscious effort. Juggling it at first, he clenched his fingers around the neck just before it would have spilled onto the floor. A splash hit his face square on his lips, then evaporated and snaked up his nose. As if presenting a hard won prize, he thrust the bottle to the ceiling.

All six Cossacks exploded with cheers, complete with applause and table slamming. Voldemars smiled, feeling accepted as part of this unique pack of men, but when he glanced at Ivan's contentedly quiet and smiling face, he felt more than just acceptance. He felt warmth. True, sincere warmth.

"Voldemars. You lucky!" Ivan waved his finger in a scolding gesture. "If you spilled that, Tatiana would make you clean!"

"And clean, and clean," A chorus of knowing voices complained from the kitchen.

"Tatiana does not like—"

Otilija screamed. Voldemars' weak smile vanished behind wide eyes. His face paled. He glanced back at the Cossacks, then to the room, debating where to go. "I must be in there!" Voldemars burst through the curtain. Another boisterous round of laughter resonated from the kitchen.

"Push!" Tatiana's shrill voice grabbed Voldemars' attention. He froze in the doorway, torn between rushing to Otilija's side and honoring Cossack custom. Two other women helped Tatiana tend to Otilija as she squirmed in a large, high-backed chair in the center of the room. Tatiana stood between Otilija's propped up legs, and like a conductor before an orchestra, directed everyone's actions with flailing arms and high pitched commands. Osipov's thin, wispy looking wife, Katya, wiped Otilija's brow constantly with a wet rag. Sergei's wife, Anastasia, stood at Otilija's side, massaging her bare, bulging stomach.

"Push, Otilija!" Tatiana ordered again. Otilija responded dutifully, her face turning red as she winced and pushed down. After a noisy, snorty exhale, she looked up. Voldemars realized she had seen him when she cracked a weak smile.

"Look at me! Again, push again!" Tatiana demanded. Otilija obeyed. Tatiana's face brightened as she weaseled in closer to Otilija. "Look! The baby."

"He's big. Big for such a small father!" Anastasia giggled, craning her neck to see over Otilija's knees.

With an obviously practiced, well-honed skill, Tatiana reached down and steadied the baby. Voldemars cautiously stepped closer, trying not to disturb the concerted effort that tended his wife.

"Push!" Tatiana ordered again. Otilija complied, then released her breath with a loud "Argh!" Voldemars jumped back, startled by Otilija's guttural sound.

"Oh, Momma. Momma's got a girl. A big girl," Tatiana chanted. Katya and Anastasia beamed wide smiles, obviously comforting Otilija.

Anxious and curious, Voldemars approached with measured steps until he stood next to Otilija. Tears welled in his eyes as he stared at the vernix-covered child.

All three of the women startled when Voldemars stepped in close to them. They glowered at him with disapproval, leaving him very uncomfortable.

"It is fine, Tatiana," Otilija mumbled. "In Latvia, men are allowed."

"They only get in the way!" Tatiana grumbled her opinion, as close to spitting in disgust as he had ever seen her.

"And I want him here," Otilija added.

Reluctantly, Tatiana wrapped the baby and offered her to Voldemars. He stretched out his open hands, gently accepted the well wrapped child, then slipped open the blanket and peeked at her face. Tatiana grabbed Katya and Anastasia, then the three of them scurried off to a corner of the room while Voldemars stood in awe at his child. He felt a foolish looking grin blossom on his face as the baby wriggled and squirmed in his hands.

"Brevite!" Voldemars said softly. "We have Brevite, Otilija!"

"Brevite," Otilija mumbled quietly, gently moving her head side to side. "Yes, we have Brevite," she added sleepily. Her hooded eyelids slid open and revealing glassy eyes. She extended her arms and let her face grow long and wanting, as if begging Voldemars to let her hold the child.

Cautiously, Voldemars leaned close enough to Otilija and lay Brevite at her side. As the infant's trembling lips slowly moved in and out, Otilija instinctively brought her baby to her breast. No sooner than Brevite's lips touched her mother's nipple, she latched on and started sucking. Otilija moaned in pleasure, trembling, then glanced up and weakly smiled at Voldemars.

He returned the smile, then leaned over and kissed her forehead. He snuck another peak at Brevite, but from the corner of his eye, he noticed Tatiana had returned, with a vengeance for his intrusion. Her stern, impatient glare was disapproving.

"I'll be back when they're a bit more tolerant of me," he whispered to Otilija.

She stared up at him with hollow, tired eyes. She wanted him to stay for a moment longer, but she was too washed out to argue. She let him withdraw. He nodded a cordial thank you to the women, then bowing graciously, left the room.

"He must learn his place, Otilija," Tatiana scolded, waving her finger, and directed Katya to fetch some water.

"He's just trying to help—" Otilija started.

"Men know nothing about babies!" Tatiana cut her off bluntly. "Especially girls!"

"They take care of things that need strength," Anastasia added. "Cut wood, get food, break horses. Raising babies needs a gentle hand."

Otilija chuckled, but too worn out to protest, she simply nodded and accepted the Cossack way.

"Now, Katya, Anastasia and me clean you. You feed baby. Later, you eat well. New mommas need strength." Tatiana ordered through a wry grin as Katya returned with a steaming pail of water. Without further delay, Tatiana and Katya started on Otilija's sponge-bath, while Anastasia helped the new mother with the baby.

In the kitchen, the pack had been whittled to two, Ivan and Osipov, with three asleep at the table, bent over on their folded arms. Voldemars, pale and wan, stumbled into the kitchen and rejoined the male bonding ritual which had continued without him. Exhausted and on the verge of collapse, he struggled to the table, then slumped into a chair next to Ivan. His head drifted down until he noticed the poorly carved, but meticulously clean table a nose length from his face. He popped his head back up and caught Ivan's and Osipov's eyes focused sternly on him. He realized his transgression.

"This was Sergei's spot, yes?" he asked politely. He started to stand.

Ivan clamped his huge hand on his shoulder, keeping him in the seat. He chuckled as he nodded toward the floor. Voldemars glanced down and saw Sergei curled up and sleeping near the fireplace.

"So, Voldemars! You see baby?" Ivan slurred. He slammed his open hand on Voldemars' back. "And because you didn't wait, you have girl, yes?"

Voldemars glared up at Ivan's glassy eyes, puzzled at his superstition. More so because it was true.

"A girl, yes. Brevite." He nodded and smiled widely.

"Bree-veet-ah? What kind of name is Brevite? Alexandra or Natalya—strong, proper Cossack names!" Osipov spit out his words in a drunken stupor. He pounded the vodka bottle on the table in front of Voldemars. Three heads asleep on folded arms bounced and dropped back to the thick hairy forearms they rested on.

"In the old Latvian, it means liberty," Voldemars said.

"I understand. She is your battle cry. You will now go home and fight for your territory, eh?" Osipov's thick, wild eyebrows danced devilishly under his furrowed brow.

Voldemars glanced up at Osipov with a confused stare.

"The war is over. Why would I—"

"Oh, no. I hear it has yet to begin."

Voldemars craned his neck forward, confused by Osipov's parable. He snapped toward Ivan, who sat in his chair, smug and approving, interrupted only by a soupy, deep belch.

"I don't think I heard you correctly," Voldemars begged for explanation.

"The word from the marshes is revolution in Latvia will be soon!"

"To be free of the Bolsheviks. A noble battle." Ivan snuck in.

"How do you know that?"

Ivan lifted his open hand diplomatically. He stared at him with a knowing glance, then winked. "Tereks travel far. We know everything all over Old Russia."

"Drink!" Osipov demanded, then jerked backwards, almost falling from his chair. He waved his hand, motioning Voldemars to drink while he giggled uncontrollably. Voldemars stood silently, jaw agape.

"Comrade Voldemars!" Ivan's garbled voice dribbled from his lips. "You wish to be part of this, then, eh?"

Latvia free from Russia, Voldemars thought. I never thought it could be possible. Maybe Ivan was mistaken.

"Ivan will prepare you to do this. To be strong. To be the winner. To be the leader. To bring Cossack tradition to Latvia!" Ivan proudly announced. "But, you need vodka. Vodka makes men strong. Now, drink!"

Voldemars locked eyes with Ivan, then dropped his back to the table. You? You are going to show me how to lead and fight? Voldemars thought, furrowing his brow. You slay me, Cossack! You do realize you are not dealing with some new recruit here!

Osipov chortled, sounding like his voice tripped on his numb tongue. Voldemars shook his head, partly disbelieving and partly indignant with what he had just heard. He locked eyes with Ivan, then silently brought the bottle to his lips.

"Ah, Brevite!" Osipov toasted, wobbling as he tried to stand.

"Brevite!" Ivan toasted.

"May she grow up to marry a Cossack. A real man!" Osipov threw his head back and gulped his drink. As he jerked his head forward, he belched loudly, then threw his glass into the fireplace, barely missing Sergei. As it smashed in pieces, Osipov slammed his fists on the table.

"Prosit!" Sergei weakly toasted from the floor without picking up his head.

Ivan remained still as Osipov's demonstration relented. He squinted his hideously bloodshot eyes and glared at Voldemars. His face turned dour as he started pensively scratching his beard. Finally, a wide grin blossomed across his face.

"You know, Voldemars. Freedom from Mother Russia can only be won with great strength. Cossack strength! Do you think your friends in Latvia have that strength?"

"Latvians have great inner strength."

"Mmm," Ivan nodded in agreement. He tugged at his beard again. "But your independence must be won in your enemy's home," he added in a grave tone.

"What is it that you're trying to say?" Voldemars asked pointedly.

"I do not feel here, in my heart, that you do not trust me, Voldemars." Ivan challenged.

Osipov stiffened, coldly. Voldemars swallowed hard. The intoxicated odor from Ivan's breath slapped him hard.

"Is it that you feel Cossacks are nothing but animals?"

Voldemars felt his face flush. Ivan was right.

"Let me tell you, Gentleman Voldemars," his sarcasm oozed in his words. "We have been free to do what we wish, ever since the days of Czarina Catherine!" Ivan proclaimed pompously. "We are nothing but a small band of Caucasian Cossacks, and all of Catherine's men could not bring us to submit to her wishes. Ever since then, no other Czar has ever tried to tame us. You are military man, Voldemars. Haven't you wondered why they choose to leave us alone? Haven't you wondered how we earned our reputation as unbeatable warriors?"

Voldemars thought for a moment. Ivan was right. The Terek had a reputation which had spread all the way to Latvia. Intently he nodded and listened more carefully, realizing that even if he did say no, Ivan was on a roll and bound to tell him.

"Tactics!" Ivan announced, slamming his fist down on the table. He stood up and began lecturing. "Every revolution needs to have special tactics! Small groups of soldiers hit enemy when not looking, then disappear before the big army can retaliate. Knowledge of the land is important!

"French revolutionaries used these tactics. And then the government used it in the Prussian Wars. We know of so many great wars that were won because of these tactics. All we did was add our horsemanship, Cossack horsemanship!"

"Guerrilla fighting," Voldemars noted, nonchalantly.

"What is this?" Osipov frowned at Voldemars. Ivan's eyes grew wide. His face contorted into a puzzled and skeptical expression.

"It's the type of fighting. Guerrilla is a Spanish word for little war," Voldemars added smugly.

"Ah, yes," Ivan smiled and nodded approval. "Many little wars make up big victory in war! But it works. Look around you. No Russians, not a one! Only proud Cossacks!"

Voldemars nodded again.

"I have no great love for Czar, nor do I have any for the Bolsheviks. But I have come to like you, Voldemars. I feel that inside, you have Cossack heart," Ivan's voice quelled to just short of a whisper. "And because I see what kind of man you are, I will teach you how to be as free of Bolsheviks in Latvia as we have been from the Czars here in all of our history!"

Voldemars nodded. He remembered Cossacks were used to teach horsemanship during his first assignment in Poland. If what Ivan said was true, that he could learn even more from him, he could become one of the leaders in Latvia's fight. A great leader. And in the eyes of his father, he would be redeemed. He would have the honor he had left the farm for. Even more, it would be for Latvia and not Russia.

"I will stay and learn all you have to teach me, Ivan," he agreed. Ivan and Osipov beamed wide, toothy grins.

"Good! Then I, Ivan Ivanovich, will be your instructor." Ivan stood and lifted his shot glass high. "But first, we must drink to our new friendship!"

"Vod-mel-mars!" Sergei slurred as he pushed up from the floor and tried to stand. Voldemars smirked impishly, then leaned over and pushed him back down. He choked the bottle's neck, tipped it vertical, then filled his mouth. As the liquor neared his throat, it spasmed. He gulped against it, but the vodka vaporized. He gulped again, trying to keep up with the urgings of his comrades. Within thirty seconds, he finished the bottle, then slammed it down on the table. He wiped his lips with his sleeve and grinned. Ivan burst out with an approving belly laugh as Voldemars felt the alcohol start dancing a tingly ring around his head.

Voldemars' eyes burned when he cracked them open and saw that the sun had already risen on a new day. His head felt like it had been entombed with a ton of square, pointed-edged bricks. He moaned and pushed himself up from the sleeping rack, which he couldn't even remember crawling into, then shuffled to his pack full of clothes. He ferreted to the bottom and pulled out a package neatly wrapped together in a white linen bed sheet. Holding it close to his chest, he shuffled out of the house and slipped into the dank, misty air.

He trudged through black, oozy mud behind Ivan's home until a narrow, hard packed pathway emerged from the swamp. Furtively, he glanced back, then slipped into a field of tall scrub. Totally consumed by the growth, he felt even more confident no one would see him. He shuffled one hundred more meters to a clearing he had prepared three days earlier.

In front of him was the scorched patch of earth he had burned into the grass. Setting the package down, he assembled the supply of dry sticks he had collected. He hastily started a small fire. At first, a chokingly thick cloud emerged like a genie from an Arabian folk tale, winding and bending as it tumbled toward the sky. A slight breeze coaxed the tiny wisps of flame larger. Carefully, he fed the orange dancers to life with larger chunks of wood. When the entire stack was engulfed in hot flickers, complete with spewing, hissing steam. He was satisfied.

He stepped away from the fire and kneeled next to the package. With the care of a surgeon, he untied the string holding the linen together, then pulled back the sheet. Hidden for months, his last Russian military uniform lay helpless and formless before him. He paused to remember the honor of wearing the tunic, then carefully he removed each of the medals that hung above the breast pocket. He inspected each decoration, remembering the exact battle that won him the honor. With a sigh, he lay each next to his dress uniform's ceremonial saber.

"But nothing for Gorlice," he mumbled, disconsolate, staring at the stripped uniform. "Good-bye, old friend," he added, then lifted the tunic by the epaulets and draped the tail across the fire. He held the tunic until fire began eating at the cloth like some ravenous animal, then folded the shoulders over the growing holes. The shirt continued to hiss and steam as he took his trousers, unfolded them, then lay them on top. Black smoke swirled up for a moment, but then flames slipped through the holes they had scored through the layers of clothes. The lingering odor of gas, a scent he thought had been left in Odessa crept up and weakly tried to insult him, but the acrid odor was swallowed by the flames as they engulfed the uniform. In quiet reverence, he glared at the thread connecting him to the Czar, watching it succumb and disappear amidst the flames.

He reached down and picked up his saber, and ran his finger along the ornate metal etching that formed the dull edge of his sword. Moving up to the handle, he turned the saber and inspected every intimate detail of the tasseled steel grip. In his hand again, after almost a year of being hidden from anyone's sight, he felt as if he was clasping hands with an old friend.

"You will need this when the weather turns cold," a scratchy voice startled Voldemars. He spun around and gasped. Ivan stood behind him, cloaked with a gaudy yellow and soft blue riding coat. A Cossack coat. Ivan's eyes turned toward the fire and he watched the last threads of the uniform disintegrate. Voldemars swallowed hard to remove the lump from his throat. "I know I should not admit this, but you scared the living shit out of me."

"Then our first lesson in becoming a Cossack will be how to keep from getting surprised so you will not be frightened," Ivan said with a wry grin. "A Cossack is never frightened. Especially a Terek."

"I remember."

"This will be your robe, your uniform, if you wish. It marks you as part of my clan." Ivan tossed the cloak at Voldemars. "You drank well last night, Voldemars. You make me proud I chose you to be my friend!"

"But my head says that I didn't," Voldemars admitted, holding his head together with his hands.

"You will get used to it. All Tereks do," Ivan said. He placed his arm around his shoulder and began to hum a solemn sounding folk song while they watched the last of the strands burn.

In the Caucasus

5 September 1917

*V*oldemars gingerly slurped at his cardamom spiced tea, careful not to burn his leathery tongue. It was still numbed flaccid from another long night of drinking with Ivan. He slurped until a mouthful slipped in and singed. He recoiled, wincing tightly. Clumsily, he set the cup back on the table.

"Eat first, Voldemars. Morning tea should be cold anyway. And you don't burn your mouth," Ivan said, close to chortling. He reached across the table and snatched the crust-stripped loaf of black bread between them. Growling, he tore off a large, ragged edged chunk, then dipped the edge into a carved wooden bowl. As he pulled it out, Voldemars watched the thick, sweet grape preserves plop back into the bowl. Ivan quickly cupped his hand under the dribble, then brought the mash to his wide open mouth and stuffed in the whole piece without losing a drop. His cheeks bulged as he mawed the food.

"Good!" he groaned, pleased. He licked the drops from his palm, then ripped off another piece of the bread and reached for the mash. "Eat, Voldemars. Eat for strength."

Voldemars shook his head and glanced back into his tea. Even after six months of living with Ivan, he still found their manners disgusting.

"You not like this, no? Well, you eat anyway. Tatiana will be upset if you don't eat. No one wants Tatiana upset!" Ivan said as he dipped another piece of bread into the bowl, this time catching two floating bread crusts with his swipe.

"No, this is fine. I just don't eat much in the morning."

"Cossacks eat good in morning, Voldemars. Eat!"

Voldemars brooded, thinking more of how to say what he had to instead of commenting on Ivan's crudeness. He brought his tea back to his mouth and tipped the cup enough for the liquid to warm his lips.

"Or do my manners still bother you?"

Voldemars gasped as a mouthful slipped in, surprised at Ivan's uncanny perception. He choked on the hot fluid, until the cardamom tingled at his nose. The mouthful forcefully back washed through his nostrils, then dribbled into a puddle on the table.

"Voldemars. A Cossack trick." Ivan bellowed, banging his hand on the table in approval. "I should have known you were just playing with me."

"Yeah, playing," Voldemars pushed the words out. He wiped off his face with his shirt. "I was thinking, Ivan. Brevite is old enough to travel now."

"Mmm," Ivan grunted again. He weakly waved his hand as he swallowed so hard that he looked like a snake swallowing a large mouse. Lifting his beer stein, he gulped twice, then hammered the cup onto the table. He wiped his mouth with a swipe of his sleeve.

"Perhaps you are right. Rains will be coming soon. Then snow. Snow will make travel north difficult."

"How long do you think—"

Ivan chugged another mouthful of beer, then let go with a soupy, guttural belch. Voldemars cringed as Ivan swallowed what he had obviously brought up.

"The question is not how long. The question is who. Let me see, now. If you head north," Ivan's voice drifted off as he looked pensively at the ceiling.

Voldemars' head spun from Ivan's parable-like words. He wondered if Ivan had ever spoken clearly.

Suddenly, the outside door burst open. They jumped in their chairs. Voldemars turned, but when he saw what appeared to be a uniformed government agent, he snapped his head back and stared into his tea. Through the corner of his eye, he noticed Ivan slowly rise from his chair.

"Ivan Ivanovich?" the officer said. His ill-fit uniform was sloppy and wrinkled.

"Yes, I am. I am Ivan of the Tereks!" His loud voice was forceful. "Why do you disturb my meal with my friend?"

The officer flinched, yet held his ground. He organized his thoughts and cleared his throat.

"I am from the Ural Soviet. We have evidence you are hiding an enemy of the state!"

Voldemars instantly froze. Panic electrified every nerve in his back as he felt the officer's eyes drill into him. The distinct odor of last night's vodka wafted up from his chest as he felt flush. If he identifies me, I'm done, Voldemars thought. He scanned the room, looking for a quick exit. His eyes stopped on Ivan's two black wolf hounds laying near the window. Their eyes were wide, fixed on the Russian. Their ears were stiff and perked. Oddly, though, they remained silent.

"You are aware of the penalties for hiding traitors, are you not?" The officer's voice lowered in pitch and grew more officious.

Voldemars glanced back to Ivan and read his eyes.

"The Terek do not recognize you. No one but Terek rule here. We rule ourselves, as we have for years." Ivan's growl grew belligerent. His eyes grew wide, filling with anger.

What the hell are you doing? Voldemars' eyes screamed.

Ivan kicked out his chair, then motioned Voldemars to do the same.

Are you crazy? Voldemars thought, furrowing his brow. Ivan insisted, nodding once confidently. Do what you have to do, his expression said.

Sucking in a deep breath, Voldemars swallowed hard. He kicked his chair out, spun around, and pulled a concealed pistol from his belt. Surprised, the officer staggered back toward the door. Voldemars held the pistol high and close to his face. He didn't know how else to keep his face hidden.

Ivan then clomped his boots heavily on the floor. The officer's face blanched. Ivan took measured steps toward the man. Terror etched ghastly creases in his forehead. He quivered and sheepishly searched with his hand behind his back for the door, but froze as Ivan's dogs darted to the door and cut him off. Between their bared teeth, their low pitched growls snarled out viciously. The officer's face waned even more. His eyes darted between Ivan, the menacing dogs, and Voldemars' pistol.

"Now, you bastard! You will listen to me," Ivan grabbed the man by the collar and with one hand, lifted him off his feet. He waved his purple stained finger at his nose.

"I said that we, the Tereks, make the laws here. Not you or anybody else. If I choose to invite someone into my stanitza, that's my business. And as for your laws—"

Ivan stopped as he released his grip, dropping the trembling Soviet to the floor. He scrambled to his feet, intensely wary of the snarling dogs only a meter away from him.

"Let me just say that I don't ever want to see you or any of your fucking friends around here again!"

The officer remained frozen.

"Did you hear me?" Ivan demanded.

Quivering, the man nodded.

"Good! Now that we understand each other, get the hell out of here!" Ivan hissed through his grape-stained teeth. He turned back toward Voldemars, grinning out of the officer's view, then strutted back to the table. The officer continued shaking under the watchful eyes of the dogs, growling so much that their jowls frothed white.

Ivan plopped down at the table, then dipped his hand into the bowl of sardines next to the grape mash. He held the head close to his lips and sucked in the pickled fish. His jaw moved back and forth a few times and he spit out a string of bones, completely stripped of their meat. He smacked his lips as he sucked each of his fingers, grabbed his stein, and swigged a mouthful of beer. He slammed it back on the table, released a stomach born belch, and peered up to the Soviet with a menacing squint.

"Let him go!" he barked.

Immediately, the two dogs stopped their growling and slowly sat back on their haunches. The officer slunk past the dogs and scurried out the door. The door slammed shut and Ivan released a tremendous laugh which shook the whole kitchen.

"I've never seen them do that," Voldemars released a huge sigh. Quietly, the dogs thrust their noses into the air, sniffed twice, then slinked to the table. After they licked up the crumbs on the floor, they returned to their spots near the fireplace.

"That's a tradition Poppa passed down to me." Ivan grabbed his stein and guzzled another mouthful of beer. He ripped off another piece of bread, and as if nothing had happened, buried it into the grape mash.

"Poppa told me to train the dogs to let anyone in. Show them you're not afraid. But," Ivan waved his finger, then stuffed the bread into his mouth. He chewed twice and swallowed hard. "But not to let anyone out unless you tell them they can go out!" Ivan burst out in laughter. Just as quickly, he fell silent. His wide blue eyes turned sad as he looked down and shook his head. He seemed to be lost in thought, staring into his empty stein.

"I had the Okhrana trained well." His voice was subdued. "None of them bothered me with any of this shit. But I guess now I just have a whole new crew of government lackeys to teach!"

Voldemars sat back down at the table and took a small piece of bread. As he dipped the bread into the mashed grapes, he swirled it around as Ivan had before.

"Manners don't matter out here, Voldemars," he mumbled, appearing to be adrift in his thoughts. "Friendship is what is important. Remember that. Friendship with the right people will make you win your freedom from these fools."

As grape mash dribbled from the corners of his mouth, Voldemars stifled his urge to quickly wipe it away. It felt strange just hanging there, but it also felt good in a rebellious sense. What would my father say if he saw this, he thought.

"Perhaps you are right. It is time that you and your wife head home," Ivan said. He ran his fingers through his beard. His eyes took on a hollow appearance. "You have learned Cossack tactics well. Yes, a good student. I must admit, though I have never taught anyone not Cossack that could handle a horse as well as you." He perched his bushy eyebrows, then twisted his eyes. "Are you sure you don't have any Cossack blood?"

Voldemars ran his hand over his scraggly beard as he inspected his Cossack friend. Their features were similar—high cheekbones, almond shaped eyes, and a rounded face with a nose tucked tightly to his face.

"Ha! Even that beard of yours is beginning to look like you belong here in Terek!" Ivan guffawed. He munched on another dripping piece of bread.

"I guess that depends on how far back we go," Voldemars pined nostalgia. "It is said that many years ago, some of Ghengis Khan's men traveled north and settled Riga, while others stayed here. That being true, I guess then you could say that we have both descended from the same stock. From a long, long time ago."

"Then we have the same roots for our tree, no? Good!" Ivan quickly replied, then grew more serious in his face. Solemnly, he added: "I can do little more to help you, Voldemars."

Ivan then rose from the table and shuffled to his cabinet. He rummaged for a moment, then pulled out a fresh bottle of vodka with two metal cups and stomped back to the table. He filled Voldemars' halfway, then filled his own and gulped down a mouthful as if it were water.

"Your journey will be difficult," he started with glazed eyes. "Cossacks honor each other's territory as sacredly as if it were our own homes. It is, you know. Land and home. Enough foolish talk. Terek are near the Caucasus. Don live up by the river, and Ingoosh live in the mountains. And then you have the Bolsheviks to deal with, but I taught you how to handle them, eh?"

"If I stay away from them, I should not have problems."

"My friend Voldemars." Ivan waved his finger in a lecturing motion. "Bolsheviks will not be a problem. But Don are a different clan from Terek. Once you reach their land, you will need to convince them you are worthy of their help!"

"Convince them?"

"Yes, what did you call it? Custom?"

"How?" Voldemars caught a whiff of the vodka as it evaporated in front of him.

"They, as any Cossack, recognize horsemanship as ultimate test. You will need to prove your ability in one of their games." A wry grin returned to Ivan's face. "And of course, you must win."

Voldemars confidently smiled back, then sipped at his vodka.

"And for God's sake, Voldemars. Don't drink like old woman in front of them!" Ivan slammed his fist down, jolting the table and rattling the cups. "In these six months, haven't you learned how to drink like man? Do like this. Drink!"

Ivan snapped his head back and drained his glass in his throat. He swallowed hard, snapped his head forward, then slammed the glass on the table.

"Take a fucking mouthful and swallow. I know them. They will tear you apart and leave you for the wolves if you don't drink with them like man. Don are not as friendly as Terek."

Voldemars followed Ivan's lead, took a mouthful of the vodka, then swallowed hard. For a moment, he felt nothing, but his wait was brief. A warm tingle flickered like a tiny flame in his stomach, then quickly ignited and crept into his chest. With little hesitation, it raced up his nape and exploded into a sharper, more prickly sensation. He felt the vodka nip at every one of his hairs as it passed from the back of his head to the front. His head grew heavy and his mind dulled as the tingling expanded to his arms and legs.

"Very good! Now that's how to drink vodka!" Ivan proudly announced, then took another Cossack-sized gulp from his own cup.

"Then—" Voldemars had to stop when his head began spinning. "Then, tomorrow we go?"

"Tomorrow? No, today!" Ivan blurted, protruding his lips through his beard. His eyes twinkled. "Riding with tingle of vodka in head is exhilarating. That is Cossack way, Voldemars."

Voldemars remembered the last time he rode with the tingle of vodka in his head. He grew nauseous just thinking about it.

"We go, then. Another drink, and we go." Ivan insisted behind a wry grin without letting Voldemars respond. He swept his hand across the table, then lifted his cup and clanged the edge with Voldemars'. He upended it and downed the remaining liquor. Voldemars mimicked his host, and he kept his mouth closed to keep from getting any more drunk that he already was.

"Nothing better than good vodka, no?" Ivan commented. "I'll roust Sergei and Osipov, and horses for you and your Otilija!"

"I'll go tell the women to bundle baby Brevite, and we'll be one with wind," Voldemars said as he stood, trying at least to sound like a Cossack.

❦   ❦   ❦

Under waves of gray, herring-bone shaped clouds, Ivan led the caravan north. Otilija rode close to her husband with Brevite nestled in a round backpack. Through the morning, they descended from the stanitzas amidst the mountains and into the valleys. By mid-afternoon, the single file of horses emerged out of the last pass between the Caucasus where the Manych River entered the grassy steppe lowlands.

Ivan remained as the head of the expedition, as he always did when the Cossacks rode on what he called adventures. Across the breast of his admittedly favorite white and powder blue tcherkaska, bandoleers filled with silver-tipped blank cartouches hung decoratively. Dangling from his left hip was his personal saber, a richly carved blade with a stone covered guard. Osipov followed, draped with his favorite emerald green tunic, one he claimed as spoils during an adventure into Georgia. Sergei's long, shirt, complete with ballooned arms, was bright blue with yellow and red-trimmed edges.

Now comfortable with the lavender tcherkaska that Ivan had given him, Voldemars felt as if he had become one of the Terek. He kept his cavalry saber, a subject of much debate between him and Ivan. But he insisted he would not part with it, and it hung proudly from a leather strap that ran from his shoulder to his waist.

Near the river, Ivan signaled them to stop. After a brief survey of the area, he urged his mount toward the rambling water, leaving everyone else on the pebbled bank. Voldemars watched him survey the territory ahead, then plod halfway across the river. He turned his horse parallel to the banks and signaled the pack to cross in front of him, as if he stood guard for their safety. Osipov lead, followed by Voldemars, then Otilija and finally Sergei.

Voldemars and Otilija continued unescorted to the other side as Osipov stopped when he reached Ivan. Sergei stopped his mount and cocked his head. A playful smirk blossomed on his face. He steadied his horse, then urged him closer to Ivan.

Suddenly, Ivan whooped twice. As he withdrew his saber, he yanked back on his reins. His horse reared, thrashing his forelegs into the air. Sergei bellowed a blood curdling scream and sharply dug his heels into his horse's ribs. Frothed water splashed and sprayed in every direction as the pair raced through the river, sabers drawn as if charging into battle.

Voldemars froze, panicked he had been duped into being the target of a barbarous Cossack attack. Realizing there was no escape, he defiantly stood his ground between the charge and his obviously shaken wife, and prepared for the onslaught. His hand twitching, he covered the grip on his saber.

Ivan emerged from the water first and raced toward Voldemars. But without so much as a swipe with his saber, he sped past, close enough that Voldemars could hear his mount's snorting. Sergei's horse pounded past with the same fervor as his leader, followed closely by his echo bouncing back from the mountain pass. As the racing pair galloped into the grassy field, Sergei captured the lead from Ivan, then let out a trilling whoop.

Awe struck, Voldemars watched the hussars play. He breathed relief, mistaken at their intentions. Back near the river, Osipov whooped with a deep, rhythmic tone, like a tavern bully urging on a fighting pair.

Ivan nosed ahead with a sudden burst of speed, then extended his lead by two lengths. He leaned almost parallel to the ground, and with one quick swoop of his saber, slashed the top half of a solitary bush, leaving it less than two feet high.

Sergei slipped in close behind and lopped off what remained to ground level, leaving nothing but stubble. His cry became victoriously joyous as he stood up in his stirrups, holding his saber high over his head.

Ivan stood up in his saddle, and spun his horse around in a remarkably tight turn, then raised his saber skyward. Sergei remained in hot pursuit until he was so dangerously close to Ivan that Voldemars thought the two might collide. Instead, Sergei yanked back on his reins, whooped loudly, and inched close enough to clash his saber with Ivan's. As if the ritual signaled an end to their joust, the men bellowed loud laughs, sheathed their swords, and galloped toward Voldemars, Otilija, and a chuckling Osipov.

"This is as far as we dare go, Voldemars," Osipov said quietly, his face suddenly turning more serious. "I know what we have said about being fearless. And I could see in your eyes you feel we are nothing more than a lawless band of barbarians. So what I say now may surprise you."

"I don't think so, Osipov," Voldemars admitted. "I have seen and heard many things over these past few months. Once, any of them may have surprised me, but now, I don't believe anything you say would—"

"We have an understanding with Don," Osipov said. He stopped long enough to swallow a mouthful of vodka from his flask. "Many years ago, Terek agreed not to trespass on Don land. In return, they promised that our sovereign claim to this land would not be challenged. Because of this, we must now turn back and head home. The river is our border. We can game here, as can the Don. But no further. You and Otilija are on your own, friend Voldemars."

He leaned over and offered his hand to Voldemars. As he did, Voldemars gazed past him and saw wide, open fields of summer-browned grasses teeming with blackbirds, each swinging back and forth as they clutched to seed heads. The fields remained without much variety, spreading out for what appeared to be miles of openness.

"It certainly is a beautiful land," he mumbled. "Who of Don should I look for? If I just go traipsing into Don land dressed like this, don't I threaten your agreement?"

"Good question." Ivan jumped in.

Voldemars caught himself, remembering what Ivan had taught him about being surprised. He watched Ivan swig from a half-bottle of vodka before surrendering it to Sergei.

"I talked to Alexiev about week ago. When you meet Don, tell them you are friend of Ivan the Terek. Tell them you are lost friend I said had come from a far place."

"But how do I know they won't believe me?"

"You still do not trust us, do you?" Sergei said, resting the bottle against his mount's flank. He glared sternly at Voldemars. His hand slipped down to his saber.

"Let me explain." Ivan interjected, taking the bottle from Sergei and passing it to Osipov. "It is sadly true that Cossack reputation is, shall we say, stained. Let me explain more about Cossacks. We've gone on pogroms, raised hell, created chaos. True, but, we do this because we were mercenaries. We've killed because we were paid to kill. It was a job, like the job you say is teaching others."

"It was our way," Sergei took his turn in the explanation with surprisingly adept control of his words. His voice was still laced with anger. "We know you feel our job is distasteful. But it is necessary one, nonetheless. We know that. We all know that. But we have kept our freedom from all Czars by doing just this one task for them."

"Why do you think we drink so much," Osipov added soberly. "Vodka has the remarkable ability to cleanse our minds of the sins that come with our job."

"And the Bolsheviks?" Voldemars asked bluntly, gasping as he let a mouthful of vodka slide down his throat.

"The Bolsheviks will not bother us," Sergei jumped in. "They know who we are and what we do. Ivan told me you saw what little they can do to us."

"I don't think we'll be much value to Bolsheviks," Ivan added with a saddened tone. He bowed his head. "We've always taken pride in who we are, not what we've done. The Bolsheviks, though, are a ruthless lot. I've seen what they've done, and they enjoy killing. It's dark times for all mankind, Cossack or otherwise when there are those who kill for pleasure."

Voldemars inspected every thread and muscle of the three Cossacks mounted before him. When his eyes met Osipov's, he nodded. Sergei's crooked grin coaxed him to smile. All was healed between them. But when he looked into Ivan's penetrating eyes, a twinge grabbed at his heart. He felt their eyes lock with mutual admiration as a tear welled in his eye.

"I will always remember you, friend Ivan," Voldemars fought back the tears. "In all of my life, I have always looked upon Cossacks much as you have just characterized me. But these last few months have shown me that you and your friends are the most compassionate, generous, and unpretentious people I have ever known. Perhaps the most I'll ever know. I know you didn't have to do what you did for me and Otilija. And for that, I am deeply grateful."

"Take this," Ivan mumbled as he rummaged through his makeshift saddle bag. He pulled out a full bottle of vodka and tossed it to Voldemars. "Cossacks honor good vodka!"

"I wish you well, friend Ivan," Voldemars said as he stashed the bottle into his satchel.

Ivan saluted in a mock imitation of military protocol. Sergei and Osipov followed, then chortled.

"Good luck, Colonel Voldemars Vechi. I hope Cossack in you will help win your Latvia brivibas," Ivan said, then swooped his saber from its sheath and sliced the air next to Voldemars, close enough that he heard the whoosh of the blade. His horse reared and thundered off, followed closely by his two companions.

Voldemars and Otilija watched the trio of whooping, yelping Cossacks splash through the river, then disappear back into the mountain pass. Alone on the steppe, they started their long journey home.

❧   ❧   ❧

For the two hours since they had departed company from Ivan and his clan, Voldemars and Otilija followed the railroad tracks northeast, taking Ivan's suggestion. As if they were on a pleasant country ride, their horses plodded through the waves of amber steppe grasses at a reserved pace. The air remained dry and touched with gentle breezes wafting the odor of musty, fallen leaves from the distant woodlands. Hidden behind thickening clouds, the sun left the day cool and comfortable.

Voldemars knew the general geography of the area, and realized that the distance to Voronezh along this route would be twice what they would need to travel if they crossed the Don territory directly. But Ivan's warnings about this clan of Cossack made it absolutely clear to him that this route would be markedly safer. Skirting the known reaches of the territory would make for fewer chances at confrontations with the Don.

"In all my years, I never dreamed I would be doing anything like this," Otilija muttered.

"Oh?" Voldemars engaged, tipping his head back and listening.

"Married, yes. With child, yes. But riding with my husband, on horseback, through Russian fields with my child strapped to my back like some sort of nomadic throwback? Not really."

"Survival, Otilija," Voldemars mumbled absently. He surveyed the landscape, but there was nothing but the endless sprawl of grass fields. "One day when we are old and gray, we will rock in our chairs at Telmeni and reminisce about the adventure these days offered."

Otilija shook her head. She urged her horse closer to him, then nudged his arm. "At Telmeni? You did say at Telmeni?"

"I guess I did."

"Does that mean you've decided?"

"Things have changed for me," Voldemars noted matter-of-factly. "They've changed in a way that—well, I guess things are just different now."

"Oh?"

"I never thought I could ever be near Cossacks, no less live with them. Yet I did. We did. We lived like Cossacks, me with the men, and you with the women, and hardly ever seeing each other. But I have to admit, I've learned alot more from Ivan than I ever thought I could. I guess I had alot of time in the stanitza to think about what I really want."

"Look!" Otilija gasped, pointing to a farm which had appeared over the horizon.

Voldemars' voice evaporated. He pulled his reins, stopping his horse. Cautiously, he studied the area more thoroughly.

No movement. No noises. No animals. Nothing but what looked like an abandoned farm. A strange tingle crept up his back, but dissipated as quickly as it had started. Increasingly curious, he turned to Otilija, nodded and moved forward. With his eyes, he told her to follow closely, then urged his mount tentatively.

When the north side of the house became visible, he stopped his horse immediately. There were two mutilated horse carcasses in the field. He gagged as the wind shifted and brought not just the rank stench from the rotting flesh, but also the sickening buzzing of a swarm of carrion satiated flies.

"Oh, my God." Otilija's gasp sounded breathless. She turned away, covering her mouth with her open hands.

Voldemars stared at the farmhouse, obviously left after heinous pillage. Windows rested half-open, their glass totally smashed out from their panes. Gaping holes pocked the siding where clap boards had been ripped away.

"Cossacks!" Voldemars heard a women shout with alarm. His eyes darted back to the front of the house where he spotted two, hunched old women. One froze as she grabbed the other's shoulder and pointed. Even from his distance, he felt intense fear in their frozen stares.

"No, no!" Voldemars started to explain. "We are,"

He stopped his approach as the women scurried like frightened rats for safety behind the house. From their haven, eyes peered out warily.

"Is there no virtue left in this world," Otilija mumbled disgustedly, then dropped her head and continued back toward the rail bed.

Voldemars stood frozen, abandoned.

"Those bastards. Those two-faced, lying bastards," He heard Otilija continue grumbling.

It can't be Ivan. If this is the Don's work, I don't know if we can trust them as we have Ivan, he thought, trying to assure himself as he turned his horse around. He caught up with Otilija at the tracks, still mired in disbelief at what he had seen.

❧   ❧   ❧

. An hour later, Voldemars stopped at a fork where the tracks split off to the east and a road wound north into a thick wooded area. He peered as deeply as his eyes allowed into the stand of autumn blushed birches and oaks, but the glen's contrasting darkness revealed little. Puzzled, he weighed the risk of heading either way, then chose. "Keep your eyes open and stay far enough behind me that you can run for cover if I tell you," he warned Otilija.

She nodded, and he nudged his horse and cautiously approached the trees until they passed through the opening below the spreading boughs. With each of his horse's measured steps, daylight succumbed to woodland darkness. He felt his nape hairs bristle. Listening carefully, trying to compensate for his limited vision, he remained keen to everything. Song birds whistled short, chirpy tunes as they flitted amidst the branches. Twigs snapped underneath scurrying feet of squirrels and rabbits. Wind whooshed through the leaves, pushing aside branches and letting slivers of sunlight slip though the canopy.

"Go back," he suddenly whispered without warning, pulling up on his reins. He cocked his head and listened closely until he confirmed what he had heard. Pivoting his head quickly side to side, he flashed his finger toward a thick stand of birches. "Over there. You should be safe there."

Otilija froze. Her eyes iced over.

"Go now! I hear horses." He ordered more forcefully, turning broadside in the open road. Otilija complied, quickly slipping behind the thin peeling trunks as Voldemars' mount snorted and danced underneath him. He was ready, fist clenched over the handle of his saber and heels poised at his mount's ribs. The distant hooves grew louder. His hand twitched. His legs ached. Even the goose skinned boots he wore seemed to suddenly shrink and strangle his calves. Breathe slow, stay calm, he thought. Everything Ivan had told him about the Don flooded his mind.

Two horsemen appeared from behind the shadows. They pulled up and sat rigidly.

His skin quivered. They had obviously seen him. He remained stolid and steadfast and sized them up. Their clothing looked nothing like what Ivan had told him Don Cossacks would be wearing.

There is something about one, Voldemars thought, focused on the one to the left. He was huge and his horse stood massive in proportion. His heavy black beard hung down far enough to cover the opening on his green tunic. His hair lay matted like a rug over his head and covered his ears. In contrast, the other horseman was clean-shaven, with long, wavy blonde hair. His tunic was the same as his partner's, but the blandness was decorated with traditional Cossack trappings, complete with silver-tipped bandoleers, crossed over his chest.

Why haven't they charged? Voldemars glanced back long enough to ensure Otilija remained hidden, then turned back and combed his mind for how Ivan showed him how the engagement needed to be done. His pulsing right hand hovered only inches away from his saber's handle, arm crossed over his body. He nervously cinched up his horse's reins in his left hand, then sucking in a deep breath, nudged his horse and inched toward the standing pair. His confidence wavered, even as he knew that with a Cossack-trained horse underneath him, he could respond as quickly as would be needed—like Uguns would.

Oh, shit! Voldemars stopped his mount with a tug. His adversaries had yet to move toward him. What if they're Bolsheviks? Christ, have I given away that I'm not a Cossack.

Don't fear the Bolsheviks. If you act like a Cossack, they will fear you, a voice said clearly in his head.

He rummaged into his supply sack, found a shiny ruble, and in one motion, flung the coin toward the two horsemen. When it fell perfectly, half-way between him and them, he drew his saber.

"Here goes nothing," he mumbled, then tried to whoop like Ivan had taught him. The sounds that emerged sounded more like a choking raven than a fearless Cossack. He snapped his reins and dug his heels into his mount's flanks. Instantly, the horse reared and bolted toward the horsemen. He crouched close to his horse's neck, trying to break the wall of air battering his eyes, but the pounding still drew a film over them. Even squinting did not help.

Instead of bolting toward him in what would have been typical Cossack response though, the pair remained nervously still. Panic paraded the thought that these men were not what he thought they were. He glanced down and noticed the ruble pass quickly under his horse's hooves. Immediately he pulled hard right on the reins.

The horse slammed his front legs into the road, almost throwing Voldemars from his saddle. Dirt sprayed up from the dug in hooves as they slid to a stop. He squeezed his thighs and pushed himself back into the saddle's hold, then glared at the pair.

"Cossack!" The large bearded one called. His voice echoed through the trees. His wide, gray eyes fired out a cold, icy stare.

Voldemars' horse pawed at the dusty road. Panic squeezed at his throat.

"We mean you no harm, Cossack. We are nomads," the smaller one explained with an odd tremble in his voice.

Voldemars was instantly puzzled. "White or Red," he demanded, waving his saber in a threatening gesture. A strange, inquisitive expression suddenly appeared on the large man's face as he stared at Voldemars' saber.

"Whites!" The large man shouted. A small, congenial grin grew underneath his scraggly beard as he cocked his head.

"And how do I know that?" Voldemars demanded as he studied the large horseman closely. There was a vague familiarity there. He was sure of that. Tentatively, he nudged his horse forward again. His eyes remained fixed on the large soldier, all the while combing his mind for where he may have seen the face before.

"You don't, but neither do we know who you are," the smaller one sniped.

"I come from Terek territory," Voldemars revealed, realizing he had nothing to lose. "Ivan Ivanovich had given me these clothes since mine were ragged and worthless."

"Ivan?"

"Yes. He told me one called Alexiev would help me."

"I am Alexiev Alexandrovich!" The bearded fellow insistently stood in his stirrups.

Like a low hanging bough on a brisk country ride everything about the huge man became obvious.

"Chenelov? Alexiev Alexandrovich Chenelov?"

"Voldemars?" Alexiev asked, squinting and leaning forward. "Son-of-a-bitch, Voldemars? Is that really you?"

Waves of relief crashed though Voldemars.

"Christ, I couldn't see you beneath that scraggly beard of yours!" Alexiev's tone skipped an octave as he stoked his beard. His grin widened to his familiar toothy smile.

Slipping his saber into its sheath, Voldemars snapped his reins and cantered toward Alexiev. He stopped next to his old comrade and extended his hand. With his typically strong grip, Alexiev grasped Voldemars' hand, pushing the blood right out of his fingers. "I never expected to ever see you again," Voldemars said as he turned and whistled two shrill notes.

"And neither did I," Alexiev said. "This is Leopold Mikailovich. He is, well, he was from the Eleventh. His entire brigade was lost at the front."

Voldemars nodded at Leopold and smiled as Otilija joined the group.

"Leopold, this is Voldemars Janovich Vechi. My commander."

Leopold dropped his head, as if in a silent prayer, then glanced back up at Voldemars and Otilija. "I know what you must have gone through, Colonel Vechi." He started with a factual, solemn coldness to his voice. "My brother died of gas poisoning at the front. You are fortunate to have survived."

"I know," Voldemars mumbled. His shoulders and neck tingled as the hellish recollections of his own ordeal at the front passed fleetingly though his memory.

"How goes the battle, Alexiev?" Voldemars pried.

"Not well." Alexiev hung his head, obviously embarrassed. "The Bolsheviks are disorganized and a sorry lot, but we haven't been able to get the supplies we need from other governments. It seems every time we win a battle, the Bolsheviks steal it back. Casualties are heavy. I don't know how much longer we can hold out the hope of ever winning."

"My God. Oleg. Have you heard from Oleg?" Voldemars blurted.

"I'm afraid not, Voldemars," Alexiev bowed his head briefly. "Ukraine is a big land, and there are many of us Whites. The problem though is that we have no organization. I suppose that is why we're in so much trouble. As for Oleg, if he's lucky, he's befriended some Cossacks and is in hiding someplace where the Bolsheviks won't find him. And if he's not…." Alexiev bowed his head again.

"If he's not, I wouldn't hold much hope for him. He's either dead or jailed somewhere," Leopold added coldly. "The bastards have shown no mercy since they've captured Kiev."

"The Bolsheviks have taken Kiev?" Voldemars asked. Alexiev nodded.

He looked up to the canopy of leaves and sighed loudly. "Sometimes I wonder if it's all worth the fight."

Brevite's muffled cry escaped her basket.

"What's that?" Leopold asked as Otilija swung the basket in front of her.

"It's what is worth the fight. My Brevite," Voldemars said proudly. "Our baby Brevite."

"My God, Voldemars. Are you crazy?" Alexiev craned his neck to see. "Why would you be traveling in a war zone with a baby strapped on your back?"

"Christ, you know what the Bolsheviks will do to you if they catch you," Leopold said.

"If the Bolsheviks catch me, well, it doesn't matter now, does it? I don't intend to be caught. We're headed back to Latvia. Ivan heard that there are some in my land that are planning to move away from Russia and become a free state."

Alexiev turned toward Leopold and raised his eyebrows. Leopold nodded solemnly. As he did, an idea sprung to life in Voldemars' head. "My dear friend, Alexiev," he started jokingly, as he thought about his idea further, the more attractive it became. "What would you say if we reformed—"

"I know you haven't seen each other for a long time," Otilija said as she pulled Brevite from the basket. "But Brevite needs to be fed, and I will not do that on horseback."

Alexiev grinned as he turned to Voldemars, who just nodded. "I see where you got your penchant for command, Voldemars!"

"Yes," Leopold nodded, then turned his horse. "Our camp is not far from here. Follow me."

❦   ❦   ❦

A damp, chilled night air rolled in quickly after sunset, coaxing nightingales to begin their evening serenade. Hidden safely deep in a thick stand of pines, Otilija sat by herself and nursed Brevite while the three former soldiers scurried about to prepare an evening camp. Leopold assembled a meager campfire, dropped a lit cigarette into a pile of tinder, then methodically propped twigs around the wisping smolder. Voldemars and Alexiev gathered armfuls of sappy pine and dropped their loads next to Leopold before turning back and scavenging for more fuel. Within minutes, the rich aroma of burning pine filled the air while flames lapped at the darkness, casting ghostly shadows on each of the huddled men's faces. Concerned for Otilija's exposed skin, Voldemars retrieved one of the colorful blankets from his supply packs and draped it around his wife and daughter. After a brief, understanding glance, he returned to his place with the other two men.

"Do you know what happened to that farm back there?" Voldemars asked, sitting on a stump near the fire.

"Reds," Leopold said coldly, and threw another stick onto the fire.

"That's why we weren't so sure about you at first," Alexiev added. "Almost all of the farms around here have been attacked. At first I figured it was Cossacks, but when I went to their camp and questioned them, they denied it."

"Then you do have contact with the Don?"

"We understand each other," Alexiev noted. Leopold cracked a knowing smile.

"Ivan said they've stopped their pogroms, too, but I found it hard to believe."

"I met Leopold in their camp that night," Alexiev said. "It was then that I believed them."

"The Reds came through here three nights ago, just before sunset." Leopold's monotone voice quivered. His eyes glassed over as he lay a larger branch onto the fire. "What seemed like a whole brigade of the bastards galloped out of the grasslands, whooping and hollering like they were Cossacks. I was with three of the Don, not far from the tracks. We hid in the brush and watched those ruthless bastards circle the farm. When the old women came out to scream at them, they chased them until they dropped from exhaustion. Two of the fuckers broke into the barn, then started shooting off rounds from their rifles like madmen. Boards splintered. Pigs squealed. Horses snorted as they escaped from the open doors, dragging their own bleeding, mutilated flanks behind them."

Leopold snuck a glance over his shoulder toward Otilija, then looked back down to the fire. He poked absently at it with a branch in his hand, waiting long enough for the end to catch fire. He pulled out the end and stared at the fading flicker. "Then a tall bastard strutted out of the house, carrying a beautiful girl over his shoulder. Her dress had been torn, her tits hung exposed, cut and bleeding. She beat the hell out of his back, screaming for help at the top of her lungs, but he wouldn't put her down. He just kept on walking with this devilish look on his filthy face." Leopold stopped and dropped his face into his open hands. Choked up and stuttering, Leopold fell silent, unable to continue.

"When he threw her down to the ground, the Cossacks had seen enough," Alexiev continued, shadows dancing on his face as he waved his hands dramatically. "They charged, leaving Leopold stunned and alone. He watched as the fuckers gunned down the Cossacks without even a second thought. They didn't even have a chance."

306   Telmenu Saimnieks

Leopold looked up to the sky. His mouth gaped open as if he wanted to continue, but nothing emerged from his mouth, other than labored sighs.

"Like animals," Alexiev said in an angry yet despondent tone, "they fucked the poor girl right in front of the old ladies, slapping and cursing at her while she fought to protect herself. Then, leaving what you saw, they carried the poor girl off. She's probably dead by now."

"The Cossacks aren't the ones without a sense of morality," Leopold said with a cracked voice.

Voldemars startled when he heard Brevite burp next to him. Otilija must have heard most of the story. She hung her head, wiped Brevite's mouth, and peered at Voldemars with terror filled eyes.

"They were looking for us, Voldemars," Alexiev concluded. His face had blanched to a pasty white. His eyes were wide saucers, reflecting the wildly dancing fire.

"Somebody told the Reds we were there, and when they didn't find us, they took it out on them!"

"Then are we safe here?" Voldemars whispered. He glanced at Otilija as she carefully placed Brevite back into her basket near the fire. He turned back to Alexiev, whose face twitched as it held back tears.

"That was a Cossack house. The Don have vowed they will carry their revenge until the last of them have been drained of their last drop of blood," Alexiev muttered.

"As long as the Don survive, we will be safe. But the Bolsheviks have much better and more powerful weapons than the Don," Leopold added.

"I see," Voldemars said as Otilija sat down next to him, holding the basket tightly. The campfire crackled and spat small, red sparks toward him, but they fell harmlessly to the ground. In the distance, amidst the howls of hungry wolves, Voldemars heard the familiar blood-curdling yips and whoops of Cossacks in a charge. He wrapped his arm around Otilija and brought her close to him.

"I never thought I would grow used to those sounds," Otilija admitted. "It's strange, Voldemars. Now they seem to comfort me, knowing what kind of man is behind them."

Gunfire echoed in the distance. More yelps and screams followed. "A Cossack's honor. I would have never believed it if I hadn't experienced it myself," Voldemars said.

Near Telmeni

19 September 1917

Voldemars led the entourage of four horses plodding along the dusty road north of Cesis and into the village of Valmiera. He squirmed in his saddle, gently massaging his sores, festering from the two weeks of continuous travel from the Ukraine. His sores, though, were merely an inconvenience compared to the emotional battle raging in his mind. Even through his exhaustion, his mind worked feverishly without respite, searching for the exact words he would say to his father. From the time the sun rose, he rehearsed what he wanted to say over and over again, experimenting with intonation and emphasis. But now that the sun was setting beyond the western hills of Valmiera, the words grew increasingly difficult to remember.

He surveyed the landmarks as he stopped at a tree-lined dirt drive which turned sharply west from the main road. He stared through the glen formed by the alley of oaks covered with golden orange leaves. To the right was an open field of cut rye, standing in pyramids like amber sentinels. Behind them a thin wisp of smoke trailed up from the house, still hidden beyond the trees.

"Is this it?" Otilija asked innocently as she drew next to him.

He remained silent. He turned his mount broadside and maintained a blank stare into the alley. A slight breeze slipped the aroma of fallen apples by his nose.

"Voldemars, is this Telmeni?" she asked again, tipping her head.

Thirteen years, he thought as he straightened. His father would never approve of such a poor riding position. He tightened his buttocks, itching his sores, then immediately stiffened his back and sat upright again. His heart fluttered in his chest, followed by a gnawing anxiousness which crept through every one of his bones.

Has he changed as much as I have in thirteen years, Voldemars' thoughts cascaded. Does he even want me back anymore? Is he still alive?

"Is something wrong?" Otilija's voice invaded his thoughts.

Damn, why didn't I write? Voldemars was consumed. Why didn't I even try try to write? I really could have found the time.

"Voldemars?"

He shook his head and glanced at Otilija, but when her piercing eyes fixed on him, begging him to share his thoughts, he turned back and peered into the glen.

"Home," he mumbled, rubbing his mouth with his open hand. Memories he thought had been lost forever appeared as vivid as the days he had lived them. The time he acted out the legend of Lacplesis, when he spent all night fishing on Bauzis with his father, hiking with him through the Gauja valley, exploring castle remains. The images flipped past as soon as they came into focus. The image of him was suddenly older as he recalled staying up all night at his first Jani, singing dainas so loud that he was hoarse for a week. Elena appeared, the first girl he ever kissed after they both had stolen a drinks from Poppa's special brew without him knowing.

"Voldemars?"

"Uh, yes. Telmeni. This is Telmeni." He returned to the present. "Let's go." He waved his entourage onto the side road and plodded forward.

"You never told me much about Telmeni," Otilija prodded, closely following him into the glen. "Or your parents, for that matter."

Inadvertently, he ignored her, more consumed with trying to catch a glimpse of the house for assurance that he had remembered the landmarks correctly.

I hope this is it, he thought, swaying side to side on his horse. Christ. If this is old man Ziemels' road, he'd probably come out and chase me with a switch. Voldemars had let all of his chickens loose at one time for a joke.

He hunched over and poised his head near his horse's throat. Finally, contorted and almost falling off, he caught a fleeting glance of the farmhouse. A tingle raced down his back, but vanished when the breeze shifted, pushing the tree branches back into his view again.

"Yes, Otilija. This is Telmeni," he muttered as he pulled himself back up. When he emerged first through the glen into the opening in front of the farmhouse, he stiffened and slowed to a measured pace. Wave upon wave of electricity trickled through his spine as if the sight alone coaxed all of his boyhood memories to rush out and greet him.

The apple orchard spread out to his left, and just like every autumn, under each carefully pruned tree lay a skirt of golden and red blushed fruit. Beyond the orchard, what seemed like one hundred coned, amber rye stacks stood in orderly rows in the fields, each of their seed-filled tops tied together and bent off to the right. In the meadow, a small herd of cows meandered through freshly cut field of hay, stooping to nibble on tied rolls of grass. Berry bushes arched over the stone walls and slat fences. Gardens seemed to fill every available spot, stretching out forever, stopping only for small buildings or stone walls.

"Oh, Voldemars, I don't know if I can ever be the farm wife you want me to be," Otilija mumbled.

"I know you can," he muttered, half-listening to her.

"But I'm used to closeness and defined limits of a city. Like Riga. I don't even know if I can deal with this openness."

"It's not as difficult as it appears."

"But will your parents accept me?"

"Momma will like you," he assuaged. "I know she will. And she'll teach you all you need to know."

It's not easy for me either, Otilija, he thought, as the haunting face of his father when he left Telmeni all those years ago returned. That same pained expression hovered close to his face, almost close enough that he could smell the sweat that oozed from his pores. His attention was drawn back to the side of the road where he caught sight of buckets hanging off taps hammered into swaying liepa trees. He remembered how as a child, he would spend hours just watching the buckets fill slowly with the dripping sap. And when they were full, he quickly replaced them with empties, then carried the full ones back to the house, sloshing at his side. All of this work just so he could watch Momma boil the ooze down into a sweet, sugary syrup. His mouth watered as his taste buds flickered with the richness of that syrup mixed with freshly churned butter trickled over hot potato pancakes.

He remembered how his father would sometimes sneak away with a few of the buckets and furtively carry them out to the smoke house. What his father had done with them remained a secret until one year his curiosity captured him so much that he mustered the courage to follow him out to the smokehouse. Careful not to be seen, he hid behind a mound of rocks until Poppa closed and locked the door. He rolled a stump next to the little house, and used it to peek through the small window that otherwise would be out of his reach.

Poppa carefully measured out some rye in a small metal cup, then mixed it in a clay pot with a jar of blackberries he had obviously hidden away since summer. When he looked satisfied at the mash, he added it to the bucket, now steaming away on the wood stove. An impish smile blossomed on his face as he inhaled the billowing steam rising from the kettle.

Each week, he followed his father out to the smoke house to watch him work with the concoction. Each time, Poppa's smile seemed to grow wider and wider, until after six weeks, he remembered Poppa's face light up. After Poppa left that day, he remembered sneaking into the shack and getting his first taste of Poppa's kvass, as he called it. His tongue dried merely at the thought of tasting the head-spinning brew.

He was startled back to reality when he heard the front door of the farmhouse slam closed. The image of him tasting the kvass vanished. He was only meters from the house. On the porch rested two chairs. One he remembered as Poppa's and a smaller one pulled up next to it was Momma's. When a figure stepped out of the shadows under the porch roof, he could not help but stare.

He walked toward Voldemars with short, stilted steps. His sun reddened face pruned as he squinted, trying to recognize who these people were that rode up to his house.

Voldemars felt his heart skip. His throat swelled. His breathing stopped. All of the disjointed memories he had relived over the past six months flashed through his mind like a repeating rifle firing off bullets. Thirteen years of suppressed emotions for his father rushed his mind like an overfilled dam bursting loose. His face grew taught and his lips quivered, lacking instruction from his subconscious as to which way to turn or what to say. His mouth dropped open, and he started to recite the phrases he had repeated what seemed one hundred times, but the words evaporated before escaping his lips.

The old man stiffened. He craned his neck toward Voldemars and squinted. Tremors shook his entire body as he revealed recognition of the face underneath the beard. He raised his quivering hands to his mouth, then turned toward the house.

"Kristine!" Voldemars heard the voice crack on the verge of tears. "Kristine, it's Voldemars! Come quick, Kristine! Voldemars has come home!"

Home. Poppa's words reverberated in his head. A cascade of relief rushed from him and through his chest like a waterfall. Festered anxiety dissipated, cycling wildly with contentment. The lump in his throat grew even larger as his father turned back and faced him with a beaming expression. An expression which Voldemars hoped for but never expected to ever see again.

He slipped off his horse, and handed the reins to Alexiev, who had pulled up next to him. Remaining rigidly at attention, he studied his father through a film of tears. As he started rehearsing each of the opening lines he practiced along the road, his father started stiltedly toward him. But when the old man stopped directly in front of him and peered up with his oval, green eyes, Voldemars' mind went blank.

Face to face, the two men stood quivering, blankly staring into each other's eyes. Voldemars tried to force out some words, any words, but nothing escaped his mouth.

"I'm sorry I haven't written, Poppa," he managed.

Janis' jaw trembled. His smile melted until his lips pursed and expression grew cold. "I see you are well, Voldemars." The life that flickered in his hollow green eyes seemed to fade.

Silence reigned as the pair stood simply staring at each other through misty eyes. The seconds seemed to linger as each man stood his ground, attempting to read the others' thoughts.

"How long has it been?" Janis asked tentatively.

"A long time," Voldemars mumbled quietly. He searched his father for a sign that everything had been forgiven, but his face had grown ashen and cold. Voldemars sighed, debating whether a calm, collected approach or a more openly emotional one was appropriate. Stiffly, he reached out, grasped his father's shoulders and drew him close.

"How's Momma?" he asked softly into his father's ear.

"She's well," Janis tentatively replied. He squirmed out of his son's grasp and slowly pushed himself away before tipping his head and staring into Voldemars' cloudy eyes.

"And Augusts?" Voldemars also stepped back.

"Fine. He's just returned from Moscow." Janis curtly replied.

"And Romans?" Voldemars asked. A smile cracked his face. "Is he chasing girls yet?"

"Romans? Oh, no, not Romans," Janis returned. "You'd be surprised with him. He has grown up to be a very serious, very studious boy. Only books for him." Janis let a wry grin slip. Voldemars caught a glimpse of it just as it shriveled back to pruned, brooding lips. "But then, his stubbornness is definitely a trait I'm used to," Janis added.

"Edwards?" A tiny grin blossomed on Voldemars' face as he sensed progress.

"He's working up north. Estonia, I think."

Voldemars felt his father's glare burrow deep into him, obviously probing. But when he looked up and caught his glance, Janis broke the stalemate and turned away.

"And who is this with you?" he asked, looking past him.

"Excuse my poor manners, Poppa," Voldemars stepped back. He reached up and took Brevite's basket from Otilija and while cradling it, helped his wife from her mount.

"This is Otilija, my wife."

"Mr. Vechi," Otilija politely tipped her head and nodded. She took the basket from Voldemars and started to pull the squirming baby out.

"Poppa. Call me Poppa." Janis glanced at Otilija and offered a warm, but short lived, smile. He turned his attention back to Voldemars. "You could have written me that you have such a lovely wife. Is one of these fine soldiers Oleg, who did write to me?" Janis asked, nodding to Alexiev and Leopold.

Voldemars recoiled, hearing Oleg's name.

"I am Alexiev Chenelov," Alexiev started, struggling not to make his voice sound intimidating. "I was a captain in your sons' brigade. And this is Leopold Petrov."

"Russians?" Janis whispered, staring grimly at Voldemars. He stumbled backward while Alexiev and Leopold hopped down from their saddles, but quickly regained his balance, and stared icily at Voldemars.

"No, Poppa. They're good Russians," Voldemars said.

"We prefer to be considered Ukrainian, sir," Alexiev noted. Janis' expression remained disapproving.

"They're not Bolsheviks, Poppa. They're my friends," Voldemars added. "They helped us get home and they're—"

Voldemars felt his words evaporate as he hesitated and concentrated on his father's expression.

"We have come to fight with your son for your Latvia!" Alexiev announced proudly.

Janis' expression melted. His eyes widened and bulged as his head snapped between Voldemars and Alexiev. He nodded politely to Alexiev and Leopold, to which each of them nodded back. His smile grew slowly, but eventually spanned his face. "How do you know?"

"The Cossacks know everything, Poppa," Voldemars noted. A tingle ringed his head as he realized he had obviously done something to win his father's trust back.

"Cossacks?"

"I've come back to fight for Latvia." Voldemars pronounced.

Janis expression blossomed as he smiled widely. A tear dripped from his eye and trickled down his cheek.

"The long barn over there," Janis turned and pointed to the stone-walled barn. "I've used that as a stable. You can take the horses there."

Alexiev smiled politely, and motioned to Leopold. Holding the reins from both his and Voldemars' horses, he started toward the barn. Leopold took Otilija's reins from her, then headed toward the stable and quickly caught up with Alexiev.

Janis maintained a wary eye on the Russians until he was sure they were out of ear-shot, then turned to Voldemars. "Then you've heard something?"

"A little, yes. But I probably don't know as much as I should. Now that I'm back here, I must fulfill my duty to you and to Latvia."

"Oh, my God. It is. It's Voldemars."

Voldemars looked up and saw his mother leap off the porch as the door slammed behind her. Tears streamed down her face and a wide smile dimpled her cheeks as she ran toward him. She ran to his open arms and plunged into his chest. Air rushed out of her lungs on impact, but then nothing except a mother's warmth surrounded him. She wrapped her arms around him and squeezed until he was breathless. When she let go, she lifted her head, and peered into her son's eyes.

"I knew you would be all right," she whispered. Her eyes sparkled brightly.

My God, Momma, he thought, studying Kristine. Thirteen years and you haven't changed a bit. Your hair, your face, your smile, your eyes. Everything is like it was so long ago.

"I knew it in here!" she added, crossing her arms over her chest. She turned to Janis and flashed a grin.

"Momma, this is Otilija," Voldemars said as he turned. Otilija had lifted Brevite from inside the basket and bundled her in a blanket. She smiled and slipped the blanket off from the top of her infant's head.

"And this," he continued, stepping toward Otilija, "is Brevite, your granddaughter."

Kristine gasped. Her hands immediately covered her gaping mouth. She shuffled on her toes toward Otilija. She peered into Brevite's brown eyes, lifted her hand and touched the baby's tiny nose. Tears streamed from her eyes, and she looked to Otilija.

"She's beautiful, Janis. Come look." Kristine said, nuzzling with the baby. Janis stood ashen and stiff. He glanced at Voldemars, mouthed the word brivibas, and turned back to stare at the baby. Tears glistened in his eyes. He whispered the baby's name again and a crooked smile cracked his pruned lips.

"We received a letter from your friend, Oleg," Janis mumbled as his sober expression returned. "We were concerned."

"I'm fine, Poppa," Voldemars said. "A little thin, but I'm fine. You need not worry about me."

"Let's go into the house, Otilija," Kristine whispered to Otilija. "I haven't had a baby in the house since Romans." She stopped to sigh. "My word, that was so long ago."

Otilija nodded and smiled. She glanced at Voldemars, and without saying a word, cautioned him to be understanding with his father's feelings. He closed his eyes and nodded as the two women shuffled toward the house.

"We have much to talk about Poppa," he blurted with a bit of formality in his voice as the door to the house closed. "I know I'm not as good a true soldier as I was before the gas, but it's my duty to you and Latvia that I become part of the militia."

"Voldemars," Janis waved his hands to stop his son, but failed.

"My injury won't stop me, Poppa. I've learned how to make up for my weaknesses." Voldemars stopped as Janis grasped his arm. He nodded toward the barn.

"We will have plenty of time to discuss what needs to be done for our independence."

"But preparations will need to be made." Voldemars protested as he followed his father. Every element of warfare he had been schooled on rushed back without so much as a hesitation. "We will need to get supplies, agree on tactics, set up reconnaissance. There are many things that need to be settled and discussed before we march off to battle."

"I know Voldemars," Janis lifted his hand to shush his son. "The seeds have already been planted. We haven't been sitting on our hands waiting for all of this to happen!"

"But—"

"Tomorrow, Voldemars. We can discuss those things with the right people tomorrow. You must be tired. Tonight, we will relax and be a family again."

Telmeni

16 October 1917

O tilija woke up when morning sunlight streamed over the hills, through the window, and directly onto her closed eyelids. She groaned, rolled onto her side, then sat up lethargically. Aching, stiff and drained, she twisted from her hips to her shoulders and tried to undo the knots in her back. The stretching, though, only seemed to make everything hurt more.

"What a night!" she mumbled. She pinched the bridge of her nose and leaned as far back as she could and rolled her head from side to side.

"She never had nights like that in the woods!" she grumbled as she stood up. Bleary eyed, she stiltedly shuffled across the room in bare feet until she reached Brevite's cradle. Brevite lay peaceful, asleep, with her tiny hand nestled close to her mouth. Otilija sighed, exasperated. "And what was your problem last night? Or was it just that you felt it was time to kick up your heels?"

Brevite snorted, then thrust her chubby arms above her head and stretched. She arched her back, brought her hands back in front of her mouth, and wedged her fingers deep into her tiny mouth.

"Oh, my little angel," Otilija mumbled as she smiled. She leaned over, unfolded the small blanket bunched up in the corner, and slipped it over Brevite. She shuffled lazily to the window and gazed out at the rippled blue surface on the lake.

Crisp air drifted in. She inhaled a lung full of it, savoring the fresh, sweet aroma of the dew-moistened morning for a moment. It was so much cleaner than what she remembered was typical for Riga. There were no choking fumes from nearby factories. There was no soot to collect in her nostrils, which would blacken her handkerchief when she blew it out. There was no dust collecting in her pores and that could have to be scrubbed from her face at night. It was all just clean air, scented lightly with crisp, split oak and freshly cut meadow grass.

Out in the fields she spotted Voldemars and Janis plodding along, side by side. Janis motioned with his hands every so often, appearing to explain something for a moment before moving on, deeper into the field. There was obvious enjoyment in his animation. Voldemars seemed to be enjoying his time with his father, as well.

"Now that's something I never thought I would ever see." She smiled, comforted that he was home and happy. In the short time she had been here, she also felt at ease. She had overcome her initial feeling of being overwhelmed by the immenseness of the farm. But when she imagined it was nothing more than a big garden, it all became much less daunting.

She heard Brevite rustle in her crib, and hurried on tiptoes to look. The little one had only rolled from one side to the other, stretching her arms out over her tiny tuft of black hair. Otilija relaxed. She draped the knitted blanket back over Brevite, leaned over and gently kissed her baby's head.

She quietly tip-toed to a small desk in the corner of the room, then carefully lifted and secured the draw. She took a piece of writing paper from the top shelf, dabbed the fountain pen into the inkwell, and started an overdue letter to her mother.

ॐ

16 October 1917

Dear Momma,

I hope this letter finds you and Augustine safe and in good health! I grow especially worried for you ever since Voldemars told me that the Germans have invaded Riga. I pray that you have been spared the chaos which I have heard is associated with front line battles.

Since this is my first letter in some time, I have much to write and tell you. We had some tense times in Astrakhan, but with the help of some of Voldemars' friends, we were able to make it out safely. Do not worry. Voldemars and I are safe at his parents' farm, Telmeni, which is nestled on a lake in Valmiera, a small village near Cesis. And you have a beautiful little granddaughter! We've named her Brevite, in the hope Voldemars says, that we will soon be free. She has your dark hair and eyes, Voldemars' round face, and my ball-ended nose. She is healthy, nurses well, and is growing like a weed as they say out here. I hope that we'll soon be able to get together, and you can see my little baby for yourself.

Otilija stopped briefly to think about what to write. Then she remembered Tatiana and the Cossacks. Momma would like to hear about that, Otilija thought and continued writing about Brevite's birth and the six months they had lived with the Cossacks. She giggled as she explained how the prim and proper Voldemars actually got along with the unruly Russians.

She stopped again and thought of what else she had to say. A scented breeze meandered through the window and reminded her of how beautiful Janis' garden was. She knew her mother would enjoy hearing about Telmeni, so she continued writing.

When she was done, she signed the letter with all her love, folded the letter, and slipped it into an envelope just as a churning queasiness knotted her stomach. She leaned back in her chair, and breathed through the nausea. All of the familiar symptoms were there—the morning sickness, the constant feeling of being hungry, and the incessant time spent in the outhouse.

Knowing that worried her immensely. This was not a good time to have another baby. There was too much turmoil going on with the Germans and the Bolsheviks. The nights she was able to sleep were haunted by the thoughts of Natalya's death in childbirth. And even when they faded, vivid memories of her first stillborn child swooped in like some raven pecking away at her wounded soul. But she also knew there was nothing more she could do but hope this one would be as healthy as Brevite.

As quickly as it had arrived, her nausea subsided. She knew though, like an outgoing tide, it was due to come back. Sucking in a deep breath, she sighed, then addressed the envelope and sealed the letter inside. Leaving it on the desk, she stood up and wearily shuffled across the room to check once more on Brevite.

The baby was sleeping comfortably. Content she would nap for some time, Otilija left the room and headed toward the kitchen to find something to quell her grumbling stomach.

❧   ❧   ❧

By mid-morning, the bright autumn sun warmed the chilly morning air to the point of actually being hot and humid. Voldemars and Janis broke from their hectic schedule of autumn chores and returned to the porch for a well deserved rest. Janis reached the porch first, removed his shirt and draped it over the rail. He melted into his chair, expelled a lung full of air, leaned back, and relaxed.

"A fine morning, isn't it?" he said as he tipped his hat back off his forehead. He wiped the sweat from his face. "It certainly goes much faster with someone to talk to."

"Not that I'm complaining, but it is much more work than I remember, Poppa." Voldemars leaned on the porch rail. Catching his breath, he could not help but wonder if the damage the gas had done was part of his problem. "But I do enjoy a good day's work."

"I hope so. We have so much to do."

Janis picked up his pipe and stuffed the bowl full. Blue clouds grew like smoke from a train around his head until he finally let loose a stream of aromatic smoke. Voldemars started pacing the length of the porch, more out of habit than nervousness. He wiped his sweaty brow with his forearm as he slipped in and out of the clouds billowing around his father.

"Winter is coming quickly and there is quite a bit that needs to be done," Janis mumbled between puffs. Voldemars stopped his pacing. "And with Edwards up north, I really need the help. The rye needs to be cut and chafed, the potatoes need to be dug."

"I was thinking." Voldemars crossed his arms and rubbed his chin pensively. "I heard that the Russians had formed five Latvian regiments, and—"

"It's a little early for the birches to be tapped, but at least we can get the buckets," Janis continued, as if Voldemars was silent and listening.

"And if I remember correctly, they were assigned to the northern fronts. Poland and Lithuania I think."

"We could get the smokehouse ready for making kvass."

"They would surely provide a solid base for a strong militia."

"I don't think so." Janis responded with terse disgust.

"All we need to do is find them."

"You won't find them." Janis' tone grew loud, irritated and icy.

"I'm sure they would—" Voldemars froze. He glared at his father, suddenly realizing what he had said. Janis drew in slowly though his pipe and looked to the cloudless sky.

"Why? Why wouldn't they fight for Latvia?" Voldemars continued. I've returned. And I'm sure others would as well!"

"A year ago, maybe a bit more," Janis' voice echoed with a hollow, calculated tone. "At the front—" His eyes glazed over.

"Poppa?" Voldemars prompted to break the sudden silence.

"Without food, munitions, or artillery support, more than forty thousand Latvians were killed. The Russian bastards who were supposed to be giving them cover, turned tail and ran."

Voldemars sat stunned, feeling a mix of anger and astonishment grow within his chest.

"The regiments you are looking for were left at the mercy of the Huns." Janis finished in a despondent tone.

Voldemars recoiled and sucked in a deep cleansing breath. Mustering his composure, he pushed his jaw closed, then rubbed his chin. He started to pace.

"How could they do that?" He lashed out, arms flailing. His pace quickened to a feverish stalk. "How could those bastards leave their own to be slaughtered like that? Where the hell was their sense of honor and duty?"

Janis did not answer. He continued silently rocking back and forth, each time clenching his teeth even tighter on his pipe.

"There must be some survivors." Voldemars pivoted smartly. "They couldn't have wiped out the entire regiment. We can form some fighting brigades out of the survivors."

"Maybe at one time, but I don't think we can do it now."

"Christ, we've got to protect ourselves somehow. We can't just let the Germans take us over." Voldemars fumed. He was so engrossed in his rage that he did not even notice that Oskars Ziemels had walked up the driveway. Voldemars jumped, startled by his sudden appearance.

"By the striking resemblance to Janis, I would assume you are Voldemars?" Oskars interrupted. He politely nodded and extended his hand.

Voldemars stood, speechless. He tentatively reached out and let Oskars take his hand and shake. When it registered who the man was, he released his grip and pulled back his hand.

"I am Oskars. Oskars Ziemels."

"Ah, yes. Mr. Ziemels."

"I don't know if you remember me, but when you were a little boy, you used to play in my fields."

And you used to chase me out of them with rocks! Voldemars thought.

"I haven't seen you in a month, Oskars." Janis broke into the conversation. "I presume you've been in Riga? Is there news?"

"I'm afraid the news is not good. The Germans have taken the city and seem to be firmly entrenched."

"We must take it back." Voldemars said.

"Many people have been killed in the fighting." Oskars bowed his head respectfully.

"We can't let the Germans have our capital."

"Patience, Voldemars. Patience," Oskars waved his hands. "The council is already working on a solution to this crisis. And if all goes well, we should have Riga back."

"The council? Listen to what he's saying, Poppa." Voldemars exploded, stomping his feet. "We're dealing with Germans, here. Huns. They don't care about laws or protocols."

"Don't tell me about the Germans," Janis retaliated.

"Don't you remember they used gas, Poppa? They used hideous gas." Voldemars raged. His eyes burned at the thought of the gas again.

"Christ, don't you think I know that?" Janis spit back. "Ever since I received that letter from Oleg, I was worried sick about you."

"And without a thread of decency or conscience." Voldemars missed his father's comment. "Have you seen what's left of the battlefields? They're wastelands. Devastated wastelands burned into oblivion."

"Voldemars!"

"They'll lay waste to all of our lands if they're not stopped!"

"Damn it, listen to me!" Janis stood up. An angry grimace covered his face. "Didn't you hear what Oskars said? It's done! It's already happened! Riga fell to the Germans!"

"Don't you realize what you're saying?" Voldemars' voice grew more cutting. "Look at me. Your own son. I was gassed by these war mongers. My lungs were ripped apart by their gas, and they—"

"I know what I'm saying," Janis yelled, standing in his son's face. "And I know what happened to you." Janis turned away. He stopped and spun around, looking even more angry.

"And as for being heartless, who was the one that didn't send me a letter or even a simple fucking note? I had to get word of what happened to you from one of your friends. No, Voldemars. We will do this the right way—the Latvian way! Everything, every logical, moral, and lawful step will be tried before any more blood stains our land! Protocol will be followed."

"Screw protocol." Voldemars flailed his arms. "Any diplomat will tell you that protocol is solely the dialogue before war consumes the masses. We are at war, aren't we? Aren't the Germans on our land? Aren't there Germans in Riga? You know the damned Russians aren't going to help us this time, as if they've ever helped us before. We have no choice but to fend for ourselves!"

"This is our home and we're going to defend it in our way." Janis glared into his son's face for a moment, then turned and stomped back to his rocker. When he turned around he pointed his quivering finger at him. "And if you can't do things the Latvian way, then take your Cossack friends and go back to the fucking hills. We are a civilized people here."

Janis dropped into his chair, stuffed his pipe into his mouth, and sucked in a mouthful of smoke. He leaned his head back, expelled a wide stream. He huffed for a moment, then seemed to settle down.

"What else, Oskars? What about Russia?" he turned back to Oskars and asked with a more reserved tone.

Oskars' head darted between Voldemars, who remained in a fuming but silent rage and Janis, smoked calmly in his chair. His rocking indicated he was still seething.

"Little news gets out, but there is something going on there. I'm planning on spending some time there to keep an eye on what's happening." He glanced at Voldemars, then perched his eyebrows and shrugged his shoulders. "I hate to say it, but I think the Latvian Bolsheviks would know more about what's happening there than we do."

"Bolsheviks? Christ, there are Bolsheviks here too? In Latvia?" Voldemars' face contorted. Janis fired a frosted glare, ordering Voldemars to remain quiet and listen.

"The association will hold it's next meeting in Valmiera in a few weeks," Oskars started, furtively lowering his voice. "Rostislavs says they may be able to dig up more information about what's going on in Russia by then."

"What have you heard?" Janis asked calmly, leaning forward. Voldemars listened quietly, under protest, but as ordered.

"Anarchy rules. Last I knew, the Bolsheviks had a majority of seats in the government," Oskars answered, disconsolate.

"And Lenin? Last I heard he disappeared from Germany. Has anyone seen him yet?" Janis prodded.

Lenin? Voldemars thought. The epitome of the continuing Revolution. He wasn't even in Russia for the February Revolt, and was still the sole cause for it.

"No one has seen him, but I'm sure he's someplace nearby. If I know him well enough, he's plotting something, but God knows what and God knows where," Oskars mumbled.

Voldemars had finally heard all that he wished to hear. He stomped off the steps and headed for the stable.

"Germans in Riga. Lenin free in Russia. Christ, chaos is just around the corner if we don't do something about this." He mumbled as he stormed down the pathway to the stable. "I can't believe my own father has softened that much to believe that politics can end conflicts. Politics? Hell, politics is only a precursor to war, every soldier knows that. Where the hell is the old Latvian blood that has been shed over the centuries not in vain, but in honor. Even our flag represents that honor. And now, we talk."

He stiff-armed the stable doors open. He stopped before his horse and saw the same fire in them that he felt. The same fire that burned in Uguns' eyes. His own confidence soared.

"I'll show them. I'll show them all. I, Voldemars Vechi, will be our Lacplesis if I have to!" He slung his belt and saber around his hips. With a quick tug, he secured the sword to his waist, slipped into the stall, and mounted his horse. As his buttocks pounded into the saddle, the stark realization of his tantrum came clear. For a moment, he stood quietly and evaluated the sanity of his thoughts.

"Who am I fooling. I'm no Lacplesis. I'm nothing more than an old soldier. And an old soldier with a family as well. But someone has to lead this struggle. It won't be won by words and posturing. And I promised Ivan that it would be me."

Smitten, Voldemars jabbed his heels into the horse's flanks and grasped the reins tightly. His horse bolted from the stall. With rippling muscles across his shoulders and flanks, the horse raced out of the stable. As the wind battered at Voldemars' bared teeth, he let the enjoyment of a sober ride at a full gallop again tingle in his veins.

Cesis

18 November 1917

*V*oldemars' long winter riding coat flapped wildly around his legs as he galloped toward Cesis castle, feeling he had to deliver the news he had heard as soon as possible. The sun tried to pierce through the heavy gray cloud cover, but failed, leaving only cold bitterness more typical of winter than autumn. His horse's hooves punctuated urgency as they thudded rhythmically onto the road, kicking up a billowing trail of amber dust. He urged him to an even faster pace and with brief complaint that sprayed his horse's froth back into his face, his mount complied and increased his already break-neck speed.

Near the castle, Voldemars veered off the road and onto a well beaten pathway. He grinned as he leaned into his turn and saw the castle turrets, peeking through the pallor of leafless brush along the edges of the swamp. Dull red ivy, the color of dried blood, limply clung to the brownstone, weathering the already cold autumn winds.

"Back to camp," he said loudly as he reached a checkpoint one kilometer from the castle. He unsheathed his saber, sliced an x in the wind, then raced by the spot where the dormant brush started rustling. Glancing over his shoulder, he spotted two uniformed sentries hastily emerge from the side of the pathway and plunge into the dusty wake rolling up from the ground behind him.

"It's been a long time coming, men," he mumbled, practicing what he had to relay. "But our time has finally arrived!"

Rounding the ivy covered turrets at full speed, he entered the castle's trampled courtyard, then pulled back on his reins. His horse immediately slowed to a prance. He maneuvered a wide circle around the grounds.

"Assemble in the courtyard!" He heard voices echo through the castle as he brought his horse to a stop at the southern most edge of the field. He turned toward the castle, and waited for the balance of his regiment to muster. The first two onto the field were the horsemen chasing him. They crossed before him, mimicking their commander's wide turn, stopped precisely at the center of the field, and whistled loudly three times. Like bees pouring from a disturbed hive, soldiers scurried out of every castle opening. As they snapped to attention in a single long row before the horsemen, they shouldered their arms, a sad array of rusty rifles and long carved sticks.

"Far cry from the bright, spotless brigade of the Eighth!" he mumbled, somewhat disconsolate. The command he dreamed of since he returned to his homeland. A militia of bright-eyed Latvian soldiers, eager to carry forward the traditions of courage and bravery of Lacplesis, a honed fighting machine unmatched in modern Europe—was nothing more than a conglomeration of refugees from the dismembered Russian army and volunteers from nearby farms with armament that was questionable at best. Among them were older men. Men too old to be considered for service in any normal army. The tears in their trousers and old, worn-out boots epitomized their lack of polish. Cloth caps sat low on their foreheads, jokingly pushing their ears out almost at right angles to their heads. Grins cracked their faces, pushing up scraggly, sparse mustaches. Teeth neglected for years peered out from behind cracked, colorless lips. But unlike the wry, forced, tired, and pained grins he remembered from his last months in the Russian Army, these smiles were determined, proud, and strong. Conviction, if nothing else, was their character.

He turned away from the rank at the midpoint and pranced back to the two horsemen standing in the center of the field. He glanced up to his friend Alexiev, tipped his head and flashed a grin. In one fluent motion he dismounted, handed over the reins, then pivoted precisely and returned to his review, picking up where he had left off.

The texture of the deeper ranks changed vastly from the first glance. He cringed, embarrassed at how young this part of his brigade appeared. Peach-fuzzed faces gazed out as the substance of the rank, young and inexperienced, even more than he was when he first joined the cavalry. But the same grit and determination from the older rank emanated from behind wide, expressive eyes.

Tough enough? he wondered, scrutinizing the boys much more closely than he did the older men. He stopped before the first boy, planted his left toe, left-faced, and stared into the young, glistening eyes. He watched for quivering or trembling, but there was none. The boy's eyes returned a cold, expressionless stare.

Excellent, he thought as he let the corner of his mouth twitch upward, signaling his acceptance. He turned to the next youthful soldier.

Underneath a smudged helmet the boy's fiery, wide, gray eyes peered out above prominent, high cheekbones. His gaunt face seemed almost ghostly. His olive green tunic looked more like his father's ill-fitted suit coat. He wore no cartridge belt to cinch the center of the shirt, and his pants ended precariously between his ankles and knees, as if he had grown three inches since he had put them on this morning. His feet appeared more like poorly covered pontoons, angled at a precise, forty-five degree angle. Voldemars moved his eyes slowly up the boy's body again and stopped at his eyes.

Christ, he can't be more than fourteen, fifteen at the most. Voldemars motioned for the soldier to step forward as he stepped back far enough so that their conversation would not be heard by the others.

The boy snapped to attention centimeters from his commander's face, then let a wide grin slip.

"Are you sure you want to be here, son?" Voldemars whispered in a fatherly tone.

"I will be there for my Latvia!" the boy announced as he proudly thrust out his chest. "I am old enough to make my decisions, and I chose to be here."

Voldemars sighed, unsure if his stomach churned with pride for the boy's elan or concern that he might very well become a burden to the rest of the brigade. The conviction he heard, though, was familiar. It was precisely that same conviction he felt when he moved away from Telmeni years ago.

"What's your name, son."

"Baronovs, sir. Aleksandrs Baronovs." The boy remained rigid at attention. He snapped his chin to his chest emphatically.

Voldemars leaned over to the young man and whispered in his ear, "You stay close to me and listen if you want to stay alive. And if I'm not there, then you listen to Alexiev or Leopold. Remember that."

Aleksandrs quivered as a frown wrinkled his forehead, but nodded and smiled. Voldemars winked back then and motioned for him to step back and rejoin the rank. Voldemars completed his review. He stepped back to the center of the field, and stood next to Alexiev and Leopold.

"How well do you know Latvian?" Voldemars asked Alexiev, as he heard artillery rumble like faint thunder in the distance. Both men nodded tentatively, but positively.

"Good. This bunch is in dire need of good direction and instruction," he noted sarcastically.

Alexiev and Leopold both agreed with a smile as Voldemars turned back to face his regiment.

All I can do is hope they're ready. May Lacplesis be with us, he thought. He marched forward and stopped midway between Alexiev and the soldiers. He drew a deep breath, then blew it out forcefully.

"Soldiers of the Vidzeme Regiment of the Northern Latvian Army." He announced with a full, booming voice. "We are on the verge of the most important historical event which has ever taken place in Latvia."

❦   ❦   ❦

Dressed in their best suits and top hats, Janis and Oskars looked strangely out of place on the rickety, wooden, horse drawn cart underneath them. Amidst the stifling, unusually warm day, both had removed their heavy overcoats and thrown them in the bed of the empty cart. When they had passed Strenci on their way to Valka, the sun slipped behind and remained shrouded by rapidly thickening cloud cover.

"You know, Oskars," Janis mumbled as they entered the village and turned toward the meeting hall. "I've read so much about the Valka which Pumpurs had written about, but I've never made it up here until now."

"Nor have I," Oskars added, absently, obviously consumed by the starkness of the north.

Janis swiveled his head right to left as he searched the horizon for any sign of the designated meeting place—the legendary castle of Valka. Leafless trees scratched scars against the bleak, overcast skies, while a slight mist conjured a medieval tone. Janis could not help feeling like he was actually traveling back into the legendary time of Lacplesis.

He remembered all of the times Voldemars sat on his lap, enthralled by the stories of the legendary bear-man of Valka. He enjoyed telling those stories, a tradition he carried on from his father. As a boy, he would spend hours dreaming he was Lacplesis, and traipse through the woods, fantasizing about saving pretty girls from ugly, fire breathing dragons and hoards of savage barbarians. He had even built his own Castle of Light out of fallen branches. It looked more like a Livi stick house, but in his mind it was a castle.

"There it is!" Oskars pointed to the castle at the end of the road. Janis stared in awe at the view and froze. As the road headed down a hill, Lielvarde, Lacplesis' immortalized castle, rose magically from amidst the swamps banking the Gauja River. Its huge white stones anchored the wall between rounded turrets, sentries at either end of the structure. Each of their picketed tops were worn, but remained proudly upright, like jagged teeth pointing toward the overcast sky.

The grand entrance to the castle remained natural and undisturbed. Red ivy clung to the stone, trailing the walls like crimson rivulets trickling from the tops. In front of the castle, adorned in new, colorful, ceremonial uniforms, a battalion of Latvian Rifles stood watch. Janis nudged his horse toward a line of other horses and wagons that had been tied to a row of naked, creaking white birches. They dismounted, submitted their credentials to the guards, and were escorted through the large, propped open oak doors and into the expansive courtyard of Lielvarde.

The pair traversed the courtyard, never taking their eyes from the massive turrets which stood proudly at the corners. Breathless, they entered a passageway lined with open rooms. The musty, stagnant air gave Janis the sense that he was stepping through a rift in time. He imagined watching Lacplesis hold his medieval court, filled with strong, stout and proud knights in shining silver armor. He thought he could even see the golden hair of his boyhood hero flow over his royal head, held together at his shoulders by two loose braids on his chest.

At the end of the corridor, they passed through another set of rounded, massive oak doors. The historical image vanished immediately, replaced with the reality of the hall's modern furniture and draperies. Janis felt frozen, even though a tiny tingling in his neck had been sparked to life. Lining a wide speaker's podium, ten guards stood at near perfect attention, five to each side of the pedestal. On either end of the stage, two of the largest Latvian flags he had ever seen, hung fluidly and majestically from guarded flagpoles. Behind the speaker's podium, an immense, red crest had been perched on a white drapery. In its center, a brilliant yellow sun emanated spiked rays toward a cloudless blue sky. Inside the sun's core rested a triangle of three golden stars touching at their points. That was what Goldmanis had said would be their icon, the symbol of the three integral parts of Latvia; Latgale, Kurzeme, and his home province, Vidzeme.

"It will be done today, Oskars," Janis whispered, choking on his rushing emotions.

"I don't follow you," Oskars mumbled, still consumed with the pomp that surrounded them.

"Independence," Janis said in a hushed voice, shifting his focus to the gathered crowd. "Just look around you. Have you ever seen so many suits in one place? Have you ever seen so many different types of people in one meeting? Farmers, businessmen, warriors, politicians."

Oskars surveyed the room silently. "I don't even remember seeing this many suits in church."

Janis turned to Oskars, who remained in a fixed, wide-eyed gaze at the officialism that seemed to pervade the room. His tingle exploded into a tremor, then raced down his neck, not stopping until it quivered through each of his toes.

"Christ, I can feel it," Janis whispered. "The whole room is electrified. Yes, something big is going to happen here. Something really big."

"Kind of brings tears to your eyes, Doesn't it, old friend?" Oskars whispered.

While Oskars stood reverently, Janis scanned the hall for familiar faces. He recognized the representatives of the Provincial Council of Vidzeme, already clustered in one corner of the room. He recognized Rudolphs Zalitis, the neighbor who only a few months back had chastised his association with the separatists.

Janis dipped his head and smiled. Rudolphs tipped his hat in reply, then flashed a knowing grin back. He spotted Aleksandr Baronovs, the old baker from Riga whose son had made such an impression on him earlier. The old man appeared animated, adamantly discussing a point with his neighbor. His arms flailed wildly as he punctuated his position with a pointed finger.

Janis' attention was drawn to the front of the room when he noticed movement. He spotted the familiar large frame of Janis Goldmanis passing the color guard. Each soldier snapped to attention and presented his rifle. Goldmanis acknowledged each salute with slight tips of his tall, black top hat without breaking his long, deliberate strides. He took the podium and faced the crowd. Worming his finger between his collar and neck, he relieved some of the stiffness in the shirt. Then, with a proud, almost presidential air hovering around him, he scanned the room. He grinned, grabbed his mallet, and pounded it three times. The buzzing in the room fell silent. All eyes fixed on the huge figure on the podium.

"Welcome to the opening session of the First Latvian National Assembly." He started with a booming deep voice, then waited for everyone to take their seats.

"We, as the delegates to the Latvian National Assembly, are about to embark on a venture of major historic import for Latvia and the world. Several times in the past we have petitioned the Russian Duma for confirmation of our right to self-determination, but as yet, have not received any reply. Therefore, as accorded by our laws, our provisional council has called this assembly together in this place of such hallowed importance to the Latvian people to vote on the question of Latvian sovereignty!"

The crowd exploded in enthusiastic revelry. Janis could not resist leaping to his feet and joining in the outburst. As the crowd chanted "Lat-vi-ja" through broad smiles, Oskars joined in the pandemonium as well. Janis cupped his hands to make more noise when he clapped. He felt his years yoked to the Russians peel away with each cheer the crowd bellowed. Vigor he vaguely remembered from his youth surged again in his veins as a sense of self-control blossomed and grew into virile vengeance. He shouted louder than Oskars.

Expecting the demonstration, Goldmanis grinned and stepped back. He took a drink and raised his hands to silence the crowd.

"My fellow Latvians." His voice echoed off the walls. "Our proclamation of independence will be published for all of our families to see. And it will be published in our language!" The crowd buzzed. Sporadic applause started. "We will not be German!" Louder and more adamant applause and cheers rose from the crowd. "We will not be Russian!"

The crowd exploded with cheers so loud that Goldmanis had to cup his hands over his mouth and call like an ancient town crier. "We will be Latvian!"

As if rehearsed, the entire assembly vaulted to its feet and cheered wildly. Janis turned to Oskars and embraced him in a victory hug. He looked up from his friend's shoulder and saw that even the stone-faced soldiers lining the walls and stage smiled, trying to reserve their excitement to vigorous handshakes and back slaps. As tears rolled from his eyes, he remembered the image of Voldemars returning home. He felt just like that now.

"If you want to fight, my son, do it for Latvia," he mumbled, but it was drowned out by the celebration.

As he headed home an hour later, Janis directed his horse along the road unconsciously. Emotionally and physically drained, he let his thoughts drift aimlessly, while Oskars quietly watched the western sky. The sun, captive throughout the day behind an ominous cloud cover, had finally broken through with shimmering rays which pierced through the clouds like the spokes of a wagon wheel. Pink tints at the ends of the incisions glowed brighter than the rest of the sky.

"The sky, Janis," Oskars noted as he leaned over and poked Janis with his elbow. "Look how bright it is. It's just like how the legend says it would be. 'Upon the return of Lacplesis, the rising sun over Lielvarde will shine over the Latvian people for one thousand years.'"

Janis felt his mind sputter as if the day's revelry had left him hungover. "I don't think it will be as easy as just saying we're free. Think about it. We've been twice German, and twice Russian, and before that we were under Sweden's control. We may have declared independence, but now we have to earn it."

"But we have leadership now, Janis. Strong leadership. Leadership that will surely bring us—"

"Leadership is nothing if we do not have a base. Kurzeme is still in German hands. And considering what the Russians will be losing, we can only hope we will be strong enough to prevent being crushed into submission again!"

"Then perhaps what we need is a little faith?"

"We may have faith," Janis added soberly. "But at what price will this independence cost us."

"Price?" Oskars quivered at the chilling comment. "What price?"

"The cost is blood, Oskars. Latvian blood—the steepest price there is!" Janis grew impassioned. "My God, how many Rifles have died at the front? How many thousands have been killed during the latest siege of Riga?" Janis' melancholy oozed. "And what do we have to show for it?"

"Sacrifices have been made throughout the years, Janis. Liberty is not free. I know that and I'm sure you do, too. If we intend to attain and keep our freedom, we must invest something. And if it has to be blood, that is unfortunate—"

"I know, Oskars," Janis interrupted. "But it would be so much easier if I knew the blood wouldn't belong to my own son."

Riga

30 March 1918

*A*ugustine shivered under a pile of loose, wet, decaying hay, partly from fear of the furious hell that whirled around her and partly from the cold dampness. She cringed as she heard the German soldiers rip, smash, and shatter all that had been her life. She peeked out from under her straw cover and saw one shadow pass by the kitchen window, then another slip into her bedroom. It stopped at her delicately sheer, white curtains, hovered for a moment, then violently ripped them from their rods. Memory etching gruesomeness peered out from behind the naked, broken pane, looking like a satiated predator after a kill.

She gasped, horrified at just the thought that this devil was violating her room.

"Get out of there, you bastard," she whispered, wishing she could run up to the house and chase him out. "Get the hell out of my room!" But she could do nothing but cower in the garden and feel vulnerably helpless. Tears streamed from her eyes. She felt the urge to scurry away to a safer place, but fear kept her hunkered down in the the dank smelling leaves and strewn hay.

She heard more glass shatter inside the house. Forcing herself to look, she spotted the demon stomp out of her room and then heard him yell and taunt the other soldiers in the house. Shadows appeared in the kitchen. More taunting and bantering. The voices then subsided and faded away as the shadows disappeared again. Relief finally waved through her as the soldiers emerged from the front door of the house, then stomped arrogantly out into the street and broke into another house further down the road.

An eerie silence shrouded her house. She was scared to go back and see what remained in their wake, but she had to find her mother. Finally, she overcame the fear which shackled her legs in the stench of the decaying vegetation and marsh-like soil, and carefully slunk toward the house. She kept a close eye on the road as she approached, but when she heard her mother's feeble sobs meandering out from the broken windows, she quickened her pace.

"Momma. Oh, my God. Momma came home," she gasped. She was beckoned by her mother's weeping. At the back door, she pulled herself up and peered inside. Her eyes jumped from her head at the appalling aftermath. Splintered, broken chairs littered the room. Curtains lay strewn near the smashed windows they once adorned. Slivered shards from broken dishes coated the floor and counters. She took a deep breath to quell her fears, then carefully slipped through the door and into the kitchen, trying to remain quiet. Her mud-caked shoes crunched on the shattered glass as she passed through the kitchen and into the parlor.

Unprepared for what she found, she gasped. Her mother lay on the floor, battered and beaten into a crooked, bloody mess. She remained frozen, but for only a second, before she ran to her mother's side and fell to her knees.

"Oh Momma, what have they done?" she cried. Tears streamed in rivulets over her cheeks. She leaned over and lay her head on her mother's chest. Doreteja's chest struggled to rise, gurgling and hissing as she tried to draw in even a mouthful of air. Blood dribbled from the froth at her mouth.

"Augustine." Her voice barely escaped. Augustine wrapped her arms around her mother's shoulders and sank into her blood stained dress.

"There's a letter...in the desk...," Doroteja struggled to get the words out. "From Otilija. Take it," she winced and groaned, then coughed twice, spraying blood into Augustine's hair.

"Go to neighbor's house. Tell Elze what happened. Take the letter. Go to Telmeni. You need to be away from here. Tell Otilija," A hard wince halted her words. Doroteja's face cringed even more. Spasms violently thrust her neck and chest forward for a moment, but then succumbed. She fell limply back to the floor. Her pained frown slipped into a dull, blank stare.

"Momma! Don't go, Momma!" Augustine protested, but Doroteja did not reply. She leaned over and kissed her mother's bruised and blood-stained forehead. Whimpering and sobbing, Augustine rested her head on her mother's chest.

Approaching voices in the street startled her. She jumped to her feet, scurried to the desk, and dug frantically for the letter. She rifled through the drawers. After shuffling through only a few papers in the side drawer, she found the letter, quickly stuffed it into her shirt, then scrambled back to the window.

"Oh, my God!" She felt her breath evaporate. Huddled together with arms around each other, the same three soldiers that had ransacked her house were heading back this way. Terror strangled her when the one face that was branded into her memory looked up and seemed to glare right at her. She felt panic fester as her heart pounded wildly in her chest.

Escape! A voice in her head screamed. She spun around and glanced again at her mother's body, then back out the window.

"Bastards!" She spit out the window, then scrambled back toward her mother's stiff body. She closed her eyes for a brief prayer, then stood up and frantically scurried back out to the garden. Remaining low enough so that she would easily be mistaken for a fox or small deer if seen, she squished through the mushy garden pathways until she emerged out the backside. She hurdled the short fence her mother had put up for rabbits, then disappeared into the mix of naked and evergreen underbrush, plunging deep enough into the woods to feel safe.

Out of breath, she dropped to her knees and inspected every bit of scrub around her. Nothing. A couple of birds chirped hesitantly. The stream churned in the distance, tumbling over the rocks and winter fallen branches. She sucked in as deeply as she could, but the tightness in her chest kept her from satiating her need for air. She concentrated on taming her heart, but the pounding continued undaunted.

The brush rustled. She dropped to her stomach and opened her eyes as wide as she could. The rustling stopped. She breathed a little easier. Then the brush exploded, scaring the life out of her as a partridge took flight.

Distant voices perked her ears again. She immediately scrambled to her feet and weaved through the cracking, winter burned branches until she reached the waterlogged stream bank. She knelt next to the gurgling water which drowned out the loud wheeze from her lungs.

Her thoughts galloped frantically as she tried to draw in as much of the stingingly cold, damp spring air as her lungs could tolerate. She knew she had to get out. She had to get to the main road somehow if she was going to get out toward Cesis, and she would need some help in finding a horse. Her mind went blank as she tried to think where she could get a horse.

A coherent thought finally slipped through her mind. Pulling herself up from the marshy stream bank, she started toward the city, following the stream, risking only brief peeks along the brush. Finally, she spotted her target. She crept closer to the barren undercover until she found a vantage point.

Studying every square centimeter between her and the house, she surveyed the area. No one. She scanned out into the road in front. It was quiet, too. Her heart raced even faster than she thought it could. Her weary legs felt stiff and immobile. She felt as if she could go no further, but she had to. She closed her eyes for a moment, whispered a prayer for strength, then bolted from the brush toward the house.

Stumbling onto the porch, she tapped at the door, weakly. No answer. She banged her fist harder on the wooden door. Nothing.

"Somebody, please answer!" she begged, banging even more impatiently. Again nothing. She bowed her head, growing fearful no one was home.

"My Lord, child. What happened to you?" a voice spooked her. As she looked up, she saw Elze Vilks, a woman her mother's age. A startled expression etched her face. Augustine caught her breath, tried to answer, but her voice evaporated.

"Poor child. You're shivering. Come inside."

"The Germans—" Augustine leaned over while she tried to calm her frantic breathing. "They killed Momma, Mrs. Vilks! They killed Momma!"

Elze gasped and covered her mouth. She shook her head, then thrust her arm out and grabbed Augustine's clammy arm.

"Come inside." Her voice was demanding. "You need some dry things and something hot. I'll make some tea."

"I don't have time for tea," Augustine felt irreverent in her protest. "You must understand, I've got to go. The Germans are coming. I've got to go." She protested, unable to escape Elze's grip. "You must understand. The Germans." Her eyes screamed, desperately.

"There is time," Elze firmly assuaged. Augustine sighed and surrendered. She stumbled into the kitchen and plopped into a waiting chair. Her soaked dress clung to her, convincing her that Elze was right. Her chest heaved. Her heart pounded. Her head spun circles as she tried to relax, but the haunting image of that one German soldier's face hovered in her mind.

"Momma wants me to go to my sister in Valmiera. Otilija wrote a letter back in the fall," Augustine muttered as she fumbled into her shirt with her cold hands. She tried not to touch her skin, knowing how cold they would feel, but the inevitable touch happened and sent her into shivers. She latched onto the letter, pulled it out, and waved it at Elze.

"Poor, dear. You must be terrified," Elze said in a calming voice as she stared into Augustine's eyes. She grabbed a woven blanket from the sofa, and wrapped Augustine tightly.

"Stay bundled in this while while I prepare your tea."

"But Mrs. Vilks, the Germans!" Augustine continued waving the letter.

"You have time," Elze confirmed sternly as she poured steaming water into a cup. "Alberts will get you to Valmiera."

Alberts? Augustine cringed as Elze placed the tea in front of her. She wrapped her hands around the cup and bathed her nose in the rising steam. The heat felt so good that her quivering stopped.

She thought about Alberts as she moved her face closer to the amber liquid, still swirling from Elze's last stir of the tea spoon. She had never paid much attention to Alberts since he was always off on his own studying something while everyone else was playing. While other boys were out playing soccer, he studied politics. While other boys were chasing girls like her, begging them to go to Jani and the theater, he walked off alone into the woods. But if there was one trait of Alberts' that everyone knew and envied, it was his horsemanship. Everyone knew he was one of the best in all of Riga.

Augustine placed her lips on the rim of the cup and slowly drew tea into her mouth. Though bitter, the fluid felt good on her tongue. Its warmth seemed to creep through her mouth and down her throat, quelling the remaining tremors in her chest.

"Alberts!" Elze yelled.

Augustine drew in a more substantial mouthful of tea. She was startled when Alberts appeared at the end of the table, as if out of thin air. She could not help but stare. The young man standing in front of her was more than just another boy. His sandy blonde hair and clear blue eyes seemed so stunning that she could not understand why she had never recognized them before.

"Augustine needs to go to Valmiera. You know the way to Valmiera, don't you Alberts?" Elze asked, smirking as she stood up.

Alberts smiled. Augustine swallowed hard. As Elze passed by him, she leaned over and whispered something which Augustine could not hear, but it made Alberts smile even more. She tapped his shoulder, then disappeared into the parlor, leaving him alone with Augustine, standing fig-leafed. He smiled shyly, then cocked his head and stared for a moment. He dipped his head politely, and shuffled off without saying a word.

"Now where did that boy run off to?" Elze huffed as she returned and dropped one of her heavy winter dresses next to Augustine. "Here, take these and go change. You must get out of those wet things. I'll fetch you a coat. I'm sure you've heard how fast Alberts likes to ride."

Augustine gulped her tea. She could never ride fast. When she rode with Otilija, she had gone slow because she always got nauseous. She finished the tea, and took the dress. As she shuffled into the bathroom to change, she gritted her teeth and tried to convince herself she would be fine this time. She grabbed the coat Elze left for her and stepped out onto the porch.

"Oh, my word!" she gasped, bringing her hands to her face. The horse Alberts sat on was massive. And the muscles were bulging so much she could see its blood pulse.

"We should go now," Alberts said, as he rolled his eyes. "Momma says Valmiera is, hmm, fifty kilometers. We can make it in, I'd say two hours." His mouth turned up into a wry grin. "Three at the outside."

Augustine swallowed hard then turned to Elze and gazed at her with wide eyes. She was scared. Scared out of her wits. If the horse were smaller, or did not look as imposing, she may have felt a bit less uncomfortable. But she knew this was not the time to back out. She had no time to argue. Sucking in a deep breath, she mustered all her courage and decided it was time. She leaned over and hugged Elze.

"Can you be sure Momma is taken care of?" she asked as she pulled away.

"Don't worry, meitene. We'll take care of your mother. It's the Latvian way." Elze assured as she squeezed Augustine's shoulders. "Now you go! Riga is no place for a young, beautiful girl to be alone now."

"But you—?" Augustine quickly turned back to Elze.

"Don't you worry about me. I know how to handle the Germans," Elze replied emphatically. Augustine weakly smiled and turned toward Alberts and his horse.

"Don't worry about Momma. I know she will manage. Now, put your foot here," he mumbled, pointing to the foothold as he leaned over and offered Augustine his hand. She hesitantly slipped her foot into the stirrup, then extended her arm and looked up with a sheepish grin. With the chivalry of a knight, Alberts carefully and easily pulled her up and settled her into the saddle behind him.

"Now, wrap your arms around my waist and we'll go," he said. Augustine froze. Her arms lay limp at her sides. "If you don't, you will probably fall off." He said a little more sternly. Tentatively, she lifted her arms and set her hands on his waist. "Around," he coaxed.

She slowly moved her hands across his hips until they reached his stomach and touched. She interlocked her fingers and sighed. "Like this?" she asked. An odd feeling tingled through her neck. She felt safe. Her breathing slowed even though a warmth crept along her shoulders. She leaned into his back and felt even more secure.

"That will do. Now hang on tight," he said. She felt his thighs flex as he gently dug his heels into the horse's flanks. She grimaced, and clenched her eyes shut as they started toward the road.

❦   ❦   ❦

As they arrived in Valmiera, the sun slipped below the horizon beyond Riga. Alberts turned his back to it and stopped his horse, then gazed back at the rippled clouds, bellies softened from the daytime gray to a pastel-like pink and blue. He turned the horse back and started up the long access road to the farmhouse.

With Alberts' help, Augustine slid down the side of the horse. She wobbled toward the door on her trembling legs, and as she stepped onto the porch, the door flung open. Blanched but ecstatic, Otilija stood before her younger sister. She seemed frozen, but she quickly regained herself and rushed Augustine. As Otilija wrapped her arms around her, Augustine paged through the hundreds of things she wanted to say to her. She pulled away and looked directly into Otilija's teary eyes, then felt her heart flutter. A flood of emotions fought to be the first one out.

"How's Momma?"

Augustine remained silent for a moment. She could feel everything that happened in Riga come rushing back like a terrible nightmare.

"Momma's dead," she said, stiffly.

Otilija's lips quivered. Her jaw tightened, then her whole body began to tremble. Stumbling backward, she dropped into Janis' rocker, hunched forward into a ball and began sobbing.

Telmeni

3 April 1918

$\mathcal{E}$dwards Vechi glanced back through the spray of mud and water kicked up by his horse from the quagmire that was left of the softened road. He had looked back each kilometer for the last ten and had seen no one, but he still needed the security that he was not being followed. He felt his horse slip a bit in the soupy mud, more so than he had before. He knew his mount was growing tired from the long trek, but he was not about to give up. They may have given up in Riga, but he'd be damned if he was going to capitulate as easily as they had.

A surge of relief trickled through him as he saw familiar landmarks of Valmiera; the old school house and Bolodnieks' sheep that always seemed to be out in his pasture. Minutes after, he spotted the road leading into Telmeni, and pushing his steed at full speed, he turned his horse up the road. But as his mount complied, his hooves slipped and he began to stumble forward. He wrapped his arms around the animal's neck, knowing a fall at this speed would surely cripple them both. Snorting and scrambling, the horse gained better footing at the edge of the road, then caught his balance just as a stiff oak bough swatted Edwards across his face and neck.

The horse again surged forward. He exhaled the stale breath he had held since the horse began stumbling, then stood up in the stirrups.

"Poppa!" He yelled at the top of his lungs. "Poppa!" He screamed again, this time cupping his hands to help his voice carry.

He spotted two figures on the porch. One he could tell was Poppa. The other, he was not sure who it was.

"Poppa!" He tried to holler over the sloshing of his horse's hooves through the mud. He saw Janis vault from his chair, then descend the stairs and stand in the watery muck, waiting. Pulling up on the reins, he brought his horse to a sliding stop, splashing water which fell only inches short of his father. He swung his left leg over the animal's flank, slipped out of the saddle and plopped ankle deep into the mud near his father's feet. He crouched over, dropping his hands onto his knees, and sucked in air as deeply as he could.

"My God, Edwards. What's wrong?" Janis asked, rushing to his side. "You look like you've seen a ghost!"

"You've got to get out of here. We've got to get everyone out of here," he said quickly, then sucked in a deep breath.

"What are you talking about?"

"The city. We're losing in the city, and I know they're heading this way."

"Who's heading this way?"

"What's happening, Edwards? What did you see?" Augusts joined the pair. A puzzled yet pained expression covered his face.

Edwards stood up and drew in a deep breath through his open mouth.

"The city council has given in. They've capitulated to the Germans!"

"They did what?" Janis frowned.

"The Germans on the council demanded that all the Latvians resign their positions." He hunched over and sucked in another deep breath. "And son of a bitch, they did. Like lambs being led to a slaughter, they just gave in."

"Jesus, that's it then. If the city council is under German control, you know they'll give in to all of the Kaiser's demands." Augusts said with a reserved, logical voice. He turned away, despondent.

"After that, the army marched right in. Nobody stopped them. They're arresting people at random. They're killing and stealing. The city has fallen into anarchy."

Edwards stopped his rambling long enough to shake his head.

"Just like in Moscow," Augusts muttered as he lowered his head in disgust. Without saying another word, he shook his head, turned, and shuffled back into the house.

"Christ, it's our city, Poppa. It's our country, and we're being taken hostage by an invading army," Edwards said as he caught his breath and stood straight up.

Janis' face flushed red, deepening by the second. Conviction etched a scornful expression on his face. Behind his pruned lips, his jaw moved feverishly.

"First Augustine, now this," Janis mumbled, then burst out, "We will fight." His arms flailed as if he were a politician at a rally. "They will not do this to our Latvia. We won't stand for it. If we need to, we will fight in the streets until the last drop of German blood is drained from their wretched bodies."

Janis turned and stomped up the steps. Kristine, drawn to the porch by the commotion, grabbed him by the shoulders as he tried to storm by her. He stopped long enough to reveal his anger consumed expression. She stepped aside and let him pass, then glanced down at Edwards. "What's going on? What in the world could get Janis so up in a tizzy?"

"They're executing people in the city."

"I should have listened to Augustine. It's no wonder she was so upset," Kristine muttered as she shook her head.

"The German council has declared martial law and anyone caught protesting their control is publicly executed." He looked toward the house, craned his neck and tried to peer inside. "We've got to get everyone out of here. Now. You have to make Poppa understand. He should realize that."

"Haven't you learned by now," Kristine mumbled, disconcertingly. "When Poppa is like this, it's of no use to say anything to him."

Edwards stared into the window of the house, his eyes aflame with passion. He looked out toward the lake, then up at the gray sky, then back to the house. He pursed his lips, just like his father had done before, and worked his teeth through his lower lip, chewing bits of skin off.

"Then Poppa is right," he said. "Now is the time that we need to be strong. If we are to be a free state, then now is the time we have to prove ourselves."

Edwards craned his neck and looked around, trying to find his father. Kristine smiled and tipped her head.

"He'll be out to the barn. He would want you to help get us packed."

Edwards nodded and walked into the house with his mother.

❧   ❧   ❧

Janis stormed toward the barn, consumed. When he heard Alberts and Romans jabbering, he stopped and pivoted.

"Get the wagon packed up, Romans! We've got to get out of here!" He said as he entered the barn, startling both of the young men. Romans peered back at Alberts silently, then continued arguing his point.

Janis burst out of the barn on his strongest horse in full stride and headed toward the house, startling Alberts and Romans again.

"Get the damn wagon packed up, I said," he ordered and headed toward the house. Romans complied, leaving Alberts until he followed him in to help.

"Augusts!" Janis rounded the corner of the house, straight-backed in his saddle as if he were a commanding officer. He pulled back on the reins and stopped the horse. Augusts ran out of the house and onto the porch, looking up to his father. "Get the women packed up and ready to go. Romans is getting the wagon ready. Take the wagon and head up to Cesis!"

"Cesis? Isn't that where the Strelnieks is assembled?

"No, not Cesis. Valka. Yes, go to Valka, instead. Find the Castle Lielvarde. There will be some men there. Tell them you are Janis Vechi's family. They will find you a place up there safe from the Germans and the Russians."

"And you, Poppa? What about you?" Augusts asked. Kristine stood at the door and listened intently.

"Voldemars and his regiment need to be alerted!" Janis stated.

"But, Poppa. Shouldn't the word of the German advance come from the military command instead of you?"

"No!" Janis shook his head. "It is my duty to tell my son that he was right all along when I argued with him. We should have chased the Germans out months ago, just as he felt we should have."

"May God be with you, Janis," Kristine bid. "I'll have everyone ready to leave."

Janis cinched up his reins and jabbed his boots into his mount's flanks. The horse reared and bolted down the muddy road in full gallop with Janis leaning left and into the horse's flying mane.

Janis spotted the winter-burned ivy which still clung to the impressively tall, round turrets as he approached the Cesis castle from the main road. He leaned into the turn in the road and bolted toward the front of the castle. As he cleared the corner, two armed soldiers appeared out of nowhere and flagged him to stop. He obeyed, pulling quickly back on the reins as the soldiers deftly spun their rifles and aimed directly at him. When his horse slid to a stop, Janis looked around and realized he had become completely surrounded without even noticing where the soldiers had been hiding.

"Where the hell did you all come from?" Janis muttered, then lifted his arms and signaled surrender. He turned completely around and surveyed the rag-tag looking, but obviously well-trained, militia.

"Let him pass. He's family." A familiar voice called from in front of him. Janis snapped his head back to the front and froze, seeing what seemed to be a complete second regiment where only seconds before were only two soldiers. Voldemars, dressed in a field green uniform, stood proudly at parade rest and grinned.

"Christ, I never saw any of you," Janis commented as he dismounted. "Where the hell were you all hiding?"

"The tactics we'll need to use are pure Cossack, Poppa. And for our purposes, they'll be very effective," Voldemars said as he strutted toward his father. "The Cossacks may be barbarians, but one thing I learned from them was how to always win, even if the odds are not in my favor."

"Voldemars, the news from Riga is not good." Janis changed his tone. His face soured. "The Germans have demanded and won capitulation from the city council. Dissidents are being arrested and executed as examples."

Voldemars face grew long as his eyes thinned to slivers. He pensively rubbed his chin, and his lips jutted as if he were brooding. "Are you saying the defense of Latvia is in our hands?" His voice deepened. This is my chance, he thought. If I lead my men toward Riga, we would surely be the heroes of this battle.

"It's not Latvia that is so important. It's your family. Your wife." Janis said.

Voldemars did not hear him. He glanced over his shoulder at his men. A fire ignited and danced in his eyes as he entertained his own illusions of grandeur, picturing himself marching though the streets of Riga, proudly waving his white gloved hand to those who honored him as a paragon. As he scanned the crowd, he saw Kristine and Janis point to him, proudly announcing to all that would listen that he was their son. Next to them stood Otilija, holding Brevite high enough so she could see him. And next to Otilija, stood Doroteja.

"What are the women doing?" Voldemars returned to the present. "Has Otilija heard from her mother?"

"Edwards is taking Otilija and Kristine to Valka," Janis avoided the question. "They'll be safe there. Augusts and Romans will be staying with them."

"And Otilija's mother and sister?"

A pained expression washed over Janis' face.

"Augustine arrived today with a boy named Alberts Vilks. I don't suppose you know him. Alberts joined the Strelnieks as soon as he arrived."

Voldemars read into his father's avoidance. Janis did not have to explain any further.

"How is Otilija taking the news?" he asked.

Janis remained silent. He pursed his lips and chewed on his lip.

"Did you know that Otilija is pregnant?" He changed the subject.

Voldemars felt his emotions overload. He sucked in a deep breath and closed his eyes. As he let it go, he regained his composure. "Please let me know what's happening with her?" he whispered. "I'll to be there when I'm needed. If I can."

Janis remained silent as he put his arm around his son. "Are you going to Valka with Momma?" Voldemars asked.

"No, I'll remain at Telmeni," Janis responded.

Voldemars' brow furrowed with disapproval.

"To keep you informed and help if I can." Janis said.

"Oskars is staying in Valmiera?"

"I'll stay in touch with him."

Voldemars nodded and cocked his head, accepting the noble deed his father was planning. His eyes glazed in a distant stare for a moment.

"The Estonians. My God, Poppa. If someone can convince the Estonians to help us, to fight with us, and that it's in their best interest, we have a chance."

"I heard Rostislavs mention that Ulmanis and Goldmanis are soliciting aid. I think they said from Britain," Janis said. "But I really don't know what help they'll get."

Voldemars nodded halfheartedly. He put his arm around Janis and walked away from his men to get out of earshot. "I hope they are successful," he mumbled in a resigned voice. "We'll need all the help we can get to win this one." Janis tipped his head and locked eyes with his son. "After all I've done with these men, I hate to admit this, Poppa, but I'm not as hopeful as I was before," Voldemars lamented. "We have few weapons, no uniforms, no real way of defending ourselves against the German or Russian war machines, regardless of how much they've suffered from the war. I really don't believe we have even the slightest chance of winning. For now, the only thing we can rely on is pure will."

"What can I do for you?"

"If you can, convince someone that we need rifles, men and horses. Then we may have a fighting chance."

Janis bowed his head and rubbed his mouth. "I will do what I can," Janis turned back toward his horse. Voldemars shuffled back to his battalion, mustering his spirit once more for his troops' benefit. He glared into the eyes of all of his men and saw in each pair the same indomitable compassion he felt for his lands' freedom.

I can't measure their determination, Voldemars thought, watching his father disappear down the road. Voldemars signaled his men to move closer. But determination is definitely the one resource we have in adequate supply.

"My father has informed me that our moment of truth is near!" Voldemars spoke with a firm, controlled tone. "The Germans have taken Riga. Our duty, though, will be to guard against the Russians.

Since the battles will soon be waged on one front or the other, we will need to be ready."

Valka

18 July 1918

Otilija woke lying in a puddle of sweat as a sudden twinge tugged at her stomach. It surged, receded, then went away. There was something vaguely familiar about the surges. She rolled over, tried to get as comfortable as her bloated belly allowed, the dozed back off.

Five minutes passed. She couldn't sleep. Another pain started the same way, it built to a level enough to irritate her, but not enough to make her wince. As the pain receded again, it suddenly became very clear what was happening.

Otilija slipped her legs over the side of her bed, then eased her weight onto her feet. She took a moment to catch her breath, then pushed up from the bed and stood. She waddled across the wooden floor to her sister's bed and rested.

"Augustine. Wake up."

Augustine didn't stir. Otilija reached over to her shoulder and jostled her sleeping sister gently.

"Huh?" Augustine startled. She quivered and then popped her eyes open.

"I need you to get Voldemars," Otilija said.

Augustine's eyes were glazed and her jaw lax. "You need what?" The words seemed to barely fall from her mouth.

"I think the baby is coming," Otilija said slowly, making sure that Augustine would understand through her stupor. "I need you to get Voldemars."

Augustine vaulted upright and stared at Otilija. She looked at her face, then down at her stomach.

"Baby?" Augustine's mouth quivered. she rustled "But how?"

"Get a horse from the stable and ride to Cesis. He's at the castle."

"But how do I get there? I don't know—"

"Just follow the main road. You remember." Otilija felt another twinge coming. She braced herself against the bed and closed her eyes.

"Are you all right? What's the matter?" Augustine's face suddenly came to life. She smiled quickly, but then frowned.

"The baby. I think the baby is coming," Otilija repeated, breathless.

"Oh, my God," Augustine started scrambling. She jumped out of the bed and scurried around the dark room, searching for clothes. "The baby. I'll wake Kristine. And Augusts. He can get Voldemars."

"No," Otilija grabbed Augustine's arm. "I need you to get Voldemars. He will know it is important if I send you."

"But, Uncle Augusts will be mad at me," Augustine's voice quivered.

Otilija sighed relief as the twinge subsided. "He will understand. This is important to me. I want to be sure Voldemars is back before the baby is born."

She handed her light jacket to Augustine and wrapped her arms around her. Pulling her in as closely as her bulging stomach would allow, she hugged her briefly, then whispered, "Go. Tell Voldemars it's important."

Augustine nodded quickly and headed out the room.

Otilija shuffled back to her bed and plopped onto the side. She sucked in as deep as she could. The baby seemed to be kicking up under her chest, stifling her breath at less than satisfying.

Another twinge tugged at her stomach, only harder. As she winced, she heard hooves gallop out of the barn. She leaned back and tried to breath deeply, hoping it would relieve some of the pressure. It helped.

As the sound of the hooves faded, the twinge did as well.

❋   ❋   ❋

Voldemars stumbled out of his field headquarters, half-asleep, exhausted after a fitful night plagued with nightmares. With his shirt untucked, he plodded up to the castle's lookout over the Gauja River valley and waited for daybreak in the muggy summer morning. He seethed about the ridiculousness of being stationed so far away from anything. He knew there was no chance he and his regiment could engage in any meaningful battle. And with no opportunity to fight his way into his country's history, he would remain just another mundane, unknown, unimportant soldier.

An hour passed before the sky lightened enough for him to see more than just black and gray in the silhouettes. And when the color of the Gauja River valley blossomed, he grew instantly absorbed. His eyes glazed over as he saw the birches which grew like a blanket on the southern edge of the ravine. Wisps of steam rose from the water and veiled the bank, hiding the brown mottled caves and rock precipices. Sunlight glinted through the green canopy of leaves, but was split into thin virga-like strands at the fog bank, then stopped altogether.

"Four months since Brest-Litovsk," he mumbled. Every muscle in his body tensed at the thought of the treaty between the Germans and Russians. "Four months since those bastards chose between them who would be our rulers. That was our liberty and our destiny for us to decide."

His voice echoed through the valley, carrying with it the same angered tone in which he had spit out. He would hate the bastards forever for doing what they did. He could have been one of Goldmanis' chosen leaders if it weren't for them.

But as his voice faded, passerines on an early morning forage chirped and sang as they flitted through the broad leaves of the majestically sized oaks at the crest of the hill. Below, hidden by the fog mist, the river trickled through rocky bends.

A sudden pang stung at his chest. He bent over, held his hands on his hips and sucked in a breath as deeply as he could. He felt the air wheeze as it slipped through his throat and pierced through his swollen passages. The pain relented, but the reminder of what the Germans had done to him in the Carpathians made its mark.

"I could be one of those commanders in the southern regiments." He stood back up, raising his fist to the sky. "Then I could rightly inflict my revenge. Instead, I was handed a rag-tag bunch of volunteers who fight with themselves just to get out of bed in the morning." He stopped again and inhaled deeply. The pain had completely retreated.

He glared out and shook his fist. He remembered what he had done with his troops. He grew more confident that the regiment was ready and able to face either the Russians or the Germans. And win.

Another hour passed. He decided he had wasted enough time wallowing in his misfortune. He knew his mission was unclear, and because of that, he could not project any solid leadership for his men. But he also knew he could debate for days what could or what should be. So instead of carrying on that debate for another entire morning, he turned his back to the river and headed toward his regiment's encampment at the castle.

He glanced down and counted as his boots stepped down each of the slate steps which wound down from the overlook and back to the castle. Each step grew harder and harder as he tried to suck in another breath of fresh air. The gas attack in the Carpathians still sapped his stamina. Finally at the third landing, sixty steps he had counted, he stopped to catch his breath.

Leaning over the stone wall, he exhaled explosively, trying to clear the mucus which had collected in his throat. After pulling in his third deep breath and holding it for a count of twenty, the spasms in his chest subsided, and he continued his descent. Halfway down the next flight of stone steps, he spotted a soldier hustling up toward him, half dressed and hurriedly taking two, sometimes three steps at time.

"Morning, Alexiev. Any news?" he said, stopping to lean back and pull in another chest full of air.

Alexiev cocked his head as if listening, then stopped and emphatically waved for Voldemars to follow him. Voldemars' heart jumped into his throat as he read Alexiev's blanched, concerned expression.

"The Russians! We're here for the Russians. We can take those fools." Voldemars' adrenalin surged as he bolted toward the massive figure. He entertained more of the rapid-fire possibilities shooting though his head. "Or is it the Germans. The Germans started an offensive and Goldmanis wants us to redeploy!" Out of breath, Voldemars stopped at the landing three steps above Alexiev. Alexiev's face was more than just pallid,it was ghostly.

"Christ, you look like death. What is it?"

"Someone has come for you," Alexiev said between deep, heavy pants.

"Who?"

"A woman. Augus—"

Voldemars bolted past Alexiev. As his boots clomped rapidly down the steps he fretted. He jumped off the last step and sprinted around the castle wall. Needles pricked at his chest as he turned the corner and ran onto the parade field, but when he saw Augustine, dressed in a nightgown and jacket mounted on her horse, their insistence grew dull and ignorable.

"Augustine!" he yelled, waving his hands. "What are you doing here?"

"Otilija said to get you. She thinks she's having the baby!"

He felt a surge in his legs and he deftly changed direction toward the horse stable. He grabbed the bridle from the stall and slipped it into place. With his free hand, he pulled out his saber and as he yanked his head back, slashed the rope that tied his horse to the rail.

"Let's go, boy!" He commanded, sliding his saber into its sheath. He slapped the horse's shoulder hard, then ripped the reins from his mouth and snapped at the leather as well.

The horse responded instantly, dancing around on his hind legs until he had turned completely around, then exploded into a gallop.

He smiled as he bolted out of the stable, thinking the horse was responding as well as the horse that saved his life in the gas attack. As he made a wide turn, clumps of grass flew up from the horse's rear hooves. He started past the castle, then noticed through the corner of his eye a large figure stumble to a stop in the field.

"Alexiev, you have command. I'll be back soon."

Alexiev acknowledged with a wave as Voldemars sped toward Augustine, who had already turned her horse and was headed for the road. With long, loping strides punctuated by pounding hooves, Voldemars' horse closed the gap. As he drew up next to her, Voldemars turned and smiled, but also noticed her white knuckled fists clenched tightly on the reins. Her eyes were wide with terror.

"Relax, Augustine," he yelled over the thundering strides. "Lean into his neck and relax. Let him run. He'll do fine on his own." Voldemars ground his heels into his horse's flank, spurring him to pick up his pace. As he passed Augustine, he glanced again at her face beaming proudly as it rocked with the motion of the horse.

Christ, that's Otomars! he thought, gasping as he felt a knot twinge in his stomach. Augustine's features were unmistakable. That face was the same as her brother's, the one he had beaten years before. At the same time, though, he saw Otilija in the young woman galloping beside him. Adrenalin surged.

"Faster, now Otilija" He caught himself. "Faster, Augustine. Follow me." He bolted ahead of his riding mate.

❧   ❧   ❧

As soon as Augustine pointed out the shack through the trees, Voldemars dug his heels into Uguns and steered him through the pathway leading to the house. When he cleared the brush, he spotted Augusts calmly sitting on the porch, puffing smoke circles around his head from his pipe. He pulled back on the reins to slow his horse a little, then swung his leg over and flawlessly dismounted with a Cossack's flair. His boots hit the soft ground near the stoop with a thud, but his momentum forced him to take three running steps before he could slow to a dignified walk.

"Whoa!" The horse planted his legs, turned and returned in an arrogant gait toward Voldemars.

Augusts stood up and walked toward Voldemars, greeting him halfway to the house with a strong embrace.

"You have a son, Voldemars!" he stated through his clenched teeth. "A strapping, healthy son!"

"A son," Voldemars repeated. He backed off and let Augusts firmly shake his hand. "I have a son."

He stood absolutely still for a moment, mulling over the idea. As he cocked his head, he started to imagine all the things he could teach his boy. A smile crept onto his face as he thought of taking walks through the woods with him, just to explore every path he never had a chance to. They would spend days fishing in the lake. He would tell him the stories of Lacplesis and of the glorious days of the Lettish royalty.

"Voldemars?" Augusts' voice pierced his daydream. Voldemars shook his head and returned to reality.

"Yes, a son. Well then, Uncle Augusts, let's go see my son."

"You go ahead. I need to speak to that girl," Augusts muttered sternly.

Still stunned, Voldemars simply nodded and drifted toward the tiny grass-roofed house. He heard Augusts start to chastise Augustine for leaving without telling anyone, and her protests as he stepped through the doorway, but he remained focused. He stiffened immediately, like a pompous general and surveyed the inside of the house. To his left, the kitchen was empty save for the half rusted pot-bellied stove in the corner. To his right was a small, vacant bedroom. He held his breath and listened closely. Ahead, in one of the small rooms three steps away, he heard cooing and high-pitched, simple chatter. It was Kristine's.

He strutted forward and entered another small room. Near the small crib he spotted his mother gently playing with the infant. By a window which seemed too large for the room, Otilija sat solemnly in a blanket padded chair, arms crossed on the sill, staring out into the woods.

Voldemars sighed to catch his breath, loud enough that Otilija must have heard. She turned her head toward him and immediately, her face changed from melancholy to joy. He walked stiltedly across the floor, all the while bouncing his eyes between Otilija and the little boy in his grandmother's arms.

"He's quite handsome," Otilija said as Voldemars kneeled next to her. "Like his father."

Kristine startled and looked up. She grinned widely, then stood up, and carefully shuffled toward Otilija. After delivering the baby into Otilija's extended arms, she patted Voldemars on the back.

"Have you thought of a name?" he asked as he pulled the blanket back from his son's face.

"Tradition says we should name him Voldemars."

"But?" He read her hesitancy.

"I was hoping you thought Andrejs would be a good name." Otilija's eyes peered wistfully at her husband.

Voldemars pulled in a deep breath. He looked down at the baby, then glanced back at Otilija.

"That was your father's name, wasn't it?"

Otilija nodded and closed her eyes. Voldemars glanced down at his son. His face was as wrinkled and pruned as the dried figs he saw in Astrakhan. The red splotches on his cheeks stood out and quivered as he moved his jaw up and down as if he were eating. Thin strands of black hair draped across the pink skin on his head, and his brow was furrowed.

Voldemars felt himself drift as he concentrated on his son. Andrejs' sons, dressed in full Russian uniforms, bloodied and tattered, paraded by in his thoughts. Otomars. Oswalds. Vilis. And little Fricis. As each face floated by, he saw their mouths drop open, calling Poppa between etched winces. When they were gone, Augustine's image appeared as she looked on the horse leading him to this decrepit shack in the woods.

"Voldemars?" Otilija asked.

Voldemars squeezed his eyes closed and opened them. He shook his head and looked back down at Otilija.

"Andrejs is a fine name." he mumbled. "A fine name."

After enduring two seemingly endless nights spent constantly tending to Andrejs' colicky fits, Otilija dropped her head onto her crossed arms and let the bright morning sun bathe her mussed brown hair. She drifted off to sleep and dreamt that she was laying on the shore of Telmeni's lake, relaxed by the summer warmth. She heard birds sing as they flitted by, and the gentle rustling of mice dancing through the dried underbrush.

Andrejs coughed. She immediately popped up and snapped her head toward him. His gurgling did not sound alarming like it had been most of the night. But to be sure, she lifted her head from the sill, then shuffled over to the crib and checked on the baby. His face looked a little pale, but his cough had not wakened him. She sighed, then tied her housecoat together and scuffed her way to the kitchen for some tea.

Kristine turned and smiled at her when she stumbled into the kitchen. Little Brevite turned her attention away from the dough Kristine had been kneading and smiled.

"Look, Brevite! Momma's awake!" Kristine said as she wiped her hands off on her apron. She bent over and picked up Brevite, much to the little girl's delight.

Held securely in her grandmother's arms, one-year old Brevite giggled as she flailed her arms at her mother. Otilija shuffled toward the pair, pecked at Brevite's head, then grinned as she mussed her wispy black hair.

"Another rough night?" Kristine asked. Otilija nodded, rolling her blood-shot eyes.

"Poor dear," Kristine added. "Why don't you sit down and relax. I'll fix you some tea."

"Mmm," Otilija mumbled and quietly sighed as she shuffled to the small chair near the window. She sat down and set her arm on the sill, then lay her head down.

"I finished the wash and it is all hung," Augustine announced as she waltzed into the house.

Otilija lifted her head and offered a weak smile.

"Oh my word, Otilija. You look terrible!"

Otilija nodded and set her head back down.

"Augustine, would you go watch Andrejs for your sister while I make her some tea?" Kristine asked. Augustine's eyes glistened and a wide grin blossomed on her face as she disappeared into the baby's room.

Kristine grinned and shook her head as she finished drawing water for Otilija's tea.

"She'll be a good mother someday, won't she?" She chuckled as she balanced the cup on a saucer and walked to the table with Brevite in tow. She set the tea on the sill in front of Otilija, then lifted Brevite into the chair next to her mother.

"Now just relax and enjoy your tea." Kristine swished her hand around a towel covered bucket. She pulled out two pirogis, dropped them onto little Brevite's lap, then patted her on the head.

Brevite smiled widely as she fondled the roll and brought it up to her mouth, but as she took a bite, Andrejs gagged.

Otilija leapt to her feet, almost knocking over her tea, but Kristine quickly placed her hand on Otilija's shoulder and pushed her back down.

"Momma!" Augustine's trembling voice called from the nursery.

Otilija's heart skipped. She tried to stand up again, but Kristine again set her back down.

"You just sit and enjoy your tea with your daughter. I'll see what Augustine is screaming about," Kristine insisted.

Through tired, reddened eyes, Otilija looked up at Kristine and smiled weakly. Still tense, she tried to relax as Kristine started to leave the room. She dropped her head back into her arms and fell asleep.

Kristine stopped as she saw Voldemars quietly walk through the front door, wiping the sweat from his brow. She pointed to Otilija and motioned with folded hands that she was asleep. Voldemars nodded and placed a finger over his lips, then tip-toed toward Otilija. He bent over and gently kissed the top of her head, then turned his attentions to Brevite as Kristine tip-toed into the nursery.

"Something's wrong, Momma," Augustine said with quivering hesitancy. Her face was blanched with fear. "He may have settled back down, but he looked like he was turning blue."

"Probably just some mucous," Kristine said as she carefully stepped across the room. "Sometimes babies take a while to clear everything out."

She peeked over the slats into the crib and watched Andrejs' tiny body lying still, covered with a thin sheet. Reaching over, she lightly touched his face, but when he did not even respond to her touch, an instant of panic surged in her heart. She frantically placed her palm on his forehead, then slipped it down to his open mouth.

"Oh, my God. He's not breathing," she gasped.

Augustine gasped and brought her hands to her face.

"Otilija! Otilija, come quick!" she cried as she watched Kristine pick up the baby and squeeze at his chest.

Voldemars bolted into the nursery. He glared at Augustine, then Kristine and then his son in her arms. The horrified expression he read on Augustine's face sparked a tingle which raced down his neck and flared through his back. A choking lump grew in his throat as he took measured steps toward his mother. He swallowed hard, but the lump in his throat remained. Reaching out as he stopped next to Kristine, he took Andrejs from her arms and held him close. The baby gasped and feebly coughed once, then fell limp in his arms.

"Momma...doctor...." His face waned. "Momma, take Andrejs. I'll go get a doctor."

Voldemars handed Andrejs back to Kristine, then spun around and scrambled toward the door, but stopped as he ran into Otilija.

"Voldemars? What's wrong?" Otilija stopped him as he passed the door jamb. "Why was Momma yelling?"

"I'm going to get a doctor." he insisted.

Otilija gasped. She hurried to Kristine's side and extended her arms.

"Voldemars, don't go!" Kristine solemnly insisted as she rested the infant into Otilija's open arms. She reached down and grabbed a blanket for Otilija.

"What?" Voldemars turned and grasped the door jamb. As he leaned back into the nursery, he felt fear consume his mind and agony tear at his heart. The image of Otilija weakly stumbling toward the sill, then plopping down in the chair drained the last ounce of hope from his heart. Still holding her baby close to her chest, she shook her head and repeated "no" over and over again through heavy sobs.

Voldemars' felt his whole life crashing in around him. The joy of having a son had vanished, taken away as quickly as his first one had been. Guilt from being absent when he was born gnawed relentlessly at him. It coldly reminded him that he was missing when his first daughter was born as well. But when he glanced down and saw little Brevite peeking though his legs, he realized he had an obligation just as important as his position in the militia. Brevite needed him. And Otilija, sobbing with their dead baby in her arms needed him.

He calmly settled next to his wife. Mustering all his courage, he rested his hands over hers.

"We still have Brevite," he consoled. "And we still have each other." Otilija lifted her head and stared at her husband through teary eyes. "I know it hurts, Otilija, but we must go on. We need to be thankful that we still have what we have."

She forced a smile, even though the cold infant in her arms burned at her breast and left her feeling cheated and empty.

Northern Latvia

11 November 1918

"Reconnaissance," Alexiev explained to the handful of soldiers huddled around him, "by definition, is the observation of the enemy and their movements without, and I repeat, without them knowing you are watching!" He grabbed a stick and started scratching lines in the dirt to help explain. He drew a series of x's in a single file on the ground.

"This is the enemy here." He pointed to his scratched diagram, then scratched another set of x's on the ground and drew a line between the groups. "For proper surveillance, you need to be hidden from them, but still able to watch all of their movements."

"Scrub along the road usually provides good cover, but if it doesn't have any leaves on it," Leopold added, grabbing a stick and holding it in front of his face, "it won't do you any good."

The scouting party smiled.

"Position is just as important," Alexiev said, holding his fisted hand in the air. "Any time you have the sun, put yourself between it and the enemy. If they look your way, then they have to shield their eyes to see you."

The sun was setting quickly. He knew they had to be in position before darkness fell. Since they still had over a kilometer to travel before they would be at the location where the Estonian command reported the Russian troop movements, he knew they would have to move soon. He looked back to the group and his eyes fixed on Aleksandrs'.

"Once into position, everyone needs to remain quiet and motionless." He held up his finger. "One move, one sound, and we may as well have been flushed like a partridge! Understood?"

Aleksandrs nodded along with all the other soldiers.

"We'll leave the horses here. Ozolis, you are to remain here with them."

Peters Ozolis, the youngest of the group, nodded with a frown.

"Let's go!" Alexiev ordered as he picked up his rifle and slung it over his shoulder. He turned and started toward the road, cutting through the mix of evergreen and leafless brush, followed by Leopold and each of the soldiers.

The early evening dimness settled as the soldiers arrived at their location and quickly took positions near the road. As the soldiers settled in, Alexiev and Leopold slipped out onto the road and peered into the area where the men were hiding.

"Patience, old friend. They have to learn," Alexiev responded to Leopold's rolling eyes.

"Christ, Alexiev. Their smell is enough to give us away."

"Consider yourself lucky then that we are downwind," Alexiev whispered as he surveyed the hidden soldiers.

"Jekabs, your rifle is sticking out too far!" Leopold scolded. Jekabs pulled his rifle barrel in.

"Aleksandrs, your hand is exposed! Pull it in!" Alexiev barked. He stood with his hands on his hips until the hand was withdrawn. They both made one last inspection, and satisfied, they slipped off the road, and joined the men.

"One last order." Alexiev wormed down into the brush. "If you see anything, do not do anything to attract their attention! The intent of this mission is reconnaissance, not engagement. Is that clear?"

Wide eyes and dirt smudged faces nodded, then turned back to the road.

"So what do you think?" Leopold badgered in a whisper as he hunkered down next to Alexiev. "Do you think Voldemars is right? Will that fat shit Vacietis roll his Red army in here, now that the Germans have surrendered?"

"Hmm," Alexiev grunted. "I know Vacietis is short, stumpy, and at times, even acts as stupid as he looks. But my friend, he is competent. That is fact. And since he was born here, he knows the land, and that gives him a distinct advantage over us. That concerns me a great deal."

"I wouldn't get too knotted up about that. I bet this is just a ruse," Leopold said sarcastically, blowing condensation rings with his breath.

"I don't think so. Think about it. The Bolsheviks want a Communist Latvia. That's been obvious since the bastards took over Russia."

"Then I guess we'll see," Leopold said confidently.

Alexiev peered over to Aleksandrs crouched in the brush next to him. His focus was intense. His eyes were as wide as a rising full moon, and a strange but seemingly confident grin etched his face. His hand twitched nervously, uncomfortably close to the trigger on his tarnished rifle.

"Watch him closely." Voldemars' words echoed loudly in Alexiev's head. "Don't let things get out of hand. He's a little too eager at times, but he has the potential to become a good soldier. Sit on him if you have to."

"Alexiev." Leopold poked him. He pointed south along the road.

"I see something!" Movement along the road caught Alexiev's attention. He wormed closer to the road to get a better view, then waited, quiet and vigilant.

"There's the proof, Leopold," he whispered, as a small patrol of soldiers appeared from around a bend in the road. Alexiev stealthily sat up on his haunches and nervously inspected his hidden rank again. He pointed to Raymonds, then motioned for him to head back and send news of the confirmed sighting. The boy stumbled as he got up, but then scurried back through the brush.

As Raymonds disappeared, Alexiev turned back toward his file. His eyes fixed on Aleksandrs. The boy's trigger finger twitched even more than before, and dangerously close to the metal tongue. His feet bounced rhythmically but quietly, digging a hole as his toe continuously hit the ground.

"Patience, Aleksandrs. Patience," Alexiev whispered. Aleksandrs nodded.

"What a sorry lot," Leopold commented in a low, hushed monotone. "Just look at their faces drawn, pale. I bet they had even less food than we did when we were at the front."

"Different time, different place. They were hungry as well as discontent with the czar. Now, they may be hungry, but—"

Alexiev stifled as he saw the lead soldier of the regiment break rank and head directly toward them. The Russian's eyes sat back in his head, stolid and cold, icy and determined. As he sauntered close enough to spit on, Alexiev held his breath, but remained at the ready with his rifle. The soldier stopped, fished through the brush with his bayonet, then slipped the weapon over his shoulder. He looked back to the regiment and waved, then moved closer to the hidden soldiers.

"Oh, shit!" Alexiev gasped under his breath. The soldier then stopped a meter from Alexiev's gun barrel and fondled his trousers. He undid himself, then released a stream of urine into the brush. A rancid ammonia smell splashed up into Alexiev's face. He cringed. He strained not to move as the stream dribbled down to nothing. The Russian sighed, fixed his trousers, and rejoined his group.

Alexiev held his breath, stifling his gagging reflex as the meager compliment of ten Russians continued down the road. Leopold silently chuckled, pointing to the urine puddle, then glanced back at the Russians. Carefully rolling over, Alexiev relaxed and let out a steady, silent breath that misted in front of his face. He pulled his legs up underneath him as he watched the last of the soldiers disappear around another curve in the road.

But out of nowhere, another soldier appeared, hustling as if to catch up with the others. Alexiev caught a glimpse of him, startled, then flopped back over on his stomach. A dry twig snapped underneath his chest. Leopold peered at Alexiev with wide, saucered eyes, like he had just been caught stealing.

The soldier turned, leveled his rifle at the bushes, and fired blindly. The bullet whizzed by Alexiev, close enough that he felt the heat of the lead near his ear. Instinctively, Alexiev turned to Aleksandrs. He was squinting, and his rifle was aimed directly at the Russian. Alexiev saw Aleksandrs' finger quiver as it squeezed on the metal tongue.

The gun went off. The sound resonated like a violent mid-summer thunderstorm. Alexiev saw an orange flame lap out from Aleksandrs' rifle barrel.

"Shit!" he yelled.

"Major!" the Russian yelled. He aimed into the brush again and fired.

Alexiev gasped as he saw Leopold's head jerk back just before his own face was showered with bloody lumps of bone and tissue. Leopold's body slumped awkwardly forward.

"You're not getting away from me, you bastard," Alexiev vowed in a whisper. Stiffening his mettle, he let his reflexes take over. Crouching over his rifle sight, he cocked his head, and squinted down on his left eye. The Russian's image grew blurry as he tried to focus through his tears, but then movement in the distance drew his attention away from the single young soldier frantically trying to reload.

The rest of the Russians scrambled around the corner and took up defensive positions on the opposite side of the road.

"We won't go down without a fight," Alexiev vowed as he noticed Aleksandrs leveling his rifle from the corner of his eye. He turned his head and aimed into the Russians.

"Fire!" Alexiev yelled as he yanked on his trigger. His rifle hopped in his hand. A red flame lapped out at the road. More muzzle flashes from the Russian side of the road startled him, but he reloaded. Deafening cracks followed each flickering tongue. Leafless, dry branches shattered as bullets whizzed by his head. The smell of scorched wood and burnt meat blended with the gagging smell of sulfury discharge. Piercing screams wailed next to him, then dulled to muffled moans, then finally faded into silence.

"Oh, my God. I got one." Alexiev heard Aleksandrs as one of the Russians crumbled to his knees, then dropped onto his face. A curtain of bullets ripped through the brush. Panic froze Alexiev as he watched blood gush from one of his own men's neck wounds while at the same time he heard air whistle from the pierced chest of another.

His stomach knotted tightly. Through his locked jaw, he tried to pull in air, but failed. His vision narrowed and blurred at the edges, like he was looking through field glasses. The trees began circling around him, then spun faster until he became dizzy and weak. He glanced down to his stomach and saw his uniform dripping blood through a tear. His stomach began burning just as he realized it was his chest that sucked air. The night went quiet and black again, like it was before the Russians marched through.

❧   ❧   ❧

Distant sounds of cracking and popping drew Voldemars' attention away from grooming Uguns before putting him up for the night. The sound seemed familiar to him, but there were so many other sounds that kept him wondering what could be going on miles away. The snapping finally stopped. Thinking nothing more of it, he went back to grooming his horse.

"Commander Vechi!" He dropped his brush and hurried out of the stable. "Commander Vechi! We've been hit!" Voldemars suddenly recognized the voice. A surge of prickles raced up his spine.

"Son of a bitch." He ran back into the stable and snapped his horse's reins free. Kicking open the gate, he jumped and slipped a foot into the stirrup and swung the other leg over his mount's back.

He yelled, snapping the reins. The horse spun around, and broke into a gallop as his hooves hit the ground.

At the entrance to the camp, Voldemars saw Peters heading at lightning speed toward him. He slowed his own mount and waited.

"Ozolis, report." he ordered.

Peters pulled back on his reins and slowed his horse.

"Commander," Peters gasped, out of breath. After two quick breaths, he continued. "Something happened. I was watching the horses as Alexiev ordered me, then all hell broke loose. There was gunfire everywhere. I heard screams. I did what Alexiev told me. Get the hell out of there if anything happens. Report back to Voldemars." Peters had to stop to catch his breath again.

"Bastards." Voldemars bit his lip so hard he tasted blood. "Go back into camp," he barked. "Get Gimines to assemble another scouting party. We're not letting these bastards get away with this one."

As soon as he finished, Voldemars heeled his boots into Uguns' sides and streaked toward the reconnaissance site.

"Christ, I should have just believed Alexiev," he grumbled, feeling the cold November wind bite at his cheeks. "We should have attacked weeks ago. We had enough proof that the bastards were bringing in troops."

He took less than five minutes to reach the site. As he rounded the bend in the road, he pulled up and slowed his horse to a trot. The animal's ears perked and pointed.

"What is it, ol' boy?" he asked. He pulled his horse off to the side of the road and dismounted.

"Stay," he ordered. The horse twitched his ears and snorted. Careful not to step on anything, he made a silent, tentative approach. Wisps of clouds dimmed the moon's light as they passed in front of it, but enough remained so that he could see everything. When he turned the corner and peered into the clearing, he froze.

Ten mangled bodies lay motionless in the road. The odor was sickening and familiar. Dead soldiers. Burnt cloth stained with clumps of flesh scoured from bodies. He surveyed the area to be sure he was alone, then proceeded. The first body he reached was a Russian foot soldier, prone and motionless. A gaping wound oozed blood over splintered bones where his spine should have been. He glanced up the road and noticed the spot where the skirmish had occurred. Oddly, though, there was a trail of blood between two shallow lines scratched into the dirt between footprints.

Ambushed? He tried to piece together the scene in his mind. He turned back to the dead Russian, and followed a line back to where his felling shot must have come. He peeked into the brush. Nothing. He needed to search further.

He split the brush with his hand. An abandoned rifle fell from out of the branches and clanked on the ground. He saw Leopold, now just a bloody, mangled mass. Next to him, Alexiev lay still. The gaping hole in his back was silent. Shocked, Voldemars stumbled over the bodies between him and Alexiev, then dropped to his knees next to his old friend. He wedged his hands underneath his huge chest, and cringed when he felt cold dampness on his uniform. Straining, he grunted as he turned Alexiev over.

The body flopped limply onto its back. In the pale moon-light, his face appeared even more ghostly. Bits of bone had lodged in his black beard. An odd, almost peaceful expression rested comfortably on his face.

"You fucking bastards." He shook his fist. "I will have my revenge for this. Mark my words, I will have my revenge if it's the last thing I do!"

❧   ❧   ❧

Two weeks passed, uneventful for Voldemars' regiment marooned in the center of the country, stagnant. He woke in the morning consumed in his thoughts, wondering why Zalitis, the acting war minister had ordered him to report to the Latvian Command field headquarters in Valka. The Russians had done nothing since their last raid. The reports from the German front were just as uneventful. By a process of elimination, he convinced himself there was only one reason for Zalitis' hasty message—a promotion. His work organizing the roots of the Northern Vidzeme Regiment was to be recognized with the overall command. He was sure of it.

Low, bleak clouds accompanied the bone-chilling north wind from the time he left Gaujiena. The light, dry snow which the cloud cover promised held off until he guided his horse onto the parade field at headquarters. As the snow began to stick to his overcoat, he pulled back on the reins and surveyed the strangely quiet campground.

"What do you think, ol' boy?" he mumbled, then nudged his horse on to start a wide looping circle around the field. Half-way through his circle, he noticed that two stiff sentries emerged from amidst three closely spaced tents and waved for him to stop. He turned his horse toward the guards and complied, quickly dismounted and saluted.

"I am Captain Voldemars Vechi, Northern Vidzeme Regiment. Minister Zalitis has ordered me here." He reached into his breast pocket, pulled out the orders he had received and surrendered them to the taller of the two guards. The sentry took the orders, gave them a cursory inspection, then turned and pointed to the cluster of three tents.

"The center tent. He's in there with a couple of other officers." The sentry folded the message and handed it back to Voldemars, then buried his hands back into his pockets.

Voldemars nodded, tipped his head to the shivering pair, then offered the reins to the sentry. For a moment, the sentry glowered at him. Grumbling, he frowned and took the leather in his bare hands. Voldemars saluted sharply, then strutted directly toward the tent as the guards headed toward the stable.

He stopped just outside the tent, primped his new tunic, straightened his cap and sucked in a deep breath. Mentally prepared to accept the honor of a promotion, he slipped through the flap and into the musty, smoke filled tent, and snapped to attention.

"Captain Voldemars Vechi. Reporting as ordered, sir!" He identified Zalitis standing between two other high ranking officers. To his right stood Colonel Kalpaks, the commander of the entire Latvian army.

Voldemars knew instantly that this had to be a truly important meeting if Kalpaks was summoned. Kalpaks had not changed much since the last time Voldemars had seen him. His closely cropped black hair stood straight, neatly brushed away from his forehead. Beneath his round, wide blue eyes, shadowed by thin crescent shaped black eyebrows, his nose sloped sharply down to a point. He had thinned the mustache Voldemars remembered as thick and unruly down to a thin, well-shaped brush on his upper lip. He tipped his head forward with a silent acknowledgment, then pursed his lips into a smile. "Captain Voldemars Vechi, we meet again." Voldemars read the conversation in his eyes. "I presume you are ready to take on this new assignment."

"I am ready." Voldemars replied through his eyes, then nodded and broke a wry grin of his own.

The other officer, though, was unfamiliar. His eyes, almond shaped and slanted slightly upward, were more strikingly northern than Kalpaks'. His nose seemed almost too large to be real, turning down at the end to hook over his thick gray mustache. A salt-and-pepper Vandyke style beard pointed forward and jutted out over his tight uniform color. As he smiled, his cheeks pushed his eyes closed to slits.

"Good morning, Voldemars," Zalitis said as he stood and offered his hand. "I'm glad you could make it. Please, sit down. We have much to discuss."

Voldemars stepped forward and shook the minister's hand, then pulled out a chair and waited until all three had seated themselves. He sat down across from Zalitis.

"I assume you know Colonel Kalpaks?" Zalitis started.

"No introduction needed," Voldemars cordially nodded to Kalpaks. "I've heard much of your successful campaigns. And I believe congratulations are in order on your promotion to Commander of all Latvian forces."

Kalpaks acknowledged with a feigned, humble smile.

"And this is Colonel Zemitans," Zalitis said, turning toward the other officer. Voldemars' eyes met Zemitans' and exchanged cordial but cold glances. "He will be commanding the Northern Latvian Army. And myself, well, I hope to enlist Estonian support for us."

Zemitans? Voldemars' heart sank. His thoughts rambled. What has he done for us? Why has he been promoted to command the Northern forces and not me? I assembled the Northern Army! I have contacts in Estonia! I could get you the support you need!

While Voldemars tried to make sense of Zalitis' choice of Zemitans over him, the minister unrolled a large and highly detailed map of the Baltic area over the table. Voldemars glared icily at Zemitans.

"If these men will be your staff, why did you order me here?" Voldemars asked with a fleeting glance. Zalitis joined the colonels in examining the map. Voldemars noticed that all the lands surrounding Latvia had been ominously shaded. Additional heavy lines had been drawn through Latvia, paralleling the Daugava River.

"Colonel Zemitans will command the forces here," Zalitis started to explain, pointing to southern Estonia and Northern Latvia. "His forces will sweep down from the north, retake Cesis from the Russians, then regroup, move on to Madona and then eventually reach the Daugava." He waved his hand in a sweeping motion as he spoke. Voldemars caught Zemitans' cold eyes peering at him.

"And Colonel Kalpaks?" Voldemars asked.

"I am presently stationed in Jelgava," Kalpaks said, his voice deep and resonant. He pointed on the map. "I will sweep south along the Daugava, then up to the river."

Voldemars studied the map and the movements they had discussed. In his mind, he shaded the areas which were each of the other commander's responsibility. Finally, it was clear to him what his assignment was to be. "And me?" He asked to confirm his suspicion.

"Protect the back door," Zalitis said, solemnly. "If we are to defeat the Red Army, we will need to ensure their supply lines are cut and our rear flank is protected." Zalitis drew in a deep breath as he glanced up and stared at Voldemars with wide eyes. The contact was sincere. "I've seen your men, Voldemars. They are not much to look at, but I commend you on how well you've prepared them. They are the best suited for this particular mission."

Voldemars looked at the map and realized something disturbing. He rewound Kalpaks' words again in his head, then followed his army's objectives. He turned to Kalpaks and frowned. "Are we allied with the Germans?" he asked.

"We have no choice," Zalitis added matter of factly.

"Don't trust them." Voldemars' eyes bulged.

"We've got to trust someone, Vechi," Zalitis interceded. "Christ, we don't have much at this point."

"Have you seen what they're doing in Riga?" Voldemars shouted back, barely holding himself in his seat. "They're uncivilized barbarians. They're animals."

"We need their arms," Kalpaks defended, slamming his fists to the table.

"At what price?" Voldemars countered.

"Without them, we will surely fall to the Russians." Zemitans joined the fray.

"Isn't there another ally we could court? What about the English?" Voldemars protested. From the cold, emotionless stares pasted on each of the officers' faces he realized he was debating what had already been decided.

"I know how you feel," Zalitis said calmly.

Voldemars chewed his lower lip frantically. Zemitans would not argue points as he would. Zalitis just thought this coalition would be the best. He didn't harbor the same ill feelings for the Germans.

"May I speak freely, Colonel Kalpaks," Voldemars mumbled.

Kalpaks nodded.

"You are a better man than I to lead the Southern Army. But, after what the Germans have done to me, I will never trust them as long as—"

Zalitis raised his hand and stopped Voldemars before he could finish. "If we are to win this war, and bring freedom to Latvia, we must trust someone. The Germans are simply the least objectionable."

"Then it will be done." Voldemars reluctantly acknowledged, adding in a cold, obediently militaristic tone.

Riga

21 March 1919

O skars Ziemels skittishly snapped his head side-to-side to be sure no one watched him, then plunged into the dark alley between two abandoned factories. He scurried along the damp brick walls which seemed to go on forever, trying not to clomp his shoes on the cobblestone street. Panting and out of breath, he reached the rear entrance of one building, then collapsed. He leaned his head against the cold metal frame, dropped his jaw open and tried to suck in as much of the pungent old town air as he could. His chest stopped before he could completely fill his lungs, so he exhaled and tried again. As the cold, damp spring air seemed to ooze into his spasming throat, dirt and soot trapped in the air scraped at his passages.

His feet throbbed. His head pounded. His eyes burned. His chest wheezed. As soon as he dropped to the cold, wet cement, his thighs burned with hard cramps. There was no way he could keep up the pace he had maintained all morning.

He sucked in a deep breath and tried to clear his mind so he could think of who could have leaked their meeting place to the Bolsheviks. That was the only way they could have known. They had held hundreds of secret meetings in so many different towns and had never been caught before. He tried to picture each of the new faces at the meeting, but even his thoughts were blurred.

The echo of boots stomping down the alley again grabbed his attention.

"He's down here!" he heard one of the Russians bark.

"Shit. They found me." He gasped. He focused enough to see the Bolshevik thugs turning into the alley. His heart pounded faster as he leaned over and peered into the darkness. He needed a place to hide.

Scrambling to his feet, he kicked open the door, then tumbled into the eerie silent darkness of the factory. The smell of urine smacked his face as he pulled himself up and stumbled across the expansive main floor of the factory, past rusting, cobweb covered machines that had laid dormant for months. At the far end of the machine room, he discovered a half open door. Straddling the door jamb, he sucked in a deep breath before slipping inside.

Rats squeaked and scurried without direction before him as he plowed through mildewed, urine-soaked flax bales. He caught his foot on a roll of baling wire and fell forward. A rat squealed as his head slammed on top of the rodent. He felt the rodents teeth prick into his nose, drawing blood as it yanked out and scampered off to another pile of dank cloth.

Beyond exhaustion, he lay on the rank smelling floor, feeling the blood ooze from the bite on his nose.

"In here!" he heard a voice exclaim. He flopped over to his back, sat up and scooted back into a large pile of rotting rags. A shadow appeared at the entrance. Another figure appeared, then a third. He peered up, slack-jawed and too tired to move. He scanned the three remaining walls, then panicked, realizing he had no escape.

"God help me," he mumbled as he clasped his hands together in prayer. The thugs converged on him, and for a moment, stood perfectly still over him, their rifle barrels aimed directly at his head.

"Pick him up," the tallest man ordered. "Take him out to the street."

The other two thugs shouldered their arms, grabbed Oskars by the shoulders, and dragged him out into the street. They released him with an emphatic shove, and he stumbled toward a collection of other men and women that must have been rounded up that morning. He looked up at their faces, but did not recognize any of them. As he looked at them closer, he saw the women all huddling together, sobbing hysterically. All of their dresses had been torn open, exposing their bleeding and grotesquely mangled breasts. He noticed a young girl standing by herself, and feeling obligated, stumbled to her side and wrapped his arms around her. Through her sobs, he heard her mumble, "Bastards," over and over again.

A sharply dressed officer stepped out from behind the group of long coated thugs, turned toward the crowd, and leered at them with a piercing stare. He strutted to the end of the sobbing crowd, then snapped his heels together. "By decree of the Riga Soviet, each of these criminals has been judged as a counter-revolutionary—an enemy of the state. The laws we have passed have been willfully violated by these bastards. Their crime is treason and their sentences have been tendered."

The officer stepped backward twice and turned toward his thugs. He raised his hand, then quickly sliced the air as he dropped it. Soldiers pushed through the aghast crowd, formed a single file facing the accused, then leveled their rifles.

"Anyone else convicted of crimes against the state will face this same punishment." The officer added, then turned back to the crowd and grimaced. He scanned the horrified faces and terrified eyes one last time before snapping his head back to his men.

"Fire!" His bellicose voice echoed against the building walls.

Gunfire cracked from each of the soldiers' rifles as flames lapped out of the barrels. Oskars pulled the young girl close to him as he felt three bullets sear into his chest. Her scream drowned out all the other screams that surrounded him, but it just as quickly stopped with a sickening gurgle. Rifle bolts clicked, followed by another deafening round of gunfire. Oskars crumbled to the ground with the girl still clutched in his arms. Then silence.

❦   ❦   ❦

Two days later, Rudolphs dolefully slogged up the muddy road to Telmeni. Having walked all the way from Riga, he still did not feel comfortable bringing the news of Oskars' death to Janis. But Janis had to know since they had all been such close friends for such a long time. Rudolphs stomped his feet on the bottom step, trying to free the mud which clung to his boots. He scraped off what didn't fall off, then continued up the steps and knocked on the door.

"Janis!" he yelled out. "Janis, it's Rudolphs! Are you home?"

Rudolphs waited for a few minutes, and when there was no response, went to the window and peered inside. He saw the parlor was disheveled looking, as if it had been ransacked, but no one was around. He felt obligated to go inside and investigate.

"Janis!" he called again as he opened the front door. He stepped inside and searched around the house. A sudden chill crossed his neck as he tentatively stepped into the parlor. He sighed relief when he realized that the room was simply unkempt.

"I guess he's fortunate to have Kristine around most of the time," he joked, trying to relieve some of his pent up tension. But as he walked out of the parlor, he grew more concerned. He did not remember Janis planning to go anywhere, and it was definitely not like him to just go and leave such a mess.

He continued deeper into the house, taking measured steps toward the kitchen, all the while listening closely for anything. The house though, was silent, except for the muffled ticking of the cuckoo clock. Carefully, he peeked around the corner into the kitchen, then froze as the sickening smell of stale kvass twitched his nostrils.

Slumped over the table, Janis sat with his head buried in his arms. In front of him, on its side, lay an almost empty bottle of Janis' kvass. A puddle of the liquor lay near the open top of he bottle.

"Son of a bitch, Janis," he gasped, then bolted to his friend and shook him hard.

"Janis. Are you all right?"

Janis grumbled and gingerly lifted his head. He craned his neck and squinted at Rudolphs, then cracked a wrinkled grin. His face had a pasty yellow color, which looked even worse with his blood-shot eyes.

"My head hurts," he mumbled, smacking his tongue.

"For Christ sakes, Janis. You scared the life out of me! How much of this stuff did you drink?"

"I don't remember," Janis stuttered and buried his head back into his arms. "I don't want to remember."

Rudolphs sat down at the table and shook his head, debating whether he should even tell Janis about Oskars. Janis picked up his head and glared at Rudolphs with glassy eyes.

"You know, I was ready for anything," he started, more in control of his speech. A slight whine tainted his voice. "I figured my son could be killed, but if he was killed at the front, he'd be a hero. I've even lost a grandson, and it didn't hurt this much."

Janis buried his head back in his arms. Rudolphs heard faint but distinct weeping from him.

He knows, Rudolphs thought, placing his hand on Janis' shoulder. Janis picked up his head again, and tried to hold it up. It wavered as loosely as a newborn's. Rudolphs noticed his face had paled even more since they had started to talk.

"Tell me why, Rudolphs. Oskars did nothing to anyone," Janis started, but stopped when he began coughing. "A senseless death at the hands of those fucking Bolsheviks. Christ. What is the world coming to? Are we destined to live in fear of everyone? Are we ever going to see freedom?" Janis started to gag. Rudolphs jumped from his chair and slapped Janis on his back.

"Are you all right?" Rudolphs panicked. He grabbed Janis under his armpits and yanked him up out of his seat. "Come on. I'm taking you to the doctor!"

Janis did not resist.

❧   ❧   ❧

Later that same day, Voldemars reported to the command head-quarters in Valka. He stood across the table from Colonel Balodis, a gaunt, crusty looking soldier who had been promoted to Supreme Commander of the Latvian army after Colonel Kalpaks' untimely death. Balodis' appearance had little to do with ability, since his reputation as a true field commander was well known. Over Voldemars' new commander's right breast pocket rested the gold rising sun of Lacplesis, a medal awarded only to those who exhibited bravery and valor in battle. That decoration alone was evidence that Balodis was experienced and knowledgeable enough of a fellow soldier that he could see eye to eye with him.

"Colonel Reek." Voldemars acknowledged the Estonian Commander standing next to Balodis. He extended his hand, and the commander clasped Voldemars' hand tightly.

"Good to see you again," Reek said. A smile flashed across his thin lips.

"Yes, it is, Colonel," Voldemars replied.

Balodis set his tea down clumsily, revealing his lack of practice with refined manner. Voldemars smirked. This man was truly field experienced.

"Gentlemen, let's get down to business," Balodis started, gruffly. He stood, and leaned on the table. "As a result of our ministers' diplomatic efforts, Lieutenant Colonel Reek has offered to join forces with us against the Russian Bolsheviks."

Zemitans nodded toward Reek and grinned.

"So far, our mission has progressed very much as we had planned," Balodis continued, calling attention to the map spread out on the table. "We've been successful in all of our efforts to purge the Bolshevik forces from Latvia. By my accounts, we have recaptured three quarters of the country. If events continue to progress as they have, we should accomplish our objectives by the year's end."

Voldemars glanced at Zemitans, who had lifted his head from the steam rising out of his tea. He grinned at Voldemars, then returned his focus to Balodis.

"I have received some disturbing news, however, concerning the Germans," Balodis continued.

Did you listen to me when I said don't trust them? Voldemars contained his thoughts as he sipped calmly at his weak tea. "Especially what seems to be happening around the renegade, General Von der Goltz." Voldemars' chest tightened at the mere mention of the German commander.

"There have been reports, as of yet, still unsubstantiated that the German forces have begun to move out of Riga and toward Cesis," Reek interjected in a low grumbling tone. He pointed to Riga on the map. "We've analyzed this move and conclude that the German Landeswehr is only moving north and east to reestablish positions—here and here."

"Nevertheless," Balodis interceded, "the deployment is inconsistent with what Von der Goltz had promised in our original agreements."

"May I speak, Colonel?" Voldemars asked, nodding politely at Reek for the interruption. Zemitans glared at him, stone-faced.

"Please do. Your thoughts?" Balodis asked Voldemars to continue.

"If we were discussing a trustworthy ally, I would feel the same as Colonel Reek. However, because it is Von der Goltz, I would consider their actions as an aggressive threat." Zemitans' icy stare at Voldemars chilled the room. "In my opinion, speaking freely sir," Voldemars added.

"But Von der Goltz has been open and forward about his intentions before," Balodis said.

"Maybe he has been before, but I submit that you would not tell your adversary what you are planning to do, especially if you felt the need for surprise." Voldemars spoke cynically, but sincerely. "I've heard from several sources their intent is not only to reclaim Latvia for themselves," Voldemars turned dramatically and looked at Reek. "But to march right up through Estonia as well."

"The Germans? A threat?" Balodis burst out angrily. His face grew red with a simmering anger. "Do you realize what the Germans have done for us so far?"

Zemitans squirmed in his seat as he glared at Voldemars.

"Believe me, I do, Colonel," Voldemars defended his position. "But I have also seen first hand what the Germans are capable of doing. And although I realize we are supposed to be working with them, I have never known the German army or its command to be so altruistic as to consider withdrawal once they've claimed a victory."

"I have a hard time believing that, Vechi," Balodis pounded the table with his fist. "I've met with Von der Goltz, and personally, I feel he is a man of impeccable character!"

"I beg to differ with you." Voldemars strained to keep his temper in check, sensing he may be bordering on insubordination. "How much do you know of the circumstances surrounding Colonel Kalpaks' death?"

"Everyone knows that was an accident," Zemitans interjected, then cocked his head and squinted his eyes. "I don't suppose you believe it was anything other than that, do you Vechi?"

Voldemars scanned his colleagues. Reek's eyes were settled enough that Voldemars felt he was open to the suggestion. Balodis' were wavering, while Zemitans, the one who knew the least of the Germans sat back with a stern, closed-minded expression.

"My information comes from the field. Men talk at the front, sir, and much of the talk is based in fact. It seems that Von der Goltz never trusted Kalpaks." Voldemars chewed his lip nervously. Zemitans grew more cold, while Reek and Balodis leaned and listened intently. "It was a German bullet that killed Kalpaks. And I, for one, believe there was a conspiracy to eliminate him." Voldemars stated coldly.

Balodis vaulted from his seat. His face had turned bright red.

"Are you suggesting I was part of this conspiracy?"

"No, sir. Not at all. On the contrary, I believe the conspiracy was completely German, now it's you who may very well be the next target."

The flap to the tent rustled open, silencing the heated discussion. Balodis waved the soldier in, and he shuffled toward Reek to whisper in his commander's ear. Reek's eyes popped wide open and his face grew sullen. The longer he listened, the more his lips pruned with disapproval. He finally waved to his aide to stop, brought his hands to his face, and palm to palm. The soldier snapped his heels and slipped out as quickly as he had arrived.

Reek was silent for a moment while Voldemars, Balodis, and Zemitans waited for a translation. Reek licked his lips and sighed loudly.

"I fear Captain Vechi has been correct in his estimation of the Germans." He started with a waver in his voice. He pointed back to the flap where the soldier had just exited. "The report I was just given was that an Estonian armored train carrying recruits to the eastern front has been ambushed and devastated by the Landeswehr."

A collective gasp rose from the table. Balodis peered across at Voldemars, his eyes wide in disbelief. He brought his hand to his face and rubbed at his day old beard. Zemitans, stunned, dropped his jaw open as his face paled.

"There were no survivors," Reek added, solemnly. "They didn't have a chance."

A pall settled over the room in traditional respect for the lost soldiers and the gravity of their new situation. Voldemars stared at Zemitans, then at Balodis.

398   Telmenu Saimnieks

"Gentlemen, this means we have a two front war now." Balodis' quivering voice broke the silence.

Voldemars glanced at Zemitans, but the officer remained glassy-eyed and rigid. Voldemars fully understood the predicament Zemitans was in, especially since his was the division that would be sandwiched between enemy forces.

"My forces will maintain against the Russians, Colonel," Voldemars offered. "But there is little support we can offer until we've eradicated them from Latgale." Voldemars thought for a moment then said, "Pincers."

Balodis cocked his head.

"Pincers, Colonel. It's worked on the Germans before!" Voldemars looked over the map of the Baltic area as he spread his hands over the ends. Zemitans and Balodis leaned over the table, listening closely. "If we soften here." He drew a line with his finger south of Cesis. "The Germans will move toward Cesis, like a bulge. Then we send troops around the bulge to the rear, and pinch it off!"

Balodis nodded. Color returned to Zemitans' face. Reek looked up, thought for a moment, then pointed to the map. "I can take the left flank. I have some forces along the Daugava which can be redeployed."

"And watch my back door, Vechi?" Balodis asked with a brief grin. "I don't need the Russians moving through and surprising me while I'm fighting the Huns."

Voldemars nodded as he sat down, then sipped at his cold tea.

Near The Russian Border

20 December 1919

L eading his men into a stiff north wind, Voldemars' cavalry regiment plowed diligently through a deep blanket of snow, frozen by the winter's inhospitable cold. The brief afternoon sun had already surrendered its heat to the Nordic blast, and as it retreated into the horizon, its light faded as well. He knew that his regiment would need to strike camp shortly less they too fall victim to the knifing bitterness.

To the east, he spotted the edge of a forest, then signaled for his regiment to stop. He motioned for his scout to come closer, not wanting to speak for fear of letting even a breath of warmth out before he could extract all the heat from it that he could. The young soldier gripped his reins with his teeth, then reached into his saddle bag and extracted a map. He unfolded the paper, traced his already reddened hand across it, then pointed to a town in the upper right hand corner of the chart.

"Rezekne," he mumbled, but the howling wind swallowed each utterance as it seeped out from between his frostbitten lips.

"Can you see any shelter?" Voldemars asked. He kept his chin buried in the collar of his coat.

"There is a forest east of here about a kilometer. On the other side is the town. We should be able to find shelter there." The boy stared up to Voldemars, and with his wide, brown eyes, begged his commander to let him put the map away and bury his hands back his sleeves.

As soon as Voldemars nodded, the boy crumpled the chart away in his coat, then carefully extracted frozen stiff reins from his mouth and slipped his extra long sleeves over his shivering hands.

Voldemars turned to his regiment, huddling closely against the biting wind, then signaled to proceed in the direction the scout indicated. One by one, the soldiers urged their horses on into the drifting snow.

After ten excruciating minutes, Voldemars spotted the tree line poking over the white blanketed hills. But as they approached, he noticed something odd poking out from the rolling snowbanks. He signaled his men to stop, then cautiously dismounted and crunched his way through the snow.

It was here! He remembered when he saw a frozen hand sticking out of the tundra. Two weeks ago, the Rifle Corps had suffered a massive defeat at the hands of the Russians here. This was the reason why Zemitans had ordered his regiment up to this God forsaken, no man's land. He needed backup to replace these lost heroes, and Voldemars' regiment was the closest.

The blowing wind shifted the snow like desert sand. Ice crystals shushed as they slipped away from more frozen flesh, revealing even more of the grim macabre buried in the piles of bloodied snow. He swallowed hard as he stared reverently for a moment at the slain soldiers, frigidly lifeless and half-buried, then soberly plodded ahead. As he reached the hand he had first seen, he kneeled next to the partly covered body. It was a boy not much older than sixteen.

A lump grew in his throat as he felt the cold seep through his coat. He wondered what he had said to his father when he left for the Rifle Corps. Did this young man callously walk away like he did, not thinking about what heartache he may cause. Carefully, he brushed off the body, then removed his warm, bulky mitten and grasped the boy's frozen hand.

For a moment it was cold, but then he felt nothing, as if the hand was as warm as his.

"For your wives and children," he heard a distant voice utter. "That is why we are fighting. Not just freedom, but for our families."

Voldemars clenched his eyes shut, then pivoted his head to look all around him. Each of his men waited patiently and silently on their huddled horses. None of them could have said those words. They were too far away. No one could have said that except—He snapped his head around and looked back to the boy. He felt his hand. It was frigidly cold again. With one tug, he pulled and turned him over. Where the body had been, two maroon streaks laid frozen into the snow, separated by a thin white patch. His head again spun and he felt like he was flying back through seven hundred years of history. Through a frosted window, he saw a bear-skinned Livonian moving the body of his own commander, revealing the same pattern. He remembered Poppa telling him that story of how the symbol became the Latvian flag, the flag he and his men were fighting for.

"Commander?" a quivering voice asked from behind him. "Are you all right?"

Voldemars turned enough to see his scout, knee deep in the snow, gazing at him with concern etched on his face.

"I'm fine," Voldemars said softly as he stood and stiffened. He gazed at the symbol for a moment, then sighed. "A sign. It's a sign that everything will be all right." Silently he turned, placed his arm around the scout, and led him back to the horses, where they remounted and headed through the woods and into Rezenke.

Voldemars approached the first farmhouse they came upon and as his men stood by, he convinced the owner to billet them for the night in his barn. As they settled into the barn, he selected sentries for the night to alert the regiment if the Russians dared try a surprise attack. He knew it was pointless, since even the cold-hardened Russians would not risk sorties on such a horrible night.

Icy bleakness quickly captured what was left of the light of day, and the winds wound up to an inhumane howl. Voldemars selected a corner of the barn to settle. He pulled out his musty, canvas tent from his pack, then wormed into the stale hay. He threw the tent over himself, then gathered up an arm full of rank smelling straw and slipped it under his head.

Exhausted, he let his eyes slip closed. What awaited his men tomorrow concerned him, but he tried to shake the thought and rest. As he drifted into a restless sleep, he pictured his regiment snaking up a hill in single file, hearing the rumbling of gunfire and the muffled screams of the fallen. The image grew clearer as he crested the hill and looked down onto the battlefield.

Through a wide veil of frozen breath, he watched a valiant Rifle Corps brigade standing firmly entrenched and under siege. The Red Army was attempting to breach the militia's lines, but he sensed their resolve weakening. He mulled over his orders and decided the best tactic he could employ was one brazen charge at the rear of the Bolshevik line. Calling his men in close, he had them form a circle.

He scanned the eyes of his men. They were ready. The farm-boys and plowmen he started with were now experienced warriors. Each set of eyes flared. Each face stood solid and confident. He knew nothing else needed to be said.

"Reform the charge line." He grinned widely. "On my signal, we will commence the battle!"

He nudged his horse back to the front of the line and watched the battle as it deteriorated into hand-to-hand combat. Rifle fire cracked and resonated like fireworks. Sabers clanged amidst screams silenced quickly by piercing thrusts. He spied the weakness he needed—the Russians' rear flank was exposed. He drew his saber and pointed it to the sky. He glanced up at his weapon, the same one which had seen him through battle so many times before. This battle, though, would be his most important.

He swooped his sword through the air and the charge was on. Through the frozen hills, whoops and wild yelps echoed, reminiscent of the thousands of Cossack pogroms which had bloodied Russia's history. Pounding hooves thundered down the hill, leaving a cloud of snow in their wake.

The Russian soldiers turned and froze with fear, totally surprised at the sudden rear-flank attack. With Rifle Corps in front of them, and this cavalry rushing in from behind, the Russians had no place to run. The Rifle Corps took command and countered while the Red Army was still startled. Their thrust severed the Bolshevik line into small pockets. More Latvian infantry poured into the battlefield and engaged the Russians.

He whipped his mount to a faster pace. His valiant regiment sealed the Russians' escape route, closing the loop from the rear. The Bolsheviks opened fire on the approaching cavalry. Shots whizzed by his head as he charged into the heart of the Russian line. He bared his teeth, defying his own mortality.

Men fell beside him. Horses heeled and dropped, pierced by return fire. Undaunted, he continued the ambush until the Bolsheviks, pocketed, trapped, and outnumbered, had no recourse but to surrender. Gunfire ceased. He slowed his mount. His charges confronted the Bolshevik commander and his officers. He brashly signaled his troops to divide, allowing him and his stallion to enter the circle arrogantly. His charge pranced onto the crest of the commander's redoubt, then stopped at attention.

"Vladimir." He gasped as he glared at his old subordinate.

"So we meet again, Vechi!" Vladimir sneered defiantly. Hatred oozed from his eyes.

He sucked in a deep breath and let his horse fidget close enough that his gleaming sword wavered centimeters from Vladimir's nose. His nostrils flared. His chest expanded.

"Cease hostilities." He commanded to the encircled troops. "Lay down your arms, or face elimination."

Towering above his adversaries, Voldemars eyed Vladimir, who clutched at and aimed his rifle at Voldemars defiantly. Momentarily, the two commanders' own silent battle continued.

"Cease hostilities," bellowed Vladimir to his men, breaking the stalemate. "Lay down your arms." He was disgusted and threw down his rifle.

Voldemars stiffened and nudged his horse toward Vladimir. He slipped down from his saddle, then strutted the last three steps. He put his foot on the embankment and glared at his old comrade.

"For the Russian army, you surrender?" Vladimir asked, waving his sword near Vladimir's face. Grimacing, he solemnly nodded his capitulation.

Voldemars woke up coughing. He popped his eyes open and peered around the barn. It was dark and quiet, save for the snoring of his men and the throaty breathing of the horses.

It was just a dream, he thought, rolling over and hunkering back under his canvas cover. But tomorrow, will be the real battle.

❧   ❧   ❧

Voldemars woke before sunrise, stiff and cold. An ammonia-like smell wafted up from underneath his cover and joined with the musty odor to insult his nose. He slipped off the tent, then sat up and shook himself clean of the straw he had buried himself in. His back and shoulders creaked around his stiff muscles. He heard his vertebrae pop and slip back into place and he felt better.

This will be my day of reckoning, he thought, remembering the dream he'd had during the night. As he stood up, the icy air knifed through his damp clothes and chilled his skin to goose bumps. He quivered at first, but as he started moving, he felt the chill relent. He shuffled over and joined a group of his men already tending their mounts.

Today is the day that Voldemars Vechi writes his name in the annals of Latvian history, he mused as he carefully inspected his mount's hooves for cracks and splits. He started to mull over what prophetic words he would use to inspire his men before they plunged into battle. They would be the regiment that secured the victory in the war for independence. They would be able to tell their children and grandchildren how they served under the famous Voldemars Vechi in that famous fight. Lost in his thoughts, he had stepped into a large pile of horse manure. He shook his head, chuckled, and tried to wipe his boot clean.

An hour later, bundled in long woolen coats, the regiment followed Voldemars out of the barn and eastward, toward the hills Zemitans had told him would be his objective. After another hour of plodding along against the biting wind, the regiment reached the back side of a secluded hill. Voldemars suddenly realized he had seen this hill before. This was the exact same hill he had dreamed of last night. His chest swelled with pomp as he realized his dream must have been a vision of his coming glory.

"Finally. After so long, standing back and watching everyone else capture the glory, this will be my turn to bask," he mumbled. He signaled his men to follow him up the hill. They snaked up the hill in single file behind him, and Voldemars again mused what quote for the ages he would enunciate before their glorious plunge into history. As he grew closer to the crest, the reality of why they were there grew louder and more evident.

He stopped at the top of the hill, and through a frozen mist, watched a valiant brigade of Latvian Rifle Corps move with ease against the retreating Red Army. Pockets of Russians resisted the onslaught, but only feebly before they turned tail and ran.

"My victory." He was dumbfounded. Grandeur had escaped him again. He wanted to be angry. He wondered what he could do to become part of this historic event. He started to wish the Rifle Corps would falter so he could lead his men in to rescue the battle. But the cheers rising from his men on each of the successful parlays wrested the anger from his heart. "For your wives and families." He heard the boy's voice again.

The Russians retreated en masse. The Rifle Corps swiftly followed as if they were chasing vagabonds from their vegetable gardens. No more shots were fired. Only threats were volleyed during the chase.

"I guess this means we can all go home now." Voldemars heard a voice quiver behind him. He turned around and saw Karlis, a man close to his father's age. Karlis smiled and revealed peg-like teeth. Voldemars tipped his head and stared into the old man's eyes. Sincerity and placidness oozed from them. He harbored no illusions that he would be a hero. He was simply doing what he had to do for his wife, his children, and his country. He was obviously comfortable with that. And that was enough.

"Yes, Poppa—" He caught himself. "Karlis. Let me clear it all with command, but I am sure we will all be going home soon."

Riga

11 August 1920

*V*oldemars waited outside the National Theater in Riga for the mixed crowd of military brass and political dignitaries converging on the marble steps to pass through the pillars and into the auditorium. He debated whether or not he really wanted to enter the halls and watch the signing of the treaty. The war was over and Latvia had won freedom, but it seemed so remote to him that it was done.

He glanced down at the modest array of medals and ribbons on the breast of his tunic. It was nothing like the display he had seen on the likes of Balodis or even Zemitans. It was even more modest than the medals he had left to burn in Ivan's field. He couldn't help but think that if he had duty at the Russian front, he would be one of those leading the mass of officers in for the signing. Instead, he was just the caretaker of a back-up unit, and a forgotten one at that.

"Are you going in, or are you going to wait for a messenger to come out and announce it is done?" Alberts slapped his hand on Voldemars' back.

Voldemars turned and feigned a smile. "I don't know. Why don't you go on ahead."

"You don't want to miss this," Alberts insisted.

You don't understand, he thought, staring into Alberts' boyish eyes.

"This is the most historic event of our lives," Alberts said, tugging at Voldemars' arm. "This is important."

Voldemars wanted to argue but instead, he followed Alberts toward the theater. As he reached the wide marble steps, he noticed a little boy looking up at him. The boy's green eyes studied him almost in reverence, dancing between his meager collection of ribbons and his knee-high riding boots. A smile blossomed on the tyke's face as Voldemars stopped and turned to him.

"Come on, we'll be late," Alberts urged, grabbing at Voldemars' sleeve. Voldemars stared at the boy, curious.

"Go on ahead," Voldemars said, absently, waving Alberts on.

Alberts waited for a moment as Voldemars crouched down to the little boy's level, but then hurried into the crowd and disappeared.

Voldemars rested a knee on the sidewalk and motioned the boy closer. He glanced up to his mother, and after an approving smile, he shuffled closer.

"Are you one of the Rifles?" he asked.

Voldemars saw awe in the boy's expression as he studied each of the medals on the uniform. "Yes, I am," he said.

The boy's face beamed. His arm quivered a moment before he raised it and pointed to the crossed rifles on Voldemars' collar.

"Momma, look. He's one of the heroes."

Voldemars felt a pleasurable rush. He called me a hero, he thought. Voldemars glanced up to the woman standing behind the boy. Her wavy black hair and dark complexion stunned him.

"Maria." he gasped. Blood drained from his face.   .

The woman's head cocked as she looked at Voldemars strangely.

My, God, you're alive, he thought. Memories cascaded through his thoughts as he glanced quickly at the boy, then back at his mother.

"Maria?" he asked more politely.

"You must be mistaken, sir," the woman said with a quiver to her voice. "My name is Jana, and this is my son, Andrejs."

Voldemars felt his face flush and his heart race. He drew in a deep breath and cleared his thoughts.

"I'm sorry. You just looked like someone I knew," he said as he stood up. Voldemars unclipped the crossed rifles from his collar, and offered them to the child.

"He can't take those," Jana said quickly.

"No, it's all right," Voldemars placed the badge in the boy's hand. His smile grew ear to ear. "I can always say I lost them someplace," he added, winking.

Jana nodded graciously, then prompted, "Now what do you say, Andrejs?"

"Paldies," the boy said, not taking his eyes off the medal in his open palm.

"Andrejs," Voldemars said as watched the boy stroke the rifles. "A fine name for such a strong looking lad."

Jana smiled. It was the same smile he remembered that Maria had shown him years ago. He wondered if Jana was lying to him about her true identity.

"We need to be going," Jana said, tugging on Andrejs' shirt.

"I'm going in for the signing," Voldemars said. "Would you like to join me."

"I would love to, but we need to be going," Jana said, backing away. "Thank you again for the medal. I am sure Andrejs will cherish this for a long time."

Jana took Andrejs hand and led him away, leaving Voldemars standing at the steps alone, thinking if it was really Maria. But as he dreamed of Odessa, boots clomping down the steps interrupted.

"The final proclamation," Alberts said through gasps. "They are about to sign the treaty."

Voldemars nodded and headed up the steps. As he walked through the doors he glanced up to the stage and saw the collection of dignitaries, their gazes fixed on Goldmanis as he read from the treaty.

"And the Soviet government renounced forever, any and all claims to the territory which is now the sovereignty of the Republic of Latvia." Goldmanis sat down and pressed the treaty flat on the table in front of him. He inked the pen before him, then with an exaggerated wave of his hand, signed the treaty. Standing, he offered his chair to the Russian commander, then offered the same pen he had used. Grudgingly at first, the Russian commander accepted the pen, then sat down, and signed the paper.

The crowd erupted in deafening applause. The Latvian delegation at the table beamed, proud and free. The Russians sat, subdued.

Voldemars felt a twinge at his chest. He could have been up there instead of Zemitans. He should have been. But he wasn't and it was done. Latvia was free.

In the eyes of at least one boy, though, he was a hero. And that was just as satisfactory for now.

Telmeni

23 June 1923

*V*oldemars leaned his shoulder into the bedroom door jamb and gazed in on his father, asleep in his bed, partly covered by a tangled mass of a down blanket and thin bed sheet. His breathing had settled into a more regular pattern and sounded much less strained than it had when Voldemars first started watching him two hours before. Janis' face was ashen. His crusted, dry and cracking lips had a blue blush to them. A matted clump of white hair seemed to ooze from his scalp, sprawling over his pillow. "I know what you wanted from me now, Poppa." He mumbled quietly enough that even a young man would have difficulty hearing.

He pushed himself up from the doorway, then shuffled to his father's bed. Janis' eyes remained closed, their wrinkled, sallow lids bulging where his irises twitched sporadically underneath. Voldemars placed his hand on his father's shoulder and looked over his emaciated frame. It was obvious to him that Janis had only a few weeks left, perhaps only a few days. But this was the man that the best doctors in Riga had said would not survive the winter. Yet, here he lay, resting comfortably in his bed.

He drew back his hand, but when a ring of vertigo tingled in a halo around his head, he quickly set it back onto the edge of the bed to brace himself. He squeezed his eyes closed and willed away the dizziness. Still a bit wobbly, he opened his eyes.

He gasped at the spectral, blurred image in front of him. He was looking into the past at a man in a bed in Odessa. It was himself. He remembered that he too was given only days before the doctors expected him to make his final retreat. And like his father, very much like his father, he defied them.

"Maybe that's why I had to find out for myself who I was, Poppa," he said as he closed his eyes again. The image vanished. When he reopened them, the reality of Janis in his own bed was there again. "I am more like you than I wanted to admit back then."

Outside the open window, Voldemars heard giggling. He shuffled to the window and looked down. Otilija and Augustine, acting like a pair of school girls, happily hugged each other tightly at the front of the house. Otilija stepped back and mothered her little sister, carefully picking out the traditional wedding wreath of daisies and young oak twigs from her auburn hair. As she stepped back, her lips quivered into a grin and then into a wide smile.

"Are you sure you can't stay at least until tomorrow?"

Augustine looked down to her feet and shook her head sheepishly.

"Jani comes only once a year, you know." Otilija prodded as she tipped her head and flashed a pixieish expression. "It would be fun, Augustine. Just like we were teenagers again!"

"You know I'd love to. I haven't been to a solstice fire in years. But Alberts has been so adamant about getting back to Riga."

Otilija held up her hand and stopped her sister in mid-sentence. She wrapped her arm around her shoulder, then led her two steps toward the carriage before stopping and turning Augustine to face her.

"We can let this go this one time, but let me give you some advice." Voldemars leaned his head closer to the window, barely able to hear Otilija's coaching. "When something is important to you, don't let him bully you into changing your mind."

"She's a good woman, Voldemars." Voldemars was startled as a ghostly hand touched his shoulder. He turned around quickly and stared at Janis behind him. "From what I've seen, she's quite a bit like Kristine. Strong when she has to be, soft when she should be."

Voldemars glanced back over his shoulder to his wife and her sister, still talking near the carriage. Alberts had joined them and was helping his new wife up to her seat.

"I guess I know that," Voldemars mumbled as his father's hand slipped off his shoulder. He watched Janis shuffle weakly back to his bed. He leaned over crookedly, then as tremors quivered his frail body, he dropped down on it.

Voldemars hurried over and helped him lay down. After a huge sigh, Janis pointed to the door with his crooked finger.

"Water," he muttered through his cracked lips. "Some water. Could you—"

"I'll be right back. Just relax, Poppa," Voldemars said as he headed for the door. He rushed down the stairs and into the kitchen. But when he walked back into the bedroom with the water, Janis had already fallen back asleep. Shaking his head, he placed the cup on the chair next to the bed.

"I'm sorry, Poppa," he whispered as he lingered for a moment. "I'm sorry for all the pain I've caused you these last years. But if it helps, I've learned who Voldemars Vechi really is and where I really belong." He hung his head silently for a moment, then turned and headed outside for a smoke.

"Voldemars?" a weak voice called. At the doorway, he stopped, turned, then froze as Janis' vacant eyes engaged his with empathy. His lips trembled as the corners of his mouth twitched into a smile.

"I am sorry too." Janis coughed weakly. "When the fires start, come wake me for the fires. It will be a good time to talk."

"I will," Voldemars said and left.

❦   ❦   ❦

As small groups of black and white storks gracefully drifted in from the bay, evening crept in. The cloudless sky grew darker in steps, settling on a rich indigo. A full, pink moon peeked above the horizon and hovered for a moment before ascending above the tree line and mellowing into a gray, cream-colored mottled ball. One by one, peepers began creaking solemnly, harmonizing a spring melody which carried through the hills.

Voldemars settled into his father's chair on the porch, packed his pipe and lit the stingingly sweet tobacco. A comfortable moistness slipped in on the air as he leaned back in the chair. On the hills in the distance, freshly lit campfires appeared like street lamps coming to life. Their light tinted the horizon with an orange glow. Across the lake, like a mythical genie conjured out of his bottle, a fire started as a willowy flicker, then grew into a yellow and orange torch. Silhouetted images circled the burning light, then started a graceful sway around the fire. The enclave moved faster and faster until single dancers broke from the group, and with a strikingly fluid grace, launched themselves into a daring leap over the lapping flame. As they gracefully touched down, they each bowed to the delight of the gathering, then continued their solos around the fire.

Throughout the hills of Valmiera, dainas passed from generation to generation drifted into the summer night, commencing the centuries old celebration of the Jani. After each melodious four-lined strain, "Ligo" erupted from the enclaves, then echoed through the valleys as the gay folk songs rose again.

Voldemars set his cold pipe down as the last cloud of rich aroma dissipated above him and melded into the night sky. Pasty white and gray ashes spilled from the tipped bowl as he stood up and turned to head inside.

"A fine evening for Jani," Janis muttered, supporting himself at the doorway.

"I was just coming to get you." Voldemars caught his breath.

"I've got to get something from the shed," Janis again mumbled with a drone as if his thoughts were elsewhere. He raised his hand

and with a quivering finger, pointed out to the wood shed. The sudden spark in his eyes told Voldemars exactly what he wanted.

"Sit here, Poppa. I'll go get it."

Janis grunted and absently stared for a moment. Voldemars caught a whiff of his stained pants as he helped his father shuffle to his chair. He slipped a thin blanket over his trembling legs, then turned and clomped off the porch toward the shed.

He remembered the time he snuck out behind his father to spy on him while he brewed kvass. The thick smoke from the fire, the gleam from the brown bottles, and his father's twitching smile as he tested his first batch all captured his imagination again as he opened the rickety wood door. Like that fateful day he stole a sip of the tingling brew, a row of brown bottles sat quietly, covered with spring dust, patiently waiting to be selected. He reached the shelf in two steps and slipped his hand around a bottle neck, then let his fingers draw lines on the dirt. He closed his eyes and blew the bottle clean. Dust itched his nostrils, much like he remembered the mildly effervescent and stingingly sweet brew had done.

"Ligo!" Voldemars was startled back to reality as the enclave across the lake punctuated their daina. As the song returned to its gay bounce, he slipped out of the shed and returned to the porch.

"A long time ago." Janis started catatonically as soon as Voldemars stepped onto the porch. His sunken eyes sat vacant in his head. "I watched a boy walk away from here."

Janis sighed noisily as Voldemars cracked open the bottle top, let the gas emanate for a moment, then filled the small wooden cups.

"When he did, I never thought I would see him again."

Voldemars lay his hand on his father's and stared into his hollowness. He saw a tear well up, then trickle down his ashen face.

"I guess I was a bit impulsive then, wasn't I?" he asked.

Janis shook his head. "Now I look at the man who has returned."

He closed his eyes. He dropped his head until the sparse hairs on his chin scraped his chest.

"You look tired, Poppa. Would you rather sleep?"

"No," he answered quickly, popping his head up and opening his eyes grotesquely wide. The sinews in his neck tried to stretch the flaccid, goose-bumped skin but left small folds hanging like jowls. "Over these last twelve years, I thought about why he left. I always thought there was something wrong with him." Janis brought the cup to his lips and sipped. He sighed heavily as his trembling hand descended away from his face. "Then I realized that he left because I was too demanding. I had always thought about what I wanted, not about what he might have wanted." Voldemars felt a chill run down his spine. "Or might have been trying to say."

"No, Poppa. When I left, I thought I knew what was right. And I was adamant about proving that."

"Ligo!" punctuated the night, followed by what seemed to be its echo across the other hills. Voldemars looked out at the dancers, leaping over the fires with fluidity like quicksilver. One figure split his legs out, Cossack style, as he straddled the lapping flames. Cheers erupted as he landed. The singing resumed.

"As the illusion of who I wanted to be was challenged time and time again, I realized that I truly had nothing to prove. I was who I was and nothing was going to change that. I only had to find out what was important—what was truly important to me."

Janis coughed then slammed down his wooden cup, spilling the kvass over the table. Voldemars whipped his head around and stared at his father. A weak smile cracked his face.

"And I did." Voldemars broke his glance and sat next to his father.

"I'm proud of you, Voldemars." Janis' words barely escaped his lips.

"I realized that I don't need to be a hero for the Russians or the Latvians. I only need to be content with who I am."

Janis slipped back into his chair and rested his head on the high back. He closed his eyes and sighed heavily as another "Ligo!" erupted from the enclave.

"Kristine will need someone to look after her soon," Janis said with deep resignation.

"So, when I returned from the front…" Voldemars said without hearing his father.

"Romans has decided to remain in Riga."

"I found a parcel of land a few kilometers from here."

"And Augusts has a job in Cesis."

"Otilija and I will build a modest house and live close by."

"I would like you to stay here."

"We could come visit often."

"And be Telmenu Saimnieks."

Voldemars recoiled, then gawked, slack-jawed and speechless. He stared at his father in disbelief. "But Edwards is the oldest. Shouldn't he—"

Janis waved his hand weakly, then bobbed his head forward. He slowly cracked his eyes open. "I've already talked to him. He has a farm in Valka that he's happy with."

Dumbfounded, Voldemars did not know what else to say. He looked deep into his father's eyes and saw the same ones that he had left twelve years ago, staring at him as he walked away on the dirt road in front of the farm. Then he heard Otilija's voice remind him of how selfish he had been. A swirl of memories cascaded through his mind as he relived each pang of failure, each knifing disappointment, each time he was passed by for someone else to be the hero.

As the kvass tingled in his head, he realized that what was truly important to him was Telmeni. And Otilija. And his dying father.

He shuffled to Janis and squatted next to him. The old man's clouded eyes followed his every move as he placed his hand on his shoulder. He saw tears well up in his eyes.

"For you, Poppa, I will," he said. A tear trickled down his own cheek.

Another "Ligo!" echoed through the night.

0-595-22448-2